Sherlock Holmes: Tales of Light

Sherlock Holmes: Tales of Light

by
Tracy J. Revels

Edited by
David Marcum

MX Publishing

First edition published in 2024
© Copyright 2024 by Tracy J. Revels

The right of the individuals listed on the Copyright Information page to be identified as the authors of this work has been asserted by them in accordance with the Copyright, Designs, and Patents Act 1998.

All rights reserved. No reproduction, copy, or transmission of this publication may be made without express prior written permission. No paragraph of this publication may be reproduced, copied, or transmitted except with express prior written permission or in accordance with the provisions of the Copyright Act 1956 (as amended). Any person who commits any unauthorised act in relation to this publication may be liable to criminal prosecution and civil claims for damage.

All characters appearing in this work are fictitious or used fictitiously. Except for certain historical personages, any resemblance to real persons, living or dead, is purely coincidental. The opinions expressed herein are those of the authors and not of MX Publishing.

ISBN Paperback 978-1-80424-506-4
AUK ePub ISBN 978-1-80424-507-1
AUK PDF ISBN 978-1-80424-508-8

Published by
MX Publishing
335 Princess Park Manor, Royal Drive,
London, N11 3GX
www.mxpublishing.co.uk

The stories in these volumes were originally published from 2016-2024

CONTENTS

Forewords

Introduction	1
by Tracy J. Revels	
Editor's Foreword: Purely Authentic	4
by David Marcum	

Adventures

The Adventure of the Empty Manger	11
The Adventure of the Furniture Collector	25
The Adventure of the Opening Eyes	42
The Disappearance of the Highgate Flowers	58
The Adventure of Merridew of Abominable Memory	73
The Adventure of the Black Perambulator	88
The Disappearance of Little Charley	103
The Adventure of the Spinster's Courtship	120
The Adventure of the Confederate Treasure	135
The Adventure of the Vanished Husband	149
The Adventure of the Queen's Teardrop	164
The Adventure of Vittoria, the Circus Belle	180
The Adventure of the Last Laugh	194
The Adventure of the Awakened Mummy	208
About the Author	225

These stories have previously appeared in the following volumes:

Volume 1
Sherlock Holmes: Tales of Light

The MX Book of New Sherlock Holmes Stories

- "The Adventure of the Empty Manger" – **Part V: Christmas Adventures**
- "The Adventure of the Furniture Collector" – **Part XXXVII: 2023 Annual (1875-1889)**
- "The Adventure of the Opening Eyes" – **Part XL: Further Untold Cases (1879-1886)**
- "The Disappearance of the Highgate Flowers" – **Part XXXII: 2022 Annual (1888-1895)**
- "The Adventure of Merridew of Abominable Memory" – **Part XXIII: Some More Untold Cases (1888-1894)**
- "The Adventure of the Black Perambulator" – **Part XXXVI: However Improbable . . . ." (1897-1919)**
- "The Disappearance of Little Charley" – **Part XXXIII: 2022 Annual (1896-1919)**
- "The Adventure of the Spinster's Courtship" – **Part XXXIII: 2022 Annual (1896-1919)**
- "The Adventure of the Vanished Husband" – **Part XXII: Some More Untold Cases (1877-1887)**
- "The Adventure of the Queen's Teardrop" – **Part VI – 2017 Annual**
- "The Adventure of Vittoria, the Circus Belle" – **Part XI: Some Untold Cases (1880-1891)**
- "The Adventure of the Awakened Mummy" – **Part XLV: 2024 Annual (1898-1917)**

After the East Wind Blows

- "The Adventure of the Confederate Treasure" **– Part II: Aftermath (1919-1920)**

Sherlock Holmes and Doctor Watson: The Early Adventures

- "The Adventure of the Last Laugh" **– Volume II**

Volume 2
Sherlock Holmes: Tales of Shadow

These stories have previously appeared in the following volumes:

The MX Book of New Sherlock Holmes Stories

- ☐ "The Adventure of Khamaat's Curse" – **Part XVIII – Whatever Remains . . . Must Be the Truth (1899-1925)**
- ☐ "The Adventure of the Headless Lady" – **Part XVI – Whatever Remains . . . Must Be the Truth (1881-1890)**
- ☐ "The Adventure of the Winterhall Monster" – **Part XIII: 2019 Annual (1881-1890)**
- ☐ "The Adventure of the Hungry Ghost" – **Part VIII – Eliminate the Impossible: 1892-1905**
- ☐ "The Adventure of the Heirloom Necklace" – **Part XLIV: 2024 Annual (1889-1897)**
- ☐ "The Adventure of the Buried Bride" – **Part XXXV: "However Improbable . . . ." (1889-1896)**
- ☐ "The Adventure of the Aluminium Crutch" – **Part XL: Further Untold Cases (1879-1886)**
- ☐ "The Adventure of the Veiled Man" – **Part XXXI: 2022 Annual (1875-1887)**
- ☐ "The Adventure of the Curious Mother" – **Part XLII: Further Untold Cases (1894-1922)**
- ☐ "The Adventure of the White Roses" – **Part XXVII: 2021 Annual (1898-1928)**
- ☐ "The Adventure of the Christmas Suitors" – **Part XXIX: More Christmas Adventures (1889-1896)**
- ☐ "The Adventure of the Murderous Ghost" – **Part XXXVI: "However Improbable . . . ." (1897-1919)**
- ☐ "The Adventure of the Undertaker's Fetch" – **Part XVII – Whatever Remains . . . Must Be the Truth (1891-1898)**

Volume 3
Sherlock Holmes: Tales of Darkness

The MX Book of New Sherlock Holmes Stories

- "The Adventure of the Faithful Servant" – **Part IX – 2018 Annual (1879-1895)**
- "The Adventure of the Folded Overcoat" – **Part XXXIX: 2023 Annual (1897-1923)**
- "The Adventure of the Seven Sins" – **Part XXXVIII: 2023 Annual (1889-1896)**
- "The Adventure of the Old Explorer" – **Part XXXI: 2022 Annual (1875-1887)**
- "The Tragedy of Woodman's Lee" – **Part XXIV: Some More Untold Cases (1895-1903)**
- "The Adventure of the Haunted Portrait" – **Part XXXIV: "However Improbable . . . ." (1878-1888)**
- "The Adventure of the Hero's Heir" – **Part XXVII: 2021 Annual (1898-1928)**
- "The Adventure of the Beauty Trap" – **Part XX: 2020 Annual (1891-1897)**
- "The Adventure of the Green Gifts" – **Part XV: 2019 Annual (1898-1917)**
- "The Adventure of the Silent Witness" – **Part XIV: 2019 Annual (1891 - 1897)**
- "The Adventure of the Faithful Wolfhound" – **Part XXXVIII: 2023 Annual (1889-1896)**
- "The Adventure of the Siren's Tower" – **Part XLIII 2024 Annual (1874-1888)**
- "The Horror of Forrest Farm" – **Part XXXII: 2022 Annual (1888-1895)**
- "The Adventure of the Aged Actor" – **Part XLIV: 2024 Annual (1889-1897)**

Introduction
by Tracy J. Revels

Dappled sunlight filtered through thin curtains as I settled on the floor and opened a short story anthology. I was eleven years old, and an only child on a farm in rural North Florida. I rarely saw another kid in the summertime, so I sought the companionship of fictional characters. This high school text had been left behind by my aunt, a reading teacher, and was considerably above my grade level, but I tackled it anyway, eager for distraction.

That's how I met Sherlock Holmes.

The opening story in the book was "The Adventure of the Speckled Band". It wasn't my first mystery tale; my shelves were filled with the exploits of Encyclopedia Brown, Nancy Drew, and The Hardy Boys. But I was growing bored by adventures featuring children and teens. I wanted in on the grown-up action – I craved murder and mayhem, not missing tennis shoes and kidnapped hamsters. Here, it seemed, was a fascinating combination of serious crime and historical detail. My pulse quickened when Holmes began examining the murdered woman's bedroom at Stoke Moran. As Holmes and Watson returned to keep vigil, I began to wonder if the killer was a (spoiler alert) snake.

And it was! I felt empowered and excited, and I immediately wanted to read another story. The anthology revealed that "The Adventure of the Speckled Band" was just one of sixty tales about Sherlock Holmes, penned by Sir Arthur Conan Doyle. Locating them, in these pre-internet days, was a difficult challenge, especially considering the limitations of our school and public libraries. The only sources of books in my hometown were the spinning rack of paperback bodice-rippers at *Winn-Dixie*, or the magazines and comics at the *Suwanee Swiftee*. My family made bi-weekly trips to Valdosta, thirty miles away, and on each trip, I annoyed my mother until she permitted me ten minutes in the burg's one bookstore, where I raced around trying to catch a glimpse of a pipe or deerstalker on a cover. Finally, my mother gave me William S. Baring-Gould's annotated two volumes of the Sacred Writings. This edition opened the Sherlockian world to me. It has since lost its covers, is tattered, torn, and marked up, in danger of falling to pieces. It remains my most precious literary possession.

During my teenaged years, I discovered pastiches, beginning with *The Seven-Per-Cent Solution*. Meyer's work flung wide a new door in my imagination. *Sherlock Holmes Through Time and Space*, edited by Isaac Asimov, Martin Harry Greenberg, and Charles G. Waugh, was equally influential in unlocking yet another vault of possibilities. I began to envision Holmes not only as a character, but as an ideal – the hero whose strength was not brute force, or strange gadgets, or irresistible sex appeal. Everything that made him wonderful was a product of his brain. He symbolized the unlimited power of the human mind.

Doyle's resentment of his own creation was a gift to his admirers and future writers. Since public infatuation with Holmes seemed to prevent Doyle's rise to a literary Olympus, Doyle felt compelled to shove Holmes into the Reichenbach Falls. But by (temporarily) killing Holmes, along with being careless as to the details of Holmes's career (not to mention the location of Watson's wound), Doyle gifted his devotees with potential ideas for prequels, sequels, spin-offs, pastiches, and parodies of all stripes. Perhaps there are some who write new stories for Holmes merely to acquire filthy lucre. But my personal experience with meeting Sherlockian authors assures me that most who pick up the pen, or tap away on the keyboard, determined to give Holmes yet another great adventure, do so out of their vast love for the character and their admiration for his creator.

What follows in these pages is my own modest contribution to that literature, my attempts to channel my inner Watson and find some new conundrum for the Great Detective to investigate. Imitation is, in my case, not mere flattery, but the sincerest way of expressing eternal gratitude to an immortal author. If any of these little stories can provide an hour's enjoyment to a reader, and bring Holmes back into the mind's eyes, then I am as happy as I was on that summer's day when I first met Sherlock Holmes.

Tales of Light are stories inspired by some of The Canon's more wistful moments. Holmes's adventures are filled with unexpected humor and quirky characters: Consider "The Red-Headed League" with the absurd client, Jabez Wilson, or the laugh-out-loud funny interview with Lestrade near the end of "The Adventure of Charles Augustus Milverton". To honor this aspect of Doyle's work, the stories found within *Tales of Light* are frothy in nature, and feature characters whose quirks and peculiarities serve both to drive the narrative and, hopefully, produce a smile on a reader's face. While mayhem and chaos may abound, the reader of the adventures within this volume may count on happy endings and justice served, as well as moments of "pawky" humor.

Tales of Shadow owe their existence to Doyle's stories which are more realistic in nature. In tenor, I have worked to mimic the canonical offerings found in the early collections, where Holmes is at the height of his powers and reputation. There's more murder, and sometimes not everything in the adventure goes as planned, for either culprit or detective. Expect surprises, and be prepared for cases to twist and turn in unexpected directions.

Tales of Darkness is a collection springing from the well of nightmares. Doyle was a master of horror as well as mystery. Holmes's cases often featured the truly grotesque, from the hellhound roaming the foggy landscape of Dartmoor to the devil causing murder and madness in the sinister atmosphere of Cornwall. But Holmes knew that all evil, even if cloaked in supernatural forms, has a purely human origin. *"No ghosts need apply,"* he warned, and these stories follow in the tradition the master established. Doyle also understood that sex and violence are often intimately connected, as he proved in "The Adventure of the Cardboard Box". In *Tales of Darkness*, the reader will find the most depraved villains, the most tragic victims, and the most challenging and disturbing resolutions.

As always, I am deeply indebted to my editor, David Marcum, whose encouragement led me to begin writing classic pastiches, and to all the good people at MX Publishing, who provide the world with delightful and diverse Sherlockian content. My dearest friends in my home scion, The Survivors of the Gloria Scott, are a constant source of ideas. I feel truly honored to have been invested as a Baker Street Irregular in 2021, which has helped me build friendships within the global Sherlockian world. As always, my students – especially the members of the 'Writer's Workout' class – inspire me. I thank my mother for all those trips to the bookstore and for the two-volume Baring-Gould.

This collection is loving dedicated to Dr. John Moeller, my husband.

Tracy J. Revels
May 2024

Purely Authentic
by David Marcum

I first became aware of Tracy Revels in 1999, by way of her Sherlockian pastiche, "The Adventure of the Empty Manger", when it appeared on the old and revered *Classic Specialties* website. (It's still there for those who want to track it down, preserved on the Wayback Machine – see the link below.)

Back in those days, I was deeply into my mostly-successful quest to track down, collect, and read every single traditional Canonical Holmes adventure available, including hundreds – nay, thousands – that were on the internet that have since vanished, except for the printed and archived versions in my collection. I was thrilled when Tracy's Christmas story appeared, as it was pure Holmes and Watson, by someone who seemed to have a solid understanding of who Holmes and Watson were and how they should behave, and how to present a post-Canonical adventure in a Canonical way.

A few years later, Tracy published *Sherlock Holmes: Mostly Parodies* (Classic Specialties, 2008), which I received as a Christmas present from my wife and son. While these tales are not strictly Canonical, they're *funny*, and I'd like to suggest here that this book be reprinted by MX. Maybe by 2025, you'll be able to read it too.

Beginning in 2011, Tracy wrote a trilogy of supernaturally-slanted Holmes novels, *Shadowblood*, *Shadowfall*, and *Shadowwraith* (MX Publishing) and, while not my cup of Sherlockian tea, they are excellently written – exactly as one would expect from her.

I was finally able to meet Tracy in person – strangely, only the first of two times – in April 2012, at *A Gathering of Southern Sherlockians* in Chattanooga, TN. I was barely getting my feet wet in relation to attending Sherlockian events, this being my second, after *From Gillette to Brett III* the previous November. An early edition of my first book had recently been published, and Joel and Carolyn Senter of Classic Specialties had very kindly sold it on their website. (Sadly, the Chattanooga event was the only time that I met them in person, too.)

Joel had arranged for me to sell some copies of my book at the event, and he arranged for me to share a table with Tracy, who was also selling a few of her titles. I found her to be fun and smart and full of useful information – particularly about MX Publishing, which I would switch to (resulting in great personal benefit and fulfillment) the following year.

After a day of presentations, there was a banquet, and Joel had encouraged me to wear my full Inverness and deerstalker, handmade for me in Scotland as a Christmas gift from my family a couple of years before. I did so, and as Tracy was attired in full-regalia as Irene Adler, photographs were made, including this one:

Afterwards, we sat at the same dinner table and enjoyed the festivities, and I also met her future husband, John Moeller.

In 2015, I came up with the idea for *The MX Book of New Sherlock Holmes Stories* as a push-back against recent infuriating modernized versions that were presenting Holmes as a damaged sociopathic murderer, and his associates in similar offensive portrayals. At first, I thought that it would be – if I was lucky – a paperback volume of maybe a dozen or so stories. Instead, word spread, and more and more people wanted to be involved, and the first set ended up being a three-volume hardcover collection of over sixty new adventures, and after that, more people wanted contribute stories and more people wanted to read them, so there were more and more books. We're currently up to forty-five massive volumes, nearly 1,000 stories, and at this writing, further volumes are in preparation. All royalties for the books go to the Undershaw school for special needs children at one of Sir Arthur Conan Doyle's former homes, and at present, we've raised over *$125,000* for the school.

To keep the books going, I've been an aggressive recruiter, going through my massive pastiche collection to identify authors that I wanted to join the party – and I remembered Tracy's original traditional Canonical pastiche, "The Empty Manger".

In some rare cases, I've used stories that appeared online if they were obscure, and if most people likely hadn't seen them. This was one of those stories, and I reached out to Tracy to see if she could revise it a bit for publication in one of the upcoming MX anthology volumes. She was very willing, and soon it was part of the overall collection. But she didn't stop there. She now had the fever. Since then, she's been one of the collection's most prolific contributors – and all of her stories are excellent. I never have to worry when she sends me a new Holmes adventure – there won't be any teeth-grinding formatting problems, and Holmes and Watson will be themselves in a Canonical way. I don't have to worry about them going off the rails (or the cliff) and Holmes being a murderous sociopath or Watson having a psychosomatic wound. Tracy writes solid, knowledgeable Canonical adventures, purely authentic, and most important – they're fun to read. Even the dark ones.

At one point, it became apparent that Tracy had written a *lot* of Holmes stories – enough to be assembled into their own books. She and I collected all of them together a couple of years ago, but then for some reason the momentum bled away. Then, this year it became even more apparent that there were a *lot more* of her Holmes stories, and now was the time to go ahead and publish these books.

Tracy sorted the stories into three themed volumes: *Light*, *Shadow*, and *Darkness* – which is something for everyone. But even if you favor one sort over another, I heartily recommend all of them.

The only other time that I've met Tracy in person was literally for one minute in January 2024, when we were both in New York for the Sherlock Holmes Birthday Weekend. It was in passing in the fabled Dealer's Room – just long enough to say hello and move along. But we've corresponded for years, and she's kept me very entertained with all of these excellent stories.

And there are more of them waiting in the wings. As I write this, Tracy has sent a few more stories for the next MX anthology volumes – and with any luck, there will be others after that, enough for a fourth volume in this collection. She's within sight of equaling the sixty stories of the original Canon, and there is no sign that her creative well is running dry.

I'll fight to hold the right to say I'm her biggest fan, but I want everyone to relish these stories as I have. Fortunately, it's easier now that they're all in one set.

Enjoy!

David Marcum
June 2024

NOTE

The web address for Tracy's first pastiche, "The Empty Manger", for those who wish to painstakingly type it in, is:

> *https://web.archive.org/web/20101223033107/http://sherlock-holmes.com/featur9.html*

Sherlock Holmes: Tales of Light

The Adventure of the Empty Manger

The adventures of my good friend Sherlock Holmes were vast and diverse. In his many years of active practice, he came to the assistance of titled nobility, decorated military heroes, and industrial tycoons. He recovered stolen art and artifacts of incalculable value, tracked down assassins and world-famous felons, and prevented scandals that would have disgraced royal dynasties on three continents. Yet, in glancing back over the hundreds of cases which I have never published, I often find that the small problems my friend resolved were more fascinating than the cases which brought significant financial reward and the gratitude of monarchs. Crimes which took only moments to unravel were, in their way, as exciting as mysteries that required months of strenuous activity on Holmes's part. And as the years of retirement creep steadily upon me, I recall my friend's dignity and kindness far more than his celebrity. Indeed, the memories that are most intense to me are not those of breath-taking escapes or dramatic revelations, but of the times when the heart, as well as the mind, of Sherlock Holmes was revealed. Therefore, I offer to my long-suffering readers this brief account of an incident that gave me a startling insight into the very soul of Sherlock Holmes.

It was Christmas Eve of the year that Holmes returned to London. I had, at his insistence, abandoned both my medical career and my home, and resumed residence in that famous suite of rooms on Baker Street. While the young Doctor Verner had purchased my small Kensington practice, I did, on occasion, receive a summons from a former patient and could not in good conscience refuse to come to his aid. Lady Amelia Hildeborne was one such sufferer, a chronic invalid – at least by her own diagnosis – who would admit no other physician to her bedchamber. The note that she was dying from a hemorrhage had roused me from a winter's nap and sent me scurrying to her mansion in one of London's more fashionable neighborhoods. The lady proved to have only a slight nosebleed, and I was just buttoning my coat and shivering in the bitter wind on her doorstep when a sharp halloo caused me to turn my head. There, bundled in a long coat and muffler, smoking a cigarette with an air of nonchalance, was my friend.

"Holmes? This is a strange coincidence."

He favored me with a look of impatience. His scowl asserted he had once thought more highly of my intelligence.

"It is not a coincidence, Watson," he said, flicking away the cigarette. "I am here because I followed you here."

"But how?" I demanded. "I received the note from Lady Hildeborne at seven, long before you were awake. And do not tell me that you had my destination from Mrs. Hudson, because the note she brought up to me was sealed, and I tossed it into the fireplace before I left Baker Street."

Holmes smirked. "There is no great mystery to the thing at all. When my friend Watson is roused from hibernation at such an ungodly hour of the morning – and I am made well aware of this fact because I can hear his muttered army oaths even through the walls of my own bedchamber – and then carelessly shaves and departs on a medical errand, it can mean only that he is destined for this fine address."

"I confess I hurried but – "

"You clattered on the stairs and slammed two doors. There was blood on the razor and in the basin, and there is spot of plaster on the left side of your jaw, just where I suspected it would be. Your medical bag, which you leave near the sofa, was missing. There was no other possibility."

"But why this address?" I asked. "I could have gone to any of the patients who remain rather inexplicably attached to me. You knew only that I was off on a medical case."

"That, I confess, was a subtle calculation," Holmes said, with a low chuckle. "But it is Christmas Eve, and just yesterday I heard you complain that you wished you had more funds for holiday libations. A particular bottle of French wine prominently displayed at Number 3, St. James Street, was mentioned. And I know that of your half-dozen former patients, only Lady Hildeborne rewards you in cash when your services are rendered. Knowing also that she is, in your own words, a 'miserable hypochondriac', but one whose 'payments are princely', it was easy to imagine that such a summons would be very hastily answered, especially since the desire for a holiday treat is upon you."

I shook my head in amazement. I had not realized just how much I had missed Holmes's gift for making fantastic actions seem so obvious. "You make it all simple."

Holmes shrugged, then turned and gestured to a waiting cab. "Life is appallingly simple, for those with sharp eyes and well-honed brains," he said, without a trace of modesty.

"But there remains a bigger question," I noted, as Holmes opened the door and then slid in beside me. "Why did you follow me?"

Holmes gave the driver orders to take us to Oxford Street. Leaning back in the seat, he frowned, mulling over my statement. For an instant, he appeared oddly puzzled, as perplexed as one of his own clients. "I can only assume that I wanted company."

I tried not to let my amusement show. Holmes could make all the deductions he pleased, work his magical trick as often as the opportunity presented itself, but I felt that in this one area I was the more observant partner. In the months since he had returned, I had noticed a change in him. He was less likely to disappear for long evenings, or to spend endless hours brooding over his index, or simply smoking his pipe in somber reflection. Instead, he had more frequently insisted that I come along with him, whether for a ramble in Regent's Park or to attend a concert of violin music at St. James's Hall. Every case that had come his way, no matter how insignificant or obvious, had required my assistance. It had become the exception, rather than the rule, for one of us not to be at the table when the other was seated. In my view, the deduction seemed rather straightforward. Whatever Holmes had been doing in the three years that the world presumed him dead, it had been a lonely occupation. He had returned to London almost starved for companionship and spiritual connection. His brief accounting of himself given on the day of his return – a tale of covert travels in Persia and Tibet, of wondrous explorations made under the name of Sigerson, and of painstaking work in a chemical laboratory in Montpellier – had never been mentioned again. I had come to believe that my friend was purposefully lying to me about his adventures, but I easily forgave him any falsehood that was required to maintain his dignity. Whatever had happened, it was clear to me that it had been a harsh time for him, and that my duty as his closest associate was to help him resume as normal a life as possible.

"So you plan to do some Christmas shopping?" I asked, as our cab rattled toward London's famous commercial district.

Holmes shook his head. "I plan to do some watching. The combination of holy days and heathen capitalism is always amusing and occasionally instructive. Or would you prefer to return home?"

"No, I'll accompany you. I'm certain that I can find something to spend my 'princely payment' on," I said, patting my waistcoat pocket and feeling the weight of the coins within it.

Holmes began to talk of other things, and I lost track of both direction and time. But suddenly there was a sharp cry and a black robed figure came dashing out of an ancient, grime-covered edifice. The man's shouts and squawks, along with the way he waved his arms and danced about at the edge of the street, gave him the appearance of an ungainly and agitated crow.

"Help! Robbers! Thieves! Help!"

Holmes twisted and gave me a predatory smile. Then, with the agility of a hound over a hurdle, he sprang from the cab. By the time I paid our fare to the startled and swearing driver, Holmes had the hysterical gentleman in his grip, shaking him firmly.

"Courage! Calm yourself." The elaborate cassock clearly denoted the hysterical gentleman as an Anglican priest of the High-Church persuasion, but Holmes showed little respect for his holy status until the clergyman ceased screeching and began to take deep, steadying gasps of air. "Now," Holmes ordered, "tell us what has happened."

The clergyman blinked, as if just awaking from a nightmare. He peered from one to the other of us with tiny, watery blue eyes. He was a diminutive person, barely over five feet tall, with small tufts of white hair just above his ears. A pair of silver spectacles swung from a chain on his neck, clanking against an ornate gold cross. His bald scalp glistened with sweat, and his thin lips trembled as he struggled to master coherent speech.

"Are you detectives?"

"Something of the sort," Holmes answered. "You say you have been robbed?"

The clergyman twisted his boney hands together. "Yes. It – it will be a scandal. A disaster! The parish shall never recover. Oh, how could it have been stolen? Why did I ever walk away, turn my back, leave the door unlocked?"

"What has been stolen?" I asked. Our new client raised trembling hands.

"Our Lord himself. The holy infant of Bethlehem! The Christ Child!"

I noted how one eyebrow rose skyward on Holmes's face. His lips twisted into an expression of chagrin. For just an instant, I thought he would turn on his heel and leave the man babbling on the sidewalk. But instead, Holmes heaved a martyr's sigh.

"Come . . . you must show us the scene of the crime," Holmes said, and the priest motioned for us to follow him inside the sanctuary.

"My name is Morley," our new client gasped as we stepped into the deep shadows of the central aisle. "I have been the vicar of St. Rita's Parish for almost twenty years. Never have we had such a catastrophe. Whatever will I tell the faithful, when they arrive for services tonight?"

As the clergyman continued to whine, I took in our surroundings. Though small, the church was lavish, with exquisite stained glass windows and plush carpeting. The smell of bay-scented candles mingled pleasantly with the aroma of ancient woodwork. Just beyond the pews were ancient marble crypts, complete with effigies of knights and ladies. I guessed that sometime in the distant past, this sanctuary had been the private chapel of a noble family. Though the neighborhood currently surrounding it was unmemorable, the little church clearly had a distinguished history.

The vicar led us to a spot just to the left of the altar. There we beheld a remarkable sight of the holiday season: a nativity scene housed in a hut made of paper and plaster, populated by nearly life-sized dolls. Each figure, from Mary and Joseph to the shepherds, wise men, and angels, was constructed of cloth and held in a realistic pose by nearly invisible wires. Animals, including a donkey and lamb, were likewise cleverly crafted from wool and burlap and positioned in attitudes of adoration. While the shepherds and the holy family were clad in simple tunics and drapes, the wise men glittered with cloaks of gold and silver tissue, their diadems winking with false gems. I was so amazed by the display's novelty and artisanship that for a moment I missed the central problem it posed.

The manger was empty.

"It is a special gift," the vicar explained, "from Mr. Harold Whitestone. Perhaps you have heard of him? No? He owns the Whitestone foundries and mills, in Yorkshire. He was born and raised on this street, a poor lad, but very devout. Since he made his fortune in trade, he has become a generous patron – he paid for our new windows and all the carpets. Just last week he presented us with this tableau."

"It is certainly a striking decoration," I said. The vicar's blue-tinged lips pulled tight in a painful rictus, the expression of a man awaiting the dentist's drill.

"Yes, it is, but such trouble for us – not that I am ungrateful, heaven forbid. Mr. Whitestone has been most kind! But, you see, Mr. Whitestone felt that we should keep the sanctuary open around the clock. He believed that people should be able to admire his gift at all hours – to aid them in their Advent meditations. But, of course, that meant my curate and I were forced to take shifts, to guard it carefully, lest someone be tempted into devilment."

I could not resist a slight chuckle. "Surely making off with the Christ Child is more of a choirboy lark than a serious felony."

The poor vicar's trembling returned with such severity that I thought he might pitch himself onto the stone floor. "Oh no! This is not a prank! A thief has taken the doll for his eyes!"

Holmes had been slowly circling the scene, inspecting the thin wines that kept several of the characters upright. He halted beside the manger. "What was unique about the figure's eyes?" he asked.

"They were sapphires, sir. True gems, not bits of paste. They were perfectly matched and said to be worth a thousand pounds each. That is why we have guarded our tableau so carefully. Everyone in the parish knows about the beautiful eyes of the baby."

Holmes cut a sharp glance at the vicar. "And the rest of the doll?"

"It was of no particular value. It had a porcelain head, but the body was cloth, stuffed with sawdust and fragrant herbs. It was wrapped in a blue silk gown."

Holmes dropped to his knees and pulled his lens from a pocket of his coat. He began to crawl around in the straw, closely examining the floor beneath the figures. "Tell me what precautions you took," Holmes said. "Clearly they failed, for such a theft to occur."

The distraught clergyman began to whimper. "I or Mr. Jones sat in the pews whenever the doors were unlocked. I watched the scene all morning – a few ladies and gentlemen came by, and I was forced to shoo away some rapscallion children. An hour ago, Mr. Jones was to relieve me, but he was running late and I fear I had a case of . . . indisposition." He clutched his belly, his face turning purple with shame. "I had no time to lock the doors, and I was in the washroom for nearly ten minutes. When I returned, the Christ Child was gone. Sir . . . sir, what are you doing?"

Holmes had dropped completely to the floor and appeared to be working at the cracks of an ancient burial slab that the nativity scene surmounted. I suspected the vicar was regretting allowing a clearly insane man to try to help him.

"Aha," Holmes called, "we are in luck! The babe has sprung a leak!"

"What?"

"See here – the traces of sawdust and the scattered herbs. For us, the trail will go cold within a few paces, but for another . . . Watson, would you be so kind as to hail a cab and once again pay a visit to my old friend Mr. Sherman at Number 3, Pinchin Lane?"

"Shall I ask for Toby?"

"No, I fear that Toby's best days are behind him. Request Patches instead – it is time that he proved his worth in the field."

I set off immediately on my task, recalling with some humor the journey I had made to Mr. Sherman's odd menagerie during the adventure of the Sign of the Four. It took me well over an hour to reach my destination and return, for the streets were horribly congested with last-minute shoppers, carol singers, snowball fights between street arabs, and general holiday mayhem. As I rode along, I tried to apply Holmes's methods and reconstruct the scene in my mind. Holmes had frequently recommended employing one's imagination in the early stages of detective work, and I gave mine full rein.

Clearly, the thief had learned of the doll's value, either while attending worship or from the idle talk of parishioners. The vicar struck me as a man who would brag about the value of a patron's gift, especially as the neighborhood around the sanctuary was a poor one and the benefactor of the dolls had once been among the lowly of his flock. But how had the thief succeeded? Had he lurked in the shadows or somehow hidden himself beneath a pew? The church was exceptionally small, making such a concealment unlikely. The vicar seemed to believe his curate was trustworthy, but was he? Could the vicar himself be a criminal? For an instant my mind ran wild, considering the web of illegal activities organized by the late Professor Moriarty. Had Holmes failed in his task of bringing them all to ground? A man who would despoil a church had no respect for any creature, and might be the most desperate character imaginable. I suddenly found myself wishing that I were carrying my revolver instead of my medical bag.

Patches proved to be a dog of promiscuous pedigree. He had the long, trailing ears of a basset, the general compact body of a beagle, and the soft, curly coat of a spaniel. His eyes were bright, and his tail wagged madly. He was clearly eager to be released from his kennel and showed no concern for the inclement weather as we returned across the city. The vicar of St. Rita's gave a sharp cry when we entered the sanctuary, protesting the dog's presence.

"Very well, we shall retire," Holmes said. "Do give my best to your patron, and be sure to explain to him that his gift could have been found, if not for your refusal to allow Patches a small sniff of the evidence."

With an annoying whine, the vicar stepped back and motioned for Patches to approach. The dog dropped his nose to the straw, sniffing eagerly. He then whirled and made an unholy braying. I tossed the leash to Holmes, and we were off.

Respectable Londoners cleared a path as we sped down the street. Patches tugged hard, and Holmes was pressed to keep up with the canine. I, likewise, had difficulty keeping up with Holmes. More than once I slipped on the ice and toppled into a dirty snowbank, but I was always able to find my companion's trail by the harsh looks and murmurs of outrage from offended pedestrians.

A man sitting among a collection of spilled packages alerted me to the fact that "a crazy fellow with a dog" had turned the corner. I followed, just in time to spot Holmes ducking into an alleyway. Gasping for breath, I picked up my pace, dipping into the lane behind them.

I suddenly was in a new and repulsive environment. Gone were the cheerfully decorated streets, the warmly glowing windows. I had entered a warren of dingy alleys and narrow pathways, a hive of grim and stench. Walls were dark and stained, filth of all descriptions was piled near narrow doorways. We were stranded among some of the most squalid tenements of London, trapped in a vast rookery of disease and vice. Spectral figures wrapped in rags and cast-off coats hovered around fires set in barrels, and a sharp-ribbed, feral dog growled at Patches as our strange procession passed. I felt the weight of angry stares, the bitterness of resentment in the lean and dirty faces that turned as we moved through them. Patches stopped before a door that was half off its hinges. He squatted down and gave a sharp bark.

"I think we have reached our destination," Holmes said. "My apologies for such a brisk jog, Watson. I trust your leg has stood the test."

I glanced over my shoulder at a party of ill-clad men who had drawn together, whispering and staring at us. "I am much more concerned for my back. In this neighborhood, I might find a knife in it."

"Not a scenic area of our great city, though I hear that tours are regularly organized for the curious – a pastime quaintly referred to as 'slumming'."

I could hardly share Holmes's wry amusement at our predicament. At that moment, however, the flimsy door opened and a young boy emerged. Much to my horror, he was barefoot, despite the bitter cold, and was in the process of applying a match to an old pipe.

"Excuse me, young man," Holmes said, "but could you tell me if you have seen a girl enter this house only a few hours ago, carrying a rather large doll?"

The boy favored Holmes with an appraising look. "What's it worth to you, Guv'nor?"

Holmes held out a shilling. The boy raised his hand and waggled his fingers, indicating a demand for more. Holmes started to place the coin back in his pocket.

"Wait! I know her! I can tell you!"

Holmes dropped one shilling into the boy's grubby palm. The coin disappeared with the speed of a conjurer's trick.

"That's Betsy – she's third floor, in the rear. What's she done? Are the blue bottles after her?"

Holmes shook his head. "Thank you for that information. If you will be so good as to watch my dog for a few minutes, there's a guinea in it for you."

The boy eagerly seized Patches's leash, squatting down to call the pup to him. In the ways of dogs and boys everywhere, Patches began to lick the lad's face, perhaps the first good scrubbing that countenance had known in months. Holmes signaled for me to follow.

"Holmes," I said, as we began ascending a narrow flight of stairs in almost total darkness, "how did you know it was a girl who took the doll?"

"Elementary, Watson. There were some indications of a small, delicate boot-print on the sanctuary carpet around the nativity scene. But even before I saw those marks, I theorized that it was a young girl who committed this crime." He turned as we reached the door of the final flat in the rear of the building. "Who else would impulsively steal a pretty doll?"

Holmes knocked gently. After a moment, the door swung open, revealing a girl who was no more than ten. Her pale face and sharp cheekbones spoke of a life of suffering. Her greasy brown hair was fixed in long, unkempt braids, and her dress and smock were ragged. Great holes gapped from her torn stockings, and her little boots were held together with pieces of string.

"Yes?" she whispered, clearly alarmed at the sight of two official-looking gentleman at her threshold. Holmes removed his hat. His entire persona changed in an instant. Gone was the stern enforcer of justice, the apprehender of felons; Holmes was suddenly a paragon of benevolence. "Miss Betsy, we have been asked to come here by the vicar of St. Rita's church. We believe that there has been a terrible mistake made, and that you have taken something from the sanctuary that did not belong to you."

The girl gasped and stepped backward. Her chin lifted and moisture filled her eyes, but she made no attempt to deny her actions.

"I only took it for Ellen. It was all she wanted, a dolly for Christmas. I went to church, to pray for her. She's so sick, and there's no money, and Father is gone and Mother . . . ."

The child dissolved in tears. I started to speak, but Holmes signaled for silence. The girl gasped against her sudden emotion.

"I didn't think . . . the Christ Child would mind if I took him. Ellen is so sick. I thought maybe . . . having a dolly . . . would make her better. Like a miracle."

"Miss Betsy," Holmes said, "my friend is a doctor. Will you allow him to treat your sister?"

She sniffed and stared down at her twine-laced boots. "I can't. There's no money."

I held up my bag and quickly borrowed a phrase from Holmes. "My dear little girl," I said, "my work is its own reward."

She looked up, the skepticism of a hard existence making her momentarily wary of my offer. Then she grabbed my hand and towed me into the only other room in the flat, a close and miserable chamber with a mattress on the floor. An even smaller girl was laid upon it, covered in an array of thin blankets and scarfs. The Christ Child was tucked beneath her arm, held as tightly as her pitiful strength would allow. Betsy reached down and gently removed the doll, passing it to Holmes with a murmured apology and then making room for me to kneel at her sister's side to begin my examination.

Holmes's way with children was always remarkable – his tone was firm, yet kind, and in no way scolding or patronizing. In just a matter of moments he was able to coax the girl's story from her. Her father, it seemed, had died from an injury sustained in a local factory, forcing her mother to go to work at an unwholesome sweatshop. The girls were left alone, and they tried to help their family by mud larking. Ellen had fallen ill while climbing about in the dregs of the Thames, looking for whatever bits of cast-off junk the children could sell. Their mother was at work, and Betsy had slipped away to the church while her ailing sister napped, at first to pray but then, upon spotting the vicar, to ask for aid. The clergyman had ordered the girl out of his sanctuary, but the moment his back was turned she had returned and stretched out along a pew. When he made his brief exit to the washroom, she scampered up to the altar and purloined the doll from the manger.

"I knew it was wrong," Betsy said, "but I couldn't stop myself."

The little sister had a high fever and was congested, but I felt that we had arrived in time to save her. I was about to say as much when I noted the expression on my friend's face. I had never seen him look so troubled.

"Watson, I must step away for a few moments. Miss Betsy, do pay attention to the good Doctor and do all that he requires."

She nodded solemnly. From long experience, I knew better than to inquire where Holmes was going or what his sudden errand might be. For almost an hour, I schooled the little girl in how to best care for her sister, instructing her on when to administer the medicine I provided, and how to prepare some plasters to keep her chest warm and aid her breathing. We gave her a quick wash, then changed her coverings and her meager gown, wrapping her properly. By the time we finished our tasks, Holmes appeared in the doorway.

"Ah, I see that the sickroom has been cleared of debris," Holmes said. "And this, I think, shall cheer it up."

He removed a package from inside his coat. It was wrapped in bright red and green paper, and topped with a spring of holly. Betsy stared at it.

"Sir, what is that?"

"Something you and your sister will enjoy. No, no, you must not open it until Christmas morning! You cannot wait? Very well. Ah, and I see that my trusty porters have arrived!"

As Betsy freed the box from its paper, a small troop of young boys and girls followed Holmes inside, each carrying a paper bag filled with groceries. One child tripped, spilling out a sack of oranges and nuts. Holmes merely laughed, rewarded each of his helpers with a shiny coin, and herded them out through the doorway.

I heard Betsy gasp. At last the box was open, and inside was the loveliest doll I had ever seen. It was a perfect replica of a young girl, complete with a pink satin dress and embroidered Chinese silk slippers. It had bright blue eyes, and its brown hair was set in enticing curls. I was struck by how much it would resemble Betsy, if life and circumstances had treated her with more kindness.

"Oh, she is wonderful! Ellen will be so happy!" Betsy's gaze took in all of the foodstuffs as well. "But – we cannot pay you."

"Father Christmas never expects payment," Holmes said. "I am merely his delivery man."

Betsy was old enough to know the truth of such matters. Yet she nodded sagely and agreed to tell her sister that they had been visited by Saint Nicholas. Holmes handed the girl a card.

"On Boxing Day, you must come to this address. A kind lady named Mrs. Hudson will give you more treats, which you will share with your sister and your mother."

"But sir," the girl sighed, "shouldn't I be sent to jail? I did a bad thing."

Holmes knelt, meeting her gaze at her level. "It is true, you did a naughty deed, but Christmas is the season for forgiveness. I think you have learned an important lesson today – and perhaps taught a greater one to two old sinners."

The girl nodded solemnly, then bobbed a curtsey. Holmes reclaimed the Christ Child doll, which had been pushed against a wall. We chuckled when we noticed that a seam along its right leg had opened, spilling out sawdust and herbs, withering the limb until the infant Jesus was lamed by his adventure. Holmes wrapped the doll in his coat, then we descended the stairs and reclaimed Patches. Holmes paid his helper, who was somewhat loathe to surrender his charge, as he had been training Patches to fetch a stick. We journeyed first to Pinchin Lane, where Mr. Sherman required a recounting of our adventure, and Patches was duly rewarded for his services with a large bone. We returned to St. Rita's at a much slower pace than we had departed it, and found the frantic vicar waiting for us at the door.

"Thank heavens! By all that is wonderful, you have saved me!" He seized the doll from Holmes's hand and raced to return it to the manger. "I cannot imagine the damage that would have been done. My career, my reputation would have been ruined. But . . . but who took it? How did you find the villain? Is he under arrest? Where should I go to file the charge against him? Tell me his name and I will have him prosecuted to the full extent of the law!"

"You will do no such thing," Holmes snapped. "You hired me only to retrieve the figure, not to find the thief."

"But – "

One icy glare silenced the clergyman. Holmes folded his arms. "Now, there is the matter of my fee."

"Fee?"

"Do you think I race around London for my health? Do you think that solving mysteries, producing stolen articles from thin air, is some variety of magic trick? Of course I demand compensation."

The vicar's brow became a virtual Niagara. Sweat streamed over his bushy eyebrows, dripped from his chin, and stained his collar. He pressed clenched hands against his breast.

"Oh, of course. How . . . how much, sir? What will it cost me?"

"Some human compassion," Holmes said. "I demand that you show some care for the people who live at this address. They are to receive food, clothing, and medicine for their sick child." Holmes thrust a card into the clergyman's hand. The vicar peered down at the address and gave a gasp of recognition.

"I know them. The father died of drink, I believe, and the mother is a harlot – the oldest girl will be a slut as well, in time. Surely there are more worthy recipients."

In a sudden motion, Holmes seized the wretched clergyman by the front of his cassock. The vicar's feet quivered in mid-air. "This family will receive aid, or your patron will be informed of how his gift was nearly lost by your irresponsibility. Is that clear to you?" Holmes hissed.

The clergyman bobbed his head. Holmes dropped him to the ground and bid him good day. We departed just as the first of the Christmas Eve worshippers came streaming into the sanctuary.

Later that evening, Sherlock Holmes fell into a black mood. He barely exchanged words with me over dinner, other than to complement the choice of vintage wine that I had purchased on the way home. He stood smoking his pipe, staring out the window onto Baker Street.

"Watson," he said, "are you familiar with St. Rita, the worthy for whom the church was named?"

I confessed my ignorance as I poured myself another glass of wine and joined him at the window. Outside, a few intrepid carolers were making their rounds, and more than one obviously intoxicated reveler staggered down the sidewalk, bobbing from doorway to doorway and trying without success to hail a cab.

"She is a patron saint of impossible causes. I am beginning to think that it is all impossible . . . or at least pointless."

A fresh, heavy snow began to fall, forcing those of goodwill and too much holiday cheer to abandon the street. Holmes withdrew his pipe. His face was a mirror of sadness, and his eyes seemed not to be gazing out at the snow, but deeply into the past.

"What kind of world do we live in, Watson?" Holmes asked. "What type of man would create gilded statues and dolls sewn with gems while ignoring starving orphans in the shadows? What kind of faith would place more emphasis on the letter of the law than the spirit of compassion? We say we live in an age of progress, but what progress have we really made?"

Something in his stance, his tone, brought me to a powerful realization. My friend was hiding something beneath his innate brilliance. Over the years, I had caught glimpses of it in the way Holmes treated his Baker Street Irregulars and in his general comradery with children. It illuminated him whenever he fought for justice for the weak and oppressed. My friend had never refused a case for lack of payment, and he could be as gallant to an old charwoman as to a duchess. In that very moment, as Christmas Eve became Christmas Day, I began to wonder if what little Holmes had told me about his youth might be as much of a falsehood as I suspected the tales of his hiatus were. What secrets was he protecting? What might have been his true origin?

But I dared not voice my suspicions. Holmes's sudden despair alarmed me, and I tried to draw him out of his dark thoughts. "Where did you find the doll that you gave to Betsy and Ellen?"

"In a toy shop not five blocks from where those poor girls resided. They must have passed it on display in the window, every day on their way to the Thames." He turned and went to the fireplace, knocking out the debris on his pipe into the grate. "I have never set foot in such an establishment. No wonder parents dread this season. Do you have any idea of how much such a babble costs?"

"Yet you did not hesitate to pay it," I said. Holmes made a face and provided a pithy description of the nearly murderous crowd in the store, all squabbling over dolls and trains and sets of building blocks. Perhaps it was this sudden spark of humor, or possibly it was the second glass of wine that I had consumed, but something caused me to blurt out the thoughts that his amusing tirade inspired.

"Holmes – you do the world a disservice by remaining a bachelor! You should marry and become a father. Your talents with children are exceptional – imagine how rewarding a family would be."

"A family! Then heaven help London!" Holmes said, with an excess of alarm. "Can you envision the Holmes tribe set loose upon the metropolis? Running amok, trying to solve every puzzle and unravel every mystery among the juvenile set? My children would be inquisitive little savages with magnifying glasses and cloth caps and pipes – even the girls! They would make the Baker Street Irregulars look like angels. No, my friend, the offspring of Sherlock Holmes would be a story for which the world would never be prepared!"

I laughed fully and poured yet another libation for us, passing a glass to my friend and thinking that, of all the gifts of the holiday, the best one of all was to have him back. "Happy Christmas, Sherlock Holmes."

The Adventure of the Furniture Collector

"My husband, Mr. Holmes, is a fool. He cannot see that the fellow who visits our shop is a rascal. This is hardly a case for the police, for I cannot say that a crime has been committed, but clearly a man who would change his name and appearance three times in a single month is up to no good."

My friend smiled as he settled into his armchair. It was a bitterly cold winter morning, and the gray, muted sky held the promise of snow. I had rather selfishly hoped that no case or client would disturb us, for it was a day when a man wants nothing more than to sit with his feet toward the fire, enjoying a glowing pipe and an all-absorbing novel. I had been questing with a medieval knight for the previous hour and was irked to leave our fair damsel in distress while Holmes permitted this dragon to invade our domicile. The repellant lady was perhaps fifty years of age, extraordinarily tall and thin, dressed in a black frock and a gray fur coat that was worn to a greasy shine. Her features were too sharp for any pretense at beauty, and her small eyes shone with a ferocity unbecoming in her sex. As I reluctantly put aside my novel for my notebook, I marveled that such a hideous woman had somehow managed to acquire a husband – even one who was, in her words, a fool.

"Your spouse is certainly fortunate to possess a supremely intelligent wife," Holmes said, clearly working not to laugh. "Watson sometimes thinks me as a sullen misogynist – " Here my friend gave me a conspiratorial wink. " – but I assure you that I value the observations of the fair sex, who are often aware of subtle elements which elude the masculine gaze."

"Hmmph! I am aware that Horatio Thornbill was *nothing* before he married me," the woman answered, with a sharp nod. "My people have been in business since the Tudors ruled. I was the one who taught him the secrets of our trade."

"Which is?" Holmes inquired.

"The sale of used furniture. Or – as I have instructed Horatio to call it – the careful curating of exceptional furnishings. We read the newspapers, and when someone of note dies impoverished, I send Horatio out to speak with the relatives who are usually eager to sell off what they can to settle debts. The elite have more taste than ready cash, and we acquire fine pieces for a pittance, especially when wayward heirs do not know the value of what they have inherited. Our store on Pancras Road displays furniture once owned by counts and knights and baronets – even by the occasional embarrassed duke or duchess." The lady lifted her long, hawkish nose. "It is a wonder how much some people will pay for an unremarkable mirror or sideboard because it once graced an ancestorial hall."

"A fascinating trade," Holmes said dryly. "How much would Watson's old chair or my deal-topped table fetch?"

Mrs. Thornbill removed a small notebook from her purse, ignoring Holmes's jibe. "I felt you would want our experience presented to you in order. That is, if what I hear is about you is not mere fiction, but reflections of your interest in all that is strange and bizarre in our city's life?"

Holmes elevated an eyebrow. "Very well, Madame. Please proceed."

"It started in November – the tenth of the month, to be precise. Just an hour before closing time, a gentleman came into our business. He introduced himself as Mr. William Sherman, and from his accent I would guess him to be an American, or perhaps a Canadian. He was a memorable man – tall, with a great head of white hair and a silver goatee, very elegantly and tastefully dressed, and softly spoken. He seemed to have very particular tastes. He asked if it was true that we had recently acquired several hand-made items from a certain estate. He picked out two items from that collection – a sideboard and an armoire – and made a down payment on them. Horatio extended him our most favorable credit."

"I take it from the coolness of your tone that you did not agree with your husband's decision."

"I fear not. He should have asked for credentials! The gentleman was gracious and pleasant, and I will acknowledge that he put down five pounds easily enough from his pocketbook as he provided the address where the goods were to be delivered. But there was something about him I did not trust. However, we sent the items to him the next day, in our van, and I later asked Teddy and Morgan – they are the two stout lads who come by twice a week to make deliveries for us – about the situation they found. They said the gentleman tipped them well, and that he was clearly in need of furniture, for the flat was almost completely bare.

"I gave it no more thought, but a week later, Mr. Sherman reappeared in our shop. I noticed that he had a black armband on his sleeve. Horatio rather clumsily asked Mr. Sherman who he had lost, and he sighed and told us that his wife had perished. 'A sudden thing,' he said. 'Her doctors think an aneurysm in the brain.' But before either of us could express condolences, he gestured to the wall behind me and asked if the mirror there, in a very unusual octagon frame, was from the same suite as his other furnishings. When I confirmed that it was, he insisted upon purchasing it. Horatio – in a moment of sentimental weakness – let him have it at a discount, on account of his recent bereavement, and insisted on adding it to his credited account, rather than demanding so much as a shilling in down payment."

"Again," Holmes said, "I sense your disapproval."

"What kind of man suddenly needs a fancy mirror when his wife has just died?" Mrs. Thornbill snapped. "He hadn't even mentioned a spouse on his previous visit. He clearly cared nothing about her! Perhaps he only married her for her money.

"Horatio agreed with me that our customer hadn't appeared overly grief-stricken. And eight days later, while I was in our back room working on our accounts, Horatio came galloping in with the news that another gentleman was interested in the same ensemble Sherman had purchased from and was willing to pay handsomely for a writing desk and chair. This aroused my curiosity and I glanced through the curtain that separates our showroom from our storage.

"Mr. Holmes, this man – who had given his name as Mr. Philip Sheridan – had hair as black as coal and was clean-shaven. He wore a green and gold checkered coat, with a scarlet tie and a purple silk vest. His voice was booming, and his manner was gregarious and boastful.

"'A fine, beautiful piece. Such elegant craftsmanship. I must have. Let us add in that bookcase, which matches the desk. You can make me an excellent price, I presume?'

"Of course, Horatio – overwhelmed by the man's familiarity – did so. He extended generous credit. And once again – "

"You felt cheated," I guessed.

"Oh no – I was *infuriated*, for it was clearly Mr. Sherman, with his face shaved, and wearing a new set of garments and an altered attitude. I had almost burst through the curtain, but I wouldn't wish Horatio to be embarrassed before a customer, and so I held my peace, though the moment Mr. Sheridan strolled away, twirling his cane, I took Horatio by the ear and pulled him into the back room, where I gave him a piece of my mind for being so easily deceived.

"'Why would he come here in such a garb and pretend to be someone else?' I asked. And, Mr. Holmes, my husband answered with the most ridiculous words that have ever fallen from his silly lips.

"'Katey,' he said to me, 'if the man has just lost his wife, he is probably in search of a new one. Women are more easily drawn to a jolly man than a grim fellow, and perhaps the word in his neighborhood is that he is cursed, or even that he did away with his lady. That is why he must adopt a disguise and take a new name. Some men simply cannot exist without female companionship. Why, Katey, if you were to suddenly die, well, I would have to find myself a new partner, and I would waste no time in doing so.'"

"Ah," Holmes said. "And where did you hide the body?"

The woman glared at my friend. "It was difficult *not* to murder him."

"I would imagine. But please go on – your tale is intriguing."

"I warned Horatio that any man who feels the need to change his face and name isn't a man who will cover his debts. And just as I predicted, Mr. Sheridan's payment didn't arrive on time the next week! I wrote out a note and sent it round, and when that went unanswered, I dispatched Jeffrey, our new clerk, to see to the collection himself. He returned looking solemn."

"'He's dead,' Jeffrey told me.

"'What!'

"'Yes, Mrs. Thornbill, dead as Caesar. His landlady said so. Seems that he was in a terrible accident, thrown from a cab and trampled by horses, right near Trafalgar Square. I asked about the furniture, but the landlady had already sold it, because he was behind on his rent when he died.'"

"That was exactly five days ago. This very morning, another man came into the store and inquired about the rest of the stock Mr. Sherman-Sheridan had begun purchasing. This gentleman was stoop-shouldered, and shabbily dressed in a long black coat. He leaned heavily upon his cane, and his voice was a broken, raspy thing, barely able to escape through the tangle of his bushy white beard. When he removed his hat, his head was completely bald and dotted all over with painful-looking sores. I couldn't tell you the color of his eyes, for he wore heavy, green-tinted spectacles. He gave his name as Grant, and Horatio was about to make him a price for the remaining objects. I fear I rather lost my temper, for I was tired of this game."

"'What do you want with those items?' I demanded, thrusting myself between my husband and our customer.

"'Why, I am furnishing my house,' the man replied.

"'But why these particular items?' I asked. 'If you need a hat stand and a curio case, we have a dozen more, in better condition and for lower prices. Will you take them?'

"'I think I know what I want!' he snapped.

"'You may want the moon, for all I care, for we will not sell these pieces to you.'

"Horatio was, as you might imagine, about to die of embarrassment. After all, the gentleman was certainly offering to pay as much as the articles were worth. And at my words, he doubled his bid for them. Still, I ordered him to leave. He shook his fist at us, then turned away and departed.

"'Katey, are you mad?' Horatio whined.

"'Are you blind?' I snapped. 'That was Sherman! Or Sheridan! Didn't you notice that he walked to our window with his shoulders high, but when he came through the door he was suddenly bent and lame? And that outrageous beard and those hideous glasses – no one with any sense would be fooled. Don't you understand – he's trying to collect the ensemble, without being able to pay for it in full."

"'But why would a man go to such lengths to purchase a single set of furniture – and not pieces that belonged to anyone who was famous?'

"'I don't know, but I would wager Mr. Sherlock Holmes does! You will go to see him, right this minute!'

The lady shook her head. "But he wouldn't, sir. Horatio argued that if I was so certain of the man's criminality, I should be the one who consulted you. As much as it pains me to say it, my husband is a fool, and a coward in the bargain."

My friend's eyes were gleaming. I knew that a trip into the bitter cold was in our future.

"Mrs. Thornbill, you are to be commended for your astuteness," Holmes said. "I will endeavor to live up to your faith in my powers. But first let me put a few questions to you. You say the furniture is all a set. Where did it originate?"

Thornbill flipped through her notes and tore off a page, passing it to Holmes. "From the household of the late Agnus Parker. His daughter, who handled the sale, still resides at this address."

"Do you know what the gentleman's profession might have been? You have said he wasn't one of your persons of note, whose former possessions might tempt a collector."

Mrs. Thornbill shook her head. "He wasn't famous, but he was talented. He was a woodworker, one of the best carpenters in London, and he made furniture and cabinetry for discerning clients. His daughter informed me that her father had spent his youth in America, but that is all I know about him. The pieces were quite lovely. The man's skills far exceeded that of an ordinary craftsman."

"Did his daughter state the reason for selling the furniture?"

Mrs. Thornbill frowned. "I didn't handle the negotiations, but I recall that Horatio said Miss Parker seemed eager to leave London. I remember this only because he said her urgency to be freed of the city mirrored her Christian name – which is Emancipation."

Holmes rose, his hands clasped behind his back. "Just a few more inquiries if you please. When Sherman-Sheridan returned in disguise as Grant, were you able to take his address?"

"Horatio hadn't made it that far in their discussion."

"And your clerk – Jeffrey. How long has he been with you?"

"He came in November, just after the visit by Mr. Sheridan."

"Are his wages fair?"

Mrs. Thornbill sat up straighter, a bright flush of indignation staining her cheeks. "Sir, that is a rather impertinent question!"

Holmes held out a conciliatory hand. "I am only curious to learn if the young man might be tempted into wickedness."

Our guest blinked rapidly. "He's paid well enough, but he is new, and he must work for a year before he earns any commissions. He drinks more than he should. I have told him that if he returns once more smelling of liquor, he will be sacked." Mrs. Thornbill shook her head. "He's annoying at times, but rather harmless."

"Then here is my advice to you. Return home immediately and close your shop for the day. Find some petty tasks for your clerk to do, to make sure that he remains on the premises. Doctor Watson and I will pay a call upon your shop by five at the latest. I think, at that time, I should be able to answer your most intelligent question."

Mrs. Thornbill seemed poised to launch a dozen more inquiries, but Holmes caught her elbow, hoisted her from the chair, and rather brusquely led her to the doorway. He then turned to me and began issuing orders.

"There is no time to lose. Pull on your warmest coat, Watson, and let us see where this curious and delightful little problem will lead."

Our first call was upon the bereaved daughter. While in the vestibule of Baker Street and just before we stepped into the frigid air, Holmes had scribbled a note. At our destination, this was passed along by a young maid, who quickly returned to lead us into the lady's parlor.

There was no need for Holmes to draw my attention to the obvious as we entered, for the room was nearly empty. Dark patches on the wallpaper revealed where pictures and mirrors had once hung, and only a few scattered porcelain figurines remained as decoration on the mantel, along with a half-dozen photographs in tarnished frames. More remarkable than the impoverishment of the room, however, was the chamber's sole occupant – a gray and black dog, some hideous blending of a wolfhound and mastiff, which immediately raised itself up to its impressive height and issued a warning growl from deep within its massive chest. Just as we had begun to fear for our lives, the lady entered through the opposite doorway and spoke firmly to the beast.

"Down, Rex! These gentlemen are friends." The creature immediately sank to the sad, much-frayed carpet, but its eyes followed its mistress's progress, and a show of teeth made it clear to us that no impropriety would be tolerated. "Forgive him, sirs. Rex is quite jealous of me."

Holmes shook the lady's hand and offered a quick condolence on her father's passing. She was still clad in black, a color which ironically flattered her fair skin and beautiful swirl of ash-blonde hair. She was barely twenty years of age, with large, innocent blue eyes, and I suddenly felt the need to protect her and lighten her burden.

"Thank you for seeing us so unexpectedly, Miss Parker. I am sorry to intrude upon your grief, and to ask such bizarre questions, but I fear some greater issue may be at stake."

"I only hope that I can help you," the lady said, glancing briefly at Holmes's note, "and I am grateful that you came promptly, for in two days I begin the most unpleasant task of moving. I have decided to live with a maiden aunt in the Lake District."

"Did your relocation motivate the sale of your furniture?" Holmes asked.

"In part . . . though to be truthful, I hadn't intended to leave this home until my year of mourning was done, but now I am afraid to stay here, with just my maid and noble Rex to look after me."

Holmes insisted that she take the only seat remaining in the room. The dog curled around her feet, still maintaining a watchful gaze at the strangers in his lair.

"And what has provoked your fear, Miss Parker?"

"A most unpleasant incident that occurred in this very room, less than a week after Father's funeral. Had Rex not been so close, I fear I would have lost my honor, if not my life."

"Your house was burgled?" I asked.

"No, sir. I endured a very distressing visit from a man who introduced himself as Mr. George Thomas. His letter of introduction claimed that he had known my father in America, and that he had some information which would be of interest to me. I received him here, and at first he seemed pleasant enough, and his memories of Father appeared authentic."

Holmes's eyes had narrowed, and a troubled look passed across his face. "Can you describe this gentleman?"

The lady gave a sharp sneer. "He was no gentleman, for all of his fine coat and silver watch chain. He was tall, and handsome in the face, but both his hair and beard were dyed a rather vulgar shade of red, as if he were trying to pass himself off as a man half his age. He moved around the room restlessly, and kept touching and examining objects, as if preparing to purchase them. It unnerved me, the way he caressed the furniture. There was a little writing desk just there, in the corner. Before my very eyes, Mr. Thomas opened every drawer and pilfered inside them! It was more than I could bear, so I rose and very curtly asked him to leave.

"'My dear,' he said, in a most forward manner, 'I cannot. Your Father, in his last days, wrote to me and begged me to come to London upon his passing and take care of you. I will love and cherish you forever.'

"It was nonsense, Mr. Holmes – foul and repulsive nonsense. I knew Father would never have sent such a letter, especially to a man of whom I had no prior knowledge, had never met before that hour. But the wretch wouldn't go away, even when I ordered him to depart. To my horror, he fell upon his knees, seized my hand in his paws, and begged me to marry him!

"I told him to leave that instant – he said he would not. I called for my maid, but he rose like a flash and threw his arms around me, begging me to kiss him. He tried to force himself upon me. I fought him like a tiger, I screamed for help – and suddenly Rex broke from where he had been tied in the next room and flew upon the man. The fellow shrieked as my dog's teeth clamped around his arm. He shook loose but Rex seized upon one leg. The last I saw of Mr. George Thomas, he was fleeing down the street in a most indecent state, for Rex had ripped away the entire seat of his trousers!

"I was so shaken I couldn't sleep that evening. I decided I would sell everything and leave London to live with my aunt. The furniture was easily dispensed with – sold to Mr. Thornbill, who understood how unique Father's handmade pieces were – but there were other details to arrange, including the sale of the house. Thank goodness I can depart soon."

Holmes nodded, then posed a strange question. "Do you know why your father gave you such a unique name? I have made the acquaintance of ladies named Temperance and Charity, as well as Europa and Americus, but never Emancipation."

The young woman smiled. "There is indeed a story, though of interest to none but me. Father was an American, born in the state of Wisconsin. He was twenty years old when the Civil War erupted, and he longed to enlist in the army, for he had a passionate hatred of slavery and believed that the southern rebels should be punished for their many crimes. But sadly, father had a club foot, and he was deemed unfit for military service. Eager to serve the nation's cause in some fashion, he moved to Washington, where he helped to build military hospitals and other necessary structures. He even met and worked for President Lincoln. Father so admired the president that he vowed, should he ever have a son, he would name the boy Lincoln, and if a daughter – " Here the lady smiled.

" – she would be Emancipation, for Father could think of no other feminine name that would better honor his hero."

Holmes thanked the lady and we exited her house. The moment we reached the sidewalk, Holmes flagged down a cab, giving the driver Mrs. Thornbill's address and promising a sovereign if the man could get us there in twenty minutes. The driver whipped the horse so enthusiastically that I was nearly pitched out of the vehicle.

"I say – Why the hurry?"

"Because," he answered, "I fear I have made a critical error. Watson, do you recall the sad fate of my client, Mr. John Openshaw?"

It took me a moment to sort through the vast cast of characters, the many people who had called upon my friend in their hour of need. At last, the young man's pale, worried face returned to my mind, but it was difficult to answer Holmes over the wild clattering of hooves. The pavement was slick and icy, and our driver was reckless to the point of homicidal.

"I do – but why should I?"

"Because I blundered. I sent him away when I should have kept him close, and he was murdered as a result. I fear I have made the same error. I should never have allowed Mrs. Thornbill to return to her shop."

"Good Heavens! What makes you think – ?"

"I didn't take the affair seriously. I was certain the clerk was involved, but I suspected a petty crime. Now, I realize a game of greater stakes is being played."

"Why are you accusing the clerk?"

"Because of the lie he told. There was no 'Mr. Sheridan' as we have learned – therefore there was no carriage accident or dispersal of the furnishings. And recall that the clerk joined the shopkeepers *after* the initial visit from the rascal in his first incarnation. He was brought into the plot – I am certain."

"Perhaps there is a female accomplice – she could have lied to the clerk."

"A possibility – but there is far more danger for the Thornbills if the clerk is dishonest or bears a grudge against them."

My head was spinning, and not just from the violent motion of the cab as we took yet another turn on a single wheel. "I still don't understand – what is the point in acquiring Parker's household goods?"

"Consider what we have learned! The man who visited Miss Parker is obviously the same man who appeared, in three different aliases, to the Thornbills. He went to Miss Parker first, he knew that her father was an American, and he made a rather sinister inspection of her parlor. Clearly, he is after something – some relic or treasure – that Parker had hidden. He was so desperate he tried to compel Miss Parker to marry him, but his clumsiness only caused her to summon her hound. Shortly afterward, she sold the objects, and this man began to purchase them. He lacked funds to buy them outright, and so went after them on credit, in different personas." Despite our cab's rough passage, Holmes's expression was calm and deliberate. "Whatever Parker possessed is a relic of great value."

"What could it be?"

Holmes made a grab for his hat as our cab skidded around another corner.

"The carpentry is the essential element. It must be something that could be concealed in a secret compartment. Perhaps a jewel or some important document."

"If such a treasure existed, why was the lady ignorant of it?"

Our cab cut between a lumbering omnibus and a regal brougham bearing a coat of arms. We were assailed with curses on all sides.

"An excellent question, Watson. Perhaps the father acquired this prize illegally or felt shame for possessing it. Only Mr. Thomas-Sherman-Sheridan-Grant knows for sure."

"What a strange quartet of aliases."

"They have a meaning."

"But what?"

At just that moment, our driver pulled hard upon the reins, and we came to a skittering halt. Holmes tossed him an ample reward. We had arrived at the Thornbill shop, a converted warehouse that dominated a corner of the grim, unattractive block. I was relieved to see a '*Closed*' sign hanging in the window. Yet Holmes gave a cry of alarm.

The door was ever so slightly ajar.

We raced inside. The showroom was illuminated only by the wane winter light creeping through the windows. There was no movement in the space, a large, open area filled furnishings of every description, a vast forest of chairs, cabinets, armoires, and bookcases. Holmes struck a match, applying it to a lamp on a countertop. Even as he did, I heard a low groan.

"Here!" Holmes hissed.

A thin, pale gentleman, who I presumed to be Mr. Thornbill, was sprawled behind the counter. His face was covered in blood, but when I knelt beside him, I quickly determined that the wound was superficial, and his pulse and breathing were both strong. He had been knocked unconscious, leaving an ugly gash upon his forehead, but he would easily recover. Holmes's fingers clamped to my shoulder.

"Let him wait – his lady may be in true peril. Move silently and don't hesitate to strike the villains down."

I nodded, melting into Holmes's wake as we tiptoed toward the rear of the shop, where a heavy curtain was hung, dividing the area for more storage. We eased beside it stealthily, and Holmes parted the fabric, peering into the back quarter. I dared not press closer, but I suddenly heard a voice, deep and firm.

"It isn't in the curio case – it must be in the hat stand! Do you have a screwdriver?"

"There's one in a cabinet up front," an eager speaker said.

"Go and fetch it."

Holmes and I stepped back. A moment later, a young, fair-haired man shot through the drapes. My friend was on him in a flash. With a chopping movement of Holmes's hand to the side of the neck, the youth fell senseless to the floor.

"Jeffrey?" the deeper voice called. "Jeffrey, what is it?"

There was a clatter, followed by heavy footsteps. A tall, robust, man stepped through the curtain, his jaw dropping at the sight of his helper upon the floor.

"What in the blazes – ?"

It was all he had time to utter, as Holmes stepped forward and delivered a sharp right hook to the fellow's bare jaw. The man dropped like a stone. In an instant we had him restrained, with Holmes's handcuffs upon his wrists. Together, we dragged him to a chair and made him more secure. Holmes then stepped to the street and blew upon his police whistle, summoning a constable.

"Where is Mrs. Thornbill?" I demanded of our prisoner.

The man in the chair glared at me. He was clean-shaven, bald, perhaps fifty years of age, and strongly built. Despite Holmes's talents as a boxer, I was grateful that we had taken such a solid opponent by surprise.

"It's none of your business. Who are you to barge in here and assault us? I'll have you arrested!"

Holmes returned from summoning the official forces. He folded his arms and stared down at the man.

"I would advise you to reconsider, Mr. Sherman. Or is it Mr. Sheridan? Or Mr. Grant? Or Mr. Thomas?" Holmes shook his head. "Really, which general of the American Union army are you choosing to impersonate today?"

"I don't know what you are talking about! I'm innocent, I tell you!"

Holmes rolled his eyes. "So you intend to be wearisome. Very well, we shall place two murders to your credit – your wife as well as Mr. Thornbill."

"I have no wife! That was merely a tale, for sympathy, to acquire a discount and – !"

Holmes smiled. His prisoner suddenly blanched, realizing he had given away part of his game. Much of the bluster instantly went out of him. He dropped his shoulders, slumping forward with a moan.

"I've done nothing wrong," he whined. "I've committed no crime. True, I told a few fibs, but it was the lad who struck his master, not me. And the lady is locked upstairs, in a washroom. No harm has been done to her, I swear it."

"The inspector will be here soon," Holmes said, "and every word you speak then may be held against you. I would suggest – if you wish any sympathy from me – that you make a full confession now. Watson, will you see to the lady?"

I hurried upstairs, into the family apartments. I quickly spotted a door with several heavy chairs pushed against it. Weak calls for help originated from inside the room as I removed the barricade. Mrs. Thornbill was indeed unharmed, though ghostly pale, her hair in disarray.

"It was Jeffrey," she gasped. "He pulled a gun from his pocket and marched me up the stairs. Horatio had gone away to the market, but I knew he would come back soon, for he left his spectacles behind – My God, tell me he hasn't been killed!"

It was easy enough to trace the train of events. The couple had closed the store, as Holmes had ordered, but the clerk had taken advantage of the husband's absence to confine the lady and admit his confederate. Mr. Thornbill was extremely unlucky to have returned prematurely. I found him at the bottom of the stairs, staggering about in confusion, and left him to the care of his wife.

The vicious Jeffrey had recovered his senses by the time I returned and was huddled beside the older man's chair. Holmes handed me the youth's revolver.

"Pay careful attention to him, Watson. Any lad capable of pistol-whipping a frail old man will not hesitate to commit future mischief." With that, he turned back to the principal culprit, who now wore an expression of exhausted contrition on his face. "Let us have it from the start, beginning with your identity. I will not dishonor the four principal heroes of the Union army by applying their names to you."

"Why did you choose those aliases?" I asked. It seemed far too intentional. Surely there was some purpose.

"Because I followed them," our prisoner groaned. "Four long years, tramping along with the Federals . . . it makes an impression on a man. My real name, sirs, is Oliver Wilson, and Agnus Parker was my friend from boyhood. When the war came, he went to Washington, and I became a sutler for the Union armies, selling newspapers, food, and tobacco to the soldiers. We chose different ways to serve our country, but we remained close, and during the war I often received letters from him.

"Agnus was master carpenter. One day, early in the war, President Lincoln came to view the construction being done at a hospital and struck up a conversation with Agnus. He admired my friend's skills and offered him a place in the executive mansion, to oversee all carpentry repairs for that house.

"Agnus was a good man, a hard worker, friendly and kind, and a great favorite of children. He made several toys for the president's youngest son, Tad – play-things which were a comfort to the boy following the death of his brother Willie. It was Tad who showed his father a wooden soldier Agnus made, one with little compartments inside, where a child could hide his foolish treasures. That very evening, Lincoln called Agnus to his office and asked if Agnus might construct something similar for him – not a toy, but a desk with secret compartments where items of great value might be stored.

"Agnus did as Lincoln requested. He wrote to me and told me that the president was pleased with his new possession and used it often.

"At last, the dreary war came to an end. April 14th, 1865, found me in Washington. By pure luck, I saw Agnus coming down Pennsylvania Avenue. We went to a saloon, where we began recounting our separate adventures. We talked for hours, until the sun went down, and the establishment became uncomfortably crowded with soldiers, newsmen, and various idlers.

"'And what shall we do now?' I asked, for both of us were in high spirits, and perhaps more intoxicated than was respectable.

"'Come – I will show you the president's home,' Agnus said. "I am known to all the guards, and the president and his lady are attending a play this evening. No one will mind, and I want you to see my marvelous desk.'

"And so we found ourselves inside the executive mansion. The residents had gone out for the evening, and the attendants were relaxed, the guards and servants smoking and playing cards together. Parker was a popular character among them, so none objected when he led me through the suites of rooms, pointing to the beautiful portraits and the gifts presented from foreign leaders. At last, we slipped into a little side chamber, a private office where the president retired when he wanted to be undisturbed. My friend's achievement was handsome and useful – for every obvious drawer there were two hidden ones, which could only be opened with deliberate precision of touch. Parker demonstrated one, and I noticed a small, red, leather-bound book within.

"'What is this?' I asked, picking it up.

"'Whatever it is, it is none of our business, Ollie! Put it back!'

"But curiosity had seized me, and I had already opened the little tome. It was a diary, such as soldiers carried, and it was filled with tiny, tight script. At the bottom of one page, I saw the president's distinctive signature – *A. Lincoln*. I was about to show it to Agnus when suddenly a loud cry went up in the house. People began shouting, there was a great tramping of running feet. Agnus went into the hallway, and was back a moment later, urging me to hurry, that the president had been shot. We dashed to 10th Street, and the humble boarding house where the nation's leader had been carried. Like so many others, we stood vigil all night, praying that God would spare him, and walking away in horror and sadness when the doctors came forth to announce that he had passed.

"'I must go.' Agnus said. 'They will want me to build a bier, perhaps even the coffin.' He turned and gave me a piercing stare. 'The book you found in Mr. Lincoln's desk – do you still have it?'

"I reached into my coat pocket and drew it forth. I hadn't realized I possessed it, as alarmed as we were when we ran from the mansion. Agnus snatched it from me, muttering that he would return the book before it was missed.

"I thought no more about that item. I moved to New York City, but Agnus met a young lady of British origin, and in 1867 he followed her to London, where they were wed. For years, I received the occasional note from him. He told me of his wife's early death, and the beauty of his little daughter, and how he was making a comfortable living building furniture for wealthy Londoners. Often, I wondered how many knights or nobles had a desk like Mr. Lincoln's, and whether those desks might be filled with documents containing state secrets or private disgraces.

"But in mid-October, I received a strange and disheartening letter from my friend. He informed me that he had a cancer, and his doctor had told him to make his peace with God and the world. The letter was something of a confession – he begged my forgiveness for several childish injustices he felt he had committed, small follies I had long since forgotten. And then, to my great astonishment, he wrote that he had never returned the President's diary. His admiration for Lincoln was so deep, and his desire to have some last relic of the great man so strong, that he had retained the little red book among his own possessions. Now, facing death, he was ashamed of his theft, but he was uncertain of how to proceed, for he had read through the diary and knew that it contained 'personal things' that might damage the late president's reputation. Above all, he wanted to shield his daughter from learning of it. He begged me for advice.

"My mind ran riot. Many people in our nation consider Lincoln a saint and collecting anything associated with him – his signature on a letter, one of his old coats or hats – is a mania. My current employer, who

I dare not name, only to say he is a hero of the war and a captain of industry, would part with thousands of dollars to own such a book. I sent a telegram begging Agnus to wait, that I would come to London to speak with him. Why shouldn't his fortune be made with this item? If not for himself, then to support his soon-to-be orphaned daughter? Agnus telegraphed back that he would place the diary in a 'secret compartment' in one of his creations and await my arrival.

"But when I reached England's shores, I learned a harrowing truth: Agnus had died while I was at sea. What was I to do? He hadn't revealed where the diary was hidden, nor had he told his girl about the book. A wiser man would have laid the case before the young woman, but greed overcame me. Why should she have a claim upon it greater than my own? I confess I tried, rather clumsily, to seduce her as an avenue to searching her home but was chased away by her dog. I considered burglary, but the dog had my scent. Then, a few days later, I learned the household furniture was being sold to the Thornbills. Now my scheme focused on getting my hands on those pieces Agnus had constructed. I had staked everything on this journey, and after my initial purchase I was running low on funds. That is why I pretended to be different men, to see what I could get on credit. Every article, I chopped up, destroyed, in search of the book. The only piece that remains is that hat rack, just behind the curtain."

Holmes pointed to the clerk. "And this man?"

"I know nothing!" the youth shouted. "This is crazy talk!"

"He came to collect my payment," Wilson sighed. "I had barely a penny left to my name, but I plied him with drink and promised him half the reward if he would help me. He had no love of his employers, especially the old lady, and he agreed to be my accomplice."

The bell at the door jangled. Inspector Lestrade came stamping inside, grumbling about the cold weather and tugging at his muffler.

"Attempted murder? Thievery? *Furniture*? What's this all about, Mr. Holmes?"

"I'm sure Mr. Wilson will be happy to tell you. And I would recommend some leniency for him – but none for his helper, who tried to knock out an old man's brains. Watson, perhaps we should go upstairs and see to the health of the victim."

I spent the next half-hour attending Mr. Thornbill, making sure the damage was, as I had initially diagnosed, more cosmetic than dangerous. His wife, who had been so quick to dismiss him as a fool, now hovered about him like Florence Nightingale, cooing over his wound and attending to his every need. Holmes took her aside and told her, in hushed tones, of her customer's confession.

"You may be in possession of an object of great historical value, hidden in a hat stand."

"Oh, please – take the awful thing with you! I don't want it in my house. Why, it almost cost *dear* Horatio his life. Oh, how horrible it would have been to have lost him . . . My brave, sweet husband! What do I care for a dead American's diary? Do away with it!"

"The hat stand is worth five pounds!" the old man on the bed croaked. Holmes smiled.

"Then I shall leave ten in your cash box. Come, Watson, I think we may depart."

The next morning, Miss Emancipation Parker arrived at Baker Street, a puzzled look upon her pretty face. Holmes explained the case to her, revealing the real intentions of Oliver Wilson, and his quest to own every possible item that might contain her Father's stolen treasure, the secret diary of Abraham Lincoln.

"I was loathe to involve you," Holmes said gently. "Clearly, your father was a protective man and didn't wish you to know about the book. But if charges are brought against Wilson, there is no hope you will be kept out of the case. Your testimony against him will be essential."

The lady stiffened her shoulders. "I understand, and I will do my best to be brave should that day arrive. What of the final piece, which you purchased from the Thornbills?"

"I have it here," Holmes said, removing a flimsy cloth that had covered the item. "I thought you might wish to witness the last element of my investigation."

"There is no need."

She spoke sharply. Holmes froze, one arm reaching for the stand, the other grasping a small screwdriver. Other tools were laid atop his table, ready to be used if he couldn't unlatch any hidden compartments.

"And why is that?" my friend asked.

The lady exhaled loudly. "Mr. Holmes, as much as I appreciate your detective work, and how swiftly you have brought two criminals to justice, I question whether you understand anything about a woman's nature. From childhood, I knew my father made furniture to keep secrets for wealthy and important people. Did it not occur to you that I would be curious, especially after Father had passed away, to find what secrets he might have kept from me? The day following his funeral, I explored every object he had made for hidden drawers and cubbyholes. Most contained sentimental items – love letters from my mother, a packet of my own baby hair, an old photograph of Father during the war. But then I discovered . . . *this!*"

The lady reached into her purse and removed a small, red, leather-bound book. Holmes and I were both shocked and, I admit, rather embarrassed.

"You have read it?" Holmes asked softly.

"Yes. And it is indeed filled with 'personal' things. Mr. Lincoln well deserves his reputation as the Great Emancipator and the savior of the American union. But I alone know how deeply human he was, and how – as a man – he loved and was loved, in ways he could never reveal." The lady considered the tiny volume in her hand. "I would never disrespect his privacy or his memory, nor would I sell this to any collector, not even for the fortune it might bring."

"What shall you do with it?" my much-humbled friend asked.

"For now, I shall keep it, but eventually I will have it returned to America, to a proper historical repository. Mr. Edwin Stanton, upon Lincoln's death, said that he belonged to the ages – This volume does as well. It should be read in some future world, when all who knew Mr. Lincoln personally are gone, and any prejudices of our time are banished." She rose with a sigh, glancing toward the final article of furniture that had caused such intense pursuit. "I did not sell all of Father's creations, of course. I retained several small, personal items to remember him by. Please keep that hat stand, Mr. Holmes and, I beg you, think kindly of me."

The Adventure of the Opening Eyes

"You must help me, Mr. Holmes! My case is so strange, my problem so baffling, that surely it will be worth your time. And if not . . . then I can only prepare my soul for death, for surely the devil is after me and I cannot escape his clutches!"

My friend, Mr. Sherlock Holmes, mastered his instinctive smirk and gently waved our overly excited guest onto our sofa. The young man was tall and pale, his almost-skeletal face bathed in sweat despite the morning's autumnal chill.

"What aspect of your recent inheritance do you find so distressing?" Holmes asked. The fellow couldn't have been more than twenty-five, but some pronounced mental disturbance had lined his face and carved deep valleys beneath his eyes. He was plainly dressed, yet carried a heavy antique cane topped with a golden griffon. A large silver watch dangled from a somewhat-tarnished chain. These were the only things which I observed to give merit to Holmes's inquiry about an inheritance, though surely more clues were visible to his keen eye.

"You come directly to the point," the gentleman said, pulling out a monogramed handkerchief and mopping it across his brow. "I see your gifts have not been exaggerated. My name is Clarence Pierpont, and I am indeed troubled by my inheritance, for it comes with a curse."

Holmes settled into his chair, nodding toward the window and the dreary October weather just beyond. "A curse? Well, it is the season for such things. Do indulge us with your story."

"My maternal uncle was Victor Lynch. Perhaps you have heard of him? No?" The nervous gentleman shook his head. "I am not surprised, nor am I offended. Very few people know of him, with good reason. He was an artist, but an undistinguished one. It isn't to say that he completely lacked talent – he could produce a reasonably workmanlike landscape, and he had an aptitude for hunting dogs and horses.

"My uncle created most of his paintings for pretentious country squires and their ilk. But back in 1860, when he was just beginning his career, he produced a large canvas that won him a brief season of fame. It is called *Sleeping Venus*. Here is a reproduction of it."

He handed Holmes a hand-tinted sketch. My friend's eyebrows rose, but he said nothing before passing the image along to me.

"Why, I know this work!" I exclaimed. It was a picture of a lovely woman stretched in mid-doze along a riverbank. She was nude, though draped in her golden, flowing hair, which strategically covered her like a magical blanket. There was much to admire in the painting, from the reflection of the woman in the sparkling water to the realistic quality of the birds that curiously observed her slumber and the supple tendrils of weeping willows which formed a bower around her. But it was more than the setting and the coy pink flesh which elevated a rather pedestrian composition to a near masterpiece. It was something about her repose, the delicacy of her closed eyes, the strange aura of lifelike sleep. Studying her face, one felt drawn into the work, as if at any moment the goddess might draw a deep breath and awaken to smile sweetly at the viewer. "Where have I beheld this enchanting figure?" I asked, as much to myself as to my companions.

"Have you frequented some of our seedier drinking establishments?" Pierpont asked. "I am told that copies of her often hang behind the bar. That she sleeps above the bottles of gin."

"She is also much favored in riotous bachelor households," Holmes chuckled. "In my university days, she graced the wall of a boarding house where several young gentlemen – of the type more inclined to the pursuit of pleasure than their studies – resided in a merry company."

"You are correct, Mr. Holmes. She has become something of a garish and questionable bit of décor these days. I have never seen the original, but my uncle assured me that the copies, as splendid as they are, didn't do it justice. He said that the real *Sleeping Venus* is superb, and quite tasteful and pleasing to look upon. She is chaste and holy. It is the men who worship her image in questionable places who are vulgar and degrade her by association! I am certain that it was this quality of both sensuality and purity which attracted her purchaser, who paid my uncle a small fortune for her."

"Who owns the original?" I asked.

"That was the great family secret," Pierpont answered, lowering his voice, as if he feared we might be overheard. "For years, Uncle wouldn't divulge who had purchased the picture. He even claimed he was forbidden to discuss its buyer. But, finally, about five years ago, he revealed the truth to me. *Sleeping Venus* belongs to Her Majesty, the Queen."

I gasped. "Surely not!"

"I assure you this is true. The late Prince Consort was, as you know, a great aficionado of paintings, and he saw it in a Regent Street Gallery. The next afternoon, a royal courtier arrived to inquire about the painting, and the gallery agent was canny enough to negotiate a higher price because he realized the purchaser was the Queen. The painting was destined to be a birthday gift for His Highness." Pierpont shook his head. "I can see you don't believe me."

"The Queen is the soul of propriety!" I snapped. "To imagine her owning such a thing, it is – "

"Elementary," Holmes said, "for in 1860 the Queen wasn't yet a widow, but a wife who was very much in love with her husband. They had their private rooms and their personal collections." He smiled at my scandalized look. "They were certainly not the first married pair to indulge a love of classical images, and they possessed the wealth to own originals, not mere copies. I have it on the best authority that the Osborne House collection is quite *extensive* in this area."

I stared at Holmes, wondering who his confidant was. Who had seen the inside of Her Majesty's most private suites? Holmes signaled for our guest to continue.

"It was the sale of *Sleeping Venus* which allowed my uncle to dedicate himself solely to the pursuit of his art. Unfortunately, lifelong fame eluded him. Oh, he made enough to buy his country house and indulge his pleasures via sales to local gentry, but actual applause and a place in the pantheon of English artists was never his, and when he died, six months ago, it was in misery and obscurity. Uncle never married, and in his later years he took to drink, so that his life was shortened both through his melancholy and his indulgence in spirits.

"I am his late sister's son, and his only heir. Dale House, as it is called, passed to me, along with all of Uncle's unsold paintings. My health has never been good – indeed I have been troubled with a weak heart all my life – and knew that I couldn't afford any demanding career. I make my living by editing books and stories for aspiring writers, so I may work from any location I choose, and it seemed to me that a house in the country might be a far more pleasant home than a flat in the city. But how wrong I was!

"I took possession of Dale House a month after Uncle's burial. The property had but a single old housekeeper, who was eager to retire, and so I hired a new staff – a butler, a housekeeper who is also a cook, a boy to see after the yards and stable, and a pair of maids, twin girls from the nearby village. There was room enough in the East Wing for them all to live in the house, and it seemed that we would suit each other fine, as my needs were few and my only occasional visitors a handful of university friends.

"But a week after we had all settled in, the first strange note arrived. Harris, my butler, found it on the doorstep one morning. It was a single piece of paper, folded over, the message composed via letters clipped from a newspaper. It read: '*I am owed a thousand pounds for Sleeping Venus. Place it in the garden folly or face my wrath.*'

"You can imagine, sir, that this missive greatly shocked and alarmed me. I took it to the village constable, who dismissed it as a prank by my serving boy. Jackie sobbed and pleaded that he knew nothing of it, and he is a good lad in all regards, quite incapable of such mischief. None of the other servants could make anything of it. Baffled, I visited the former housekeeper and presented it to her. She took one look and nodded.

"'Oh, yes, the Master received many like these in the last year that he lived. Never any clue as to where they came from. Always asking for a thousand pounds, always threatening revenge. Drove him to distraction, it did.'

"'And did he know the sender?'

"'He claimed not, but I thought otherwise. Once, I heard him shrieking in a drunken tantrum that, "Venus is mine, you shall not claim her, no matter how you harass me!" But that is all I know.'"

"And have you continued to receive these messages?" Holmes asked.

"Only one more was found, three days after the first. I somehow misplaced the first letter, but I have the second one. You may read it for yourself."

I rose and moved to look over Holmes's shoulder. The letter read: *The eyes will open until my debt is settled.*

"How bizarre!" I said. "Whatever can it mean?"

"Whisky, please," our client murmured. His body had begun to sway, his hands were shaking as if he had been seized with a palsy. Holmes quickly procured a glass, while I took the man's pulse. He was in a state of such nervous excitement he seemed likely to faint.

"You must understand," he whispered, as he allowed the bracing alcohol to take effect, "that my uncle wanted nothing more than to reclaim the success he had known with his *Sleeping Venus*. To this aim, he painted almost a hundred portraits, studies of celebrities, local villagers, and his servants. In each face, the subject's eyes were closed, for that was the aspect most praised in his *Venus*. But he was never satisfied with the effect, and so the portraits remained scattered about the house, most hanging unframed, each a silent rebuke. I saw them at first as a novelty that would amuse my friends, and so I didn't move them. Now . . . I wouldn't touch one for all the money in the world. For, you see, *they are opening their eyes!*"

Holmes and I exchanged a startled glance.

"The portraits?" I asked.

"Yes. The eyes of the people in the pictures are opening, as if awakening from sleep! It began on the morning after I received that note which you hold. I had just settled into the dining room with my breakfast, and I lifted my gaze to the wall across from me, where a portrait of Lord Melbourne hung. The picture had amused me, for the statesman looked as if he had dozed off while listening to some boring speech in Parliament. But now he was staring at me, his eyes ablaze, as if at any moment he might step down from his frame. I freely confess that I screamed and fainted. My butler and cook were terribly alarmed, and then equally frightened. Harris finally worked up the nerve to throw a canvas over the thing, and I paid a local boy a sovereign to haul the monstrosity away and burn it."

"You didn't examine the picture? You didn't note the wet paint?"

"Mr. Holmes – that would have been the action of a sensible man. But to see unreal eyes suddenly boring into me – it was too much, and I gave the order to destroy the thing before I was rational. Finally, late that evening, a friend came by and convinced me it had been a prank. The next day, all was well, and my friend returned to London. But the following morning, as I was passing along the corridor outside the great hall, I felt as if someone was watching me. I turned about and looked at the little shepherdess, who Uncle had portrayed dozing beside her lamb. She was now awake and leveling an unfriendly gaze at me.

"I confess my nerves gave way again, but before I allowed Harris to carry me off to bed, I asked him to inspect the eyes. Surely, if someone in the house was talented enough to pry them open, as you say, the paint would still be fresh. But no – it was all original. Harris even dared to take a knife and scraped about the face, but there was only one layer applied. Somehow the original paint had become flesh, and capable of movement.

"It has been like this, sir, for a week! Every morning, a new individual is found with his or her eyes alive and following me. I can bear it no longer." He leaned forward, his face in his hands. "A thousand pounds would break me, for Uncle left genuine debts to be settled – money that is owed to flesh-and-blood tradesmen, not to spirits! Please, sir, you must come and rid me of this torment."

"I will be happy to do so, for your case is rather unique," Holmes said. "But allow me to pose a few questions to you first. You mentioned that the painting of Lord Melbourne was in your dining hall, and the little girl was in a hallway. Have the other affected pictures been in these rooms as well?"

"No sir. They have been scattered about the house."

"Please try to recall where in the house each was discovered."

Pierpont looked grieved, as if such memory caused pain. But he dutifully put his head down and began counting on his bony fingers.

"After the shepherdess . . . the next was the butcher, who hung in the kitchen passageway. After that was an unknown goddess, whose image graced the foyer. I believe the portrait of Sir Walter Scott in the parlor, and after that – my God, this was the worst, this morning, the thing that drove me to throw my predicament before you – a self-portrait of my uncle, which hung above my bedroom mantel. He was now glaring at me, as if to know why I permitted such mischief in his house."

"Were the any of these pictures in frames?"

Pierpont considered. "No, none of them."

"That is intriguing," my friend murmured. "I would assume these diabolical doings are robbing the entire household of sleep."

The man scowled. "I confess to you, sir, that after the first two incidents, I haven't gone to bed without a dollop of laudanum. The servants have been taking shifts – Harris was first, and then the boy, and the maids sit up together. Last night, it was poor Mrs. Ellis who took the watch, though Harris told me that he found her asleep on the sofa this morning. My housekeeper was exhausted. It is fair to say that all of us walk around rubbing our eyes and yawning. We cannot continue such vigils for much longer."

"Nor shall you have any need to do so," Holmes said, rising and assuring Pierpont that we would follow him to Dale House the next morning. As the man prepared to depart, Holmes asked him to send the references that each of his servants had provided as soon as he returned home.

"You suspect the servants of this strange blackmail?" I asked once Pierpont had exited our rooms. I watched from the window as he did a nervous jig to hail a cab.

"You know my maxim, Watson. Once you have eliminated the impossible – "

"Yes, yes, I recall something of the sort."

Holmes grinned around the stem of his pipe as he struck a match. "Shall we give spirits any latitude this time?"

"Of course not."

"Then the deed is most likely being done by someone in the house, someone who can move easily from room to room and replace the paintings with exact replicas."

"What?"

Holmes nodded. "It is the only explanation. Otherwise, there would be evidence of newly applied paint, some retouching of the older masterpieces."

"But to copy such unusual works of art would require great talent."

"Indeed – though seeing as how Mr. Pierpont and all his staff are new residents, it is unlikely that their knowledge of the paintings is exact. A skillful forger could probably recreate one with passable details, especially as our client is so excitable and nervous, and unlikely to have an eye for observation . . . beyond noting the obviously opened ones, of course."

Holmes refused to speculate further. That evening, a small envelope arrived, containing the references that the servants had provided. The maids were only seventeen, and as this was their first employment, there was nothing except a glowing letter from the local vicar, testifying to their good character. Likewise, the stable boy had a letter from his schoolmaster, and the butler came with stellar recommendations from two former employers.

"Nothing for the housekeeper, I see," Holmes muttered. "But Harris, the butler, interests me."

"Why?"

"Because he was previously in service as a footman for Lord Hensley, and as a butler for Sir Edward Ayers. Both gentlemen are noted patrons of the arts – Sir Edward is a rather prolific, if supremely untalented, portrait painter. What might Harris have learned from them, hmm? I fear, Watson, that this will not be one of your more intriguing adventures."

But in that regard, my friend couldn't have been in greater error.

When we arrived at Dale House at exactly nine on the following morning, we found the household in turmoil. A physician's carriage was waiting at the door, and the stable lad was walking around with a tear-stained face. Harris – tall, solemn, and black-bearded – answered our knock. He was the essence of respectability, but he was clearly suppressing a strong emotion. As we stepped inside, I heard feminine weeping from deeper in the house.

"Yes, Mr. Holmes, Doctor Watson, my Master told me to expect you this morning. But I fear there was a tragedy in the nighttime. Mr. Pierpont isn't long for the world – he is grievously injured."

"May I be of assistance to him?" I asked, feeling immediately drawn to the case in my medical capacity. Harris motioned for us to follow him toward the large central staircase.

"What has happened?" Holmes asked. His keen eyes were taking in the bizarre décor on every wall. It was all so strange that for a moment I was frozen in my tracks. Then – embarrassed by my reaction – I hurried to catch up with my friend.

Everywhere around us were painted sleepers. My blood ran cold as we passed picture upon picture, of all shapes and sizes, having nothing in common except the closed eyes of their subjects.

"Very early in the morning – I would say about one – the entire household was awakened by a bloodcurdling scream. I rose immediately and, by the time I had thrown on my dressing gown and slippers, the maids and Mrs. Ellis were standing at the doors of their rooms, the girls holding each other in terror. Mrs. Ellis had the good sense to bring a lamp, and together we hurried here, to the landing." Harris paused, pointing downward as we reached the top of the stairs. "At first, I saw nothing, and was about to go on to the west wing, and my Master's bedroom, when Mrs. Ellis gave a cry. I looked where she pointed, and saw Mr. Pierpont. He had fallen down the stairs and struck the bottom of the bannister. Upon reaching him, I thought he was dead, but then I realized he was still breathing. Jackie had run down in his nightshirt, and I sent him at once for the doctor, who is with him now. If you will come this way?"

We followed Harris down a dark, rather dismal hallway lined with even more macabre pictures. He pushed open a doorway, admitting us to a cavernous bedroom. The doctor, a brusque, red-faced man, quickly informed us that Pierpont's prognosis was grim.

"A cracked skull, perhaps bleeding in the brain, and a broken right arm. Only time will tell, and we can but wait and pray."

I feared I had nothing to add after a brief examination of the patient, though I was grateful that the man's breathing wasn't labored, and his pulse was strong. Holmes gave the sufferer only the briefest glance before stalking about the room, gesturing to the discolorations and empty nails on the walls.

"I take it once Mr. Pierpont woke up to his relative's visage, he had the rest of the paintings in the room removed."

"Yes, sir," Harris answered.

"Yet the other paintings in the house remained."

"He felt it best to leave them in place until you were consulted. He told me last evening, as Mrs. Ellis and I were laying out his dinner, that once you were finished, he would have all the paintings destroyed."

"Exactly the course I would have encouraged," Holmes said. "I will have a look around and then I will wish to speak to the staff. Perhaps you can assemble them in the kitchen?"

"At once, sir."

Holmes hummed softly to himself as he stepped into the hall. It was a raw, dreary day, and rain had begun to patter on the roof and rattle at the windows. The house was so old that gas hadn't been laid in it, and we were guided solely by sputtering candles. Holmes moved slowly, examining each picture along the wall. A cold chill crept over my skin. While many of the subjects were portrayed in attitudes of repose – a student slumped on his desk, and baby in a cradle – other posed as if for traditional portraits, sitting or standing upright, but with their eyelids firmly pressed shut. Holmes scowled.

"I will need much better illumination if I am to study the brushwork. However – My word, *this* is a striking composition!"

I almost leapt backward as a sudden bolt of lightning threw an erratic illumination on a nearly life-sized picture that hung on the wall at the top of the grand staircase. I barely noticed it coming up, for my mind had been consumed with concern for the patient. Now I was nearly paralyzed by the emotion the painting provoked.

It was a devil, complete with a stark white face, a pointed black beard, and a red robe. He held a pitchfork above his head, poised as if to lash out and pierce a victim's soul. His ruby lips were pulled back, exposing sharp teeth and a forked tongue. Black horns grew from his brow, and a tail snaked around his waist, seeming to flick and dance with evil vitality.

It was the eyes, however, that pinned me down. Never had I seen such malice and diabolical intent expressed with such realism.

Holmes caught my arm.

"Steady, Watson!"

I realized that I had almost mimicked the Master of the house and plunged backward over the well-worn stairs. Harris was coming up from below and noted my agitation.

"Sir, are you . . . *My God!*"

Holmes lifted an eyebrow. "Has this picture always been in this place?"

"Yes, sir. We called him the *Sleeping Satan*. And now he is *awake!*"

"Did you notice what condition he was in this morning, when you came to your Master's aid?"

"No, sir. I fear we were far more worried about getting Mr. Pierpont to his room to notice the picture. And it was very dark last night – cloudy with no moon."

Lightning flashed again. Holmes reached out and tapped the devil's eyes.

"Dry. Intriguing. You have gathered the staff? Excellent. Would you object to me seeing the interior of their rooms? No? Splendid. Watson, if you will handle the interviews?"

Sometimes Holmes placed me in rather uncomfortable positions. I was uncertain what questions he wished me to pose, or whom he suspected. It dawned on me, as I followed the directions to the kitchen, that perhaps Holmes wished to be alone with the butler to accuse him of the crime. I worried, for Holmes hadn't requested to borrow my revolver, nor had he brought one himself, and Harris was a large, muscular man. While Holmes's abilities in physical confrontations were excellent, I didn't like to leave him with such a fearsome opponent. But what could I say in protest that wouldn't give my friend's game away? I mentally pledged that I would listen intently, and that so much as a squeak would bring me up the stairs in a flash, my gun at the ready.

The household servants had gathered around the table where they took their communal meals. Clearly the home had once required a much larger staff, for there were many more chairs and empty places. I noticed a rather splendidly decorated cake resting in the center of the table. It was a lovely bit of work, covered in pink icing with flowers so intricately shaped that for an instant I thought they were real roses, though of course such quaint spring flowers wouldn't be in bloom in the gloomy autumn season.

"Oh, sir, it is our birthday," one of the little maids said, upon my inquiry. "Mrs. Ellis was so kind to make it for us. Of course, we hardly feel like celebrating now."

"Naturally," I said, asking them their names. Ellen and Abigail answered my questions quickly, with only a slight and natural show of girlish nervousness.

"Mr. Pierpont is such a nice man. It has been a pleasure to work here," Abigail said. "He is so very neat and tidy, it hardly feels like work at all, except on those weekends when his friends from London come to visit."

"They tracked in a lot of mud last time," her quieter sister agreed.

"Have the pictures frightened you?" I asked.

The girls looked to each other, then clasped hands. A tear slipped down Abigail's face.

"They are horrid, sir! We almost gave notice when their eyes started to open. We felt like we might turn a corner and find some painted man staring at us! We wondered . . . Can they really see us? Might they see us when we are asleep, or while we are dressing? I was all for running back home to Mother."

"And I told her how silly that would be," Ellen countered, with a show of sudden spirit. "Papa needs us to work, for the doctor says he will never be well enough to go to the mill again. No ghost or painted ghoul will ever stop us from taking care of Papa."

"And what of you?" I asked the stable lad. "Were you alarmed?"

"Only by that scream last night," he said. "I heard it all the way up in the attic, where I sleep. I'm not afraid of any silly paintings, but that scream – they said it was the Master, but it sounded like a banshee, coming for our souls."

"It woke me from a very deep sleep," Mrs. Ellis volunteered. Even as we had talked, she had been minding her pots. The savory smell emanating from them was almost enough to make me forget that I needed to focus on my questions and take careful notes for Holmes. "I was dreaming I was with my late husband, and we were going to take ship to America and . . . Well, I was ripped away from that lovely dream. I had fallen asleep with my book. It only took me a moment to light a lamp and scurry to my door, but I believe the girls were ahead of me. And Mr. Harris wasn't a second behind them. Sir, would you mind if I set the table? No one had a bite of breakfast earlier, with all the worry about the Master . . . ."

"Of course!" I answered, and in a twinkling the plates were pulled down and napkins folded. I looked through the doorway but there was no sign of Holmes. The ladies insisted that I join them, and soon I understood why Pierpont had been so satisfied with his servants. They were clearly dedicated to him, making constant inquiries as to whether I felt Mr. Holmes could solve the mystery. They seemed to think that should Holmes unveil the secret behind the opening eyes in the paintings, their Master would recover.

"Watson – not missing a meal, I see!"

I turned with some embarrassment to find Holmes standing just behind me. I stammered out quick introductions, noting as I did that Harris was hanging back in the doorway. His face had gone ghastly pale, and I feared that perhaps Pierpont had expired moments before.

"Is there something wrong, sir?" Ellen asked. I realized that Holmes was making an intense study of the cake on the table.

"I am merely admiring the lovely confection," he said. "If it is as tasty as it is charming, it should be the most delicious cake ever cooked." Holmes turned and nodded to Harris. "I see no reason to detain the staff further. I am certain that the physician could use some further towels and bolsters for Mr. Pierpont's comfort, and the doctor's horse also requires attention."

Harris wasted no time in barking orders to his underlings. He followed them out of the kitchen with a quick snap of his heels, leaving us alone with Mrs. Ellis, the cook. She stood stiffly, regarding my friend, whose gaze remained fixed upon the ornate dessert.

"Is there something I can do, sir?" she asked.

"Yes, I believe there is. You can tell me the truth." Holmes lifted his head, meeting the woman's steely gaze. "Are you merely the creator or – as I suspect – both the creator and subject of *Sleeping Venus*?"

I must have made a sound of utter astonishment. The lady sighed and gathered up her apron, wiping her hands upon it.

"Is it so difficult to believe that I was once that beautiful?"

Holmes pulled out a chair and, with a gracious motion, guided Mrs. Ellis into it. I leaned closer, and now I saw what Holmes had deduced. Though age had taken its toll and added heaviness to her frame, the lady's skin was as fair and as pure as the sleeping goddess's flesh. Her hands, roughened by domestic labors, still folded into the elegant lines of the painting.

"I will tell you all. There is no use to hide any longer, and I swear upon my soul that I never meant any harm to come to Mr. Pierpont. You cannot imagine the horror I felt when he screamed and tumbled backward down the staircase. Had it been his wicked uncle, Victor Lynch, I would have exulted in it, or given him the fatal push myself. But the young man was good and kind, and I only hoped to frighten him into giving me what I was owed."

Holmes settled across from the lady. "Victor Lynch stole your painting."

"Yes. I was a village girl from the Lake District. In my youth, I was a good sketch artist, and came to London to make my name – a decision which cost me the love of my parents, who disapproved of women's independence. My ambition quickly outstripped my funds, however, and I was soon desperate for employment. The artist Eugene Delarosa – There is a name the world should remember! – hired me as his model. He was a kind and good man, almost thirty years my senior, and he never allowed me to be exploited. My heart was soon given to him despite the great difference in our ages, and we developed an understanding between ourselves, so that I was his both his muse and his protégé. He helped me hone my skills, and I became a skilled painter. It was in his studio that I met Victor Lynch, an only moderately talented student who was paying for lessons. I foolishly allowed Lynch to see my masterpiece, my self-portrait as the goddess. He became obsessed with it and offered to buy it from me. I refused, even though the money would have been welcome.

"Not long afterward, my beloved Eugene fell ill. We journeyed to Bath for him to take the waters, but much to my despair he suddenly weakened and died there, in a lodging house. By the time I was able to return to our London flat, I found that our careless landlady had admitted Lynch when he claimed to have left a canvas in the studio. My *Venus* was missing, and I knew immediately that he had stolen it. I went to him, demanding its return, but it was too late. He had submitted the painting to a gallery as his own work, and it had almost immediately been purchased by the Queen's agent. I was incensed – I threatened prosecution! – but he in turn argued that without my protector, my word was nothing. I was an artist's model – A woman who shamelessly disrobed for men! – and no one would believe my claim that he had painted over my name and signed his own. He gave me a mere ten pounds and promised that if I swore a complaint against him, he would accuse me of being a common harlot.

Though my heart was broken, I felt I had no choice, for I had no friends or advocates, and no good reputation of my own.

"I moved away. I became a cook and a housekeeper, instead of the artist I had dreamed of being. I was married for a time, but my husband died young. With each passing year, I grew angrier at the injustice that had been done to me. From time to time, I pondered how I might get revenge. By a stroke of luck, one of my friends, Mrs. Jane Moore, gained employment with Lynch as his housekeeper. It was she who told me of his obsession with painting sleeping figures, hoping to recreate the most magical aspect of my work. She told me also of his descent into melancholy and drunkenness. I saw my opportunity. With her help, I sent the notes, which drove him almost to madness and shortened his life. When he died, I thought my work was done, but the more I considered, the more I felt I was still owed for the theft of my work. Jane told me about the new Master of Dale House, how he was frail and nervous. In that I saw my chance.

"Jane recommended me to replace her. I came to Dale House ahead of the others, which gave me time to observe the paintings. I worked fast and created a dozen duplicates, for if I had waited to merely modify the existing pictures, the deception would be easily discovered. I was fortunate that almost every picture was unframed. Once the time was right, I placed the two notes, and then I began to replace the pictures."

Holmes, who had listened to this recitation with an expression of admiration, rather than condemnation, now gave a brisk nod.

"It was obvious that the instigator was inside the home. The delivery of the notes could hardly have been accomplished otherwise, and certainly the images couldn't have been exchanged unless managed from within."

"I never meant to harm Mr. Pierpont – only to see if I could frighten him into giving me the money."

"Tell us what happened last night."

"I had been saving the Satan for a dramatic moment. When the young Master returned, he told us that you would arrive the next morning. He also said that if you couldn't solve the mystery during your visit, he would order all his uncle's paintings to be burned. I felt this was my final opportunity to manipulate his emotions. His confidence in you was such that he relieved us of any duty to watch during the night, which was helpful to my plan.

"I waited until I was certain the Master and every other member of the staff was asleep. It was almost one when I slipped from my room, bearing the canvas, which had been hidden – as they all were – inside my mattress. I carried a candle with me and worked as quickly and quietly as possible. But then, just as I had completed the exchange, I heard footsteps coming down the hallway from the Master's room. I had no time to flee, but I flung myself behind the curtains to the left of the picture and blew out my candle.

"Mr. Pierpont was clad in his nightshirt and dressing gown and carrying a single candle of his own. He stood on the landing, looking all about, clearly confused by the noise he had heard. He sniffed, and I heard him mutter, 'I smell smoke.' Then he turned, and at that moment lightning flashed close by. He spun around and looked up at the picture. Another flash followed hard, less than a heartbeat after the first. He threw up his hands, his eyes went wide, his mouth opened in a silent scream. To my horror, he dropped his candle and toddled backwards, and then fell and went bounding down the stairs.

"I stepped out. By some miracle, no one had awakened or heard the fall. I retrieved the candle and stamped out the place where it had begun to smolder upon the rug. God forgive me – I seized the painting with the closed eyes, as well as the two candles, and thrust them all into the closet in my room. Then I stepped just far enough into the hallway so that my voice would carry and gave the loudest scream I could manage. I was back inside my room before anyone could arise. Then I pretended to be awakened and followed Mr. Harris in his investigation."

Tears slowly drifted down the elderly lady's cheeks. "I swear I didn't push the Master, nor had I any intention of causing such a hideous shock to him. I only hoped he might restore what was mine. But now I am sorry, and would give anything for him to recover, so that I could beg his forgiveness."

Holmes reached out and gently patted her hand, then signaled for me to rise and follow. We retired to a small library, where a half-dozen portraits, all with their eyes closed, hung on the walls.

"How did you know?" I asked.

Holmes settled into a red leather chair by the fireplace. His expression was unusually troubled, though he answered my question with a quick wave of his hand. "It was elementary. Paintings don't open their eyes. The fact that the paintings were duplicates, rather than merely 'retouched' originals, confirmed that they were the work of a true artist. The fact that they seemed to 'awaken' at odd hours confirmed that the switch was occurring from within the house. Therefore, the artist and culprit must be a member of the household. Only a talented artist could have created the replicas of the paintings, and only an artist could have crafted such an amazing dessert. Surely you noticed how realistic the roses were upon that cake. Art in the blood takes *many* forms. Therefore, the cook was also the artist and culprit. The cake caused me to look more closely at the lady, and when I did, I immediately saw the reflection of the sleeping Venus."

Holmes shook his head. "What I didn't note was the burned spot on the carpet, where the Master dropped his candle. But I shall blame that on the abysmal lighting of this ancient home."

I settled opposite to Holmes. "What an amazing story the lady provided."

"One which may be impossible to confirm," Holmes said, "as all the participants are deceased except for the lady. Perhaps a discreet inquiry to Her Majesty's closest confidants would enable us to learn whether there is another signature beneath the paint on the *Sleeping Venus*."

"But who would have the privilege to ask such a thing?"

My friend smiled coyly. "I may know a certain individual whose previous services to Her Majesty's government are legion. But as for now . . . ." He shook his head. "I am loathe to give Mrs. Ellis over to the authorities."

"You believe her? That she didn't push Pierpont?"

"What purpose would murder have served? A dead man couldn't reimburse her, and clearly, she bore him no personal ill-will."

A sharp rap on the door interrupted our discussion. Harris stepped inside, his face ruddy, his eyes wet.

"Sirs! My Master has awakened!"

Of the many strange and bizarre cases my friend handled in his long and distinguished career, this one had a resolution which brought joy to all concerned. Mr. Pierpont made a full recovery, and once he was on the mend and assured that there was no devilment in his home or occult influences in the artwork, Holmes mediated a confession. Mrs. Ellis fell to her knees before her Master and told him everything she had related to us. The young man's jaw dropped. His eyes went wide.

"It is like a novel!" he gasped. "A fair maiden, so cruelly wronged. I always knew Uncle Victor was a wicked, sinful man. How mean and dirty of him to have forged his name upon your art!"

"I wish I had never frightened you, sir. It was wrong to abuse you for another's crimes. I should go to jail."

"And then what would I have to eat?" the young man laughed. "No, dear Mrs. Ellis, please stay. We will say no more about it, and as soon as I can, I will make things right. Is that possible, Mr. Holmes? Is there some way that Mrs. Ellis may receive the proper credit for her beautiful painting?"

I am happy to say that Holmes made a visit to the "certain individual" who could make inquires of Her Majesty's Curator of Pictures, who in turn was able to examine the painting and determine that the name signed to it was indeed the wrong one, and one layer beneath was the signature of the lady as she had been at the time – *Eliza Martin*. Mr. Pierpont in turned helped his housekeeper craft a memoir, which became a best-seller, so that the lady was more than repaid for the theft of her work.

Perhaps most satisfying, one year after the event, Holmes and I attended a celebratory bonfire at Dale House, where the entire collection of sleeping pictures was destroyed, so that no future haunting of master, staff, or home should ever occur.

I leaned back and took down the great index volume to which he referred. Holmes balanced it on his knee and his eyes moved slowly and lovingly over the record of old cases, mixed with the accumulated information of a lifetime. "... Victor Lynch, forger ...."

– Dr. Watson and Sherlock Holmes
"The Sussex Vampire"

The Adventure of the Highgate Flowers

It was a dour, damp afternoon in early May, and I felt myself encumbered by the sense of an unfinished obligation. An old acquaintance from my university days, Doctor Fulton Winston, had been killed in a carriage accident and buried in Highgate Cemetery a month before. I could claim no special intimacy or ties of friendship with Winston, but he had kept abreast of my literary as well as my medical career and had, from time to time, sent me notes of congratulations and expressed a keen interest in the adventures that I shared with Sherlock Holmes. I had been shocked to learn of his passing, which had occurred while I was away from London on a case with Holmes. I missed Winston's funeral, and though I had written the expected condolences to his widow, I was nagged by the feeling that I had not honored a good man as he deserved. Holmes – whose patience for any outward expression of mourning was limited – was busily engaged in some chemical research. I donned my hat and coat and was putting my hand to the doorknob, engaged in drawing the breath to inform him of my intentions, when his voice rose sharply from behind his philosophical instruments.

"For what it is worth, Watson, you may give the late Dr. Winston my regards as well. It is always gratifying to know that one has admirers, and rather disheartening to learn that they have passed on."

I would be prepared to swear that I had given no indications of my plans for the day, nor spoken a word of Winston's demise. Muttering yet again that Holmes would have been burned alive had he lived in an earlier century, I departed.

A short time later, having paused only long enough to purchase a spray of lilies, I found myself navigating the great avenues of the dead at Highgate Cemetery. It was truly a Valhalla of the age, filled with majestic markers, stone testimonies to lives of heroism, service, and piety. A sexton directed me to my friend's grave, which had just been marked with a small marble column topped with an urn. The ground was still overturned, black rather than green, and bore the sad remnants of a few faded flowers. I cleared these away and left my offering in their place. Winston had been my own age, and there is something about the death of a contemporary that perhaps causes one to pause and reflect at greater length. Many memories rose from that reverie, not only of Winston, but of other friends, relatives, and one most dear who awaited me in some better land. It was difficult to think of them, yet as I did something of the weight that had oppressed me seemed lifted, even as the sun dared to peek around the gray clouds.

I turned to go back and was halfway to the gate when I heard the distinct sound of a woman crying. Such a noise would not, of course, be uncommon or unexpected at this hallowed place, but there was a quality to the wailing that gave me pause. It was not mere grief. I felt I heard something within, something more to the quality of terror. I paused and oriented myself towards the weeping. I made my way through the labyrinth of tombstones until, at last, I located the source of the sorrow.

A woman was kneeling beside an ornate stone monument, her face sunk into gloveless hands. She was clad in full mourning garb, though her bonnet had fallen away, revealing a long plait of nearly white hair wound tightly around her head. She gave a start at my approach, and I quickly doffed my hat and begged her pardon.

"Forgive give me, Miss," I said. "I did not mean to intrude. I only feared – from the sound – that you might have been injured."

She wiped roughly at her face. She had been beautiful once, but grief had scarred her. Her eyes were so sunken they appeared bruised, and her cheekbones seemed ready to protrude through gray-tinged skin. I guessed her age to be almost forty, though I later learned she had not attained thirty years.

"No, sir, I am not hurt. Only sad – and perhaps angered. I do not understand this strange persecution, and there is no one I can appeal to for help, no one who can aid me."

"Persecution?"

"Yes. Tell me, sir, why would anyone leave flowers on a stranger's grave – flowers bearing notes that seem, by turn, to plead and threaten?"

I looked to the stone she knelt before. It bore the name of Azreal Pooler and a death date of only eight months past. "Your father's grave?" I asked.

"Yes, he who had not a friend in the world. And yet, almost every day for a month, I have found *this*."

She pointed to a strange, almost gaudy arrangement of flowers, all held together with a white satin bow. They looked more appropriate for a bridal bouquet, or perhaps a centerpiece for a lady's luncheon, than as a tribute to the dead. The woman began to weep again.

"Oh, if only someone could help me! If only someone could make it clear!"

"Dear lady," I said, "I know someone who can."

"My name is Zora Eaton," the young woman said. I had returned to Baker Street with her in time for tea and was grateful that Mrs. Hudson had taken it upon herself to send up a generous selection of sandwiches, for upon closer inspect, Miss Eaton was not only suffering from grief, but also from malnourishment. "Thank you for agreeing to hear my story, Mr. Holmes. I hope I'm not intruding upon your work. As I said to Dr. Watson, what seems to me a terrible torment may be nothing more than a mistake, but if so I cannot account for its bizarre regularity."

My friend had been examining the bouquet with great interest, murmuring the names of the flowers it contained. He dropped it carelessly back onto his desk.

"Do begin at the beginning, Miss Eaton. Your father's name was Pooler?"

A tiny hint of color came into her cheeks. "It was, sir. Twenty-five years ago, Azreal Pooler was a young architect hired to supervise some repairs on Elmwood Manor where my mother was in service as a chamber maid. The two of them were taken with each other – my father promised her marriage – and then, most cruelly, he abandoned her when the work at the manor was completed. Alas, by then my mother was carrying me. She was dismissed from service when her condition was known. She wrote most piteous letters to my father, who at first insisted that I must be given away. My mother bravely refused. At last, through the good offices of the village vicar, my father conceded to settle some money on my mother and myself, but not to marry her or give me his name. And so I was born into a kind of village infamy, and grew up being tortured by my schoolmates. Father provided just enough for us to rent a small cottage, but never enough for all the things we needed. Mother worked herself into an early grave, doing sewing and nursing and whatever job the local women would send her way. She died and was buried there in the village churchyard when I was fifteen.

"I had thought I would be sent to a workhouse or an orphanage, but on the day of my mother's funeral, my father appeared, nicely dressed and riding in a fine carriage. He took me to my old home and looked me over, the way one might inspect a hound or a horse.

"'You're my girl, all right – there is no mistaking the Pooler hair, so fair as to be white, even in youth. I will admit I've been no father to you, but now that your mother has died you must live with me. I'll not have it said that I was cruel and put you in the streets. There now, dry your tears and pack your things. You will not be coming here again.'

"And so, before my mother's grave was even covered, he took me away to his home in London. At first, it seemed like a fairy tale, for everything in the house was beautiful and there was plenty to eat and new clothes for me to wear. But Father's kindness lasted less than a month. Once he saw that I could clean and cook, he dismissed his servants. He went out to his office every day, and each morning I would find a list of things he expected to be accomplished. I barely had time to swallow a cup of tea, for woe be it if a domestic task was neglected.

He was a difficult man, and he did not hesitate to strike me, with his hand or with a stick, for even the smallest infraction. Once, when he caught me laughing with a handsome young lad who had come to collect a tradesman's bill, he kicked the poor boy across the yard and then beat me so badly that a doctor had to be called, and for almost a week my life was despaired of. After that day, I swore that as soon as I was twenty-one, I would leave him and make my own way in the world."

"You must have hated him," I said softly.

"I tried not to, sir – for my mother always taught me that hatred was the pathway to darkness and Hell. I struggled to forgive Father – to tell myself that he had been made hard and mean by the dogged pursuit of wealth. I saw that he had no friends, no one who visited or called upon him, or sent good wishes upon his birthday or compliments of any season. Even the men who were employed in his firm avoided him as much as possible. He drank, but never immoderately, and he did not deny me adequate food or clothing, though he would not spend so much as a farthing for a book or a matinee performance at the theater. He did not allow me to attend church, or to venture out alone beyond a walk in our small garden, so that I made no friends and certainly cultivated no gentleman callers. I merely marked out the time until my twenty-first birthday.

"When it came, I informed Father that I was leaving him. He was furious, and told me that he would disinherit me, that I was throwing away a fortune. I told him I did not care – that I could no longer bear being worked to death inside my own tomb. I ventured out with no more than a carpetbag and my ambition. I found a place in a boarding house only a short distance from Highgate Cemetery. The landlady had a small business in making ornaments for mourning – fixing hair into broaches, engraving names into brass lockets, and such. She took me on as a helper, and in this simple way I lived.

"After a year, Father came to see me, and we made amends. He sent me miniscule monetary gifts from time to time, and I visited him occasionally, but I never stayed for long. It was clear to me that Father was a man without the capacity for love, and that nothing I could do would change his nature. He continued to live alone in his fine house until he suddenly sickened, some eight months ago. The doctor called me in, and I had just time to ask Father's blessing – which he gave only grudgingly – before he died."

"Yet surely he made you his heir," Holmes said. "His name was not unknown to me when you stated it, and he was among the most successful of his occupation in the city."

The lady's answering smile lacked humor. "Father left very precise instructions, and quite a good deal of money, to see that he was put away in style, though all of his wealth could not purchase an excess of mourners for his funeral. His house was not his own but rented. Everything he owned was sold and the money put into a trust for me, from which I am not allowed a shilling until I reach the age of thirty, and I have just turned twenty-four. Until I attain thirty years, nothing but my own labor and the kindness of my elderly landlady stands between me and complete impoverishment. Perhaps that is why the notes and the flowers on Father's grave seem so cruel."

"Tell us how it began," Holmes said.

"I live only a stone's throw from the cemetery, and I make a point of walking over to visit Father's resting place every day if the weather is not too harsh. I realize this will seem strange to you, but for all his sins, Father was the only family I had left in the world. There is comfort in that cold and lonely place, and I have grown so familiar with every stone and epitaph that I could name the entirely of Highgate's residents. It was a month ago that I first noticed the bouquet on Father's grave. I was certain that it had been placed there by mistake, for Father had no friends or living family besides myself. I picked it up and took it to the sexton, inquiring if he had not erred in its placement, and he told me that no one had given him flowers to deliver. Not knowing where they belonged, I decided to bring them to my rooms, for they were very bright and gay, and looked lovely in a vase. It was while I was arranging them that a folded note fell out. For an instant I thought the mystery solved until I read the paper.

"The sentence was: *'If you love me, you must not bear it'*."

Holmes and I exchanged a puzzled glance. "What did you make of it?" I asked.

"I made nothing of it. I thought about returning the flowers to Father's tomb but decided that since they were clearly left there in error, it would do me no good to return them. Two days passed, and on the third, I was shocked to find another bouquet left on the soil, its white ribbon flapping in the breeze. Once again, I pondered whether Father might have had some admirer from his profession who was grieved at his death. But surely, such an individual would have placed roses or lilies on the soil, not this bright spray, so alive with color. I plucked it up, searched it, and found yet another folded bit of paper. This time, the message read – *The sacrifice is for the best.* Once again, I went to the sexton, who was rather vexed with me, and asked why I even thought someone would be so ignorant as to place flowers upon the wrong grave. Again, not wishing to return them to the grave, I took them home."

Holmes leaned forward. "How many more times has this strange event occurred?"

The lady began using her fingers to count upon. I noticed how red and chafed her hands were – in places they looked raw and bloody. I imagined that in her line of work, using needles, wire, and pins to create cheap mourning jewelry, it was inevitable that her hands would be tortured.

"At least eight more times, counting today – so ten messages in all."

"Do you visit your father's grave at the same time every day?"

"Perhaps not at the same minute, but always between one and two in the afternoon."

"And the flowers are fresh?"

"As if just picked from a garden." The lady shook her head. "After the fourth occasion, I began to look closely for anything that would give a clue as to my Father's visitor. I have seen boot prints, and lady's shoeprints, but there are such marks everywhere when the ground is wet."

"Indeed, in a public venue, such marking would not be instructive," Holmes mused, leaning back in his chair. "You have never seen anyone near the grave?"

"No, sir."

Holmes waggled a finger. "You said you were very familiar with the tombs in the vicinity. If I gave you a paper, could you write down the names?"

"I will try sir."

Holmes handed her some foolscap. Deliberately, she marked an "*X*" for her father's resting place, then began to draw other marks and names around it.

"Imagine yourself facing Father's tombstone," she said. "There is a large cedar tree to the left, which Father is buried beneath. To the immediate right is the Hoyle family mausoleum, with its great brass door. Behind Father are three members of the Neville family – Edward, Allan, and Abigail – a father, son, and mother. Before Father, behind any visitor, are the tombs of Manuel Jose, the South American general, and his wife, then another large stone in honor of Mr. James Seymour, the philanthropist."

"Nothing that honors maidens, I suppose?" Holmes asked.

"Hardly, sir – though about twenty yards beyond, past the Hoyle mausoleum, is a large and very beautiful statue of an angel, which I have seen many people stop and admire."

Holmes nodded. "Have you disposed of the notes?"

"No sir, I have kept them, though I threw them into a drawer, and I cannot swear to their order."

"Allow my friend to escort you home, retrieve the messages, and send them back to me by him. There is nothing more that can be done today, but perhaps if I can see the notes – "

"You could make some sense of them. I will do so immediately. Thank you, sir – I feel much better already."

"Do let me know if more of these strange bouquets are found." Holmes caught me by the sleeve as the lady stopped at the door, exchanging a kind word with Mrs. Hudson. "Your professional opinion, as a physician?"

I understood why he was asking, and why he was insisting that I accompany Miss Eaton rather than merely hailing her a cab. She had grown paler as we talked and had pushed her tea away with a single sip, flinching as if the beverage pained her when swallowed.

"Perhaps some cancer," I said. "I fear she will never live to claim her inheritance."

I returned to Baker Street feeling even more mystified than before. Miss Eaton had been so weary and ill that we had made little in the way of conversation on the journey to her lodging house. Her landlady was a very motherly sort, and immediately took charge, assuming that I was a doctor her boarder had gone to consult.

"She's been ill, on and off, for almost a month now, she who was never strong to start with. Her hands shake too badly to work some days, poor girl," the lady said, as our client climbed up to retrieve the notes. I recommended some hearty broths, and plenty of rest, then bid Miss Eaton goodbye. I will never forget her gentle smile and sincere thanks.

I resisted the temptation to open the notes. Each was folded twice and written on sturdy paper that felt expensive. I had no doubt that Holmes would immediately know where it was made, what it cost, and where it might have been purchased. As I entered our rooms, I found my friend brooding over a large book.

"Hello, Watson. Tell me, when you were a romantic young swain, did you know that flowers spoke a language? Or that this study is called *floriography*?"

I chuckled. "I have heard of such, but never felt the need to investigate further. A simple rose or carnation was usually enough to charm a pretty girl when I was a lad. But what messages are contained in that bouquet? You seem intent upon deciphering it," I noted, as Holmes had taken the arrangement apart and laid the flowers out across his table.

"Indeed, I have, and I find myself none the wiser. This bouquet bears quite the mixture of sentiments. In it, we see the morning glory which, according to this *Ladies' Almanac*, signifies affection, as well as tulips, which indicate passion."

"A strange code to place on an old villain's grave."

"Indeed. The hydrangea is more fitting, as it speaks to heartlessness, as well as the wolfsbane for misanthropy, the foxglove for insincerity, and the marigold for jealously. Yet entwined with them is the yarrow for everlasting love."

I considered the colorful blooms. "Surely not all of these are native plants, or bloom in the same season."

"A wise observation, Watson. These are not flowers readily acquired in city gardens, yet they were fresh in the middle of the day"

"They must have been grown in a greenhouse!"

Holmes settled in with his pipe. "Elementary. You have the notes in your pocket? Will you read them aloud to me?"

I cleared my throat. Each card was brief.

>*If you love me, you must not bear it*
>*The sacrifice is for the best*
>*For God's sake it must be soon.*
>*If you tell her, you will kill me.*
>*Will you do it or not?*
>*I will not break my vow.*
>*She will cast me out if she learns.*
>*You will not suffer.*
>*I love you more than life.*
>*M is the problem.*

Holmes frowned. "No wonder the poor young woman is terrified. Whatever is afoot, it sounds like a bad business. Now, Watson, would you be so kind as to take down my index books? Let us see what, if anything, we may learn about Mr. Pooler's eternal neighbors."

"You think there is an error in the placement of the flowers?"

"No – I think the placement is purposeful, but for what purpose I have yet to surmise. An error might have been committed once, but surely not a further nine times."

"Clearly," I said, as we divided up the relevant volumes, "the message was meant for someone other than Miss Eaton. Do you think that person received the messages?"

"I cannot theorize without data," Holmes reminded me. "Let us see what we can learn from these pages."

We spend the remainder of the evening pouring over the books. We learned a great deal about the distinguished career of General Manuel Jose, who had battled guerillas in the Andes before retiring, covered with honors, to his wife's homeland. We also learned of the many hospitals, orphanages, and museums which had benefitted from the benevolence of Mr. James Seymour, the owner of a dozen factories in the north of England, a man who had buried three wives, five sons, and all his grandchildren before passing away at the age of ninety-nine. The Neville family proved singularly uninteresting, though Holmes made a note to do further research, as he believed a Neville cousin had been associated with certain unpopular Parliamentary reform measures in the 1870's. It was only when we turned to the volume containing his collection of H's that Holmes became animated.

"Ah, at last – a thread of hope, even if a very thin and fragile one. See here, Watson. The mausoleum holds the mortal remains of Bradley Hoyle and his wife, as well as two sons. There is a widowed daughter-in-law and one grandson still in the land of the living."

"Why is this hopeful?"

"Because Bradley Hoyle was a noted botanist," Holmes said, his eyes gleaming with triumph. "His home in St. John's Wood contains one of the largest greenhouses in England."

"But surely his descendants would have a key to the mausoleum, and if they wished to leave floral tributes, such would be placed within its chamber," I challenged. "And anyone wishing to somehow salute the family's achievements could hardly miss such an imposing structure and lay the flowers on Pooler's grave instead."

"As you say, it seems unlikely that the grandson – he would be twenty-eight years of age – or his mother would leave a bouquet propped against a brass door, for the wind to blow away. And yet . . . ."

Holmes collected the notes that had been tucked inside the bouquets. He mumbled, "Written by a man, on paper that is at least five shillings a packet . . ." and then wandered off to the window. Great swirls of smoke emerged from his pipe, making the atmosphere of the room so oppressive that I wished him a good evening and took myself off to bed. I had barely managed to tug my nightshirt over my head when the door was unceremoniously banged open.

"Watson, into your clothes again! Make haste, man – our client's life depends on it!"

It was early morning before we returned to Baker Street. Many was the time we had raced through London, but rarely had the stakes felt so high. It was difficult to hear Holmes's words over the wild snap of the whip, the swearing of other drivers, and the great clatter of hooves on pavement.

"Poison!" Holmes shouted in my ear. "Every one of those flowers is poisonous. There are even a few I have not yet identified, but I would wager my soul that they also leak dangerous sap or grow toxic leaves."

"Many flowers are deadly if eaten."

"Yes, but these, if merely touched by a person with delicate or broken skin, can do harm. In a hale and hearty person, a mild rash might be produced. Taken together, on the skin of a woman already malnourished and sickly . . . ."

I found myself shouting at the driver to go faster. At last, we reached the boarding house. Our frantic knocks were met by the worried countenance of the landlady, who had been on the threshold of sending for me. Holmes raced up the stairs. The poor girl was gray-faced and clearly in great peril. I did what I could, and a few hours later, as her breathing grew less labored, Holmes carried her down the stairs and together we saw that she was made comfortable in a private hospital operated by a friend from my days at Barts.

"I will never forgive myself if she dies," Holmes growled over coffee. "I am a damned fool, not to have realized it from the start."

"Who could bear her such a grudge? Do you suppose someone could have hated the father enough to take revenge upon the daughter?"

"If so, it is indeed the coldest of dishes," Holmes whispered. He turned again to the notes and began to rearrange them.

"It is only a suspicion, but if we now place the messages in this order . . . ."

If you love me, you must not bear it
The sacrifice is for the best
I love you more than life.
I will not break my vow.
You will not suffer.
M is the problem.
She will cast me out if she learns.
If you tell her, you will kill me.
For God's sake it must be soon.

Will you do it or not?

"It is clear that something is building. A crisis is about to come to a head."

"What should we do?"

Holmes gulped down the last of his coffee. "I must return to Highgate and place myself where I can watch the Pooler grave. If the flowers are fresh, they must be placed there in the morning."

"We will both go," I insisted. "I feel equally responsible for Miss Eaton's fate."

Holmes nodded wearily. "Then let us try and solve this mystery, for if we cannot save the lady, we may perhaps avenge her."

And so we departed our rooms to make the journey to the great City of the Dead. As ill luck would have it, an omnibus was broken down, and the streets jammed with carriages, cabs, wagons, and their assorted irate drivers. Because of this, we did not reach Highgate until nearly ten that morning. The Pooler grave was easily found, thanks to the markers of the tree and the massive monument to the general and the public benefactor. Holmes froze as we stepped into the narrow pathway that faced Pooler's tomb.

"On the Hoyle mausoleum steps. Look!"

A bright bouquet, almost an exact mate to the one that Miss Eaton had received, was resting against the brass doors. It looked new, freshly cut. Holmes scowled.

"There appears to be more than one step in this dance. Very well – Watson, I think if you take a position behind the general's tombstone, I shall loiter behind the tree."

It made for a quiet morning, and more than once the effects of the evening nearly lulled me into sleep. But then, just before noon, I heard the rustle of a lady's dress. Cautiously, I peered out from behind my post.

A striking young woman was standing before the Hoyle mausoleum. She was wearing a gay, pink-checkered dress that clashed with the solemnity all around her, and a straw hat with an absurd festooning of yellow silk flowers. Her face was round and sprinkled with freckles, and her wiry hair, the color of a prize pumpkin, hung long and untamed down her back. She seemed to consider the brass doors for a moment, then glanced around and picked up the bouquet with purple-gloved hands. She plucked out the note, read it, and gave an angry growl. Returning the note to the blooms, she purposefully bent down and jammed the stems of the arrangement into the soil by Pooler's tombstone.

She looked up to find Sherlock Holmes standing over her.

"Good morning, Miss – ?"

"It's no business of yours!" she snapped and turned to march away. Holmes, however, had her fast by the elbow. "Let me go, you masher! I'll scream!"

"You will do no such thing – not unless you wish to be arrested for the theft of the Hoyle family's flowers."

"What? Theft? No – no sir. What are you, some kind of a constable? I've done nothing wrong!"

"I believe that Dr. Watson can verify your perfidy. He was also a witness," Holmes said, signaling for me to step forward. The young woman's reaction was immediate.

"Watson? Not . . . not *the* Dr. Watson? What writes the stories?" At my nod, she whirled back, her thick jaw bobbing open. "Then you're Sherlock Holmes."

"I am indeed. And you are a murderess."

"What! No! No!" The girl began to weep. "All I've done is move Billy's flowers. Billy was the one who set it up. I haven't hurt anyone. I would never hurt anyone, especially not now."

My doctor's eyes told me the truth, just as I suspect her unconscious communication, the way she suddenly clutched at the front of her oddly gathered skirt, made everything clear to Holmes.

It was perhaps the strangest luncheon Mrs. Hudson had ever served. The young woman – whose name was Nellie Morgan – ate like a ravenous wolf. Holmes, I, and our other guest watched in bemusement.

"I worked in a music hall," Miss Morgan said, between bites of her chicken. "Billy used to come there all the time. His mother didn't like it – she's a snob, all for the opera and such fancy things – but Billy likes to drink beer and sing. He fancied me right from the start. I know there were much prettier girls there, but somehow, I caught his eye and stole his heart. He promised me he would marry me. See, he even gave me this ring." She held out a chubby hand, exhibiting a cheap silver circle with a piece of blue glass atop it. "At first, we didn't even think we needed a priest to make it right. We stayed in my rooms over the hall, except of course Billy had to go home at night. Then his mother went to someplace in Germany, to take a water cure, and Billy had the whole house to himself. Ta, didn't we have fun, making merry everywhere, even in the greenhouse. Truth be told, I think our little stranger was sent down from heaven right there, amid all those beautiful flowers."

"Miss Morgan – "

"No, let me finish, Mr. Holmes. You said you wanted to hear it all and, quite frankly, I'm sick and tired of this sneaking around. Billy loves me. Maybe we didn't do everything prim and proper, but he's going to marry me and together we're going to raise our little one with more love than that sour old lady called his mother could ever provide. As soon as I knew for certain that the stork was paying us a visit, I told Billy. And that's when he turned queer. He stopped coming to the music hall. He stopped sending letters and gifts. It made me so mad I went to his house in St. John's Wood one day – something he said I must never do, on account of the old lady – and he took me out back and told me how he couldn't come to the music hall no more, but he would make up bouquets and put them on his family's tomb in Highgate and put letters in them. I said that was all right, for a time, but with the baby on the way he would have to stand by me. That's when . . . well, I shouldn't say any more."

Holmes took the messages from his pocket and laid them on the table. Miss Morgan's breath caught in a hitch.

"But how did you get them?" Her eyes were wild. "Billy told me to make sure I threw them away."

"You placed them back in the bouquet, and put the bouquet on Mr. Pooler's grave. Why did you do that?"

The girl shrugged. "It looked lonesome, that's all. And I didn't want to get caught with the flowers. They always made my gloves sticky. I prefer roses – I never understood why he didn't give me roses when he knows I fancy them!"

I thought of Miss Eaton's poor, gloveless hands, already covered in sores and wounds from her work making jewelry.

"Did you reply to the messages?" Holmes asked.

"I did. I used to write notes back to him and put them in the lion's paw. You know that lion on Mr. George Wombwell's grave?"

Holmes nodded. "Billy asked you to rid yourself of your baby. You told Billy you intended to be a mother."

"Yes. It would be a sin to kill our baby!"

"And you threatened him."

"You make it sound wicked, sir. I told him to be ashamed of himself. And then, a few days ago, I told him if he didn't meet me at the Registry Office next Monday, I would go straight to his house and tell his mother everything. He knew he couldn't stop me."

Holmes slipped open the final note, the one he had removed from the most recent bouquet. "'*I cannot come, you must be patient. Smell the flowers deeply, know my love is true.*'"

The girl sighed. "I do love him but – I meant what I said. If I'm not a bride on Monday, then his old battle ax of a mother had better be ready to buy a mourning dress." Miss Morgan cocked her head at the individual across the table from her. "Are you a constable?"

The motherly-looking woman who had also joined us shook her head. "I am only a matron at Scotland Yard, though I hope one day to be on the force. It seems strange that they will not let women help, when we could do so much good."

"But does this mean I'm under arrest?"

"No, dearie, but it might be necessary for you to come in and tell your story to the inspectors. We will discuss it more, in the cab."

Miss Morgan stuffed a large spoonful of pudding into her mouth. "Very well and – oh, this pudding is so good. Might I run down and ask for the recipe?"

The moment she vanished through the doorway, our guest, whose name was Mrs. Galt, turned to Holmes. "You were right to send for me, I think."

Holmes nodded. "As the girl lacks a mother or even a close female relative, I felt it would be better for her to learn the news from a sympathetic individual. Be sure to impress upon her the danger she and her child were in from young Master Hoyle's actions. In this last note, he instructs her to smell the flowers deeply. Angel's Trumpet, which featured prominently in the bouquet, can sicken from inhalation."

"Miss Morgan will either break down herself or . . . let us just say that I understand why you wish her to be informed in a room with no fragile objects in it." Mrs. Galt said, indicating Holmes's chemical apparatus and his violin with a swoop of her hand. "If she refuses to swear out a warrant on the lout, however, there is nothing we can do."

"Unless Miss Eaton dies," Holmes agreed. "Let us hope it will not come to that."

Later, after the women had departed, Holmes began to pace. He talked through the case so briskly, so absorbed in his own thoughts, it was as if he had forgotten I was in the room.

"I should be kicked from here to Charing Cross – no, from here to Canterbury or Coventry – for such a blunder. I assumed the flowers were a code, when the flowers were a weapon. Thus, the dangers of theorizing before all the data could be collected. By shifting my mind to think of some type of message in the flowers, I neglected to see the intensity of the written messages. I dismissed them as trivial love letters, when in fact, they were merely a blind to the dangers inherent in the bouquets."

"So, the boy wished to kill his girl? It seems a rather inefficient way to commit a murder."

Holmes scowled. "No, Hoyle never intended to murder Miss Morgan. His goal was to make her sick enough that she would lose the unborn child, and thus he could deny the evidence of any liaison with her. Note that he was careful to tell her to dispose of the notes, but not the flowers. It was her own simple and genuine goodness, her sadness that a tomb looked neglected, that spared her from suffering."

"Holmes," I said, as gently as I could, "this sad situation is not your fault. It is a terrible misfortune, caused by the selfish nature of a spoiled young man. And besides, Miss Eaton had already become ill before you met her." I nodded toward the now withered remains of the flowers. "Had you not retained those for study, she surely would have died. You have saved her."

"Have I?" my friend muttered. "I fear I have not, for if I had recognized her peril immediately, you could have treated her in these rooms, or taken her to the hospital immediately. Surely, Watson, you cannot write this case as one of my successes."

Fortunately, my friend was in error. The next morning, we received a message from the hospital that Miss Eaton had rallied and would make a full recovery. A short time later, we received another message that Miss Morgan, upon learning of her beloved's perfidy and intentions towards their unborn child, had indeed sworn out a complaint against him. The boy confessed all, but a sympathetic magistrate, unmoved by Miss Morgan's delicate condition, freed him. The events caused such a scandal in the newspapers that Mrs. Hoyle sent the boy off to Australia, supposedly to collect specimens for the family gardens, and while in the hinterlands of that wild country, he met his death. Luckily for Miss Morgan, a young barrister who had been assigned to the case was quite smitten with her. I learned, sometime later, that they were married and happily raising her little daughter as his own.

Miss Eaton lived to come into her paternal inheritance. In time, she founded a number of institutions that cared for mistreated children. When she died, just before the Great War, her funeral was one of the largest the city had ever witnessed for a private citizen, and her grave, marked by a simple stone, never lacks for flowers.

The Adventure of Merridew of Abominable Memory

"I hope you'll forgive me for knocking you up so early this morning," Inspector Lestrade said as we made our way through a bitterly cold London metropolis. "I would have waited until a more decent hour, but the family is anxious to move the corpse, and I know your obsession with viewing the scene before – as you once put it in the Doctor's hearing – a 'herd of buffaloes' tramples it."

My friend Sherlock Holmes chuckled. "You need not apologize to me, Inspector, but Watson may be, at this very moment, deeply regretting his decision to return to his bachelor abode for a few days. I am certain that when he crossed my threshold last evening, carpetbag in hand, he had no inkling that he would be drafted into service again on such short notice."

Truthfully, I was not in the proper mood to appreciate Holmes's sly wit. Circumstances which delicacy prevent me from recording had necessitated a reoccupation of my old rooms. It had been kind of Holmes to never seek out another flatmate, or to transform my bedroom into a chemical laboratory or a shooting gallery. However, renewing my residency had come at the cost of being shaken awake at five in the morning. Lestrade had appeared on our doorstep only moments previously, asking my friend to assist in looking into the tragic death of Professor Lawrence Whittle, who had been found dead inside his greenhouse. I pleaded a terrible headache, for I had imbibed a bit too liberally the night before, but Holmes would have none of my excuses.

"What? Are you no longer an old campaigner, Watson? Come now, there's no time for you to malinger."

And with that pronouncement, Holmes simply whisked the covers off the bed with the flair of a magician who removes a tablecloth without upsetting any of the crockery. I had little choice but to dress and follow. I might have been a soldier in the cause, but rather mutinous thoughts curdled in my brain on that exceptionally bitter morning.

"Whittle," Holmes mused. "A strange name, yet oddly familiar. Why do I know it?"

"Because I read his *Index* article aloud while you shaved," I muttered.

Lestrade was clearly amused by my lack of enthusiasm for the work. "Cheer up, Doctor. Perhaps one day some great inventor will come up with a machine to do the job for you. Just push a button and a voice will read to Mr. Holmes every article ever published!"

Holmes scowled. "Let us leave such idle fantasies for Mr. Verne and his ilk. According to the *Index*, Professor Lawrence Whittle is – or rather, was – a relic of the Enlightenment, a gentleman naturalist and an early advocate and defender of the theories of Charles Darwin. If the date given in the *Index* is correct, Whittle missed his ninetieth birthday by less than a week."

I wondered if I had heard Holmes correctly. Even though I had read the words aloud, I had been so groggy and befuddled I had made little sense of them.

"Ninety! Inspector, what makes you think that his death was anything other than natural?" I asked, perhaps with a bit more heat than I intended. It might have been the darkness of the carriage, but it seemed to me that a hint of smugness crossed the man's ferret-like features.

"Oh, let's just call it a bit of intuition. When one has as many years on the job as I do, one develops a sixth sense about these things."

"And Sir William Paltrow insisted that I be consulted, because the death is suspicious," Holmes said.

"Well, that too, but – wait!" Lestrade jerked as if his seat had just been electrified. "How in the blazes did you know about his involvement? I didn't tell you!"

Holmes tilted his head, looking out the window of our elegant conveyance. "Just an intuition, I suppose. One does develop these things after so much time in the game."

For a moment I thought the inspector might toss us from the carriage, which bore the coat of arms of the gentleman Holmes had named. Even with a slowly receding headache, I had worked out who was truly behind the summons.

"Very well. I might as well tell you all I know," Lestrade muttered. "You are absolutely insufferable at times."

Holmes accepted this as a compliment. "But I am always willing to give you the credit, Lestrade. We should have another half-hour before us. Do inform me of the particulars."

Though his feathers appeared well-ruffled, the representative of Scotland Yard launched into a thorough recitation.

"Professor Whittle was indeed a naturalist, a chum of Darwin's and other great men, though he never made much of a splash in the academic world himself, or so I'm told. Only taught for a few years at Cambridge. Then he inherited money, published a large volume on exotic animals, and spent the rest of his life puttering around in the jungles of the empire, collecting specimens for his scientific friends. His home is called

Hallowhill, and as best I could tell from the two times I was there, you'd be more comfortable sleeping in the greenhouse or the barn or the groundskeeper's cottage than the house itself. Old, run to seed, needs repair. I'd guess it costs too much to keep the plants warm to mind about the family."

Holmes raised a hand. "You've been to Hallowhill before today?"

"Yes. A week ago, Sir William made a complaint to my superiors and I was sent out to open an investigation. Sir William is Professor Whittle's neighbor, and rather fond of the old gentleman, which is more than I can say for Whittle's kith and kin. Seems that Whittle claimed to have seen a shadowy figure skulking around his greenhouse at night, and a pane of glass in the roof had been shattered. But when I got there, of course, there was no clue. The glass was broken but there were no discernible footprints, or ashes, or – "

"Inside or outside?"

Lestrade huffed, annoyed to be interrupted. "What do you mean?"

"Was the glass broken from the inside or the outside of the greenhouse?"

The inspector scowled. "I don't know. From the outside, I assume."

"You assume?"

"Well who would break glass from the inside? It's not as if a person is being kept prisoner in there. Nothing inside that greenhouse but fancy tropical plants, a few birds, that kind of thing. Sorry to disappoint you, Mr. Holmes, but there's no murderous pygmy running around."

Holmes sighed and signaled for Lestrade to continue.

"The nephews said their uncle was growing daft. He'd been that way, they claimed, ever since he came back from Brazil a year ago with Beatrisa in tow. He was always seeing shadows, hearing spooks, thinking someone was out to steal his prizes."

"Was anything missing from the greenhouse?" I asked.

"Not that the Professor could account for," Lestrade answered. "And I can't imagine why anyone would creep out into this lonely neighborhood just to swipe an orchid or two. You know how bad the weather was last week. A storm probably broke the glass."

"Is the greenhouse near any trees?" Holmes said. "Was there any debris found around it?"

Lestrade frowned again. "No . . . none at all."

Holmes rolled his eyes. "Then the storm is an unlikely culprit, unless it was far more intense than what we felt in London. And surely if lightning had struck the dwelling, the entire household would have been buzzing. Speaking of household – who is Beatrisa?"

"The source of much of the mischief, if I'm any judge," Lestrade said. "Whittle never married, but he adopted his two great-nephews, Jason and Reginald Whittle, when their parents were killed in a railroad accident. He sent them to Eton, then Oxford – hoped they'd amount to something, but they've been nothing but wastrels, at least to hear Sir William tell it. Half-a-dozen times, Whittle threatened to cut the lads out of his will, but they'd mend their ways just long enough to weasel back into the old fellow's good graces. There was also the advantage that Professor Whittle was rarely about long enough to admonish them. Then, when he returned from his trip to Brazil, it was with more than butterflies and palm trees in his baggage. He brought home a young woman – Beatrisa by name – who claims to be his daughter by a native lady he met while in the Amazon hunting butterflies, two decades ago."

"You doubt the validity of her claim?" Holmes asked.

Lestrade shrugged. "It's not my business to judge a man for his adventures in foreign fields. I suppose he knew she was his daughter, or at least believed it likely when he took responsibility for her. But I must say I don't see any English in her features. She's barely more than a savage, too dark-skinned, with markings on her cheeks and chin. She is the right age, though, and the professor was quite fond of her."

"Fond enough to change his will?" I said.

Lestrade smirked. "You have an evil mind, Doctor, and you may well be on the right scent! Sir William confided to me that Whittle said he had recently revised his will. But the professor wouldn't tell his noble friend exactly how he reworked it. I suppose that only the old man's solicitor knows the truth, and he is currently in France! Otherwise, I would have woken him up as well – spread the suffering around a bit."

Holmes noted that we were approaching Hallowhill. "One final question – how is the lady's English?"

"Broken at best. As I said, she's still trying to learn our ways. According to the nephews, she'd never even worn decent skirts before the professor took her in."

"She has no maid or companion?"

"None that I am aware of."

The wane winter's sun had just begun to throw weak illumination as the carriage pulled up to the front of a rather decrepit Georgian house, all soured bricks and slate grey tiles, the entry flanked by a pair of lichen-coated statues of dogs. The steps were warped, the door needed paint. A butler with a long, sad visage ushered us inside.

"Best we speak with briefly Sir William and the family first," Lestrade said, after refusing to surrender his greatcoat. "But I know your ways, Mr. Holmes. You'll be eager to see the body. I've stationed two of my men out there. We threw a blanket over the corpse for decency's sake, but nothing else has been moved or altered."

Holmes nodded his acquiescence, though I could tell by his expression that he would have preferred to go directly to the scene. The butler, who gave his names as Yates, directed us to a downstairs parlor.

I knew Sir William from his pictures: He was a tall, regal man with a mane of silvery hair, formerly a royal official in India, and a noted writer of travel pieces for the best magazines. Though his eyes were red-lined, he had clearly subdued his own distress to hold mastery over the situation. This was perhaps a blessing, as the two other gentlemen in the room appeared incapable of any respectable emotion. They were perhaps in their thirties and bore every sign of dissolute living, from their long, unkempt hair to their sagging bellies and pasty skin with broken veins tracing unwholesome red maps across their noses. Neither had bothered to properly dress, but instead lounged about in dressing gowns and carpet slippers. Reginald puffed on a cigarette, while Jason had to quickly put aside a glass that contained some libation much stronger than coffee or tea. Neither offered a hand as introductions were made.

"I do regret that you were be brought into this matter, Mr. Holmes" Reginald drawled. "It was only at our *friend's* insistence."

"And surely, Sir William," Jason added, with a curled lip and a dark look at his elder, "you knew Uncle's advanced age?"

Sir William's expression made it clear he would like nothing better than to turn both of the nephews over his knee and administer a sharp caning, despite their years.

"I knew your uncle was in remarkable health for a man of his decades, with a clear mind and a strong will. True, he had begun to show some frailty in his legs, and his eyes were bad, but there was absolutely nothing wrong with his wits."

Jason snorted. "He was jumping at shadows, imagining that someone was out to destroy his life's work – as if anyone actually cared about that queer collection besides himself."

"You are referring to his greenhouse?" Holmes asked.

"Yes, and there's nothing in it except – Oh, there you are! About time! How long does it take to fetch a few biscuits, you stupid wench?"

A young woman had entered the parlor, bearing a tray of food and a pot of coffee. Reginald snatched it away from her. She simply dropped her head and drifted, ghost-like, to a chair in the corner.

She was a remarkable figure, completely at odds with the frayed carpets, tarnished mirrors, and worn furniture of the room. Her dress was in the latest fashion, brilliantly colored in purple and green, with a sapphire broach at her throat and delicate boots peeking out beneath her voluminous skirts. But her thick, coarse black hair was worn loose and flowed almost to the floor, with a distinct curtain of it cut across her brow. Her skin was red-brown, and her features were those of a South American aboriginal, with inky black eyes and a compressed mouth. Strange tattoos drooped from her lips and accented her sharp cheekbones. Her earlobes had been stretched and deformed, so that they hung almost to her shoulders. As Lestrade had observed, there was nothing English about her, no hint of mixed blood. Indeed, the only thing that marked her as belonging to our nation was her dress.

Holmes stepped forward, executing a polite bow and reaching for her hand.

"Miss Beatrisa Whittle, I presume? I am most sorry for your loss."

She flinched instinctively, then looked up at my friend with wondering eyes as he kissed her fingertips. Her lips trembled. I sensed that no one in the house, besides her father, had ever treated her with any of the kindness or the civility due her sex.

"Thank you . . . sir."

"We'd better be getting outside, to view the scene," Lestrade muttered. "If I could ask everyone to remain in this room, we will be back shortly."

"Sir William could be of assistance to us," Holmes said, "if he does not mind going out in the cold?"

"I will be glad to help," the gentleman said, signaling for the butler to retrieve his coat. As we walked down a long central hallway, he pointed out the great age of the house, and how it had been in the Whittle family for six generations. Once we had passed through the rear doorway, his words became frank and focused.

"It wouldn't surprise me if one or both of those ingrate nephews killed Lawrence. They've been furious ever since he came back with the girl. You see how they treat her, now that they are at liberty. Lawrence wouldn't tell me what exactly he planned to do with his will, but I have every suspicion he was finally cutting them out."

"Sirs!"

We all turned at the cry. It was Beatrisa, who had clearly run after us, huddling in the doorway without so much as a shawl. "Please . . . find Merridew. Cold . . . for him . . . very bad."

"And who is Merridew?" Holmes asked. Jason Whittle suddenly appeared, snatching the lady back inside. Sir William frowned.

"No doubt one of the exotic birds. Whittle had a dozen or more in the greenhouse. Come along."

The greenhouse stood in the middle of a courtyard formed by the wings of the home. It was not as large as I had expected, only about the size of a significant gazebo or bandstand. One large pane above the door was shattered, allowing the sharp wind to whistle in and whirl about the roof. A burly, gnarled man in a canvas coat stood just outside the door, stamping his booted feet against the cold.

"Beggin' your pardon, sirs, but when can I get about with cleaning up and replacing that pane?" he asked. "Professor Whittle might be dead and gone, but I know he'd want his life's work taken care of. Bunch of them sensitive plants will freeze if I don't get started."

Sir William waved the man aside. "We shall be done shortly, Burton. Go and tell the footmen to get ready to transport their master's body to his bedroom and summon the undertaker."

The man favored us with a sour look but trudged away obediently.

"The groundskeeper," Sir William said. "He's thoroughly unpleasant and has done nothing but complain since Lawrence returned from Brazil. I advised Lawrence to sack him a dozen times – he drinks excessively, but Lawrence said he was a good worker and could keep the greenhouse in order."

Holmes digested this information with a slight nod as we moved inside. With the large pane of glass above the door broken, the area had grown bitterly cold. There was a strange odor in the air, an unpleasant smell that assaulted my senses before a chill wind whirled through the broken glass and bore it away. I lifted my head and noted two bright parrots on a tree limb, huddled together, pitiful in their distress. I wondered which of them was Merridew. Holmes pointed toward the central burner.

"Why is it not ignited?"

"I asked the same question," Lestrade said, puffing out his chest a bit. "The groundskeeper said a part broke yesterday afternoon. He was supposed to go to London today, to find a replacement."

Just a few paces inside the doorway was the sad scene. Inspector Lestrade's men were standing at a respectful distance to a figure covered with a darken woolen cloth. The body rested below the broken glass pane, in the shadow of a sturdy palm tree. At a signal from the inspector, the policemen lifted the blanket.

The cause of death seemed obvious: Large, jagged shards of glass had fallen into a long tray of soil, some of them coming to rest in an upright and perilous position, especially should an elderly individual be stumbling around in the darkness. Whittle's cane lay a short distance from his left arm, and his outstretched right hand showed that he had clearly tried to catch himself but failed. He had collapsed atop the largest of the broken glass pieces, which had sliced into his carotid artery. The amount of dried blood was conclusive, as was the wound. Elderly and frail as he was, death had come quickly.

"Who discovered him?" Holmes asked, crouching beside the corpse. The old man had was clad in nothing more than his flannel nightshirt and a loose Indian silk robe, with threadbare velvet slippers on his feet.

"The woman," Lestrade growled. "Her bedroom is across the hall from his. She said that he heard him leave his room at about three in the morning and became concerned when he didn't return in a few minutes. He had taken to the habit of going to the rear door of the house to check for 'prowlers' and 'ruffians'. Usually, a quick glance and a few deep breaths of cold air brought him back."

Holmes looked up at the broken pane and inquired as to the positioning of the old man's chamber. Sir William pointed it out. The professor's room had a large window overlooking the greenhouse.

"Perhaps he heard something that gave him the alarm," Lestrade added. "If only he had roused his nephews, this all would have been avoided. What is it, Mr. Holmes?"

My friend had gently brushed back the collar of the dead man's robe. Holmes gave a low whistle and, with great delicacy, pulled the fabric further down, directing our attention to what was revealed.

At the juncture of the professor's neck and shoulders were several distinctive marks, deep and small incisions, as if someone had driven sharp fingernails into his pale, fragile skin.

Lestrade hovered over Holmes. "My God! Why did I not see that? This changes everything!"

"And how so?" Holmes inquired, pulling out his lens to better examine the wounds.

"Why, it is as clear as day. Beatrisa must have followed him outside and hit him, knocking him onto the glass. That is the mark of her nails! The savage! I will arrest her immediately! Come along, men."

"Lestrade, wait!"

There was no use to protest. The inspector was racing through the greenhouse, slapping at the branches and vines, setting panicked parrots into flight. I saw one disappear through the broken glass. With a loud "See here!" Sir William gave chase toward the house. The policemen shrugged and languidly followed.

"Intriguing," Holmes whispered, returning to his examination of the marks. "Oh, let them go, Watson. I need just a few more moments to close my case."

I frowned, thinking that this was very damning to the lady. Perhaps she had learned that she was indeed an heiress and was tired of enduring abuse at the hands of her ungracious cousins. An accident to the old gentleman might be readily accepted by all, and Beatrisa would be in control of the house, able to remove her obnoxious relations.

"Did she also break that glass?" Holmes asked me. There was no point in asking him how he had followed the trail of my thoughts. "Admittedly she seems strong enough, but to do so would have required a ladder and some blunt instrument – the glass above the door is much too sturdy to have been shattered by the mere throwing of a stone. And there is the curious incident of the conveniently malfunctioning burner. But come – there is no need to wait any longer. Lestrade will have worked himself into a frothing fury by now."

Lestrade, Sir William, and the two constables had entered the house, but Burton remained just outside the greenhouse door, along with the shivering footmen.

"Can we move things along now, Mr. Detective?" he growled. Holmes halted.

"This is the second time greenhouse glass was shattered," my friend said. "What is your sense of the first time it occurred? Was it deliberate?"

The man tugged on his scraggly, tobacco-stained beard. "Probably the work of those tramps about the neighborhood. Seen a few of them sleeping rough. Guess they thought it would be warm enough in that greenhouse. 'Course, once they got a whiff of it, they changed their minds."

His comment caused Holmes to raise a brow, but my friend did not speak. I wondered how strong the odor I had noted upon entering the greenhouse would have been, without the chilly air diffusing it.

Giving a curt nod, Holmes led us back into the house. We could hear raised voices, the sound of a terrible row.

"Let us hope your medical services are not required," Holmes said, gently tugging me into the lead. With some reluctance, I pushed through the door.

The poor young woman was prostrate on the rug, sobbing as if her heart would break. Sir William had interposed himself between Beatrisa and Inspector Lestrade, while the two policemen stood awkwardly in a corner. Jason and Reginald Whittle lurked behind the sofa, glaring down at their young relative. If murder could have been accomplished with eyes alone, the woman would have been lying in a pool of blood.

"Of course, she did it!" Jason shouted, just as we stepped inside. "Look at her – she's nothing but a damned savage. Her people are headhunters, I've heard!"

"Headhunters and cannibals," Reginald echoed. "Have you checked for a weapon? Father brought clubs home with him from Brazil – maybe she used one of those."

"No! Me love Papa!" the pitiful creature cried. She had to struggle for her words between hiccups of terror. "Love Papa! No hurt him! He dead when I find him!"

"A likely story," Lestrade said. "I've seen the wounds. A woman's nails made them. You clawed at his back and knocked him into the glass."

"This – this is an outrage!" Sir William said, his long face now flushed with emotion. "This poor child has lost the only person she has in the world, and you accuse her of his murder! I suggest you look a bit more closely. If there was anyone who had a motive to kill my friend, it would be one or both of his nephews."

The men began to sputter protests in unison. Beatrisa curled up, the picture of misery, clasping her knees to her chest like a child. I looked for Holmes, and found him standing by a bookshelf, peering down at a ponderous work on biology. This hardly seemed like the time for reading.

"Well, I know what my eyes tell me," Lestrade said, "and they say I see a murderess before me. Constable, give me your darbies."

Holmes snapped the book's sides together. The act rang like a pistol shot in the room.

"Lestrade, if you lay one finger upon this lady, your men will have to arrest me as well," my friend said.

"On what charge?"

"For assault on an officer. Touch her and I will put you on the floor."

A terrible silence descended in the small room. Lestrade stepped back from his victim.

"Here now, Mr. Holmes," he snarled. "I give you more latitude than I should, but there is no reason – "

" – For you to inflict any more distress upon this poor lady," Holmes finished. "I am going to step back outside. I will return shortly. Watson, please see to her comfort. And someone get the fire stoked up."

With that, my friend was gone from the room. I gently raised Beatrisa to her feet, helping her to the sofa. She eagerly claimed the fresh handkerchief I pulled from my sleeve.

"The man is mad," Jason Whittle whispered to the inspector. "He threatened you!"

"Aye," Lestrade said, and I could sense his discomfort. He did not appreciate Holmes's words, but their relationship had been a long and, for him, profitable one. He dared not react out of pique and ruin a case. As ineffective as Lestrade was, he wanted justice for the poor old man in the greenhouse and knew that Holmes was his best means of acquiring it. He turned and snapped at his underlings to stoke up the fireplace, which had been woefully underfed.

Sir William moved to the sofa, offering his hand to Beatrisa.

"Do not worry, child. Mr. Holmes may seem an odd person, but he will get to the truth."

Reginald grumbled a curse, then caught his brother's arm and towed him into a corner, their heads nearly pressed together. I wondered whether I should part them, to prevent some dark plotting of mischief or revenge. But at just that moment, Holmes strolled back into the room. He had something in his arms, covered by the blanket that had once shielded Whittle's body.

"What the blazes is that?" Jason demanded.

"It is the murder weapon. Or, if you prefer, the murderer himself."

Holmes threw back the cloth, revealing what he held.

It was a large, hideous lizard, with green scales and a thick hide, it's back covered with evil-looking fins. The monstrous thing's whip-like tail dragged almost to the floor. Its feet were capped with long, frightful nails, and even from a distance I could smell the unpleasant odor that its body emitted. It was as if Holmes held a dragon's hatching in his arms. Beatrisa gave a cry.

"Merridew!"

The beast appeared dead. It was stiff and made no response to Holmes's handling of it.

"A green iguana, native to South America, and an unusually large one. No doubt it was Whittle's greatest prize, as he had organized his greenhouse to its comfort. Indeed, the hot glass box was paradise for the creature – until the pane of glass was broken, and the cold air came in. Iguanas are not inclined to English winter."

Holmes set the fiendish lizard before the fireplace.

"Had anyone bothered to give the professor's wounds more than a cursory examination," my friend continued, "they would have noticed that their spacing and depth prevented them from having been made by a woman. However, they are a perfect fit for the claws of this species."

Jason peered around the sofa. "The lizard killed him?"

"Not intentionally," Holmes said. "If you will observe, our cold-blooded friend has gone into something of a catatonic state. This is a survival mechanism, which – according to Whittle's own book upon the subject – allows them to endure the occasional dip of temperature within their environment. However, once the lizard goes into this strange stupor, he loses his grip upon a branch or tree trunk. Surely, Lestrade, you noted the palm tree just above the professor's body? Our lizard friend was perched there. The professor was roused by the sound of breaking glass and came out in hopes of finding his pet before it perished. As he crouched, no doubt calling to it, the iguana slipped into unconsciousness and plummeted onto the frail old gentleman's shoulders, knocking him into the glass, with fatal consequences. The fall jarred the creature from his sleep, and as the lizard scrambled away, his claws bit into the professor's back, leaving those incriminating marks. But the greenhouse grew colder and so the lizard returned to his hibernation. I found him tucked beneath a large fern, which has also been a casualty of the cold weather."

Beatrisa rose from the sofa and knelt beside the ugly creature, stroking its repulsive hide.

"Poor Merridew, poor . . . look!"

The lizard's eyes had opened. A long, slimy tongue flicked out of his jaws.

"Ah, he rouses," Holmes chuckled. "Will you arrest him, Lestrade?"

The inspector snorted. "I'd be the laughing-stock of Scotland Yard. Clearly, this was all a tragic accident!"

"In which case, I believe you owe Miss Beatrisa an apology. I trust you are gentleman enough to make it. Watson and I must take a quick detour, and then we shall be ready to depart."

"Where are you – "

Lestrade did not get to finish his question, for at just that moment Merridew came fully to life and scrambled across the floor. The Whittle nephews screamed louder than any terrified pair of maidens, leaping onto chairs to avoid the clumsy beast's attack. The constables made for the bookcase ladder and the window seat. Lestrade scrambled onto the back of sofa with the agility of a circus rider mounting his steed.

I think I would have enjoyed watching the farce, but Holmes was escorting me from the room with a grim warning.

"Our job is not finished," he said softly.

"But you said the lizard caused Professor Whittle's fall."

"Yes, but who caused the lizard's fall? The greenhouse window didn't break itself. I think, Watson, that a brief interview is in order."

"But . . . who are we . . . ."

Holmes was walking fast, and my question was lost in the howling winter wind. We made our way down a wide lawn and over to a cottage that was tucked into the shadow of the forest behind the house. Holmes halted for a moment and, with the merest flick of a finger, drew my attention to a stout ladder and a mallet that had been abandoned beside a shed, just a short distance away from the cottage. Silently, Holmes pressed on and knocked on the door, opening it before he could be properly answered.

Burton sat inside at a rough-hewn table, still wrapped in his canvas coat. He glared at us as we entered.

"What do you gents want? We brought the professor up. There's nothing more that can be done for him . . . God rest his soul."

"Yes. *Requiesce in pace.*"

Holmes sat in the chair opposite to Burton, stretching his feet toward the fire. "I have it from good authority that you have an appreciation for a refreshing libation, Mr. Burton."

The man grunted, clearly uncomfortable and uncertain of what Holmes was implying. My friend drew a silver flask from inside his coat.

"I also am something of a connoisseur of invigorating beverages. I have, in this flask, a sample of a rather potent Irish whiskey. I employ it to 'keep out the cold', and we must both admit that it is an exceptionally chilly morning."

Holmes took a rough mug from the table and poured the flask's contents into it. Burton licked his lips, his eyes beginning to shine. Holmes lifted the mug but paused before drinking. He put it down on the table before Burton's eager gaze.

"It is yours, if you can but confirm a few deductions of mine."

"I – I will do my best."

"Very well. You gained a comfortable position here at Hallowhill after your wife died. You did very little in the way of maintenance of the grounds, but your employers didn't care, for they were far more interested in carousing in London than in the appearance of the family estate. Unfortunately, a year ago the true owner, Professor Whittle, returned. He ordered you to make repairs to the greenhouse. You worked night and day, and at the end of your labors, the professor installed his exotic plants and birds into the chamber. This was acceptable – it would be far easier to tend to a garden inside a warm room than scattered about the manor. There was just one problem, and that was Merridew."

The rough man started. His shoulders began to quiver.

"You hated the creature. It was monstrous in appearance, foul-smelling, requiring constant care and cleaning of its limited space. The reek of the thing was more than you could stand. But you dared not leave – you are well past your prime and have a bad reputation in the neighborhood for your drunkenness. No one would hire you. Yet the lizard was – "

"An *abomination*," Burton growled. "I told the professor, nothing that ugly could be of God. The devil made it – it was an unholy beast – it was Satan's lapdog! But the professor wouldn't listen."

Holmes nodded slowly, inching the mug toward Burton's curled, crabbed fingers. "Somehow – perhaps an overheard conversation – you learned how cold could kill this 'abomination'. You thought how easy it would be to break a pane of glass and blame it on a tramp. You were trying to murder the iguana, not its master."

Burton sniffed. "I thought the first time, when the copper came, that the beast had slipped out, had maybe run off in the road and been killed. But the professor found it under the bushes. The damned thing – it was just . . . sleeping."

Holmes pushed the earthen cup into Burton's hand. "You never meant to harm your master."

"No. No, I swear to God and all the saints . . . I just wanted that damned beast to die!"

"Drink," Holmes urged, and the man swallowed the draught in one gulp. "You will be relieved to know that Miss Beatrisa Whittle has been cleared of the crime."

The man began to weep. "I wouldn't have let them take her away, I promise. She's a good girl, for being from a savage race. She's always been kind to me. I promise, I would have spoken out, just . . . . Does the devilish thing still live?"

Holmes rose. "I suggest that if you wish your actions to be dealt with leniently, you take a vow never to harm Merridew again. The lady, like her father, is much attached to him."

I followed my friend from the cottage, leaving Burton weeping into his folded arms. I looked toward the sad edifice of Hallowhill. The sun had just begun to clear away the thick clouds, and a tepid ray of light shown down into the glass panes of the greenhouse. A brightly colored bird flitted overhead, and I was relieved to see it find its way back through the opening into the meager shelter of the tropical chamber.

"Holmes," I asked, "how did you know Burton was a widower?"

"A magician must not reveal *all* his tricks, Watson. But you see what becomes of a good man, inclined by nature to matrimony, who loses a spouse? You see how easily he falls into snares, loses his way, even takes to drink? It is a pitiful tale."

My eyes narrowed. It was difficult at times to be Holmes's friend, to accept that he would always understand more about me than I knew about myself. But I digested the words in the spirit they were offered, for Holmes was, indeed, the wisest man I had ever known. By the next morning, I had returned home, and could sleep until almost noon in my own warm, good bed. My dear wife smiled when I told her the entire story.

"I will not write this one, I fear," I said to her. "Sir William Paltrow swore Holmes to secrecy for the sake of the family name, and Lestrade is unwilling to tell his superiors that he nearly arrested an innocent heiress when the cold-blooded murderer was actually the intended victim!"

"But what a fascinating tale it would make," she said, her smile lighting her entire face. I touched her soft cheek, thinking of how Holmes had described the culprit in his *Index*.

"Holmes referred to the creature as 'Merridew of abominable memory'! Shall I write this story just for you, my dear?"

"Yes, John. Please do!"

> *"My collection of M's is a fine one. Moriarty himself is enough to make any letter illustrious, and here is Morgan the poisoner, and Merridew of abominable memory . . . ."*
>
> – Sherlock Holmes
> "The Adventure of the Empty House

The Adventure of the Black Perambulator

Over the course of his many years as London's greatest consulting detective, my friend Mr. Sherlock Holmes welcomed humanity's spectrum into our rooms at Baker Street. Morning might find Holmes speaking with a baroness who perched grandly upon our divan, and at noon that same sofa might be occupied by a fishwife, a costermonger, or a schoolboy. Old and young, of all social ranks, brought their problems to him. Some paid in him handsome amounts. Others could offer only their heartfelt thanks. My friend had no prejudices, and the good fortune that came from solving the conundrums of the rich and well-connected allowed him time and energy to devote to the poor and friendless. It was with an individual of this latter category that one of Holmes's most unusual cases began, on a crisp autumn afternoon.

Jethro Jones was a tall man with a craggy face and a thick, unkempt black beard. He was dressed in a pea coat and a sailor's cap, with heavy brogans on his feet, and he carried various nautical aromas about his person. I could only imagine Mrs. Hudson's displeasure when she escorted him up the stairs.

"Forgive me, sir, I'm not accustomed to being in gentleman's houses," he said. "And I wouldn't dare to call upon you except – my heart is broken, sir. It's bad enough to lose sweet Jenny, though at least I could bury her and mourn her. But to lose my babes as well, and have the policemen tell me there is no hope for them – that they've been thrown away like rubbish. No, sir, I cannot sleep at night thinking of it. If there is any hope, any chance of finding them, why I will part with every farthing I earn from now until Doomsday. If you can make it right – bring them back to me – I will be your willing servant forever."

Holmes waved aside the dramatic offer. He insisted that Jones be seated, and that Mrs. Hudson bring up some coffee and biscuits for him. How Holmes deduced it, I don't know, but clearly the man was famished, and tore into the food.

"You are good to me, sir."

Holmes settled into his armchair, leaning forward, his bright eyes leaping about, studying his guest. "I knew why you came the moment you spoke your name," he said. "I have followed your case in the news, and I must agree with you – the conclusion the official forces came to was most unsatisfactory."

"Then there is hope?" he asked.

"Perhaps, though we must take every element upon its face. Let me have your story, as I suspect the sensationalistic reporters have blotched the truth."

Jones sighed and swallowed the last of his coffee. "They turned me into a monster, Mr. Holmes. They claimed I killed sweet Jenny – with all they wrote, I should be sitting in a jail cell, and no doubt would be if my best mate hadn't been with me every minute of that dreadful day and could swear that I hadn't left his side. But – no, you want it all in order, I suppose, and I will try to tell it to you that way.

"I'm a simple man, sir, and a rough one. I was born in Whitechapel, though to honest folk. My father died when I was just a lad. Had he lived, perhaps he could have applied the rod of correction, for when I was eight, I fell in with a bad gang and did many a foul deed – picked pockets, broke windows, snatched handbags – for a wicked old man who paid us a pittance for our loot. Mother tried to keep me in school, but I ran away at every chance. When I was fifteen, I decided to go to sea, and was taken on a vessel in the India trade. For almost ten years, I was as good a sailor as any captain could want, and then I came down with the enteric fever while we were in Calcutta. I don't suppose I have to tell you what a bout of that does to a man?"

I cleared my throat. "I have had some experience – I too acquired it, while serving in India."

Jones nodded sadly. "Then you know you are never the same. Oh, your strength and flesh may return, but never do you feel as you did before you had it. I recovered aboard my boat, though I could no longer work as I had, and once I even dropped down senseless from the rigging. I was done with the sea, a nearly broken man of less than thirty years.

"But there was one stroke of luck – my captain gave my name to Sterling Shippers, and I was hired to supervise the loading and unloading of their cargo on the docks. It was a good job that suited me well. I was often awake at all hours, keeping watch over the goods. A lively little pub next to our offices, The Blue Mermaid, made it bearable. It was there that I met Maggie and Jenny. They were both the nieces of the publican, orphaned girls who had grown up on the docks. They were as different as night and day, those two – Jenny was fair-haired and pale. Maggie had raven tresses that fell to her waist, and the warm brown skin of a gypsy. Jenny was prim and proper, but Maggie was wild and free with her favors, always winking at me over the plump round shoulder which her tattered dress left bare. Like so many before me, I couldn't resist her. I hardly knew how it happened, but suddenly Maggie was living in my rooms, acting as if we were husband and wife."

The man's face turned red. He twisted his big hands together, and his eyes dropped to his boots.

"It shames me, sirs, to tell you this."

"You aren't the first man to have such an arrangement with a woman," Holmes said, his voice gentle. "How long was she your lover?"

"Almost a year, sir. During that time, I was reconciled to my mother, and not a moment too soon, for she was dying of cancer. I begged her forgiveness – I had been a poor son to her. She held my hand, and with her last breath she pleaded with me to be a better man, to turn my heart to God, to be more sober, to marry, and have children. I promised her I would, and as the angels carried her soul away, I saw my path clear. I sent Maggie packing. I joined the church. I will not claim to have earned a Blue Ribbon, but I stopped my heavy drinking – no more than a pint for me in the evening. Yet things remained undone to keep my oath to my poor mama.

"I was at The Blue Mermaid when it came to me, as clear and bright as if a heavenly choir was singing in my ears: Sweet Jenny, so spotless – she would be the perfect bride. I set my cap to woo her, and to knock aside all the rivals for her hand. It took some doing, but in six months, she was willing to let me slip a ring upon her dainty finger and escort her down the aisle."

Holmes raised a hand. "How did Maggie react?"

"Well, Maggie was an alley cat – she hissed a bit when I first began to step out with Jenny, but she came around quickly enough, for she had a half-dozen sailors and rough fellows on her line. She even served as bridesmaid at our wedding. But then . . . ." Jones's face darkened. He gave his head a quick shake. "No, I shouldn't speak about the incident, as we never knew – "

"Out with it," Holmes demanded. The big man meekly obeyed, and I had the distinct impression that he was grateful to be ordered to reveal an unsettling event.

"Maggie brought Jenny a cake, just before Jenny was delivered of the twins. I put it on the table, while we went upstairs to show Maggie the nursey. When we came back down, I found our cat eating the cake, so I threw it out. The next morning, our cat was dead on the hearth – but he was an old thing, and perhaps it was merely his time. Still, I told Maggie not to bring more treats to our house, saying our doctor had forbidden Jenny to eat any sweets.

"Just a few days later, Jenny gave birth to our twins, Eddie and Eliza. You never saw such beautiful babies, sir. Perfect in every way, except," he gave a fond father's laugh, "Eddie had a birthmark on his bottom, a stain in the shape of a heart. We said he must have been kissed by Cupid, and surely one day he would be the most handsome boy in London. But then . . . ."

Jones sniffed. He pulled out a large handkerchief. Holmes rose and seized a pile of newspapers, tossing pages aside until he found the sheet he wanted.

"Allow me to summarize from the reports," Holmes said, "and correct me where they err. On the morning of the first of October, you bid your wife goodbye and left her in the care of Mrs. O'Grady, an elderly lady whom you had hired to assist with the care of the twins. It was the last time you saw your wife alive."

Jones nodded miserably.

"Around one that afternoon, your wife announced her intentions to pay a social call on Maggie, her cousin. She donned a pale blue walking dress and placed the twins in a sizeable black perambulator."

"It was special one – a pal had made it for us, extra-large."

Holmes paused for a moment, as if mulling over a sudden idea. Then he shook his head briskly and returned to the paper.

"Your wife arrived at Miss Maggie Sullivan's house at one-thirty – this fact was verified both by the hostess and a Mrs. Salazar, who resides across the street."

"A nosey old widow woman," Jones muttered. "She does nothing all day but sit at her window and watch the thoroughfare."

"Yet it is helpful to have her testimony," Holmes said, "as she established both the time of your wife's arrival and her departure at just before three in the afternoon." He frowned at the paper. "'*I saw Mrs. Jones depart in her pretty blue dress. She gave me a wave and went west toward the docks. I presumed she was going to join her husband.*'" Holmes glanced at his client. "But your spouse had no such plans."

"Indeed not. Jenny knew the office was no place for her or the babes. She might have gone to the park for some air, but she never came to my door."

"And she wasn't seen again?"

"Not by any who knew or remembered her. I had some late business to handle and didn't come home until seven. Mrs. O'Grady was in a frightful state, for Jenny had promised to be back no later than five. I ran door to door, I called out the lads who work with me. We searched high and low all that night, and in the morning, I took my fears to the police. They searched too. How could a woman with two small babies just . . . disappear? And then . . . they implied that perhaps I . . . ."

Jones dropped his face into his hands and began to audibly sob. Holmes brought him water, and stood for a time in silent support, his lean hand resting on the man's burly shoulder.

"Forgive me, sir," Jones said.

"You have lost your world," Holmes replied. "It would be strange if you didn't grieve. I will describe the details of what followed as briefly as I can. Your wife's body was found late on the second evening, below a bush in tiny park near the Grand Surrey Canal. The coroner's verdict was that she had died from a blow to the head. She was found clad only in her undergarments, her shift, stays, stockings, and her boots. Yet there was no indication that she had been . . . abused by any man. The bloodstained perambulator was found nearby. The children are still missing."

Jones scrubbed his big hand over his face. "The police have told me there is no hope, that they were murdered and cast into the canal."

Holmes crossed the floor, flipped his coattails out, and leaned forward with his elbows upon his knees. "I am not certain that I agree with their conclusions. Forgive me, Mr. Jones, but I must ask you some pointed questions."

The man lifted his head. "You have hope?"

"Hope is a weak thing," Holmes said. "Let us see if we can give it strength. Did your wife have any jewelry on her person?"

Jones shook his head. "Only her silver wedding ring, which was still on her finger. "

"Did she carry a purse with her?"

"No. Mrs. O'Grady said that she found it on the table just after Jenny left. There was nothing in it besides a house key and hatpin."

"What of her hat?"

"She wore a small straw hat with a spray of silk cornflowers. It was found about ten paces from where she lay."

Holmes nodded. "Just a few more questions. What was the nature of the relationship between your wife and Mrs. O'Grady?"

"Most friendly – the dear old woman is like a second mother to us both."

"Had your wife any other close friends whom she might have visited on an impulse?"

"No. I cannot imagine that she would have taken the babes to someone else's home with no notice. Jenny was still recovering. She was tired most of the time. I had urged her not to call upon Maggie. Had I been at home, I would have prevented it.

"Ah . . . and why would you have done so?"

The man's face turned red in spots. "Sir – I don't wish to cast aspersions, but – I feared that Maggie might be jealous of Jenny. After Jenny announced she was with child, there was something like a wild animal that came into Maggie's eyes. Oh, she claimed she was happy. She made quite a fuss when Jenny was brought to bed. She even came to the baptism. But just last week, she said that she never thought I would be a father. 'You aren't meant for it, Jeddy,' she said, and then she laughed in a cruel way. 'No, you aren't made to be a family man, not you.' That was when I told Jenny she should never be alone with her."

"Yet your wife didn't listen."

"She knew I had lived a wicked life with Maggie, but Jenny was sweet and kind and could never see the badness in anyone. Maggie had sent a note over the day before, begging for her company, wanting to see the babes. My wife felt an obligation, I suppose. She and Maggie grew up together in that pub. They had shared a room for many years, and they were as close as sisters. And when Maggie was bright and gay, she was good company."

"A final question," Holmes said. "Was there any person who would profit by your wife's death?"

Jones's face clouded. "Not to my knowledge. We had a small insurance policy on my life, but not on hers. And my sweet Jenny had no enemies, only people that loved her. The crowd at her funeral overflowed the church."

After this statement, Holmes dismissed his client with great gentleness, urging him to go back to his home and resume his life as best he could. He promised Jones he would do all that he could to help him. Holmes then closed the door and went to the window, not speaking again until he could see Jones walking down the street.

"What do you make of it, Watson?" he asked.

"A simple enough case," I said.

"Indeed? How so?"

"The lady visited her cousin, and then – for some reason known only to the female of the sex – decided to take her babies to visit their father at his workplace. On the way, she was set upon by a lustful criminal who killed her and her infants."

"Yet there was no sign of assault, beyond the wound which killed her." Holmes turned, folding his arms. "And where was her frock? What fiend, committing such a crime in a public place, would take time to undress his victim? Your theory presents some difficulties."

"Perhaps he wanted the clothing as some perverse trophy," I countered. "Or he left her clothed and some other criminal came along and took off her garments to sell."

"A rather bold way to earn perhaps a shilling or two – stealing clothes from a corpse on a footpath. And one wonders why this imagined beast didn't seize the hat and boots as well – items much easier to sell, and perhaps worth more than the presumably torn and damaged frock." Holmes hummed a bit, continuing to gaze through the window. "Would you fancy a trip down toward the docks? I think a few interviews are in order."

I was naturally glad to accompany my friend, and soon we were tucked into a hansom cab, mufflers around our necks, plunging deep into the dark heart of London, where ships from all countries of the world made port. The houses grew smaller and sadder, the businesses shabbier. A yellow miasma rose as we turned a final corner to the street where Miss Maggie Sullivan lived. Its dankness was oppressive, and I felt sorrow for the vast host of men and women who, by misfortune of birth or breeding, were forced to make their living in this undesirable sector. A fresh young matron in soft blue dress, pushing twin babes, must have seemed like an angel to all she passed.

"Stop here, cabbie," Holmes called. "Now, let us get a grasp of our surroundings," Holmes said as the hansom rattled away. "That house, with the crumbling red bricks, is where Miss Sullivan dwells. According to the papers, she occupies the rooms on the ground floor, and lets the rest to sailors and longshoremen. Just across, in the narrow house with the green shutters, is Mrs. Salazar, who verified Miss Sullivan's testimony as to when Mrs. Jones came and went. Let us pay her our regards to this witness first."

Holmes knocked and was met by a slovenly maid who told him that Mrs. Salazar was out doing the marketing. A shining sovereign convinced the woman that we were reporters who had come to interview her mistress about Mrs. Jones's murder. The maid led us up to a sitting room with a window.

"Did you also see the lady coming or going with her large baby carriage?" Holmes asked, taking a notebook from his pocket and scribbling eagerly. The red-faced woman puffed up a bit.

"Tah, I wish them other reporters or the bobbies what came banging on our door had cared as much as you, sir. No one asked, 'Now Becky, has you seen anything?' Well, sir, I saw them leaving. I was just coming in from the market, and I saw them across the street. Mrs. Jones was having a time of it, she was."

"What do you mean?" I asked.

"Oh, only that the pram was so heavy. She was having to push hard to go up the hill, and what with her hair all down in her face like that, I don't know how she saw where she was going."

"She was pushing a pair of twins in the carriage," I said. "I would think that would take some effort."

"Yes, but – they were just wee things, I heard, and she was pushing like she had a load of coal. Maybe the buggy wheels needed oiling. Anyways, I saw her, just as the fog closed in, and I thought how nice it was she still had all her pretty yellow hair. Mine went gray when my boy was born."

Holmes's pencil few over the paper. "So the afternoon was foggy?"

"Not so one couldn't see, but so's you wouldn't know someone unless you knows 'em – if that makes sense."

Holmes snapped the book closed. "It most certainly does." He motioned to a comfortable chair at the window and a pair of heavy spectacles on a table beside it. "Does Mrs. Salazar wear glasses all the time?"

The maid shook her head. "Too vain, that one. She won't go out with them on her face, or even wear them if she has company. Says menfolk don't like the looks of women in them. As if *she* will ever find another husband! Can't see a thing in the house, even with them peepers on, most of the time. I'm surprised she hasn't fallen into the Thames, blind as she is without her spectacles."

Holmes had picked up an embroidery hoop that rested beside the glasses. It was set with a sampler cloth. He chuckled as he put it down.

"I fear Mrs. Salazar will cause us to miss our deadline! Perhaps we had best check with the other neighbor instead."

"You mean Dark Maggie?" the maid asked. "Good luck with that sir! And mind you watch out – there's a dozen or more men what boards there. Rough sorts, they is. They won't take kindly to two reporters nosing about the place."

Holmes thanked her for the warning. Traffic had thickened on the street, and we paused, waiting for a safe moment to cross.

"Did you note the sampler, Watson?"

"Good Heavens, what does a bit of sewing have to do with this?"

"Only that the lady possesses a single pair of glasses and they are obviously not bifocals, but instead set to improve her distance viewing. Her embroidery suffers as a consequence – *Himo Sweat Ham* is the result."

"Are you implying that she didn't see Mrs. Jones exit the home?"

"She saw a lady with yellow hair and a blue dress pushing a large perambulator exit the building – the same individual who was spotted by the maid-servant. What an astute observation about the nature of our London fogs. Those who demean the innate intelligence of the laboring classes do so at their peril."

With that announcement, Holmes clasped my elbow and towed me across the street. He halted on the doorstep of the lodging house.

"Now you must take the lead. Once I have introduced us and gained our subject's confidence, you must use all your wiles to keep her busy while I confirm a few of my pet theories. You understand? Excellent." Holmes rapped loudly with his cane before I could object that I most certainly didn't comprehend what his game might be. The lady of the house opened the door without hesitation, though the instant alteration of her features – from expectation to disgust – did not go unnoticed.

"You lot. What are you, reporters? Haven't I told my tale often enough?"

Holmes removed his hat and spoke in his most ingratiating tones. "Forgive our intrusions, Madam, but we fear that public hasn't heard the true side of your story. I cannot imagine how difficult it must be, to have suffered the loss of a lady so dear to you, within hours of spending a pleasant afternoon in her company. If we might trouble you for just a few minutes of your time?"

"What's it worth?" she sneered.

"A guinea, for a mere quarter-hour?"

Reluctantly, the woman nodded and led us to the rear of the dwelling. It was a dark, ugly place, with peeling wallpaper and warped floorboards. The rank smell of old pipes and unwashed flesh nearly caused me to lose my breath. Holmes, meanwhile, trotted behind our guide as lightly as if waltzing through a springtime garden. He peppered her with questions: Where she had been born? How long she had lived in London? She snapped back answers, indicating that we should be seated inside her kitchen, on two rather fragile-looking cane-backed chairs. Holmes abruptly sneezed and, in a rush, put his handkerchief to his nose. I was alarmed to see the white linen suddenly spotted red.

"Blast – another nosebleed! Madam, if I might trouble you for directions to a washroom?"

She grunted and gestured skyward. "On the second floor. Mind you, keep it neat for my gents' use."

Holmes bowed himself out. Left alone, I tried to use my friend's tricks of close observation on the lady.

Clearly she had once been a woman of some beauty. There remained a brightness to her eyes and a sharpness of chin that indicated former pride, and her figure was still striking, even in a common brown housedress and apron. But her expression was one of wariness, and when she spoke, I noted the yellowing of her teeth, and that two were missing in her lower jaw, just where a smoker would hold a pipe. Her hair was cut short, with no attempt at a style, and she wore threadbare carpet slippers on her feet. Her hands were large, red, and calloused, as one might expect to find on a woman who made her living cleaning and feeding others.

"So?" She caught me staring at her. "What do you want to know?"

I pulled out my notebook. "My colleagues said you were a friend of the deceased. How long had you known her?"

"Since we were girls. We were cousins, both orphaned and taken in by our uncle."

"And how would you describe Mrs. Jones?"

"Blonde, small, pretty."

I waved a hand. "I do not mean in a physical sense. I mean – what was her soul like?"

Miss Sullivan snorted. "Just what kind of journal do you write for? Some of that church tripe? Oh, I suppose you'd say she was an angel, never missed a Sunday service. But angels don't steal men, do they?"

I shrugged to indicate that I didn't follow her thoughts. She banged her fist on the table.

"I should have been Mrs. Jethro Jones, not her! He loved me first, and if he'd had a family with me, then . . . Oh, I get tired of hearing what a heavenly creature Jenny was. If you'd known her as I did, since she was in short skirts, you'd see she was a schemer. Could play a long game, that Jenny. Wait and pray and hope and then look at a man with those great doe eyes! Pshh!" This last word was accompanied by a harsh expectoration into a spittoon. "If they knew her as I did, they'd not mourn for her so much."

"But if not for her, then for her children. Those two innocent little babies!"

"Aye, but who says they are dead?"

"They must be! The pram was found bloody."

The lady's eyes suddenly narrowed. "Where is your friend?"

"He will be back in a moment."

"He's been gone too long. I don't like strangers in my house." She stomped to the door and shouted at the top of her lungs. A few moments later, a heavyset man staggered into the doorway, pulling up his braces and rubbing his eyes, clearly just awakened from a deep and perhaps drunken slumber.

"What do you want, Maggie?"

"There's a man upstairs, in the washroom. Bring him down here, by the neck if you have to."

The huge fellow frowned, still rubbing at his face. "All right, but . . . Ah, why'd you cut your hair off, Maggie? You was so pretty in it!"

"Hang my hair!" she screeched. "Drag that man down here!"

"Watson!" a voice hissed. I turned to see Holmes at the kitchen window, signaling for me to retreat through the rear door even as our hostess and her henchman went stomping up the stairs. I bolted with alacrity, and together we made our escape through a narrow, untended garden. Holmes gave a happy laugh once we were two streets away from the scene.

"We must be thankful for drainpipes," Holmes said. "I knew when I heard her caterwaul that the game was up. But see what I have found."

He pulled a bag from beneath his coat and opened it. Inside was a glistening pile of golden hair.

"A wig," Holmes said, "which explains Miss Maggie's new and rather unbecoming coiffure – her long locks had to be trimmed to don this aspect of the disguise. Also, I discovered a most interesting bottle. Is this familiar to you?"

I examined the small, dark container. Though some of the label had been peeled away enough remained to make the contents clear.

"*Godfrey's Cordial*. Holmes, this is laudanum and syrup!"

"Given to soothe fussy babies to sleep. Sadly, the dose is frequently misjudged, and the slumber becomes eternal. Obviously, the Jones children are dead."

It was a shattering pronouncement. I stopped in my tracks, and Holmes turned a few steps later, frowning at me. I shook my head.

"No. They are still alive!"

"Watson, the evidence is clear. Maggie Sullivan, in a fit of murderous jealously, lured her victim to her home and murdered her with a blow to the head, perhaps delivered by one of those sturdy iron skillets that dangle about her fireplace. She then removed the woman's distinctive clothes and donned them herself, over her own attire. She put on the wig and hat, knowing this would be enough to fool the nosey but poorly sighted neighbor. She placed her victim's body in the oversized perambulator, covered it up, and made her way to the footpath. It is a lonely, out of the way place, and there she hurriedly dumped her victim's corpse.

"Perhaps she intended to redress her victim and found the process too onerous – dressing a dead body is quite a bit of labor, as any undertaker will tell you. She left the hat and the perambulator at the scene, but carried the dress further away, placing it in a rubbish bin, where it is yet to be found. She then returned home and did away with the children – it is the only answer. Hers is a busy house, and no matter how gracious she might be with her favors, she couldn't count on every inmate of the dwelling to ignore two infants being hidden on the property. Most likely, when we alert the police, they will find the bodies beneath the kitchen floorboards, or buried in the garden, or secreted in the odorous pool beneath the outhouse."

"Holmes, no," I said, my voice strained and painful. "The children are still alive."

My friend favored me with a dubious look. I repeated the murderess's words to me. There had been something in them, a unique quality, one that I felt certain hinted at the truth.

"Her wicked heart was broken by him having children by another woman. Perhaps she had truly longed to be a mother – and, no matter her original intentions, she found she couldn't kill two infants. The bottle suggests that they were drugged, but it doesn't mean they were murdered," I argued.

"She couldn't keep two infants a secret in that house. She would have to – "

"Farm them out," I said.

Holmes stared at me. His eyes grew wide, then his hand slapped to my shoulder. "Watson, you scintillate! Let us hurry to Baker Street. Perhaps there is still time to save them!"

The next day was spent in a fury of planning and scheming. Holmes wrote messages, dispatched his Irregulars, and poured through the back issues of the newspapers that cluttered our rooms. As luck would have it, the following morning I was called to an old patient's home, and when I stepped out to return to Baker Street, I was waylaid by one of Holmes's urchin boys, who passed me a note, tipped his hat, and scampered off into the crowd. The message directed me to another address, one I had never been to before. It was a cheerful and prosperous-looking dwelling in Westminster, and Holmes met me at the door.

"Is this one of your secret lairs?" I asked. For several years, I had known that Holmes maintained various lodgings and bolt holes. It looked remarkably well-furnished for such an affair.

Holmes chuckled. "It is the residence of someone familiar to you, a heroine from one of your more sensational tales. Come into the parlor, where the lady of the house waits."

We stepped through an archway, and I was delighted to see that my hostess was none other than the former Miss Violet Smith, now Mrs. Cyril Morton. Though a few years had passed since we rescued her from villainous abductors, she remained lovely and fresh, as regal and boldly poised as she had been when riding upon her bicycle.

"It is just the two of us, Cyril and I," she said in response to my question. "Mother passed away last year. Of course, I was hoping for a family of my own, but Cyril feels he must be more established in his new business and – "

"There is no time for chatter," Holmes rudely interrupted. "You're late, Watson, and our prey should even now be arriving." He directed me toward the back of the parlor. "I am now Mr. Morton, and this is my lovely wife, Violet – we long for the children Heaven doesn't see fit to bless us with. Your role should be easy enough to play, I think."

I nodded. I was to be the family physician, called in for this very special occasion.

The doorbell jangled. Holmes hurried off to answer it. Mrs. Morton cast her lovely gaze upon me and gave my hand a conspiratorial squeeze before settling into her assigned chair.

"How good to see you again, Doctor Watson! Oh, I do hope I don't disappoint Mr. Holmes – I mean, 'my husband'!"

Voices echoed in the hallway. It was amazing how Holmes could, with just a slight alteration in his tone and accent, become a completely different person. His voice became higher, more strident, and harried, as he welcomed a "Mrs. Dowdy" into the home. I fought not to smile, for my bachelor friend was utterly convincing as a henpecked spouse attempting to reassert his authority on a domestic situation.

A moment later, Holmes ushered a stout, red-faced woman into the room. She was overdressed in a heavy coat, with a fluffy boa around her neck and a wide-brimmed hat decorated with artificial doves and purple silk roses. She was huffing and puffing from the effort of carrying a large basket on each arm. To any outside observer, she was nothing more than a pretentious matron doing her own shopping, but Holmes had identified her as the premiere specimen of that class of dubious females known as 'baby farmers' – women who, for significant fees, found homes for unwanted infants. While some of these professionals were a blessing to unfortunate mothers, many more were cruel, neglectful, or even murderous – especially if the funds for the child's care weren't forthcoming.

"You are certain the children are healthy?" Holmes asked, with the brusqueness of a man conducting an important business negotiation.

"Oh yes, Mr. Morton. Nearly four months old and fit as two little fiddles." She placed the baskets on the floor at Mrs. Morton's feet. The lady gave a cry of delight as Mrs. Dowdy drew off some towels, revealing the sleeping faces of two infants.

"They are perfect!"

"Now, dearest, don't get your hopes up," Holmes warned. "Allow the doctor to inspect them. Start with the lad, please," he continued, motioning toward the child wrapped in a warm red cloth. "You must be frank with us," Holmes said to his guest. "What are the circumstances that brought them to your nursing establishment? I will not raise the children of drunkards or thieves."

"Cyril!" Mrs. Morton cried, her face turning pink with embarrassment.

"Dearest, we have discussed this," Holmes snapped, whirling back to the baby farmer. "What is their origin, Mrs. Dowdy? You come highly recommended, but I need the entire story."

"These are the children of a respectable family, sir, but theirs is a very sad story. Their mother, poor thing, died giving birth to them. Their father is a ship's carpenter, a hard-working and honest man. He did the best he could, but the poor mites were wanting a maternal touch, and his ship was to go to sea in less than a week, so what could he do? He brought them to me and bid me see if I could find a loving couple to take them. Most people, of course, aren't in the market for two babies at once! It seemed a blessing from above when I received your kind note."

"I do so want twins!" Mrs. Morton said, her voice soaked with a woman's maternal longing. She had taken the girl from the basket and the baby was cooing in her arms. Meanwhile, I had removed the male child's clothing, under the guise of a quick physical. I nodded to Holmes.

"He is perfect," I said. Holmes smiled, understanding that I'd confirmed the presence of the birthmark.

"Thank you, Doctor. Ah – well, hello, Inspector Lestrade," he added, as pocket door behind me slid open. "Here is the murderer you are looking for."

Mrs. Dowdy turned ghostly white, her hands flying to her face as the inspector moved to arrest her.

"What! No – no, I am an honest woman! I've committed no crime!"

"Perhaps, but you are lying about the origin of these children," Holmes said coolly. "Tell us how you acquired them."

She shuddered free of Lestrade's grasp and slammed her back into the wall, nearly knocking free a pair of pictures. "Saints preserve me, I have told you the truth! A man brought them to me – he said his name was John Benter. He came with the woman who had helped nurse the children – I don't recall her name. Please, sir, how was I to know? Are they stolen or kidnapped or – "

"Describe the woman who came to your house," Lestrade barked. "What did she look like?"

"A small, proud piece of work. Her black hair was cut short, she smoked a pipe – she said perhaps later she would come back to me with a husband, and take the children to raise, if no one else had."

"And the man?" Lestrade demanded.

"Oh, a big fellow, with yellow curls. How was I to know it was a bad business?"

Holmes turned to the inspector, holding out a card. "Do take Mrs. Dowdy to this address. If she recognizes the lady, she is telling the truth, and may go free. And Lestrade, you should probably take a few constables with you in case this 'Mr. Benter' or any of his housemates decide to defend the lady's honor."

Lestrade nodded. "And it is truly the missing twins?"

I had settled beside Mrs. Morton and was bouncing the fine little lad upon my knee. "It is most definitely the Jones children."

A few minutes later, after the official forces and their sobbing prisoner had exited, a pale-faced young man with a handlebar mustache poked his head around the door.

"Is the coast clear?" the real Mr. Cyril Morton asked. His wife eagerly recounted the adventure in their living room. Holmes knelt beside the lady, allowing the baby girl to grasp his finger.

"What a strange start in life these two have had. It does me good to think how overjoyed their father will be when we deliver them to him."

"And he will have you to thank," Mrs. Morton said.

"Oh no," Holmes gently corrected. "He will need to thank the Good Doctor, whose understanding of human nature surpassed my own. He heard the suggestion in Maggie Sullivan's voice that they might yet live. And Watson certainly has a better grasp on the practice of baby farming than I do – it came to him immediately as a solution to our murderess's problem. I cannot swear that it would have occurred to me that the children might still be within our grasp to rescue. Well, shall we collect our babes in arms and return them to their home?"

Mrs. Morton sighed as she placed the little girl back in her respective basket. The couple walked with us to the door and, as we stepped into the cab, I noticed that the lady was caressing her husband's arm. Unaware of my scrutiny, she suddenly lifted on her toes to kiss his cheek.

"If you will permit me another deduction?" I asked.

Holmes chuckled. "And what is that?"

"Before a year is done, I suspect their household will have grown by at least one more Morton!"

The Disappearance of Little Charley

"You see before you the most miserable creature on God's earth," Mr. Cullen Hart muttered. "My life, it seems, is nothing but a series of misfortunes and tragedies. First my Annie, then Christopher, and now Charley. If you can shine no light into my darkness, I swear to you I shall leave these rooms, go immediately to London Bridge, and throw myself into the Thames."

These words, spoken with great earnestness, were countered with a flurry of soft, matronly objections. The gentleman who sat upon the sofa looked like a soul teetering on the abyss, his face ashen, his eyes raw and bloody, and his chin covered in several days of stubble. He was well-dressed but his clothes hung loosely on his frame, and his dark brown hair stood about wildly on his head. He was perhaps thirty-five, though his haunted expression made him look older than his natural years. Seated next to him was an elderly lady clad in black, her soft chin quivering while her plump hands fluttered in distress.

"You must not say such things, Cullen," the lady gently chided. "Please, gather your strength and recall what the inspector told you – you must have faith in Mr. Sherlock Holmes."

My friend had been standing before the fireplace and studying this strange tableau silently. I knew he was taking in every detail of both his visitors

"I am not surprised to see you, Mr. Hart. I only expected you to come sooner."

I flinched inwardly at Holmes's comment. My friend's nature, to those who did not know him, could at times seem cold and unfeeling, and indeed the pair on the sofa looked up with expressions of shock. Yet I understood his words, for Holmes had been following the case through the newspapers for almost a week, as had the rest of England.

Sadly, the world has changed so profoundly since the passing of our good Queen and the dark depths of the Great War, that readers of these narratives may not realize that there was once a time when the possibility of a child being kidnapped was a remote one. It was a fate that one might, if possessed of an evil imagination, envision for the son of a lord, but not for the offspring of some solid *bourgeoise*. The details of the case were therefore a feast for the more sensational press, which Holmes avidly devoured with his morning coffee.

"I should have, sir. Inspector Gregson advised me to seek your assistance and told me that you have had much success in your endeavors. But you must understand that the matter is so delicate – so shameful – that for days I couldn't stir myself to come to you. Even now I fear that when you hear my story you may refuse to help me."

Holmes settled into his armchair. "The life of a six-year-old child is endangered. No scandal could dissuade me from bring all my powers to bear to find him. I shall state to you all I have learned from the papers and you may correct me if I err." He paused with one eyebrow slightly raised. "Mrs – ?"

"Cassidy, sir."

"You are the neighbor lady."

She nodded eagerly. "I have lived next to Mr. Hart for three years. I am the one who saw the strange men in the landau."

"Then we shall come to you in due time, Madam. I have gathered that Mr. Hart is a solicitor of great promise, having worked in the city for seven years. There was a Mrs. Hart who sadly died just after giving birth to twin sons. You have been a widower ever since, raising your boys with the help of a small staff. Is this correct?"

The man licked his lips nervously. "Yes."

Holmes frowned. Even from my position at the desk, where I was taking notes, I could sense how disingenuous the answer was.

"This is perhaps a point we should return to. All was well until six months ago, when young Christopher sickened and then perished."

Again, the man gave a jerk of his head. Holmes wove his fingers together.

"Since that time, your staff has been reduced to a housekeeper and a nursemaid for the remaining child. Both are mature women of unimpeachable character. Charles – known affectionately as little Charley – was kept strictly at home. No neighborhood children were allowed to play with him, nor was the nursemaid permitted to take him to the park or on any other outings."

"It was a cold day in the park that killed Christopher," the father muttered. "Our garden was good enough for Charley."

"Yet it was from this garden that the child disappeared, five days ago, at approximately one in the afternoon. The nurse had been outside with the child but was called inside to receive a package delivered by a commissionaire. As this man proved to be a former neighbor of hers, some idle chatter was made, and perhaps five minutes passed before she returned to the garden to find the boy missing. No immediate alarm was raised, as the nurse assumed her charge was in the kitchen with the housekeeper, and she was grateful to have a span of time to do some tidying in the nursery.

When she learned that the boy wasn't with the housekeeper, a rapid search commenced. The child wasn't found, you were summoned from your office, and soon the entire neighborhood was turned inside out in a quest for the missing lad."

"That is all correct, sir."

"And there has been no message – no note or demand?"

"None, sir. It is as if Charley has vanished into thin air."

Holmes shook his head. "Let us not immediately leap to impossibilities. As I understand it from the quite comprehensive diagram in one of our London dailies, your home is on a corner lot. An eight-foot-high wall protects the garden on the street side, and Mrs. Cassidy's home, which borders yours, has a similar garden. Your rear lawns are separated only by a whitewashed wooden fence. The back of the garden consists of another stone fence, though this one is lower, perhaps only six feet in height. A tree just at the wall would also make it quite easy for an active lad to escape confinement in his own yard."

"That is true, sir, but the property behind my house, which commands an entire block, is patrolled by three of the most savage mastiffs you have ever seen. They can be set into a ruckus merely by hearing Charley's laughter on the other side of the wall. I assure you my boy was terrified of them, and under no circumstances would have climbed into the neighbor's property."

"Is it possible, Mrs. Cassidy, that the child might have come into your garden?"

The lady shook her head brisky. "I was outside, puttering about with my flowers, when I heard the cry being raised. Charley is such a dear, sweet child – of course I would have seen him had he come over."

"Did you hear him with his nurse?"

"Oh yes. Until she was called inside, I heard him pretending to be a pirate. She was, I think, the English sea captain he was about to capture."

"And afterward?"

The lady shook her head. "I heard nothing. But that's Charley's way. He always plays quietly when alone."

"Is he a shy child?"

I noted that the lady looked to her companion before answering. "More so since his brother passed away. But he has a great imagination and is much taken with ideas of adventure in faraway places."

"Too much," Hart abruptly snapped. "Mrs. Cassidy, if you wouldn't mind stepping out. Perhaps the lady who admitted us – "

"Mrs. Hudson will no doubt be delighted to entertain female company," Holmes said, "especially of the respectable, genteel type. Our good landlady finds her halls too often filled with criminal characters, as well as two somewhat disreputable boarders. But before you go, Madam, I would like you to tell us what you told the police about the strangers in the landau."

The lady had already risen, clutching her little velvet bag to her chest. "I saw them three times before Charley vanished, always in the middle of the day. There was a driver, and two men who sat facing each other. One was an Indian, in a white costume with a great black beard and a blue turban with a red feather sticking up. The other was a Chinaman, wrapped in yellow silk, with his shiny hair all in a long train."

"And the driver?"

The lady shrugged. "An Englishman, I supposed, in a black coat and a high hat. I could see little of him, but I had the impression that his skin was pale, and he had just a hint of a red beard, kept short and neat. The horses were very beautiful, both of them pearly gray and perfectly matched."

"No coat of arms or markings on the vehicle?"

"None that I saw."

"And how did they behave?"

"They drove very slowly down our street. The first time, I only noticed them because they were strange. The second and third time, I noted that they had stopped before Mr. Hart's carriage step and appeared to be talking with Charley. I saw him wave his arms as if he had given them directions, and I saw the Chinaman hand him something in reward. I assumed it was a shilling, for he put it into his pocket very eagerly."

"Did you hear of these visitors?" Holmes asked Hart. The man groaned.

"Not a word, until after Charley disappeared. He was only allowed to play on the walk immediately in front of our door, so it would have been easy to hail him from the street. But he had been warned not to converse with strangers, and the nurse should have been watching him."

"A small boy is difficult to watch every moment of the day," Holmes said. At a nod from him, I rose and escorted the good Mrs. Cassidy down to the kitchen, where she began to chatter with Mrs. Hudson. By the time I returned, the atmosphere of the room had changed. Holmes had lit his pipe, and Hart was smoking a cigarette. Hart's face was even paler than before.

"And there you have it, sir – all that the newspapers could print. The police told me that I must hold some things back, so that if a demand was received, we could sort the true villains from the pranksters. No one knows that when he was taken, Charley was wearing a silver locket with a picture of his grandmother in it, or that he has a strawberry-shaped birthmark in the small of his back."

"These were wise precautions," Holmes agreed. "But now you must tell us the rest – the aspects you are unwilling to share with your motherly neighbor."

The man dropped his head. "It is most shameful, and if there was any way I could avoid speaking of it, I would. But I fear that it may have a bearing on my son's disappearance.

"I married when I was barely a week out of the university, before my prospects were clear. My parents, God rest their sainted souls, warned me against tying myself to Annie Reddon, but I was young, rash, and convinced that they held her humble origins against her. Annie was beautiful and, I thought, spirited – it hardly mattered to me that she had been a barmaid. At first everything went well for us when we moved to London, but soon Annie became frustrated. She had no flair for housekeeping, she bored easily, and she missed the free companionship of the public house. Then, when she found herself in a family way, things seemed improved. I was certain that motherhood would change her.

"But it did not, sir. She suffered greatly giving birth to twins, and for weeks she would do nothing but lie in the bed and stare at the walls. She showed no interest in our infants, wouldn't even rouse herself enough to nurse them. They were nearly a year old before she finally seemed well again, but instead of being a loving mother, she returned to her disreputable ways. She began to drink heavily. It was all I could do to retain servants when their mistress stayed intoxicated. This went on for almost two years. At last, I had enough, and I threatened to have her committed to an asylum. There was a terrible row, and it ended with her packing her bags and storming out of the house. I thought she would return when her temper cooled, but she did not. It was shortly after this terrible event that I hired Mrs. Waverly and Mrs. Brown, my housekeeper and nursemaid, who have been with me ever since. It was also just a month or so later that Mrs. Cassidy moved into the house next door.

"God forgive me, but I didn't know what to do. I was still up to my eyeballs in debts, working almost around the clock, and my boy Christopher was sickly. There was no money to hire a private agent to track Annie down. When a year passed and I didn't hear from her, I began to tell people that she had gone to America, to visit a relative, and had died during the voyage. This was the story I told my boys, when they grew old enough to ask why they had no mama."

"But you have seen your wife again," Holmes said.

"Yes. I remember it well. It was the week after the boy's fourth birthday. I had a client who was interested in buying some property in Whitechapel and wanted my opinion on the investment. We were riding through that neighborhood in the middle of the day – it is hardly a place a decent person would visit after sundown – and as we passed by in a cab, I saw her, standing with a half-dozen other slatterns, all of them washing their linen in a horse trough. For a moment I didn't believe my eyes. Her hair, coal black on our wedding morning, was now streaked with gray, her figure was coarse, her front teeth were missing. Indeed, I might not have known her if not for her tattoo. She has the image of a fiery bird, a phoenix, upon her right arm. She has possessed it since before our marriage. It was one of the many things that my parents held against her. I must have given some cry or incoherent shout, for she looked up and saw me, and though she didn't speak, I was certain I had been recognized.

"I don't know who put the idea of blackmail into her head, for Annie was never particularly intelligent. Perhaps it was one of those other drabs standing at the trough. A few days later, I received a letter, very poorly written, stating that she needed money. I would have done anything to protect my boys from learning the truth about their horrible mother, and indeed I began to send money to her, on the sole condition that she never show herself at my door."

"How did you send the funds?"

"A rough man named Sully was our go-between. He came once, sometimes twice a month. I never gave him much, but he seemed satisfied, and each payment bought silence. One occasion, however, gave me a fright. I happened to be at home, laid up with a sprained ankle, and when I looked through my window, I saw a heavily veiled woman watching the boys play on the walk. I called them in immediately and gave orders that they never be allowed outside again without their nursemaid by their side. The woman vanished, and I haven't seen her since, nor has the man, Sully, presented himself again in almost a year."

"Tell me about Christopher," Holmes said. "What claimed his young life?"

"The doctor told me it was a weak heart, a condition he was born with. The boys weren't identical – Charley was always larger and healthier. One morning Christopher complained of a pain in his chest, but before the doctor could even be summoned, he had slipped away."

"And in the six months since his passing, has your life been altered in any way beyond your sad loss? Has there been an inheritance, a sudden shift in fortune – anything that might tempt an evil man's jealousy?"

"No, Mr. Holmes. My cases have increased, but I haven't been promoted, or handled business for nobility, or come into any especially confidential information."

Holmes gave his pipe a few meditative puffs. "Then, Mr. Hart, we must face another rather unpleasant possibility. If your soon wasn't kidnapped, he ran away."

Mr. Hart leapt from his chair. "Impossible! Charley is a good and obedient boy!"

"I wasn't implying that the problem lies with Charley's character."

The man's face turned scarlet as he digested Holmes's meaning. He wasn't a large or physically imposing specimen, but his hands immediately curled into fists.

"How dare you insinuate that – "

"If you don't wish me to assist, the door may be found directly behind you."

Hart gasped, and then exhaled in a long, shuddering breath. Slowly, he resumed his seat.

"I didn't mean what I said to my son – it was only an angry retort. Surely Charley wouldn't have acted on it."

"Be precise, Mr. Hart."

The man nodded. "After Christopher's death, Charley was very glum and morose. It was sad to see the little fellow so blue, but after a month passed, he seemed to rally, even enough to complain about his mourning jacket being 'itchy'. I resolved to treat him not as a child, but as a little man, to show more interest in his lessons. But, Mr. Holmes, I confess I wasn't created to be a schoolmaster. I have no natural talent with children. I lost patience as Charley worked over his letters. I was too critical when he took up his pen. I tried to teach Charley how to sit with me at dinner, to use proper manners. But he taxed me with his constant talk, his foolish prattling. He was always making up stories, wild tales, and I am more for practical things.

"A month or so ago, he became obsessed with stories of America – of the Red Indians and the cowboys who fought them. He would talk of nothing else at the dinner table. Much to my annoyance, he began to build castles in the sky, fantasies that we would leave England, travel together, become cattle rustlers or bandits on the great frontier. I had a terrible headache the other night, when he suddenly abandoned his chair and jumped up beside me, tugging on my sleeve in a crazed, animated fashion.

"'Oh, we must go, Papa! Now, we should pack and leave, before the next cattle drive begins!'

"Mr. Holmes," the man sobbed, "I didn't mean to be so cruel, but I had been worn thin with work, with the loss of my other boy, with the fears that my estranged wife might appear on my doorstep. Without thought, I slapped Charley's face and told him that he was too old for foolishness, and that the only place he was going was to Eckardt's School, in the north, as soon as the winter term began. His eyes grew wide, his lips trembled, he turned and fled up the stairs. I am ashamed to say it, but that was the last time I laid eyes upon my son, for I didn't see him at breakfast and, just after noon that day, he vanished."

Holmes's expression made his contempt for the situation clear, but his voice remained even and neutral. "Had he ever spoken of running away?"

"Never."

"The strange men that Mrs. Cassidy mentioned – were they ever an object of conversation?"

"Not that I can recall, though . . . in truth, I only half-listened to most of Charley's prattle."

Holmes rose and knocked out his pipe. "You have heard nothing from the former Mrs. Hart since your son disappeared?"

"Not a word."

Holmes reached for his coat. "Very well, Mr. Hart. I will accompany you to your house. I could have made more of the field had I been called in immediately, but perhaps even now there is some detail which may have eluded the official forces. Will both of your servants be home?"

"My housekeeper will. Mrs. Brown, the nursemaid, went out to visit her invalid mother, but she should return shortly."

"Very well. If you will retrieve Mrs. Cassidy, I will be down momentarily." Holmes waited until Hart had slipped through the door before taking my arm. "Watson, I must deputize you. I am expecting a report from Wiggins."

"On another case?"

Holmes shook his head. "I knew about the missing wife, Watson. Gregson sent me a note yesterday, asking for help in finding her. The police have nothing as efficient as the Irregulars, and I wouldn't wish any news that Wiggins might bring to go astray. I honestly expect nothing to come from this journey, but I feel I must make it. There's a good fellow."

And so, an hour later, I wasn't surprised to hear the ringing of the bell and light footsteps on the stairs. I was shocked, however, when the person who appeared in the doorway wasn't the disreputable little leader of Holmes's street urchins, but a sensible-looking middle-aged woman in a tweed walking dress.

"Mr. Holmes is not in?"

"No, Madam, but he may return shortly."

The lady shook her head. "I cannot wait, I am overdue already, and they must never know I have made this call. When I learned that my employer was seeking Mr. Holmes's help, it gave me hope, but I know that Mr. Holmes can only work if he has the truth."

"You are the Hart family nursemaid?"

She nodded tightly. "My name is Eleanor Brown. I was widowed young and have worked for several families, taking care of children until they were old enough to go to school. I have been with Mr. Hart for three years. I loved the boys dearly." She gave herself a tight shake. "But I will not screen anyone, not even Mr. Hart, especially if there is any chance that Charley might yet live."

I sat down across from her. "You think that Mr. Hart has harmed his own child?"

"I don't know what to think! I only know that he was a harsh and cold father. He much prefers to be with his law books and papers than with his boy – that is the nature of many men, I suppose – and he blames everyone but himself for Christopher's death."

My blood ran cold. "He killed the other lad?"

"Not directly, but he was hard on him. The child was thin and frail. Something was wrong with his heart, but Mr. Hart insisted that he take hard exercise and eat more than he wanted. He was often ill as a consequence, and that only annoyed his father more. I think Christopher broke down under the pressure, poor tyke. I will not accuse Mr. Hart of willful murder, though he was infuriated when he couldn't force his son to grow and thrive simply because he willed it. But – I must speak quickly! – it is what happened to Charley that is so upsetting."

I had grabbed up my notebook and was feverishly scratching in it as she spoke.

"After the funeral, Mr. Hart came into the nursery and began gathering up all of Christopher's toys, his tin soldiers, and his books. When I asked what he intended, he said he couldn't bear the sight of anything that reminded him of Christopher. He carried off the boy's clothes, stripped the linens from the bed, took away the little pictures on the wall. I protested that these things might give Charley comfort, especially as the boys had shared everything. Charley is a precocious boy. He can already read very well, and he loves the books that were filled with tales of American outlaws, pirates, and the Arabian nights. Mr. Hart wouldn't be moved – by the time he finished, the room was nearly barren. I assumed he would bring Charley new books and presents that would help make up for the loss. But he never did. I saved a few pence and was able to buy Charley some little toys and books myself. Otherwise, he would have had nothing.

"At the same time, Mr. Hart forbade me to take Charley on walks, or let him play in the park. He ordered that Charley was to have no friends, and that no company might visit. Charley's entire world was the house, the garden, and, on occasion, the pavement before the door. Mrs. Cassidy, who had become like a grandmother to the boys, was the only ray of kindness. She let us come over on some mornings, and Charley enjoyed playing in that big old rambling house of hers. She knows what it is like to lose a child, and when she heard how cruel Mr. Hart was being, she brought out her late son's playthings and storybooks. That is all I know. Everything else I have told to the police.

"I don't wish to speak harshly, sir. Mr. Hart has been good and fair to me, though I did fear he would dismiss me when Christopher died, as he wanted someone else to blame."

The clock chimed, and she rose. "Do tell Mr. Holmes this – the housekeeper and I, and even Mrs. Cassidy, know about the wife in Whitechapel. Mr. Hart thinks we are ignorant, but we have learned the story. We all have some sympathy for the woman, even though we have never met her, for among us we agree that while Mr. Hart might appear a respectable gentleman, he would be the devil himself as a husband."

She departed, and I was just getting my notes on her remarkable narrative into order when Holmes reappeared, looking profoundly weary. He slumped into his chair and listened to the nursemaid's story, occasionally giving a nod.

"I have no doubt as to the veracity of her statement. The entire house speaks of meanness and a kind of pettiness, the way a youthful Ebenezer Scrooge might have lived, had he married before his instructive evening with the ghosts. Young Charley's room looked more like a monk's cell than a nursery. An inspection of the grounds reveals that he could hardly have climbed over any of the fences, and the mastiffs on the back neighbor's property rival any hellhounds of legend. There is a little gate that connects Mrs. Cassidy's yard to the Hart's garden, a detail that wasn't mentioned, but the old lady was very pleased to talk about how the child enjoyed romping around her domicile." A smile flickered on Holmes's face. "I can understand the child's natural curiosity about the old lady's house – do you recognize the address?"

I stared at the card that Holmes had flipped upon the table. "Why – surely this is the old Sutton Hospital for the Insane!"

"Indeed. The Hart's home once belonged to the caretaker, while Mrs. Cassidy's house made up the main complex of the private hospital."

"If those walls could talk!" I said, shaking my head in amazement. I looked toward my friend. Holmes's eyes were suddenly bright, and he surged forward in his chair.

"What was that, Watson?"

"I am only imagining the stories that building might tell. It was quite the infamous place until it closed a decade ago. They said one of the Queen's deluded, would-be assassins was given the cold-water treatment there."

Holmes was about to speak when there was a sharp rap on the door. It flew open a moment later, revealing young Wiggins.

"Ah, good lad! You have found her?"

"Yes, Mr. Holmes – but you won't like where!"

The St. George in the East Mortuary was surely one of the grimmest places in London. Many have described it as the antechamber of hell. They do not exaggerate.

The attendant showed us to the innermost chamber, where a young doctor in shirtsleeves was washing the corpse of a woman. Immediately, I spotted the telltale tattoo on her bruised and battered arm. It was fortunate that this mark remained, for her skull had been crushed and her face so badly broken that it was hard to realize she had ever been human.

"What happened to her?" Holmes asked.

"Fell from a rooftop is all I know. There's a policeman in the next room, talking with her fellow lodger."

We followed his gesture and found, of all people, Inspector Lestrade. He loomed over a ragged, frightened woman, and was uttering threats about Brixton Prison and the rope. Holmes touched his shoulder and drew him aside.

"Lestrade, are you accusing this woman of murder?" he asked, his voice lowered.

"No, no – half-a-dozen folks saw the suicide. But I think she knows where the boy is! The dead woman is – "

"Charley Hart's mother."

"How the blazes did you know? Wait – Gregson told you!"

Holmes sighed. "Still rivals after all these years? If you will give Watson and myself five minutes alone with the lady, I think we can provide you with clues that might give you an edge upon your opponent."

Lestrade snorted, but promptly left the chamber. Holmes offered the sobbing woman a drink from his flask, and his handkerchief to absorb her tears.

"Bless you, sir. I thought that man would slap the cuffs on me, and I've done nothing but share a room with Annie Hart all these years."

Holmes nodded, seating himself beside the woman. "Annie's husband was cruel to her."

"Yes. Lord, the nights we've laid awake, after our paying gents were gone, she telling me all the things he's done. That's why she left him. She thought maybe he'd be better to the boys if she was gone. She knew she was weak for the gin, she couldn't change. Why do people say we have to change when we can't, and no one will help us?"

"A mystery beyond my feeble skills to unravel," Holmes said, his voice so soothing it was almost a purr. "Was it Annie who demanded the payments from her husband?"

"At first it was. But then she felt bad about it, said it was 'soul money' and she wouldn't write to him no more. But that rascal Sully, he kept it up – until he got coshed in a brawl at the King and Key, more than a year ago. Hasn't been able to strong-arm anyone since."

"That explains a good deal. How did Annie react when she learned about one son's death and the other son's disappearance?"

"When Charley went missing was the first she knew of Christopher being dead, sir. Oh, how she wept and took on. She kept saying she should go to the house, but I told her 'If you do that, they'll arrest you.' Who would believe she hadn't stolen him away, maybe in revenge or something? But she just got worse every day, and this afternoon she swallowed half a bottle of gin and then she climbed onto the roof and before I could get to her – "

"No, no, keep the handkerchief," Holmes instructed. He reached into his pocket and forced several coins into the woman's grubby hand. "There is enough here to see that Mrs. Hart is decently buried. When her body is released, you must take care of the arrangements. I will make sure that rather unpleasant policeman troubles you no more."

"What do you propose to do?" I asked Holmes, as he closed the door on the weeping woman.

"I will send Lestrade to Mr. Hart's house to collect the grieving husband and bring him here for the essential identification. Gregson must remain behind to guard the home in case any further tips arrive."

I eyed Holmes. "That is not the real reason."

"You are far too astute today, Watson, so I must play my cards close to the vest," Holmes said, hailing Lestrade as we turned a corner. He rattled off the instructions, and I could see that Lestrade was none too pleased with the thought of a trip across London.

"I should file a report first. Clearly, the dead woman kidnapped her son, did away with him, and then killed herself in remorse."

"That is your theory of the case?"

"It makes sense!"

"There is no harm in giving such a theory a few more hours to percolate," Holmes replied. "Do bring Mr. Hart here – an inaccurate identification would be dangerous. And make sure that you do not allow the solicitous Mrs. Cassidy to return with you, no matter how much she volunteers. This is clearly no place for a respectable lady."

Grumbling, Lestrade set off. Holmes hailed the next cab and directed the driver to Baker Street.

"There is no more to be done?"

"On the contrary, there is much to be done, but I shall require a tool. It will take only a moment to procure. Do wait in the cab for me when we arrive."

Holmes was as good as his word, dashing up to our rooms and lingering no more than five minutes. I had assumed he would hurry back to the location of the crime, but instead he insisted that we pause at a small shoppe and have a cup of coffee.

"Let us review the key elements of the case," he said. "We know that the boy went missing just after his lunch on Monday, and no one has seen him since. There have been no demands for ransom, or threats directed at his father, who is an unlikely target of vengeance. Let us therefore dismiss the kidnapping for ransom scenario from our deck."

"The child's home was a sad and rigid one," I said. Holmes nodded.

"Indeed, the father hints at his own cruelties and failures, even if he refuses to take full responsibility for them. I was able to have a private moment with the housekeeper earlier this afternoon, and her story corroborates that of the nursemaid. The house is sad and lonely – a torturous place for a spirited little lad to live."

"So, the child ran away."

"A much more likely possibility."

I snapped my fingers. "The Indian and the Chinaman that Mrs. Cassidy saw. Two such exotic figures would easily have temped him to fly with them."

Holmes shook his head. "It won't do, for several reasons. What would a wealthy Indian and a silk-clad Chinaman want with an ordinary English boy? If they needed a child, for whatever vile purpose they might concoct, it would be far easier to pluck up a street Arab than to risk snatching a well-dressed youth from a suburban street, especially as their striking appearance would be memorable to all the bored ladies glancing through lacy curtains."

I understood Holmes's point. "No one else saw them. Yet according to Mrs. Cassidy, they had appeared more than once." A chill ran across my skin. "Mrs. Cassidy is lying."

Holmes smiled as he settled the bill. "I think enough time has passed. Let us pay the good lady a call."

When our cab deposited us before the Cassidy home, I was immediately stunned that a widow with no family would choose to live in such a large dwelling. It had indeed been a former asylum and bore all the sinister markings of such a place, including that most famous phrase from Dante, "*Abandon Hope All Ye Who Enter Here*", engraved upon the lintel.

"How many servants does such a pile require?" I whispered, as Holmes sounded the knocker.

"Half-a-dozen – all of whom, according to the Hart housekeeper, were sacked about two weeks ago as an economy measure. As the housekeeper is a cousin to Mrs. Cassidy's cook, she found the explanation most unsatisfying. As do I."

The door opened. Mrs. Cassidy was red-faced, her hair damp and her sleeves pushed back. She clearly appeared to have been dragged away from some strenuous activity.

"Mr. Holmes, Dr. Watson – has there been some news?"

"Might we come in?" Holmes asked, with a furtive glance down the street. "I wouldn't wish to be overheard."

"Of course, of course! This way." She ushered us into a parlor that was in a state of disarray. Wooden boxes were everywhere, carpets were rolled up and stacked against the wall, pictures were resting in a pile. "Please excuse me, sirs, I have been doing a bit of sorting, in preparation for selling a good deal of my furniture. At least there is somewhere to sit. Would you like some refreshment?"

"That would be delightful," Holmes said.

"I will need to get it myself," she said. "Do make yourselves comfortable."

The moment her black skirt whisked through the doorway Holmes leaned over to me.

"Drink nothing that she brings, but in a few moments ask her to show you something in the house – stay there and allow her to return to me."

"Why?"

There was no time for Holmes to answer. The lady had reappeared with glasses of water. A slight elbow nudge from Holmes sent me into action.

"Mrs. Cassidy, I understand that this was once the home of Dr. Sutton, the great alienist?"

"Yes, it was. I made modifications, of course, but his office with his splendid collection of books is still on the first floor."

"Might I trouble you to see it?"

She looked wary. "But if there are any new developments in the mystery . . . ."

"Do show him up and allow him to knock about, Mrs. Cassidy," Holmes said. "Watson asks such inane and stupid questions that I find it much easier to speak to important clients alone. I will wait here."

With a slow, hesitant nod, the lady rose, and I followed her up a twisting staircase. She almost shoved me through the office door, pausing only to light a single lamp before hurrying back downstairs. The office was oval in shape, a magnificent sanctum filled with books, cabinets, and antique medical devices. There was one rather unexpected item in the room – a small black and white puppy with pert upright ears. It was tied to the doctor's desk with a leash, which it strained against, whimpering piteously.

"Hello, pooch," I said, petting its soft coat. "What's wrong? I see you have food and water here. Why are you so unhappy?"

"Watson!"

I spun around and raced down the stairs at the sound of my friend's shout. Our hostess was sprawled on the floor. Holmes quickly slid a pillow beneath Mrs. Cassidy's head.

"The lady has fainted?"

"No, the lady has been drugged." Holmes waved a rag over his head, and I caught the odor of chloroform. "Thus the detour to Baker Street. A thousand apologies for my unkind words earlier, but it was quite essential that the lady leave the room long enough for me to take up a post behind the door, from which I could easily seize her."

"Holmes!"

"This is no time for chivalry, Watson. Her intentions are clear – she will be departing soon, for heaven knows where. Look at that trunk – note that it has unusual holes in it. She has the lad and intends to transport him with her."

I stared down at the motherly face. "Why?"

"She can explain later, once we have freed the boy." Holmes removed a silver chatelaine from her belt. "The only question is, where could Charley be? A home this size, that had once been an asylum, must have cells and padded, even soundproof rooms. It was simplicity itself to keep Charley confined, but it may take us hours to locate his prison."

I snapped my fingers. "I can take us there directly."

Holmes lifted an eyebrow. "You have a clue?"

"I have a puppy."

"The breed is known as the European toy spaniel," Holmes said, as he gently stroked the silken ears of the small dog. "But it is more commonly known as the Papillon, or 'butterfly dog', and was a favorite gift among royals in the sixteenth century. You may see a number of this little gent's ancestors in the paintings of Titian, and the most famous of the breed was rumored to have accompanied Marie Antoinette to the scaffold."

Mr. Hart turned his head, looking at Holmes with great, red-rimmed eyes, clearly confused by this delightful narrative on canine heritage. He had barely ceased weeping since we carried his son into his home and placed him back in his nursery bed. Gregson had taken the chore of escorting the semi-conscious Mrs. Cassidy off to Scotland Yard, while Lestrade now hovered in the corner of the room, making notes. The nursemaid and the housekeeper also lingered, warmly embracing each other, overjoyed that their young charge was unharmed. The child was sleeping, for he had been drugged with laudanum, but otherwise he bore no physical injuries.

"Why?" Hart croaked. "Why would she do this?"

"Perhaps she considered herself a heroine," Holmes said. "No doubt she saw herself as rescuing a child from a cruel father. I regret the frankness of my words, sir, but too many sources – including your own confession – paint a picture of a household from which a child would wish to escape. No one blames you for your wife's sad demise, or the loss of your other child, but if you wish to retain the love and respect of little Charley, you must examine your own soul."

"She seemed so kind."

Holmes nodded. "A quick inspection of her papers told me that she was the relic of Captain James Cassidy, commander of the *Fair Maid*, a vessel in the China trade that was wrecked off the coast of New Zealand a decade ago. All hands perished, including the captain and his child, the couple's only son, a lad of just fourteen. The vessel was well-insured, and there was a substantial settlement for the widow, but nothing could mend her heart for the loss of her boy. She invited Charley into her home, she watched the deterioration of his life, and finally – wickedly – she acted upon it, stealing the child, locking him in one of the padded and soundproof rooms in the mansion. She intended to flee the country with him at the first opportunity. It explains why she abruptly dismissed her servants, and the packed baggage that we found.

"And, most pathetically, young Charley tried to save himself before he was ever taken."

At this pronouncement, all eyes turned to Holmes. "What do you mean?" Lestrade asked.

"I mean only that Mr. Hart told us how his son begged for the two of them to go away and have adventures together. What would have planted such an idea in the child's mind? I find it likely that Mrs. Cassidy did – that she lured Charley with tales of adventure in foreign lands. A number of pictures in her house are of American scenes. Indeed, we may learn that the lady was originally an American, or spent time there in her youth. Be that as it may, the boy naturally thought such adventures would be more delightful in the company of his father than with an elderly widow. But when his father reacted to the invitation by threatening to send the child away to a dull boarding school – that sealed the bargain. Charley slipped through the gate the next day. Now the lady had only to restrain him until she could make arrangements to leave."

"Remarkable," Lestrade breathed.

"Ah, but such deductions must be tested, and I think the quickest way to verify them would be to awaken Charley, assure him of his safety, and let him tell his story. Afterward, a long holiday in America with his father might prepare the lad for a bright future." Holmes rose from his chair. "No injection of stimulant will be necessary, Watson. I think our Papillon pup may do the trick. Ah, see how readily he licks the child's face. No doubt they were the best of friends in imprisonment. The lady probably procured the puppy as an additional enticement to the lad to cast his lot with her. Taking the dog away was surely an act of discipline, once she had Charley in her snare. When we arrived, we found that the puppy wanted nothing more than to return to the child, leading us to the hidden room that we might never have found otherwise. Ah, the dear faithfulness of dogs – see, Charley awakens. Watson, I believe our work is done, so let us retire from the scene."

The Adventure of the Spinster's Courtship

"Let me be perfectly clear, Mr. Holmes – I do not approve of this consultation, although I will indulge my wife by covering whatever fee you may charge for your advice. Mine was offered for free but rejected as being insensitive. I counter that my dearest Corinna is the one being insensitive to the future happiness of her friend. This sudden concern for Miss Emily's welfare is misplaced. For Heaven's sake, the woman has little enough joy in her life. Why spoil things for her now? But I have been overruled. I shall putter around Regent's Park for exactly an hour, and then I will return. Let us hope, Corinna, that your mission is completed by that time."

This speech, delivered in the coolest and most patronizing of tones, was punctuated with sharp cane taps from the deliverer, a tall, thin, raven-haired man in an Albert coat, with a golden *pince-nez* highlighting the blueness his eyes. His card proclaimed him Lord Chester Winthrop, and surely readers of these chronicles will recall him as one of the great esthetes of the age, a man whose trendsetting was the talk of three continents. But on this morning in Baker Street, he was no more than a greatly aggrieved husband who had learned, as most husbands eventually do, that his opinion mattered little when it clashed with the ideas held by wife. His spouse, Lady Corinna, a mesmerizingly beautiful blonde woman in a fashionable mauve dress, merely nodded a dismissal at him. He departed our suite with a mocking bow. Holmes's amusement tugged at the corner of his lips.

"Dear me, I suspect he also disapproved of the draperies. Or was it the rug?"

Lady Corinna offered a thin smile. "He disapproves of most everything, sir, though usually not of me. It is uncomfortable for us to quarrel – and undignified to do it before strangers – but I couldn't sleep another night without putting my problem before you, especially as it concerns the life and future happiness of one so dear to me, who lacks any family to advise her or – let me be frank – any decent gentlemen to defend her."

Holmes chuckled as he settled into his armchair. "Never let it be said that Dr. Watson is anything less than a true *chevalier*. I am merely his meager squire. But as your husband seems the impatient type, please give us a succinct statement of the case. What crime has been committed against your friend?"

"None, yet. However, I fear – oh, Mr. Holmes, that is the worst of it! To have a sense of doubt and dread, to be so sure that something is amiss and to not know why. But enough! You have asked me for a statement, and I will seek to give it to you clearly.

"Before I was Lady Corinna Winthrop, I was merely Corrina Bray, of Brayford Castle," she began. Holmes interrupted her.

"Then yours is a heritage much older and richer than your husband's," he said. "There have been Brays in Surrey since the time of Richard III. Your husband's title is of Georgian extraction, bestowed by a German-speaking king in dire need of funds."

The lady half-raised her finger to her lips. "I am grateful for your knowledge of history, Mr. Holmes. Indeed, my family is an old one, loyal retainers of the Crown, though never ennobled for our services. Our home – calling it a castle is rather pretentious, though it does date back to the fourteenth century and has the requisite high walls and moat – has been well-preserved for generations. It is perhaps one of the finest medieval castles outside of the royal collection of estates. There were once many Brays in the countryside, but the Bray line sadly dwindled over the past two centuries, due to misfortunes in war and a tendency to contract consumption. Of my family there was only my father, Anthony Bray, my mother, Julia, and my young siblings, Marion and Ashton.

"An ancient castle is a far from pleasant place to grow up in, despite what fairy tales imply. There were no modern conveniences in the house, and it was perpetually cold, damp, drafty, or oven-like, depending on the weather. Over the generations, much of the estate had been sold, so we lacked any kind of deer-park or woodlands to play in. Indeed, there are now much finer houses on either side of the small estate. Our castle suddenly appears like something ghostly and haunted, dropped down on its little hillock from another era in time.

"Father attended medical school and became a noted Harley Street specialist. He felt it best that his children be brought up in the country, in the family home, despite the fact he could rarely be with us because of the needs of his patients. Mother much preferred city life, so we were raised principally by nannies and tutors, but we felt the closest connection – almost familial in nature – to Mr. Crow and his daughter Emily.

"Mr. Crow was an old retainer, a combination of steward and historian. He was a rather queer-looking gentleman, with a long, hooked nose and a shiny bald head. He always wore black, and with his hunched back and his strange, hopping gait, he truly reminded everyone of his namesake. He was a widower and dwelt in a small cottage just behind the castle, along with his daughter, who is ten years my senior. Crow, as we called him with childhood familiarity, was the dearest old fellow, full of tales of adventure and the great accomplishments of our ancestors. It was from Crow that I learned how Mistress Alice Bray had been a 'tiring woman' to Queen Elizabeth, responsible for handling and cleaning her gowns and jewels. There was an old, dark portrait of Mistress Alice in the hall that I loved to admire, and as a young girl obsessed with her dresses and ribbons, I used to stand before the ancient silver mirror in the castle and imagine that I was Good Queen Bess, and that my sister was Mistress Alice, who had to serve me.

"But it was Emily Crow who was my dearest companion. I was much closer to her than I ever was to Marion. It was Emily who taught me my letters – she never grew impatient with me, even when I proved the dullest of students. I don't know why, Mr. Holmes, but sometimes the letters that I see aren't in the same arrangements that others see them! It makes it most difficult for me to plough through a book or an essay. Emily alone seemed to understand, and for that I loved her!

"But I must leave off this childhood reminiscence and come to my point. Some three years ago, Father passed away. Sadly, he had more of a brain for infectious diseases than for investments, and my family was facing financial embarrassment. Mother, however, came up with a most unusual scheme: Both my sister and I were recently wed, and my brother was just beginning his studies at Oxford, so there was no family member in residence at Brayford Castle. Mother turned the entire estate over to Crow, instructing him to convert it into a kind of architectural and historical attraction, and to charge admission. When Mother first told me her plan, I thought it was fantastical. Imagine, people parting with hard-earned shillings to see our old house! But Crow immediately went to work, and soon Brayford Castle had become the talk of the Surrey countryside. Crow was the chief tour guide, and I think it was the combination of his amusing appearance and his great enthusiasm that people appreciated."

"Did Miss Emily serve as a hostess as well?" Holmes asked.

A sudden shadow came over our guest's lovely features. "No, Mr. Holmes. Crow forbid it. You see, Emily isn't an attractive woman. She has a golden heart, a sweet voice, and a compassionate character, but she is sadly formed, low and squat, and her hair is the color of a pumpkin. She suffered from smallpox as a child, and later had a great deal of blemishes, which left her skin pitted and scarred. Her teeth are uneven, and her eyes – I don't have a name to put to the condition, but they seem permanently crossed. All her life, she has been the victim of cruelties. Wicked boys have been known to throw stones at her. Now in her middle years, she is pitiful, a woman who deserves to be loved, but whom nature has given no favors that might spark romantic devotion in a man. So you see, Crow didn't wish her to 'turn away' any paying customers. Instead, he hired a very attractive young man – I believe his name was Copper or Craft something, and I only met him once, and for less than an hour – to help with the tours.

"All went very well until last winter, when Ashton returned to Mother's London house for the holidays. He has become quite the student of history and, according to my sister, who was there for dinner that night, he began to ask Mother many questions about some of the old bits and baubles in the castle. The next day, my mother and brother spent time in the British Library before embarking for a visit to the castle. Much to my surprise, they were away for three days, and when they returned, both were in sour moods.

"'What has made you so irritated?' I asked when they dined with us.

"'I have sacked Crow and that young scamp who worked for him,' Mother said. 'He'll never see another penny of Bray money, not as long as he lives. And I've served him notice, that he had best be out of the old cottage by Boxing Day, or I'll have him thrown into the streets, along with that ugly baggage of a daughter.'

"I was horrified, of course. I begged Mother to tell me what had happened, but she refused – Mother can be quite haughty that way, and because I was so slow at learning my letters, she presumes that I am too stupid to be entrusted with any family secrets. I took my brother aside and tried to twist his arm, but Ashton would say only that Crow had endangered the Bray family honor. Ashton bragged that when he completes his studies at Oxford, he will return to the village and operate the castle himself. Mr. Holmes, my brother may have the makings of an excellent historian, but he is so slothful I know he will fail to keep our family business afloat. I tried to impress this upon him, but he was most insistent that Crow was no longer welcome on the estate.

"'Then think of Emily!' I said to him.

"'I would prefer not to.'

"'Be ashamed! She was kind to you, a good nurse when you needed care and Mother was too busy with her society friends in London to be bothered by a sickly boy. How dare you talk of throwing Emily into the streets!'

"But nothing would move him. At last, I turned – reluctantly – to my husband for help. He agreed to give me enough money to help Crow and Emily establish themselves in a little home in the village. I found them a small house with a good garden, for I knew Emily took great pleasure in growing roses. She wept at my kindness but could say nothing of what had caused such a row between my mother and her father. I could only guess that she, like me, was kept ignorant of the situation. Meanwhile, Mother hired a small troupe of actors to serve as tour guides at the castle. Actors, sir! As if people of that ilk could be trusted not to steal the silver!

"Not even a month passed before this terrible and mysterious event exacted a heavy toll. Crow died suddenly in his sleep, leaving poor Emily all alone. I wanted to bring her to London as a paid companion, but my husband refused. Ashton and Mother wouldn't assist, but my sister and I pooled some money to provide the poor woman with a small annuity. She also mends and does fancy needlework for ladies in the village, so she isn't entirely destitute. Which brings me, I suppose, to the reason I have come to you."

Our client drew a deep and dramatic breath.

"You see, Mr. Holmes – a gentleman is making love to her!"

I confess that I looked up from my notes with a start. My friend's eyebrows were fixed into their most astonished angle. His voice was low and sardonic.

"Indeed?"

"Yes. It is the scandal of the community. This man – Professor Alexander Whipple by name – is old enough to be her father. He arrived two months after poor Crow was lowered into his grave and took lodgings in The Hart and Crown public house. He is bent nearly double, has the most ludicrously thick spectacles, and wobbles along with the help of a heavy cane. He wears long black frock coats and a thick scarf, even though the weather has warmed. He made Emily's acquaintance at church and claims that he fell in love with her at first sight. Can you imagine!"

Holmes seemed to be struggling not to smile. "From your description of the maiden, it seems that a man might be struck with horror rather than with *amour*."

"Exactly, sir! Only a blind man might be able to make such a statement, that he was 'taken with her beauty' and 'worshipping at the altar of her fair face'. Those are exact quotations!"

"So you have been taken into Miss Emily's confidences."

"Yes. Right from the start, she wrote to me and told me of her swain. She begged for my help, for she has no experience in such matters. I raced home immediately and spent a few days with her. Why, Mr. Holmes, I thought nothing short of a broom would chase the man from the house. When I arrived, he was holding yarn for her to roll, staring up into her face with the devotion of a dog. It was horrible."

I cleared my throat. "Is there something suspicious about the man?"

"Beyond his choice in lovers?" Holmes added.

"He claims to have been a professor of biology at a small college in America, and that he has returned to his native country in retirement. He revealed to the men at the pub that he is an old bachelor, has a good pension and some investments, and now wants a 'charming lass' to make his home complete. In and of itself, there is nothing objectionable to him. He was dignified and polite to me during our visit, and he has slipped a darling little ruby ring upon Emily's hand. They plan to marry on Sunday."

Holmes shook his head. "Madame, as much as it grieves me to say this, perhaps your husband is correct. As strange as your friend's romance may appear, if she is happy and the gentleman is besotted, then what legitimate objection can you make?"

The lady's face turned red. Her fingers curled into fists.

"But it is wrong! Oh, Mr. Holmes, if you could only feel the certainty of my intuition. Women understand these things. Emily would understand them too if she hadn't been so sheltered. She is far too innocent. She actually believes these things he scrawls on his chalkboard and – "

Holmes held up a hand. "Scrawls on a chalkboard?"

"Oh – oh, did I forget to mention it? That is the oddest bit. He is mute! He isn't deaf, but he cannot speak. He claims to have been that way since birth. He carries around a small board, upon which he marks his words."

"Ah . . . that is indeed an intriguing detail," my friend agreed. "How, might I inquire, did he manage a successful academic career with such a handicap?"

The lady frowned. "I don't know. I suppose his students were as enamored of him as Emily is. He can be very charming – he is quick to bow and kiss one's hand, and some of the things he writes are so witty and expressive. Indeed, even I felt drawn to him, as if by a magnet, and yet – it is wrong! He has some vile intention, I am certain." She leaned forward, dropping her voice. "Emily told me that he has plans to change her garden – that after the wedding he will replant it with a 'better variety' of flowers. And she has the finest roses in the village. Tell me there isn't some evil there, when he is so eager to destroy the things she loves the most?"

Holmes took out his pocket-watch. "Your tale intrigues me, but your husband will return in a moment. Indeed, that may be his tread I hear upon the stairs."

"Will you investigate?"

My friend smiled. "The countryside is so charming this time of year. Watson, I do believe we could amuse ourselves for a day or so, could we not?"

The next afternoon we found ourselves in the quaint little village of Brayford. It was one of the most picturesque destinations in the district, alive with flowers and budding trees. A short drive took us to Brayford Castle, which Holmes insisted on exploring after we placed our overnight cases at The Hart and Crown. As Crow and his daughter had been dismissed from their jobs, and the castle was now under the control of a new set of guides, I didn't see the purpose in this excursion. Still, it made for a pleasant two hours as we rambled around the old stones and listened to the docent – a young actress in a replica of a Tudor maid's costume – describe the dwelling's history.

"In this hall," she said, rather breathlessly, and with her eyes fixed on a handsome young gentleman who had arrived with his elderly parents, "are relics from the time of Roger and Alice Bray. Roger held several stewardships, but his wife was the more favored of the pair, as she was a tiring woman to Queen Elizabeth. Here – " She gestured to a gown, one displayed on a mannequin which had been roughly painted and bewigged to resemble England's most famous monarch. " – is a dress from the period. Family lore says that it was given to Alice by the Queen herself. Now, if you come this way, I will show you the room where King Charles . . . ."

She had already slipped through the doorway, but I hung back with Holmes. Much to my surprise, and some embarrassment, he had taken out his lens and was using it to inspect the details of the antique garment. He fingered the elaborate ties and twinkling stones.

"Holmes! The party will miss us."

"But this bit of history is quite intriguing." Holmes straightened, his eyes roaming the gallery, with its wealth of poorly executed paintings. "This display suggests a theory to me, but I must wait until I have more data."

"Sirs, if you will step this way?" the girl called. Holmes gave me a playful shove.

"I fear my friend has fallen in love with the Queen!" he said, and laughter erupted all around us. I shot him a sideways glance and got a wink in return. As annoying as Holmes could be at times, to see him in such a rare high humor was a pleasure, and so I took up my role to the point they were all assured that I was a blundering idiot before the tour ended.

Afterward, we enjoyed a leisurely stroll back to the heart of the village. Lady Corrina had given us the number of Miss Emily's home, and we found it to be a sweet little cottage at the end of the westernmost street, not far from the little church where the lady planned to be wed. The garden was one that might put even Hampton Court to shame, for its rich assortment of roses. Holmes hesitated for a moment at the low brick wall that surrounded the lovely flowers.

"Dear me. This is as troubling as it is suggestive."

"What do you mean?"

Holmes gave a quick shake of his head and moved on. I took another glance over the wall, my mind now racing. What had Holmes seen that I had missed? The garden looked so charming, but now I began to imagine that every petal was poisoned and that venomous vipers lurked in the shadows of the blossoms.

A notice on the church door announced a children's musical recital that afternoon, and – much to my dismay – Holmes insisted that we attend. Two hours of poorly performed songs and screeching violin solos must have been torturous on my friend's sensitive ears, but just after the event began, I deduced his reason for coming: Miss Emily Crow and her suitor, Professor Whipple, had slipped inside and silently occupied two chairs in a corner. As this was the only social occasion of the day, and Miss Crow was a devout member of the church, it was natural they would attend, and Holmes could covertly assess their relationship.

Sadly, the lady was exactly as her friend had described. I have rarely seen a more ill-favored woman, and her choice in attire – a red checkered dress and a bright yellow hat with a stuffed bird mounted atop it – did little to improve her appearance. Her fiancé was also rather odd, with his great mass of unruly white hair, tiny peering eyes behind thick spectacles, and a heavy black coat which might have been fashionable in the days of the Sailor King. He carried a schoolboy's slate, and from time to time he scrawled upon it and showed it to the lady. I couldn't read the words from my position, but they were amusing to his beloved, who blushed and giggled and once even daringly planted a kiss on his check.

Following the recital, the crowd made its way onto the lawn where a treat was being set up. Holmes waited until the couple had collected cake and lemonade, then trailed them to the secluded spot they had chosen within an arbor. Asking me to stand back, he charged forward.

"Professor!" Holmes cried. "Can it be? Professor Whipple! I am so happy to see you, sir!" Holmes thrust out his hand. The little man nearly fell backwards from his chair, he was so startled. I, meanwhile, was astonished by the ease at which my friend adopted his posture and accent to fit the look and sound of a brash American. "Don't you remember me, sir? John Sherrinford, from your class on invertebrates? It was the best class I ever had at the old college."

The gentleman gasped for breath and then pulled up his board. He wrote out, "*I don't recall you.*"

"Really, Professor? But you said I was one of your finest students. Why, you even gave me credit for discovering a new *genus* of roaches."

The man frowned, then scratched out another line that read, "*Of course, but you have changed.*"

"Indeed, I have, sir! I'm not the scrawny, callow youth I was back then. But I am being rude – Please, Professor, introduce me to your lovely companion."

At this compliment, Miss Emily blushed. Holmes took her hand and kissed it. For almost ten minutes he stood and chattered to the professor, referencing old friends at the school, and reminiscing about amusing incidents in the classroom, including one in which the "naughty boys" set the professor's trousers on fire.

"But I am taking up too much of your time, sir. I am staying at The Hart and Crown – You are there as well? Excellent! Perhaps you will stop in and drink a class of port with me tonight, for old times' sake. Here's to the old school motto – *Conquer and prevail!*"

I caught up with Holmes just outside of the churchyard. "That was amusing," I said.

"Indeed, I can rarely recall having so much fun watching a villain squirm. But let us dismiss the cad for the moment, give our battered ears a rest, and enjoy a good dinner and a cigar. I expect we will have company this evening."

The food at The Hart and Crown was uninspired but substantial, and by the time we retired to our suite, Holmes was in a relaxed and talkative mood. He conversed on a variety of subjects, including fox hunting, the mythic origins of the Druids, and the artistic sensibilities of the pre-Raphaelites. At last, I was able to guide the discussion back to the case at hand.

"I will never completely dismiss a woman's intuition," Holmes began. "For what we males call 'female intuition' is often a careful, though unconscious, set of observations. Women have honed the skills of making deductions from clues, even if they give the results a different designation. Lady Corrina was quite right to observe that Miss Emily Crow is as unappealing as her family name. Her beauty is of the interior sort, and few men are willing to seek out such hidden gems as kindness and compassion. We males are, by and large, a shallow lot when it comes to the qualities we desire in mates. The former Miss Mary Morstan was the exception to the rule – as beautiful in face and figure as she was in soul. You were a very lucky man."

To this I wouldn't disagree. Holmes waved a hand airily.

"It was incomprehensible to me, from the start, how a man who couldn't speak could control a schoolroom. Not impossible, perhaps – there are many talented academics who labor under handicaps – but rather improbable. Thus, I needed to see for myself if all the things that smacked so heavily of a disguise were, indeed, a façade. Surely you recall the unfortunate Miss Mary Sutherland, also an unattractive maiden lady, who was made love to by her own stepfather incognito."

"So this man is someone known to Miss Crow."

Holmes nodded. "Yes, but he is someone who lacks the confidence of the odious Windibank, who blamed swollen glands for his whispery voice. This fraudulent gentleman felt it best to remove his voice all together."

"But Windibank, if I recall, wanted to prevent his stepdaughter from leaving the household so he could keep control of her money. Does this false lover also intend to abandon his betrothed at the altar?"

Holmes snuffed out his cigar and moved to look out of the window. "No. I think there is a more dangerous evil at work. How fortunate we are that Lady Corrina recalled Whipple's intentions to dig up the garden! The devil plans to wed her and then – Ah, he returns. He has but two choices now: To pack his bags and flee, or to come to me and offer a partnership in his crime. Unless, of course, he intends to kill me. That would prove entertaining."

"Holmes!"

"Fortunately, I am well protected. You have your revolver, I trust? Excellent. We shall give him five minutes to decide his fate."

Within seconds of Holmes speaking these words, there was a rapping at the door of our small suite. Holmes rose and opened it, bowing as he ushered the bewhiskered man into the room.

"Professor, how good of you to join us. We have so much to discuss. Please, take the easy chair, I know your old bones are tired. Let me relieve you of all unnecessary burdens."

As deftly as a magician, Holmes snatched the slate from his guest's hands. I stepped beside my friend, folding my arms across my chest and twisting my features into a menacing scowl. Whipple threw up his hands and then, after a moment's consideration, dropped them with a sigh.

"You have me, sir." His voice was shockingly youthful. "Might I ask if Sherrinford is your true name?"

"It is not, just as Whipple is not yours."

"Shall we be honest with each other then?"

"I find honesty is usually the best policy," Holmes said smugly, "but as I have a certain advantage, I am loathe to surrender it. Neither one of us is what we seem, yet perhaps we can use that to our mutual advantage." Holmes settled into the opposite chair and casually lit a cigarette, then offered one to our visitor who, with a shaking hand, took it. Holmes even did the honor of lighting it for him, as if they were two businessmen about to settle into comfortable negotiations.

"Tell me," Holmes said, "why this elaborate charade? Surely if a man loves a woman, he has no need to play such a preposterous game."

Our visitor removed his hat and then his wig. He peeled away the beard, pulled putty from his nose, and scrubbed roughly at his face with his handkerchief. These actions revealed the young and rather handsome youth who had hidden beneath the mask of age.

"My name is Randall Collins," he said. "Five years ago, I was a university student, down on his luck, unable to afford another semester's tuition. Old Crow, Miss Emily's father, hired me to help him manage Brayford Castle. I was a combination clerk, tour guide, and custodian, and Crow treated me more like a son than a hireling.

"Crow loved history, especially the legends and lore of the castle. The Bray family showed little interest in their heritage, beyond how they could use it to finance their life in society. Crow had a theory: That one of the Bray ancestors had been a thief, and had stolen gems and baubles from none other than the Virgin Queen herself!"

"Alice Bray, the tiring woman," Holmes interrupted. Collins started.

"Why . . . yes. But how could you have known?"

"A close inspection of the dress in the castle," Holmes said. "It was obvious to my lens that some of its adornments had been snatched free, leaving aged threads dangling and unravelling. The paste replacements were poorly and very recently sewn in. But even before I saw the frock, the knowledge that an ancestor had served as a dresser suggested a person with great opportunity for – shall we say – *personal enrichment*?"

The young man nodded eagerly, caught up in the story despite his awkward position. "Yes, yes, you understand! Queen Elizabeth had so many jewels – more than any monarch before her – and she was a careless person. Pins, pearls, broaches, sparkling things were always going astray. A cunning tiring woman could easily pocket a fortune, if she dared, and this woman did. Crow deduced from her portrait that she was wearing pieces that also appeared in a lesser-known image of the Queen. Mistress Alice did have the good sense to wait until after her mistress's death to have her own picture painted, however."

"And I take it that these gems had never been found."

"No – and then, one day while searching amid the castle's archives, Crow found the journal kept by Edwin Bray, the tiring woman's son. In the entry dated on the day of the lady's funeral, Edwin noted that it had been his mother's last wish to be buried in the '*great dress*' given to her by her mistress the Queen. I don't know if Edwin didn't realize the dress was decorated with precious stones, or if he simply was determined to honor his mother's last request, but he noted that Alice had been buried wearing the gown." Collins grinned. "Crow speculated that the request had been a way to spite Mistress Alice's daughter-in-law, whom Mistress Alice loathed, and who might have inherited the jewels if they hadn't been placed on the lady's corpse."

Holmes arched an eyebrow. "And so you and Crow sought to validate this theory with a bit of grave-robbing."

Now the young man offered a guilty nod. "We were mad with curiosity, and what harm could it do? The lady was buried in the vault of the family chapel. Imagine our astonishment when we pried open the sarcophagus and found some strange atmospheric conditions within the chamber had preserved the lady and her gown. It was like viewing the body of an incorruptible saint. But once we exposed the corpse to the air, it quickly became obvious that such a miracle wouldn't last for long. We removed the gown and wrapped the body in a fine silk shroud. I assure you there was no disrespect intended.

"Crow mounted the gown for display. Since no one knew its provenance, it was simply another artifact for Crow's little museum. He took the jewels from the gown, but the damage was too evident, so he replaced them with paste replicas. Miss Emily could have done a much better job on the gown, as she is a talented seamstress, but Crow was determined that she would know nothing of our crime. He warned me that she was 'too religious' and 'too honest' for what we were doing, and I was sworn to tell her nothing about it."

"But your perfidy was discovered."

"Yes, by Ashton Bray. While poring over his books at Oxford, he caught the resemblance between the jewelry in the portraits of the Queen and Alice. He turned up unexpectedly one day and examined the gown, demanding to know where it had come from. Crow wasn't a good liar. He babbled something about having found it in a trunk. The Bray heir was having none of it, and when he brought in his mother, things only got worse. They were certain we had stolen from them but lacking the key document – which Crow had wisely put into my keeping – they couldn't prove where the dress had come from, or the jewels gone off to. Still, we were given the sack in disgrace."

"And Crow pawned the gems," I said. The young man snickered.

"Clearly, you aren't a detective," he said to me.

"Crow kept the jewels," Holmes countered. "And now his daughter has them in her possession, without her knowledge."

"Now *you* are the clever one," Collins laughed. "Crow couldn't overcome his love of history. Not even the thought of immense wealth could tempt him to part with items that had once been caressed by the greatest monarch of our isle. He kept them in an iron box, and when he and his daughter moved to the little cottage in town, he planted them beneath her roses. He assured me that when some time had passed, he would begin to pawn them and divide the proceeds with me. I was loathe to wait that long, as his health was poor, but he gave me one large pearl as a show of good faith. I left the village, sold the pearl in Edinburgh, and set myself the task of finishing my degree. Just a few weeks later, I received word that Crow had perished.

"You can imagine my conundrum. Miss Emily had no idea that a treasure lay beneath her roses. But what would happen if she changed her lodgings? Or if, in digging about, she found it? She was too innocent and naive, she would no doubt turn the box over to the authorities, and what would happen then? I thought about sneaking into town and digging up the box by moonlight, but the village is so small and folks so nosey that I dared not. The woman is such a homebody, luring her away seemed impossible. At last, I hit upon the scheme of making love to her. Poor soul, she is ugly and lonely, I knew she would respond – jump at the chance to alter her spinster status. As I had lived and worked with the Crows previously, I knew my disguise had to be an impenetrable one. An actor friend suggested the character of the mute old man, so that I wouldn't struggle to conceal my voice as well as my face. It all worked very well until . . . I suppose it was her friend, the older Bray daughter, who must have become suspicious."

"So you planned to wed Miss Emily and – " I shook my head. As a formerly married man, I saw some difficulties with maintaining his illusionary character past the ceremony itself.

"Some poison placed in the nuptial wine would no doubt have solved the problems," Holmes said. Collins's face went white.

"No! No – I may be a rogue and a grave-robber, but I am not a murderer!" the man insisted. "My plan was to insist that we spend our first night together in the cottage. I would drug her – I had the powders ready – and that night retrieve the treasure. I would depart in the darkness, leaving behind a note claiming that I had been recalled to America by the sudden death of a wealthy relative. I planned to send her a portion of the proceeds from the sale of the gemstones, just enough to keep her comfortable. She could have the respectability that came with marriage, even if she never saw her strange little husband again!" Collins leaned forward, rubbing his hands together. "Now you have it. We three are the only men who know where a treasure – which Crow estimated at over ten-thousand pounds – lies buried. I am supposed to escort Miss Emily to the church in less than forty-eight hours. What is there to prevent my plan from proceeding if I include you gentlemen as partners?"

His greedy smile was sickening. Holmes rose and flung his cigarette into the fireplace.

"Nothing, perhaps, except my name. Do you still wish to know it?"

Collins's lips began to twitch. His grin faltered. "Well, yes, it is always best to know who one is working with."

"My name is Sherlock Holmes."

The man's cheekiness collapsed into terror. He gasped, choked, and then made an awkward attempt to bolt for the door. Holmes tripped him easily, leaving him sprawled on the carpet.

"Rarely have I met a more cunning sneak and villain," Holmes said. "Your participation in the desecration of the dead is repulsive, but your plans for robbing rightful heirs and breaking a poor woman's heart is even more disgusting. Crawl back into that chair, you worm. My experience of women is intellectual, not emotional, but I am sure the good Doctor Watson – yes, you recognize my chronicler now, I take it – is far more insightful. Watson, do you think our friend's plan would have pleased Miss Emily Crow?"

"No," I said, sharing Holmes's sense of utter loathing. "It would have torn her apart, and probably killed her."

"Then what should we do with her intended murderer?"

Collins began to weep and beg for mercy. Holmes considered him with cold grey eyes.

"If we bring the police into this matter, it will only cause more heartache and scandal. There is some paper on the desk. Watson never travels without both his trusty revolver – " At this the man's eyes widened in alarm. " – and his best pen. We shall begin with a complete confession, in your handwriting, with which your fiancée is undoubtedly familiar."

It was a delicate business, but Holmes had a more than capable ally in Lady Corinna, who had arrived in the village to attend the wedding. After a consultation the next morning, the three of us arrived at Miss Emily's cottage, where the lady was excitedly putting the final items into her honeymoon trousseau. I shall spare my readers the painful reception of the hurtful revelation, and how copiously the lady wept when she read the confession and learned she had been cruelly deceived. With her permission, Holmes and I shed our jackets, rolled up our sleeves, and went to work with spades in the garden, digging in the precise spot where Crow had buried his loot. We were soon rewarded with the ringing of the tools against an iron box. We removed it from the soil, cleaned it, and brought it into the kitchen, placing it upon the table. Miss Emily, leaning on her friend's arm, tottered in to watch as Holmes broke open the lock.

Within was a jumble of Tudor era jewels – loose diamonds, pearls, rubies, and garnets, a golden broach in the shape of a phoenix, and another in the likeness of a snake biting its tail. Beneath some tattered velvet was a string of jade beads that alone would have purchased a mansion in London. Holmes opened two books, one with a portrait of Queen Elizabeth, another with the picture of Mistress Alice from Brayford Castle. It was clear that the former tiring woman had rather boldly worn her ill-gotten gains sewn into her gown.

"Oh, Corrina, I am so sorry!" Miss Emily sobbed. "How could Father have done such a terrible thing?"

The lady shook her head. "Do not apologize. In fact – I am grateful to Old Crow."

Miss Emily dabbed at her eyes. "Whatever can you mean?"

"Why, he discovered my ancestor's perfidy. She didn't deserve to spend eternity with these jewels. These precious stones once adorned the woman who famously and gloriously put duty above love – and they should once more."

With that pronouncement, Lady Corinna pushed the box in her friend's direction.

"This belongs to you, Emily. No, say nothing, I want you to have all of it! Mother and my brother need never know the missing jewels were found. Take them, Emily, and live well. You can come to London, join me in society, and if anyone asks how you came into your fortune, you may rightfully tell them that you discovered it in your own rose garden."

Even now, so many years after the fact, it warms my heart to think of Lady Corinna's goodness and Miss Emily's innocence. Holmes and I took a vow of secrecy and left the ladies plotting as to how to best change antique jewels into modern pounds. A year later, I noted Miss Emily's appearance in the society pages, where she was hailed as one of the most fashionably dressed women of the season. Later, I saw that she had embarked on a world tour. And perhaps two years after that, I saw a wedding announcement – that the former Miss Emily Crow was now Lady Emily Lawson. Holmes and I were inspired to visit the photographic studio on Oxford Street where images of celebrities and beauties were displayed. To our delight, we found the wedding portrait of the couple. Sir Richard Lawson was a large, stout man, balding with sizeable muttonchop whiskers and slight crossed eyes. The pair stood with arms linked, his huge, flipper-like hand laid with great delicacy over hers. The newlyweds focused on each other, mirror images of devotion and love. Holmes smiled as me as we turned away from the window.

"I think it is fair to say, Watson, that I have rarely seem a more splendid couple, or known a happier end to a story!"

The Adventure of the Confederate Treasure

It was a lovely morning in the spring of 1920 when I received a note from my good friend, Sherlock Holmes, bidding me to come to our old Baker Street abode that afternoon. Though retired, and more generally engaged with his bees than the pursuit of criminals, Holmes had retained his famous lodgings to facilitate his occasional trips into the city, whether to visit his brother Mycroft – these days a sometime-invalid, though with a mind as sharp as ever – or to simply enjoy the company of his former Irregulars and his erstwhile rivals at Scotland Yard. I knew it gave him great pleasure to receive a summons to the police headquarters, to deliver a lecture, or provide practical demonstrations to the young inspectors.

This communication, however, set all my nerves to quivering. It was delivered in two parts by a fresh-faced messenger who had been duly instructed on how to handle the components. I first read the note, written in Holmes's firm hand:

> *Watson – I have need of you. A young lady proposes to call upon me at four today. As you know, I refuse most cases, but in the second envelope you will find the reason I find myself inclined to hear her story. I will see that your favorite chair is cleared of debris for your arrival.*

I nodded for the youngster to give me the yellow envelope. I split it open over my desk. Five orange pips dropped out.

My knees complained as I slowly climbed the well-worn seventeen steps, but my friend's cheerful call for me to enter quickly made me forget my aches. Holmes's manner, as always, was kind if not effusive. Though he was in his mid-sixties and his hair was gray, his spine was straight, and his eyes were bright.

"Really, Watson, still fond of games of chance? At your age?"

I would not give him the satisfaction of knowing how straight his little deductive dart had flown. I had just lost half-a-month's pension on an ill-advised wager.

"Tell me of your client," I said. "I was startled by the contents of the missive."

"As was I," Holmes said. "But since her note arrived yesterday morning, I have been doing some reading at the British Library. It seems our assumption – that the last remnants of an invisible empire of terror perished in the Atlantic aboard the *Lone Star* – was premature. The Ku Klux Klan has returned."

"How?"

"Do you recall a motion picture called *Birth of a Nation*? It played in our cinemas five years ago."

I shrugged. "It was a melodrama about the American Southland, was it not?"

Holmes settled into his chair. "Of a sort. Directed by the notable auteur D. W. Griffith, it is based upon a novel called *The Clansman*, which celebrates the activities of the scoundrels who sent my client, Mr. John Openshaw, to his doom."

"But what possible relation could a book or a cinema feature have to these pips?" I asked, removing the envelope from my pocket. Holmes took the packet from me.

"They have inspired a re-awakening of the strange society," Holmes said. "New chapters of the infamous Ku Klux Klan have been organized, and have become quite powerful across the American nation. It is a disgrace that citizens of a country which so recently joined in our Great War – to 'make the world safe for democracy', as their president declared – are now eager to embrace villainy. From what I have read, the Hun couldn't have been more abusive to his victims than these 'respectable' men in robes and hoods are to Negroes, immigrants, and Catholics – all those they deem 'un-American'." Holmes sighed and placed the withered pips on the little table at his elbow. "But as to my potential client – I know only that she has received these pips, along with a threatening note, which she sent along to me. Here it is."

I took the small, folded paper. I will not offend my readers by recording the vile language it employed. Only one line was direct and not tinged with vulgarity:

> *Leave the spectacles and the map at the feet of Apollo at the stroke of midnight on Saturday, or you shall meet your brother's fate.*

"To what does this refer?"

Holmes spread his hands. "I have no data. But I think that shall soon change, for I hear the lady's footsteps upon the stair."

A few moments later, a lovely young woman of African blood, Miss Celia Howard, was seated on our sofa. She was smartly but discreetly dressed and carried a fashionable alligator bag.

"Thank you for agreeing to see me, Mr. Holmes," she said, with some shyness. "I know you are a very famous man, one who is surely not accustomed to being called upon by a distressed person of my race."

"Problems and predicaments do not discriminate, and neither do I. Besides," he said with a chuckle, "Lady Morley would no doubt be displeased if I were to refuse her private secretary."

The client gave a little start. "How could you know? I did not mention her in my communication to you."

"There is no great mystery," Holmes said. "Your employer wrote to me on her own, and her letter arrived in the post just after yours. She is incensed that you should be so persecuted, and virtually orders me to bring your torment to an end. As she is a third cousin by marriage to the King, I have no choice but to obey."

Miss Howard smiled. "Lady Morley is kindness personified, sir. I begged her not to worry herself about me, but she was greatly offended by the letter. She has taken this bizarre business to heart."

"As well she should." Holmes gestured toward the pips. "We have seen this warning before, but in another context. Please, tell us your story, from the beginning."

The lady nodded. "To do so, Mr. Holmes, I must begin with what will seem like a fable, but I promise you that every word is true.

"My people were enslaved in the state of Georgia for many generations, until freedom came to us at the end of the Confederate rebellion. My grandfather, Jim Howard, lived on the Greenbriar Plantation, near the little town of Washington – he was a widower with only one child, Eddie, who grew up to become my father. When the master went off to war, and many of the other slaves ran away, my grandfather remained – not because he felt his enslavement was deserved, but because he was a devout, godly man who pitied the mistress, a weak and foolish woman who would have starved had not some of the people stayed behind and tended to the crops.

"As you know, the war ended in April 1865, but news of the surrender only trickled into the countryside. My father was just a boy at the time. One night in early May, an event occurred that my father would remember very clearly for the rest of his life.

"It was after midnight when my father was awakened by a cry of pain. He tumbled from his cot to find his father half-carrying a wounded white man into their cabin. The man was clad in a blue uniform, but it was ragged and dirty. My grandfather gave the injured stranger what little whisky he had and offered to run to fetch a doctor, but the man grabbed his shirt.

"'No – if you call someone, the Rebs will come, and I must not let them get it. Ha! I have fixed the rascals, even if I die! Stay, do not leave me.'

"My grandfather did all he could to help the sufferer, but the soldier grew weaker, and it soon became clear he would perish. As he began to struggle for breath, he pulled my grandfather to his side.

"'My name is Hiram Johannsen, and I have lived a wicked life,' he said. 'I deserted the Union army; I betrayed my country for pillage and plunder. But I will make amends now, and perhaps God will forgive me. Listen – draw close – I will tell you my secret!'

"My father could not understand what was being said between the two men, but he saw his father shake and pull away as the soldier's soul departed. Warning his son to stay quiet in his bed, my grandfather picked up the dead man and bore him from the cabin. My father heard the hoofbeats as his elder galloped away. It was almost daybreak before my grandfather returned to the cabin, and he would say nothing of what he had done with the dead man or his horse. Instead, he instructed my father to forget what he had witnessed – an impossible task for a curious boy. A few days later, word came to the plantation that the war had ended, and that Jefferson Davis, the rebels' president, had been captured.

"Hard times followed. Though free, the former slaves possessed no money, no land, and no knowledge. They had little choice but to continue to labor at Greenbriar, receiving nothing but the right to remain in their cabins and a small division of the annual crop. My grandfather worked without complaint, but he insisted that my father attend a nearby school established by some missionary ladies from the North. At night, by candlelight, using sticks and the dirt of their floor, my father would teach his father. My grandfather struggled with numbers and it took him great effort to learn his letters, but he was gifted with a prodigious memory. He loved the stories of history, and soon he could recite the names of all the presidents.

"One of the teachers at the school, Mrs. Julia Mather, was a free woman of color from New York City, a young widow with no children. She took a special interest in my family's welfare and often visited the cabin. My father hoped my grandfather would marry her, but my grandfather laughed at the very suggestion.

"Then, three years after the war, the terrible Ku Klux Klan began its reign of terror, threatening the Negroes, the Republicans, and even the gentle ladies who wanted nothing more than to educate the freedmen's children. After a noose was left in the schoolroom, Mrs. Mather told her students that she was leaving for New York on the next day's train. My father came home in tears.

"That night, my grandfather vanished for more than an hour. When he returned, he packed a meager satchel of clothing for my father, as well as a pair of warped spectacles that had belonged to his late wife, and a map he had drawn. Then he taught my father a strange poem, which he made him promise to share with no one, except any children he might have. The poem ran:

> *It rests where only the trumpet shall make it rise*
> *Beneath the stony angel's eyes.*
> *Place the right glass above our father's name*
> *And due west, the left glass, place the same*
> *There you shall find the ladies' baubles*
> *To make an end to all our troubles.*

Miss Howard said these last words with a sad smile. "I fear my grandfather was no Shakespeare. Once he was certain my father would never forget the verses, he hitched his old mule to his little wagon. They hurried to the train station, arriving only moments before the teacher's departure. My grandfather took Mrs. Mather aside, talking with her seriously, away from all the others. My father saw him press something into her hands. Then, to the boy's astonishment, his father put him into the teacher's care, instructing him to always be a good son to her. My grandfather embraced his child and told him he must not return to Georgia. With a kiss goodbye, he sent his son away, knowing he would never see him again."

The lady sniffled. With gentle dignity, she opened her purse and brought a small lace handkerchief to her eyes.

"Once aboard the train, Mrs. Mather showed my father what she had been given. It was a diamond pendant, set round with rubies and sapphires.

"I can condense many years into a few sentences. Mrs. Mather was a good and loving adoptive mother to my father. They lived in a neighborhood called Harlem, and my father continued his education, finally becoming a teacher himself. He would write letters to Georgia, and from time to time, small packages would arrive from home. Inside these packages, Mrs. Mather would find bits of broken jewelry or a clutch of precious stones. These she quietly sold, investing the money to great profit, even as she and my father continued to live comfortably but modestly. She raised my father to believe that this unexpected wealth was not a thing to be flaunted, but a tool for raising the fortunes of their race, and that is what they did, enabling many other children of former slaves to be brought North, to receive an education or train for careers.

"The one thing Mrs. Mather would never reveal to my father was why he had been sent away, though my father often suspected it had something to do with the jewels which arrived in the mail. In 1890, Mrs. Mather developed a fatal cancer. On her deathbed, she summoned my father, by then a married man with a home of his own. She said it was time to tell him all that she knew, the things my grandfather had asked her to keep hidden in her heart.

"The man who had been carried into grandfather's cabin that night was a Yankee 'bummer', one of Sherman's troops who had deserted the general's march to the sea and had since been a fugitive, living off the land. He had come upon the caravan that was bearing Jefferson Davis through Georgia. Suspecting that Davis might be travelling with Confederate riches, the bummer slipped into the camp at night and stole a chest, which he found brimming with jewelry. The next day, the bummer was spotted by Union men who recognized him as a deserter. They fired on him, mortally wounding him, but he rode as far as my grandfather's cabin before toppling from his horse. As a dying penance, he had given the treasure to my grandfather, who carefully concealed it that very night. My grandfather had been returning to this spot whenever he felt safe to do so, and removing the jewels bit by bit, sending them to Mrs. Mather to aid both his son and her good works. But in 1888, Mrs. Mather had learned, from another missionary, that Jim Howard had died. She assumed the secret of the treasure was lost with him.

"My father knew otherwise – faithful to his promise, he had told no one about the poem, and had always claimed that the spectacles and the map were merely relics of his childhood. His life was a busy one, and he had no wish to travel to Georgia; not even the thought of still-buried riches could tempt him to the place where our people had been oppressed for generations. My brother William was born in 1893, and I followed in 1895. Our mother died when I was eight, but otherwise we were a very happy, close and loving family.

"During the war, my brother served with 369th Infantry Regiment, which won fame as the Harlem Hellfighters. William hadn't yet returned home when our dear father fell ill with the Spanish Influenza. In his last hours, Father shared his most remarkable story with me. I think I might have dismissed it as the deluded ramblings of a fevered mind, had he not directed me to a small safe on his wall, which contained the spectacles and the map. I have them here."

She removed the two objects from her purse, placing them in Holmes's hands. I rose and examined them over his shoulder. The spectacles were antique, with one lens broken, and the yellowed map was a hand-drawn thing, showing a region of the southern state of Georgia, with crude marks indicating roads, streams, and houses, along with swamps, cemeteries, and half-a-dozen little towns.

"Remarkable," Holmes said. "Your grandfather was quite the cartographer."

"I cannot imagine the labor he must have given to it, he who could barely form his letters. But my father said no one knew the country better."

"And did you try to find the treasure upon your father's passing?" Holmes asked.

"After William returned home, I told him the story and showed him these items. I thought chasing after the treasure would be a very irresponsible thing to do – Georgia is not safe for those of our race, and Father hadn't explained to me what the mysterious poem implied. But I could tell the idea of looking for a buried treasure appealed to William's adventurous spirit. He spent hours toying with the map and spectacles, scribbling down thoughts and theories. As I packed for London, where I was to join Lady Morley's staff, William insisted that I take the spectacles and the map for safekeeping, that he had all the information he needed inside his head. He said he would write to me if he ever went to Georgia. I told him not to be a fool.

"A month ago, much to my surprise, I received a letter, postmarked from Savannah, with William's name on the back of the envelope. For just an instant I imagined that he had found the treasure and was now a rich man. But this is what fell out."

She passed us another piece of paper, a clipping from a newspaper. The headline read "*Negro Neck Stretched*" and the story claimed that a black man named William Howard had "*acted too saucy by far, while visiting in the country*" and was reprimanded by "*the swift justice of Judge Lynch, as administered by our noblest Klansmen*".

"My God, what a horror!" I said.

Holmes's brow was furrowed, his palms flattened together.

"Miss Howard, what do you believe happened?" Holmes asked.

"I believe my brother went in search of the treasure and was apprehended by those who, after two generations, are still seeking it. He must have dug in the wrong place. They captured him, and my address and information about the articles I possessed was tortured out of him before he died. It is possible they know about the poem as well."

"I agree," Holmes stated. "It is the only explanation that makes sense. The lynching was merely a cover for the Klansmen's crimes. This clipping was sent to strike fear into your heart. But the next note, the one with the instruction for giving up the clues, was postmarked from London, as I recall."

"That is correct. You can imagine my horror when that awful letter arrived. The instructions made it clear the author had been watching my movements. Lady Morley's London home, in Bloomsbury, has a large garden, with a replica of the Apollo Belvedere – this is the *'feet of Apollo'* to which it refers. I have no wish to bring trouble upon myself or my gracious employer, but I refuse to betray my brother's memory. Tell me, Mr. Holmes, what should I do?"

My friend frowned, and then asked his client to reprise her grandfather's poem, signaling for me to write it down.

"It is a curious wording," Holmes said. "Though the first part of it is rather simple."

"Simple!" both the lady and I exclaimed.

"Yes. '*It rests where only the trumpet shall make it rise.*' What does that suggest?"

"A battlefield," I said. "The American war had just occurred."

Holmes shook his head, gently tapping the map. "Is there a battlefield indicated here? Try again, Watson. And consider the second line as well."

"'*Beneath the stony angel's eyes*'," Miss Howard quoted. "Wait – a trumpet and rise, an angel . . . surely this refers to a cemetery."

"Much better," Holmes said. "Taking the Biblical reference to heart, and the fact that I count at least eight cemeteries or burial grounds on this map, the deduction seems rather obvious."

"But why would he put it there?" I asked. "Wouldn't it have made more sense to have hidden the treasure in or near his home?"

The lady shook her head. "From what I have learned, none of my people would have felt safe keeping something valuable in a cabin, no matter how well concealed. Father told me that the Nightriders, as they called the Klan in those times, would invade and take whatever they pleased, even down to the last morsel of food. No, he would have needed to secure it at a safe distance from himself."

Holmes hummed softly. "Let us imagine ourselves the gentleman's place. On the night he buried his treasure, he needed somewhere to which he could easily return, but also a place where overturned earth might not draw attention. What better place than a cemetery – which is also a location that most individuals would avoid, especially at night."

Miss Howard had taken up the map. "But there are so many cemeteries – and surely several of them have angel statues as landmarks. How can we know which one he meant?"

"Ah, now we come to the crux of the problem. We are clearly supposed to place the eyeglasses on the map, with the right lens over a location and the left lens 'due west' of it. But which location? How does the next line run – *'Place the right glass above our father's name'*? Your grandfather's name was Jim Howard, correct?"

Our client nodded, then abruptly shook her head. "No – I mean, not always. His master called him Pompey, which was a name he despised. His mother had named him Juba, for the day he was born. Just after the war, he was recorded as Jim Wilson by the Freedman's Bureau, but grandfather didn't wish to bear the surname of the people who had enslaved him. A nearby farmer, Mr. Howard, had been kind to my grandfather, loaned him some tools and a mule to work with. When that man died in 1866 with no family, my grandfather took on 'Howard' in his honor."

"This does present a complication," Holmes said. We took the map and placed it on Holmes's desk, so that we could all three study it. Look as we might, nothing on the paper was labelled with any of the names that the lady's grandfather had borne in his lifetime. No Pompeys, Jubas, Jims, Wilsons, or Howards appeared anywhere.

"Wait," the lady said. "Perhaps we misunderstand the wording. If my grandfather said, '*our* father's name', could he be referring to *his* father?"

"What was that gentleman's name?" Holmes asked. The lady looked woeful.

"I do not know I ever heard it spoken."

A dazzling thought suddenly came to me. I slapped my hand to my head. "What are we thinking? *'Our father'* – it is clearly a reference to *God*!"

Holmes snorted. "Watson, I have already considered and dismissed it."

"Have you?" I asked, perhaps a bit more irked in my tone than I intended. Holmes merely smiled and tapped his finger to the map.

"Indeed, it was the first thing that occurred to me, especially as Miss Howard told us that her grandfather was an exceedingly devout man. But it is the map that makes such an interpretation of the poem problematic. See here, there are over a dozen churches indicated – which one does the poem refer to? The entire point of the poem is to allow us to place the spectacles in the precise spot. Having over a dozen spots to choose from defeats that purpose."

I feared we had reached the end of our rope. Holmes folded his arms, staring down at the map as if it had offended him. Just then, there was a knock at the door.

"Ah, I see Miss Howard's bodyguard has arrived."

"Bodyguard?"

"Yes, dear lady," Holmes said. "I have previously crossed foils with the fiends who send out orange pips. As ridiculous as the threat might appear, I have learned, to my everlasting sorrow, that it must be taken seriously. Ah – young Billy – do come in. Watson, perhaps you recall our former page?"

How long it seemed, that the youth had been nothing but a boy-in-buttons, bringing up tea and carrying messages. Now he was grown into a rather handsome and sturdy man, taller than Holmes, with broad shoulders and a military carriage.

"It is good to see you again, Doctor," he said. "Mr. Holmes has been giving me instruction in his line of work. I hope to hang out my own shingle as a consulting detective before much longer."

"And Billy is an apt pupil," Holmes said, making introductions between him and the lady. "My adventuring days are behind me, but – "

He froze. We all turned, wondering what was amiss.

"My God," Holmes whispered. "I am such a *fool*! Why did I not see it instantly?"

The color had so suddenly drained from his face that I feared for his health. I was about to reach out to take his pulse when he threw out his arms.

"Out! All three of you! No – I don't mean to throw you into the streets – only to the kitchen. Perhaps the cook – wretched girl, burns everything – can fix a few sandwiches. Yes, sandwiches, that's what is needed. You appear famished. Give me but an hour, and I will set it all to rights!"

I confess that Holmes's sudden agitation startled and alarmed me, but Billy only smiled and gently herded us down the stairs.

"I think Mr. Holmes misses the old days, the drama of the game," he said. "And Agatha's cooking is not nearly as terrible as he implies. I'm sure she can manage some refreshment for us."

And so, for the next hour, we found ourselves in a companionable knot in the kitchen, sharing some fine roast beef and beer as we waited for Holmes's revelation. Billy had been in the Great War and regaled us with stories. Miss Howard again mentioned that her brother had also served.

"In the Hellfighters? I saw them in action – they were some of the most courageous men who ever carried the American flag. I never saw chaps I admired more."

I leaned back in my chair. It became clear to me, in only a short time, that Billy and Holmes's client were immediately comfortable with each other. He asked her what I had been curious to know – how she came to be employed by Lady Morley.

"She is a collector of what is called 'folk art' – I was working at a gallery in Harlem and I helped her locate and negotiate a number of pieces while she was visiting New York. She is planning more trips to America soon. I had hoped to accompany her, but after these threats – "

"Do not worry," Billy stated. "Mr. Holmes will put it right. And if he will give me the names of these felons, I'll thrash them all for you."

A bell rang, signaling Holmes's readiness for our return. He was himself again, his long legs stretched toward the fireplace. He gestured languidly toward the map on the table.

"It is indeed elementary!" Holmes proclaimed. "Miss Howard gave us the key to the key, if you will." He smiled at the lady's obvious confusion. "You said that your grandfather was a lover of history, that he memorized the history of your nation, including all its presidents. Tell me, who would Americans refer to as their father?"

"Father – the father of our country? Why – George Washington, of course!"

Holmes motioned for us to look. He had settled the spectacles over the small town of Washington. Due west, in the middle of the other lens, was "*Freedom Hill Baptist Cemetery*".

"While you three leisurely dined, I sent inquiries to a bookseller friend of mine, who specializes in travel volumes. Fortunately, among his collection was this little book, *Rustic Georgia*. See here!" Holmes opened the tome to a sketch of a country scene. It showed a small chapel, large oak trees, and a strange monument, a grim-faced angel. "The angel is dedicated to Ebenezer Wilson, a plantation owner who perished in the war."

"Mr. Holmes, this is wonderful," the lady said, "but if these evil men are seeking it as well, how would I ever feel safe in trying to retrieve it?"

"You will be safe because we will set a snare for them. Tonight, you will give them what they want – spectacles and a map at the feet of Apollo." Holmes smiled at our shared looks of surprise. "But not this map, nor these spectacles. Instead – you will place this facsimile out as an offering."

He opened a wooden box. Inside was a crinkled, aged paper and a rusty pair of eyeglasses. I removed the paper, marveling at the crude map.

"How on earth did you find a paper so old and worn?"

"I did not have to find it – I created it. I haven't enjoyed working with my philosophical instruments in some time. It is simplicity itself to make paper seem old and decayed." Holmes pointed at Billy. "You will return to Lady Morley's with Miss Howard. I have already sent word of our plans to friends at Scotland Yard, so that they will be prepared. Billy, see that Miss Howard is able to place these items on the statue unmolested, and assist the regular forces in any way that you can. I note you smacking your fist into your palm, but do not let your emotions overtake your reason. Once these villains are arrested, the field will be clear."

"For what?" I asked.

"For Billy to escort Miss Howard to retrieve her patrimony," Holmes said. "I suspect he may have to take Lady Morley along as well – she is a feisty dame, as I have reason to recall. Hit me with a parasol once, but I bear her no ill will! You must go, so that there is plenty of time to prepare."

The lady gathered her things. "Mr. Holmes, how I can repay you?"

"My work is its own reward – now more than ever. A successful conclusion to this case will be all the recompense that I require."

After our guests departed, I was about to take my own leave, but Holmes caught my sleeve.

"Is the game still afoot, Watson?"

I knew exactly what he meant. "Where you like and when you like," I answered.

"Well, we are both too old to be scaling fences and burgling houses, and I would not trust myself with my pistol, though I would very much enjoy cracking a Klansman's head with my cane. Ah, but action is for the young. Still, we might watch the show from a discreet distance. I know a most obliging cabman who specializes in skulking."

And so, just before the stroke of midnight, we found ourselves lurking in a motorcar in the deep shadows of an alleyway near Lady Morley's stately home. Even in the darkness, Holmes's eyes glittered, and his hands worked compulsively, as if filled with the desire to grab hold of a miscreant's collar.

"I hope we aren't disappointed," I said. "I've seen nothing but ladies and gentlemen returning from the theater."

Holmes chuckled. "I doubt that our prey is stupid enough to wander the streets of London in their Klan regalia, Watson! But I have recognized several of these late night ramblers as men of the Yard – and at least one female detective as well! I do not think – "

At just that moment, a whistle blew and three men – two in evening attire and one dressed all in black, with a knitted cap pulled low – came running down the street. Immediately, a half-dozen other well-clad gents bolted from where they had waited, in doorways and behind lampposts. The two rascals in finery were easily captured, one seized by the flaps of the red-lined cloak that he wore. Much to our chagrin, the third ruffian escaped. He appeared to be clutching a bag as he fled.

"Should we give chase?"

Holmes leaned back in the seat. "No, I think not." He told our driver to deposit us at Lady Morley's door. There, we found the house alight, and were quickly ushered into a front parlor, where Miss Howard was binding a cloth around Billy's bloodied right hand, while the ever-eccentric Lady Morley puffed nervously on a cigarette.

"It's nothing," Billy said, "I barked my knuckles on one fellow's teeth. He was hiding behind a bench when Miss Howard went out to place the bait. He jumped for her. I gave him the business, but his companions rushed me. I fear they got away with the glasses and the map."

"Indeed, we saw the bearer of those items elude the police."

Billy shook his head. "Should we track him to the docks? Post men at the train stations? I wouldn't think he would stay in London."

"No – we will let him go back to America."

"But the treasure! What if he's worked out the clues?"

"Billy," Holmes said, in a voice of supreme disappointment, "do you really think I duplicated Miss Howard's map, or the dimensions of the spectacles? If he believes he knows the way to work the key – "

"He will dig in the wrong place!" Miss Howard said. "Oh, what a wonderful comeuppance."

Holmes smirked. "Especially if he digs where I planted."

Spring had turned to highest summer before I found myself in Baker Street again. Holmes's invitation for a small jollification was welcome, as I had been curious as to the outcome of Miss Howard's case. I was delighted to be escorted inside by Billy, who looked like a man brimming with adventures.

Holmes indicated that Billy should tell his tale.

"Well, Doctor, the two Klansmen we arrested kept their silence. They refused to give anything to the Yard, and the Americans at the consulate put up such a fuss that they were released a few days later, and made contact with their accomplice, who had laid low. They boarded one of the White Star liners, never knowing that their watcher was in the salon just a few paces down from them. I adopted the persona of an American – my cap is off to Mr. Holmes, who played the part of Altamont so well before the war. That accent is brutal on an Englishman's jaw!

"I made my opponents' acquaintance. One was a sot, and while in his cups, he revealed their entire plan to me, bragging that they had a map to a lost Confederate treasure. It seems that rumors of a vanished chest filled with jewels had long circulated among the men of the Ku Klux Klan. Now I understand why Jim Howard never tried to use his own windfall: Everyone was suspicious, and a Negro man with sudden wealth would not have enjoyed it for long. My new 'friend' also told me that they had tortured the secret poem out of young William Howard, and that they had broken its code. He showed me on the map where they planned to dig. I had little to do after that, Mr. Holmes, except to alert the appropriate military authorities."

"Why the military?" I asked.

Holmes gave a satisfied puff on his pipe. "Because when I redrew the map, the only 'Washington' on it was in the District of Columbia – and the spectacles landed the erstwhile treasure seekers in the middle of Arlington Cemetery."

Billy laughed. "The servicemen were not amused by a trio of Georgia crackers attempting to dig up one of their war heroes! Those yokels are all behind bars and will be for some time."

"And the real treasure?" I asked.

"Miss Howard and Lady Morley arrived in Savannah two weeks later. We went out together, late at night. We found the treasure in less than a foot of red Georgia soil. Jim Howard had placed it in an old iron box."

"And?" I asked.

Billy's lips twitched. "Doctor Watson, do you recall the Great Agra Treasure?"

I gasped. "It was gone!"

"I believe that Celia's grandfather had exhausted it," Billy said.

"You recall the poem," Holmes echoed. "The loot was referred to as *'ladies' baubles'*. I believe that the women of Richmond donated what remained of their jewelry to their fleeing president, to finance his escape. By that point in the war, there could have been very few ornaments remaining to be contributed to such a hopelessly lost cause. Over the years, Howard senior had been breaking the pieces apart and sending the treasure away bit by bit." He pointed to Billy. "And did I just hear . . . *Celia*?"

The young man abruptly blushed. "Yes, Mr. Holmes, you did. You should know that there was one item left in the container. A single, rather remarkable stone. I have it here."

He pulled a small box from his pocket and opened it, revealing an exquisite yellow diamond set delicately on a band of gold.

"I love her, sirs, and she has done me the honor of agreeing to be my wife."

The Adventure of the Vanished Husband

"They say he is dead, sir. The police have told me to abandon all hope, to accept that he is surely gone, never to be seen again until Judgement Day. My employees, my neighbors – all tell me to turn my thoughts to the future. Even my pastor tells me that I am sinning to pine so for Teddy, and that I must accept this misfortune with Christian fortitude, but I tell you I cannot bear it, for it is not true! A wife would know – she would feel it when her husband perishes!"

This outburst came with a full-bodied howl of pain, a sound that seemed impossible for such a thin, bloodless woman to produce. Mrs. Edwina Etherege rocked back and forth on the sofa with a black handkerchief clutched to her face. She was a lady of some forty years, tall and as thin as a scarecrow in a field. Her sharp, pale face was marred by a birthmark almost the size of a strawberry on her left cheek. Her dark hair was shot with gray, and her gown bagged in awkward places, indicating a sudden loss of weight. As a physician, I had immediately suspected a cancer, or some other cruel disease, might be attacking her.

"Madame, please, calm yourself," Holmes pleaded. "I am willing to hear your case. But you must gather your nerves. Doctor?"

"No, I not wish a sedative," she hissed. "I have been given too many pills and draughts. I only want to be heard, by someone who will believe me."

"Some cool water then," I suggested. With trepidation, she accepted a glass as Holmes continued to reassure her that he would listen to her problem. My friend could be gallant when he chose to be, and as soothing as a nurse if the occasion required it. The lady composed herself.

"Forgive me, sir. It is only – so many people have tried to convince me that I am insane for believing as I do, that he yet lives. My husband – Theodore Etherege, my Teddy – went missing a month ago today. He left home for an evening's entertainment and never returned. They found blood, and his clothes, his bag, and his gold watch, in his room at the Langham Hotel, but they did not find his body."

Holmes nodded. "I recall reading something of it in the newspapers. But let us have it from you, from the very beginning."

"Then I must tell you things that are humiliating to me," Mrs. Etherege said. "I fear that if I withhold them, you might lack some essential clue. I told these things to the police and was openly mocked. I pray you will be more charitable."

"I promise I will only seek to help you," Holmes replied.

Reassured, the lady began her tale.

"I am London-born. My father operated a clothing store on Tottenham Court Road. We sell both new and used attire for working men and women – sturdy boots, painters' smocks, maids' uniforms with aprons and white caps, as well as a large selection of mourning attire for ladies. I was an only child and raised in the business – it became my schoolroom, my world. As you can tell, I have no beauty, and I know that I lack any feminine charms. My entire life was given to assisting my father in the shop. I suppose I entertained some girlish fantasies of a wedding day, but when I turned twenty and all my female friends had married and were becoming mothers, I accepted the spinster life as my cross to be borne, doubling my efforts to be a good daughter and businesswoman, if I was never destined to be a wife."

"On the very morning of my thirty-fifth birthday, my poor mother died. Father mourned only until the funeral was past. Then, to my horror, he began going out to music halls and pubs, as if he were a young man again. Mother had been in her grave less than a season when Father revealed to me that he had fallen in love and wished to remarry. His intended was barmaid from a tavern who would not agree to share a house with a stepdaughter who was almost twice her age. Father ordered me to find a husband – As if such a matter were as easy as going out to buy a bouquet of flowers! – or consider becoming a nun.

"It was in this time, in such a dreadful state of mind as you might only imagine, that I met Teddy. He had been hired as a clerk at the jewelers' next door, and often we would find ourselves sitting on a bench behind our respective businesses. He was such a young man – he had just turned twenty-one – and so thin, so I began bringing food to him out of pity. We fell into companionable conversation, and in this way, I learned something of his life. His father was a Scottish baron, but Teddy was the product of an indiscretion, born on the wrong side of the blanket. His father had never claimed him, though he had provided for Teddy and even sent him to the University of Glasgow. But Teddy's high spirits had led to his expulsion from school and his estrangement from his natural father.

"'He says he will give me a portion to set myself up, if I marry a respectable girl. But it must be soon, for he has allowed me only until the end of the year to find a bride.'

"I could not help to laugh at the way his situation seemed a strange reflection of my own. I told him of my father, and of the horrible slattern who had turned his heart against me.

"'Will you take the veil?' he asked.

"'No – I have no wish to embrace the Roman faith.'

"'Then . . . do you suppose you could see your way to marry me?'

"Mr. Holmes, it was the strangest proposal in British history. I objected that he was a young and healthy man, and I an older lady. Besides, we were not in love with each other.

"'Do you not think we could see our way to love, Miss Edwina?' he asked. 'Let us play at it for a fortnight. I shall be your gallant suitor and you shall be my sweetheart. Let us see if the roles become us.'

"And, so, we did, Mr. Holmes. For two weeks we courted as earnestly as any young lovers might. We went to dances, we attended religious services, we were tourists at the Tower. Through it all, we came to enjoy each other's company. At the end of the allotted days, Teddy asked me again if I would marry him, and this time I said yes.

"However, I was too much of a shopkeeper not to haggle to some degree, and Teddy likewise felt that we should have some special agreements between ourselves since ours was a most unusual union. I was to retain control over the shop should I inherit it from my father, and he would retain a portion of his father's settlement, which he would keep in a separate bank account, for his own use. The strangest part of our pact, however, was the understanding we had about his 'sabbaticals'."

"Your husband was to become a teacher?" I asked.

"No – we merely chose the term because others seemed . . . offensive. Teddy freely confessed to me that he would need time apart, that he had a great many intellectual interests which I clearly did not share. Teddy loved music, theater, and art. It made sense – he had been to college. He had been exposed to the life of the mind. I am as dull as a brick. Teddy enjoyed attending the opera. My idea of a pleasant evening is one spent at home, knitting by the fireplace. All Teddy asked was that, twice a year, he would have a week to himself, where he might spend his time away from home in a nearby hotel, here in the city, and I would not follow."

"And you agreed to this?" Holmes said.

"Yes. Do you think I am a terrible wife?"

"On the contrary, Madame, I think that if more spouses were amenable to a sensible measure of freedom, we would have fewer separation cases, and definitely less murders. But do continue."

"We were married at Christmas and moved into the rooms right across the street from the store. A modest but comfortable allowance arrived from my husband's natural father, and my own father began to plan his nuptials. However, I never acquired a stepmother."

"Your father changed his mind?"

"No – death claimed his bride! She was killed when an omnibus overturned on Regent Street. My poor father was heartbroken. He followed her to the grave not long after, and so I inherited the store and our old home in the apartments above it.

"For five years, Teddy and I were happy. I ran the store while he enjoyed himself, reading books, painting pictures, playing the cello. We were contented and peaceful. Even when Teddy took his 'sabbaticals', there was never any hint that he had broken his marriage vows. He would return from his little adventures with programs from the theater and museums, sketches that he had made, and always some kind and thoughtful little trinket for me."

"Your husband was – *is* artistic?"

"Oh yes," the lady said, her face suddenly alight with pride. "He calls himself a mere amateur, but he has wonderful talent, even if pursued only as a hobby. But now I must brace myself, for this part of my tale is . . . difficult, even now.

"Last year, in the spring, we had the sudden, unexpected, and joyful hope of a child. Teddy was giddy with excitement and painted a nursery with a ceiling full of stars. Then one morning I awakened with a dreadful pain, and the child was no more. I nearly died in the weeks that followed. When at last I recovered, the doctor was firm in his ruling – I was foolish to long for a baby at my age and, with my fragile health, another would kill me.

"After this, a coldness developed between us. I think that Teddy, who had so gamely embraced a rather unconventional wife, now began to see clearly the differences in our ages. He asked for more and more time apart, and I meekly gave it to him, as I threw myself into my work at the store. I prayed that he only needed time to adjust his mind to our new restrictions, and that we could still be a faithful pair, even with the changed circumstances.

"Exactly one month ago, I woke before daybreak to find him pulling his carpetbag from our wardrobe. I asked him where he was going.

"'Madame Miranda plays tonight at the Royal Albert Hall – her last stop before America. I must see her!' He noted my frown, and as a placating gesture he held open the bag. "See, it is packed for only one night – I am just taking my evening clothes. I will stay at the Langham, my usual abode.'

"I forced myself to smile and bid him to enjoy himself. He kissed me and was gone.

"I thought nothing of it the rest of the day. Jack, my chief shop clerk, was hot – he claimed that some wares had been stolen. I served our customers while he fretted, and at night I took a lonely meal before retiring early. I was surprised, upon waking, that Teddy was not home – he usually returns in time for breakfast. Then, to my horror, a police inspector and a pair of constables came knocking on the door, asking me to identify a bag, a watch, a wallet, and two suits of clothes. I protested that while these were indeed Teddy's things, he surely would not have abandoned them. At that instant, one constable muttered that there was a great deal of blood in his room at the hotel. I fear that I fainted."

"Since that time, there have been no developments. I have my store, which is successful, and there is an insurance policy, which I cannot bear to look at yet, much less to place a claim upon. I am not embarrassed by any financial need, but . . . Mr. Holmes, I love my husband! I have searched my feelings and I cannot believe, for one instant, that he is dead!"

My friend has listened to this recitation most intently. He began to waggle his fingers in the air, like a conductor about to summon his orchestra to tune.

"Mrs. Etheredge, will you be guided by me?"

"You are my last resort, sir."

"As I have been to many. This is what I would have you do: Tomorrow, you will retire to the seaside for a short holiday. This is not beyond your means, I take it?"

"No sir. I have a childhood friend who lives in Brighton and who has been imploring me to call on her."

"Excellent! Do you have servants?"

"Only one maid."

"Take her with you. Lock your rooms when you go, but leave the key with your man at the store, along with instructions to permit us entry. Doctor Watson and I will visit your abode while you are gone. We will disturb nothing, I promise. I will also pay a call on the inspector who handled your case. I believe that you mentioned upon your arrival that it was Gregson?"

The lady scowled. "Yes."

"An old acquaintance, which is fortunate. He will be more candid with me than he might be with another. Do leave you friend's address, so that I may reach you quickly if necessary. And finally – do you have a photograph of your husband?"

"Yes. I thought you might require it."

She gave Holmes a *carte de viste*, which he in turn passed to me. It was an image of the couple made, I presumed, on their wedding day. Theodore Etherege was a short and reed-thin man, clean-shaven and with such a youthful face he could easily have been mistaken for a son rather than a husband. Mrs. Etherege had been somewhat stouter on her bridal morning, making it all too clear how grief had taken its toll on her health and looks.

"You have hope?" the lady asked my friend.

"Your case presents some intriguing qualities, Madame. I do not wish to make promises, but I think I can throw some light into your darkness."

"Then bless you, sir. All anyone else does is call me a fool."

"Tell me, Gregson" Holmes said, "how does a gentleman as naked as Adam in the Garden of Eden depart from a London hotel and not be noticed by its guests, desk clerk, or porters?"

The inspector nearly spat out his coffee. We three had been enjoying a most delicious repast at Simpsons and had just moved to the dessert.

"Ah, I should have known you had something up your sleeve, Mr. Holmes. It's that blasted Etherege business, isn't it? Poor old crow, taking on so over a young husband who's been dead for – what, a month now?"

"I have heard the story from the lady. Now let me hear it from you."

"There's not much to tell. Mr. Etherege checked in about four in the afternoon – he was something of a regular. The desk clerk knew him by sight. Etherege mentioned that he would be going out to hear Madame Miranda play, and at seven the clerk noted his departure in his evening clothes. He came back just before eleven and asked to be awakened at six. The boots was sent up to roust him when the time came. There was no response to his taps, but then the door, which was unlocked, swung open. The poor lad got quite a fright – there was blood in great arcs across the walls. The gentleman's attire was thrown about the room, but his gold watch and his wallet were on the nightstand. The room's key was later found beneath a chair."

"Was there any money remaining?" I asked.

"Less than a shilling. Robbery was clearly a motive, as we later learned Etherege had closed out his personal bank account and had a great deal of cash on his person, perhaps as much as five-hundred pounds."

"Yet the thief and presumed murderer left a fine gold watch behind." Holmes lifted his cup, favoring the inspector with a sardonic eye. "The abandoned attire was complete – not tattered or torn?"

"Yes. A grey tweed business suit, which the clerk recalled Etherege wearing, along with a white shirt, brown tie, and a bowler hat. The pieces were thrown about the room. The evening suit was also Etherege's – his initials were on the linen – and while it had not been damaged, it was found flung to four corners. And before you ask, there was no broken furniture, but the chairs were all upended, and the washbasin spilled out."

"Was the footwear also found?"

The inspector rolled his eyes. "You have quite the obsession with fashion! Yes, we found two pair – grey boots and black shoes."

"What about a nightshirt or pajamas?"

Gregson scowled. "We found none. Perhaps he was carried away in them."

Holmes arched an eyebrow. The Scotland Yard man sputtered.

"It is the only thing that makes sense! As you said, he couldn't have exited the building in a state of nudity! We have his wife's evidence that he had only the two sets of clothing with him, and that he was at the hotel for just one night. And then there was the blood." Gregson stabbed into his slice of cake. "It was like that business from Lauriston Gardens, blood all about. I remembered how you figured the blood had come from Jefferson Hope's nose. This was much the same, though more of it. My theory is that someone came back to the room with him and cut his throat after he had changed into his sleeping clothes. The murderer then carried his victim to another room and hid the body in a trunk. I spoke with the night porter – as you know, he unlocks the doors for any guest who departs after eleven p.m. There was a lady or two – one in deep mourning – a family of six with an Irish nurse, and several fellows who left for the late trains, taking luggage with them. I've tracked down five of those men, but as one departed for India on a packet – well, there's more work to be done."

Holmes's expression was that of a man with poor digestion, despite the remarkable cuisine we had just consumed.

"Gregson, do you mean to tell me that you are looking for a man who carried a dead body in a trunk all the way to India?"

The inspector bristled. "I'll have you know that the man I have in my sights has been a suspect in three other strange disappearances. Plus . . . ." Here he lowered his voice and cut his eyes around at the neighboring tables. "I have my suspicions about Mr. Etherege. I do not believe his 'sabbaticals' were as innocent as his wife claims. And all that love of art and music – such a man is bound to meet an untimely demise."

The next morning, we found ourselves at the Ethereges' shop in Tottenham Court Road. It was a sizable establishment, with a look of comfortable prosperity. The clerk, who introduced himself as Jack Keller, was a spry older gentleman with greased hair who immediately brought out his mistress's key and led us upstairs.

"I feel very bad for her, sir. I don't think she's had a solid meal since it happened, and I hear her crying in her office every afternoon."

"Mrs. Etherege mentioned that on the day her husband departed there had been a theft in the store, one that distracted you throughout the day."

The old man sighed. "I am ashamed that I worried her over it, sir. It's just that I despise a thief. Lower than a rat, a thief is! I have to keep a good eye on the shop, especially our used items. I always check my inventory, every day, I do. And to think a lady would do such a thing!"

"If you did not see the thief, how do you know the villain's sex?" Holmes asked.

"By what was stolen, of course! It was a widow's ensemble, for a slender lass, with a big hat and veil, a shawl, and black boots to match. Plus, a little purse, all of it used, and not terribly fine, though respectable enough. Worth maybe a pound or two, no more, as it was last year's style."

"How did the thief get in?" I asked, trying to imagine some poor woman in desperate need of a black dress. "Had any window been broken?"

"No, sir, and the doors were locked. That's what puzzled me so much. How could a whole dress walk away like that?"

"How indeed?" Holmes mused.

The Etherege apartments were perhaps some of the strangest we had ever explored. They seemed to be completely divided by taste rather than utility. There was a small parlor, stuffed with bric-a-brac, potted palms, a gilded birdcage, and a mantel covered in silly trinkets. But a second room was airy and vast, well-lit and designed to showcase a Turkish rug and a collection of Oriental divans. Several large paintings hung on the wall. Holmes observed them with the care he usually devoted to bloodstains.

"They call this new style 'Impressionistic'," he said. "I do not recognize the artist, and the choice of scenery is rather unique – no field of flowers in France, but the smokestacks and dreary lanes of Glasgow." He turned away and together we explored the rest of the chambers. There was only one bedroom, with a single wardrobe, which held a meager amount of both masculine and feminine garb. Holmes moved on to a room fixed up as a study, with a sizable library and a cello propped beside a chair. Holmes opened a desk drawer and riffled through some papers.

"I had hoped for something revelatory – perhaps I have found it. Listen to these notes, Watson. *'Sunset at Cliffs'*, fifty pounds. *'Birds and dogs'*, five pounds. *'Field below Old Gate'*, fifteen pounds. *'All must be paid to St. Clyde'*."

"*'Paid to St. Clyde'*? That has an ominous ring to it, like some type of code. Perhaps Mr. Etherege was being blackmailed over this secret life he led."

"You scintillate today, Watson. But we have learned enough here, I think. Let us take our leave."

We returned the key. Holmes took a moment to walk around the store, pausing only to ask the clerk a final question.

"Did Mr. Etherege help with the business?"

The man sneered. "Does the Queen do her own cooking? Much too fine for the trade, that one was! If you ask me, Mrs. Edwina is better off rid of him. Only thing he ever did right by her was that insurance policy."

"Indeed?" Holmes leaned on the counter with the air of a practiced gossip.

"Oh yes – took it out about eight months ago, just after the . . . well, it's not mine to say but . . . ."

"After their hopes of a child were disappointed."

"Exactly, sir. I think he felt guilty in some way. Told me he wanted to be sure she was always provided for in case he should die. Only decent and manly thing he ever did!"

Holmes thanked the clerk for the intelligence and then led me from the store, swinging his cane jauntily.

"Do you have plans for this weekend, Watson?"

"None to speak of."

"Excellent! Let us take a brief journey and savor some Scottish Lowlands air."

"And Mrs. Etherege's case?"

He smiled. "I am engaged in solving it."

Holmes could be the most maddening of companions when he chose. At times, he would grasp a mystery to his person, concealing his clues as deftly as any magician ever palmed a coin. Holmes insisted on spending the remainder of the afternoon on an idle ramble through a number of picture galleries. Later, Mrs. Hudson provided such a savory supper that I nodded off on the sofa, only to be awakened by Holmes shaking my shoulder and bidding me to take up my bag, as our cab was at the door. A short time later, we were aboard the Scotch Express to Glasgow, along with a number of weary business travelers. I tried to engage Holmes in conversation, but he waved away my questions and recommended a book to me, the *Lives of the Artists* by Giorgio Vasari.

Needless to say, I was soon asleep as our train chugged through the countryside.

"It is simplicity itself," Holmes finally said. We had secured rooms at a small hotel and set out on foot to the city's outskirts. The weather was fair and the sky a sweet shade of blue that a Londoner seldom sees. "The entire case began with a basic question – where does a man go without his clothes on?"

"To his bath, one would hope."

"You are the soul of wit this morning! Clearly, Mr. Etherege did not exit the hotel in such a state of undress. So the gentleman changed his attire and, with it, his entire person. No one noticed his exit because he did not exit as himself. He returned to his room after the concert and removed his evening suit, but did not don his business attire. Instead, he put on clothing that made him invisible. Tell me, how does a male guest in a hotel become invisible?"

"He adopts a disguise that makes him fit in. He appears to be a clerk or a porter."

"It won't do, Watson. The Langham, while large, is still too insular. A strange porter or clerk would be hailed by a regular employee as an imposter. What other types of individual might depart?" He elbowed me, none too gently. "Think of the most obvious, Watson. A man will not be recognized by his fellows, even by men who knew him well, from his previous stays at the hotel, if he exits as – "

"A woman?"

"Exactly!"

"But – where would he have acquired women's clothing?"

"That perplexed me for a moment, especially as the gentleman was not of such proportions that he might have taken one of his wife's cast-off dresses. But the theft from the shop solved that difficulty, especially when the clerk revealed what had been stolen. A black dress, a heavy shawl, a thick veil – the costume of mourning would shield a male nicely, especially a male as delicately made as Theodore Etherege. Since he possessed keys to his own establishment – even if he rarely assisted there – he could merely grab the desired items on his way out early that morning, after making a point to his still-abed spouse that he had only a suit of evening clothes in his bag."

"But why such an involved deception?"

"Let us work through it. We know that Etherege left the hotel sometime between when he was last recognized, just before eleven at night, and before the boots found the disarrayed room at six in the morning. Recall that at the Langham, the doors are locked after eleven p.m., so that the porter sees all who exit after that hour. The porter mentioned opening the door for several individuals, including a lady in deep mourning. Mr. Etherege clearly did not intend to go home in such garb! It could have been possible he was bound for some unsavory assignation, but the blood in the room hints otherwise. He was leaving forever, and he wanted everyone to think he had been murdered, so that his wife would receive his insurance settlement. But why leave just after eleven – what was essential about that time? Here, imagination is necessary. Clearly, our friend Teddy would wish to put distance between himself and London. What train would he be most likely to take if fleeing the metropolis, keeping in mind that if secrecy was of the essence – and clearly it was – he would hardly want to exit the train at a lonely station, where some bored agent would notice a lone 'woman'. No, he would need to make his exit with a crowd. What train would satisfy that requirement? A quick consultation of railroad schedules tells us that the great Scottish expresses bound for Edinburgh and Glasgow leave just at midnight. Now, could I discover which one he was on?

"Mrs. Etherege remarked on her husband's skill as an artist, and the paintings in his apartments confirmed that this was not mere spousal flattery. Artists frequently return to sites of inspiration, and Mr. Etherege had painted the same scene of Glasgow at least three times. When one considers that clue, along with the fact that he had emptied his bank account a day before his departure, one sees the strong probability that he intended to trade his London life for one in the Scottish Lowlands. A-ha! – here is an inspiring vista."

We had stopped in a field only a mile from the old city. There were several artists at work, all of them in loose smocks and rugged trousers. Holmes slipped the photograph of theEthereges from his vest.

"Do keep in mind that he may have, in the interim, begun to change his appearance further by growing a beard. Do you spot our man?"

"Good heavens! I do – that one!"

Together, we crossed the field and came up behind the thin little fellow. He was so obsessed with his brushes and palette that he did not even react until we stood just behind him, blocking his light.

"Would you step aside?" he asked.

"If you will tell me why you abandoned your kind and loving wife, perhaps I shall," Holmes answered, his tone as dark as a judge pronouncing sentence. The man spun around and went white beneath the first hint of a copper-tinted beard.

"I – I am sure – I do not understand – "

Holmes gestured toward the other painters. "Shall we tell them of your flight northward in widow's weeds? Or do they know it already?"

"No! Heavens, no – lower you tone – for God's sake, do not . . . ."

He dropped his head. His brushes fell into the grass. After a moment, he began to sob.

"Am I under arrest?"

"I am no representative of the official forces," Holmes said. "Only an agent employed by a most noble lady, whom you have grievously wronged."

"Yes . . . God forgive me, but . . . I thought it would be better. Please, sirs, give me just a moment to gather my things. Sit with me, and I will tell you my story."

A half-hour later, we were seated at a small café. Mr. Theodore Etherege ordered coffee. Holmes sat across from him with folded arms.

"I suppose Edwina has told you how we met. It is true, I am the natural son of the Baron of Strathclyde, who gave me one year to find a bride and turn from my 'dissolute way of living'. My father knew that I preferred a much more Bohemian lifestyle, with the freedom to express myself in my art. I wanted to live and to love the way that I pleased, but I simply could not afford it. I confess I only married Edwina because my time was running out and I had no practical talent for making a living.

"I did not expect to love her – but I did, at least at first, when being married was a novel status. Edwina is pleasant and kind, and completely devoted to me. But I also found her dull and boring. I have a mind meant for higher things, sharper thoughts, a greater enjoyment of life's pleasures, no matter whose god they offend! Can you imagine the torture it was, year after year, to keep company with a woman whose idea of art was a picture on a teapot, and whose idea of a beautiful song was a music hall ditty? When I married her, I thought my unconventional nature would be content to be compressed into a few weeks a year, but I was soon growing restive. And then . . . when I thought I would be a father . . . a new and more fulfilling life appeared to be opening before me. I imagined a child with my gifts, my insights, my joys. But as you surely know, our hopes were crushed."

"And you abandoned your good wife," I snapped. "You made her feel responsible for your selfishness!" Holmes raised a hand, preventing me from further speech, even though I found myself boiling with outrage. The man nodded, his face bloody with shame.

"Yes, I did wrong, and I know it. But the loss of our child showed me a bleak future. I could imagine Edwina growing old, and my time for painting, for art, for living life, for my other loves, running out as I waited patiently for her to die. I began to plot a way to be free of her. I had my father's settlement – he was faithful to his promise, and I had barely touched those funds – and I was also having some small success as an artist."

Holmes inclined his head. "You are becoming well known as 'The Glasgow Impressionist', though under the pseudonym of St. Clyde. I saw a number of your pictures in a gallery on Oxford Street. Yet your wife never knew of these commissions – she who was so proud of your talent."

Etherege passed a pale hand over his brow. "She was . . . patronizing me. She did not understand anything."

"You do her a disservice," Holmes said.

"Truly I did not wish to hurt her!" the man wailed. "That is why I took out an insurance policy. It will pay handsomely, if only the police will pronounce me dead."

"Thus, the blood in the room, to stage a murder scene," Holmes said. "Animal blood, of course?"

"Yes, bought that day from a butcher in Whitechapel. I had an urchin lad make the purchase for me, in a bottle, and paid him well for his silence. I wanted to make it look as if some terrible fight had occurred in my room. It struck me as rather hideous, which was the effect I wanted. I threw the bottle out of the window when it was done."

"And the dress was stolen from your own store."

"Edwina's store," he corrected. "I was familiar at the Langham. I could have gone to another hotel, but I always went to the Langham, and didn't want Edwina to question any change in my habits. I needed to leave on the night train, to come back here, the place where I was educated. Where I have friends, and where my best work has always been done. In school we would act out Shakespeare as they did in the olden days with lads playing the female parts – as I was so slight, I was always cast as Juliet or Ophelia. I knew I could manage a dress and a heavy veil. It was merely a matter of slipping out of the door of my hotel room when no one else was around. I had no luggage, of course – nothing more than the purse – but I had closed my bank account and so I had plenty of money. I also have a friend here, who was much astonished to see me in such attire, but still admitted me when I arrived."

"You have behaved most disgracefully."

"I . . . I know. Perhaps you will not believe me, sir, but every day that I have been away I have . . . I have regretted how I treated Edwina. I thought I would feel free, like a prisoner released from his shackles, but I do not. I thought I would find love, but I have not. Even my pictures seem wretched to me now. It is as if my hand no longer knows how to hold a brush, or my eyes the way to see the light as it falls upon the scenery. But what can I do?"

"Go home," my friend said.

"I cannot. She has given me up for dead."

Holmes scoffed. "The police have given you up. Your neighbors, your employee, your wife's pastor have written you out of the land of the living. But would I be here if your wife truly believed you dead?"

The man stared at my friend. "No, of course not. But . . . she . . . is not . . . angry?"

"Women are incomprehensible creatures," Holmes said. "I have learned that they are impossible to predict. Some hate with the fires of hell, others love with greater purity than the angels. You have deserved the former and have been granted the later."

My friend rose from his chair as the pathetic man gaped up at him in surprise.

"Come, Watson. It has been some time since I have been in Glasgow, and I should very much like to visit the University, to examine their collection of medieval charters. Mr. Etherege, I give you good day. My companion and I will return to London on Monday."

"And my wife?"

"I leave her fate in your unworthy hands." Holmes removed a folded paper from his vest. "She is currently visiting a friend in Brighton. Here is her address."

When we returned to Baker Street, Holmes found a letter from his client, as well as a substantial cheque for his services. Holmes glanced at the letter, then handed it to me with a command to read it aloud.

My Dear Mr. Holmes,

My husband has returned. I confess I screamed very loudly when he suddenly appeared at my friend's doorway, all bearded and rough like some Scottish highwayman. He explained everything. He spared me nothing. He told me how he felt he had no longer loved me, and that he had hoped I might be comforted by a financial settlement, instead of his presence. He said he should go and live his life apart from me, that he was unfit to be my husband. He was a most pitiful specimen.

I have asked him for only one thing – a fortnight to see if I may convince him that there is more to our love than he imagines, that his presence is more valuable to me than all the riches of India or China, and that I would never ask him to suppress his talents or his nature. We have discussed this at some length and have agreed to the experiment.

Thank you, Mr. Holmes, for believing in me, even as I have believed in him.

Yours very gratefully
Edwina Etherege

"A remarkable and formidable woman," Holmes said. "Let us hope the gentleman realizes the prize he possesses. I wonder if I shall ever hear of them again?"

> *"I came to you, sir, because I heard of you from Mrs. Etherege, whose husband you found so easy when the police and everyone had given him up for dead."*
>
> – Miss Mary Sutherland
> "A Case of Identity"

The Adventure of the Queen's Teardrop

"Ring for tea, Watson," said my good friend, Sherlock Holmes, dropping the newspaper he had been reading into the pile of clutter beside his chair. "We will have company within the hour."

"Oh? You have an engagement?" I asked, rather surprised, as he had not mentioned any pending cases on this lovely autumn afternoon. "A client?"

Holmes shook his head. "It has been three days since the theft of the Queen's Tear from the Lellouche Museum of Mineralogy. Three days since this singular event which, if our correspondents in the press are to be believed, has baffled all of Scotland Yard. Seventy-two hours is normally approaching the limits of Inspector Lestrade's patience and – aha, here is the man himself. His footsteps are most distinctive. Come inside, Inspector, and make yourself at home."

Our friend from the official forces had indeed materialized in the doorway as Holmes spoke. He shot a rather chagrinned look at Holmes's smug face, then tramped inside and dropped onto the sofa with a disgusted huff.

"You know it all, I suppose?"

"Only what has been published in the newspapers," Holmes answered. "Why don't you tell us the entire story, especially the parts of it which the press has omitted?"

Lestrade's sharp cheeks turned dusty red with frustration and embarrassment. He tugged roughly at his shirt cuffs as he spoke, his voice crabbed and irritated.

"Barney's a bad egg, no doubt. Petty thievery, smash and grab. He's done five years in prison for making off with a countess's jewel box when he was a footman in her employ. He's like a raven with eye for anything that sparkles, and he's full of charm, I'll give him that. He's a handsome devil, too. He talks like a gentleman, and he could probably make an honest living if he wasn't so light-fingered. True, I never took him to be especially clever, but I'll be damned if I can figure out what he did with the Queen's Tear."

Holmes gave a pointed cough. "From the beginning, if you will."

Lestrade snorted. "Then we'd need to go back to the days of the French Revolution, where the story starts. But your history is better than mine, I'd wager."

"Let us consult a reliable source," Holmes said, and leisurely stretched out his arm to pluck down the good old Index. He flipped through it, muttering softly, until he found the entry. He read aloud from the text.

"*The Queen's Tear is a teardrop-shaped blue diamond, twenty carats, said to have been in the possession of Marie Antoinette when she was imprisoned in the* Conciergerie. *According to legend, she offered the diamond as a final bribe to her jailer, in hopes of escaping the guillotine. When the wretched sans-culotte took the stone and betrayed her to her executors, it was said that the diamond acquired a curse.*'"

"Rubbish!" Lestrade snorted.

"What rare diamond has not collected bad luck and misfortune?" Holmes asked, before returning to the Index. "'*The jailer was himself executed during the Thermidorian Reaction, and the diamond was briefly in the possession of the unhappy Empress Josephine before being returned to Louis XVIII, who feared it as an ill omen. Thus it was passed along to a series of notables and each,*'" Holmes read with an arch smile, "'*has come to some unfortunate demise, including suicide, murder by brigands, and falling overboard during a storm in the Channel. The diamond's current owner, the Comte du Castlenau, permits it to be exhibited at various museums.*'" Holmes glanced up from the Index. "Clearly, this entry requires some updating, as the gem is now in the possession of a thief. The stone is valued at over fifty-thousand pounds."

I gave a low whistle as Holmes returned the Index to the shelf. "When did the Queen's Tear arrive in London?" Holmes asked.

"A little over a month ago," Lestrade said. "The owner of the Lellouche Museum of Mineralogy is a distant kinsman to the Comte. The Museum is a single room, nothing more than an attachment to a shop, Lellouche & Company, which trades in jewelry with historical significance. The shop sells antique and estate pieces, and jewels associated with royalty. Anytime a special piece is on display at the Museum, it attracts a crowd to the shop, which is accessed through an archway. Monsieur Etienne Lellouche, the proprietor, said they'd had quite the flood of people in to see the Queen's Tear, but three days ago the museum was empty at the ten o'clock hour. The old soldier who watched the display had stepped away to the lavatory, and Lellouche was assisting one of his regular customers in the shop when he heard the sound of glass shattering. Lellouche raced through the archway to see the display case on the floor and a man bolting into the street."

"Did the proprietor recognize the man?"

"He did. Barney – full name Bernard Reginald Thompkins – had been nearly a daily visitor, so much that Lellouche had begun to suspect him of devilry and more than once had shooed him out of the museum.

Fortunately, Herring, one of our lads, was on the corner when Barney came flying out of the store. Herring heard the shouts, saw the rascal, and gave chase. Herring's a flyer and plays on our rugby team, and he's the size of a steam engine! I don't doubt that when Barney looked back he was alarmed to see who was bearing down on him.

"They made five blocks before Barney took a turn and crossed a street. At just that moment a nurse with a perambulator got between them, but Herring had Barney in his sight the whole time, even if the near-accident slowed him a bit. There was a young woman standing in an open doorway, as if she'd come out to see what all the fuss was about. Barney sprung up the stairs, pushed the lady back into the house, and slammed the door.

"Herring ran up and banged on the door. He could hear the lady screaming and crying for help – he said it was the most awful racket he'd ever heard, and he was afraid the blackguard was killing her. He tried kicking the door in, but it was too stout. Another constable, Hill, came up at just that moment. Together, they forced the door open and found the girl swooning on the floor. The brute had mauled her, but she was brave and pointed them toward the hallway and the back of the house. The men caught Barney trying to shimmy over a high brick wall in the garden. They pulled him down and turned him inside out, but couldn't find the stone." Lestrade gave a tired sigh. "Might I beg a cigarette?"

Holmes nodded and passed over his silver case. I caught an odd expression on his face, part amusement and part dismay. "I assume you subjected the nefarious Barney to a more thorough search once you had him in custody at the station."

Lestrade shook out a match and pitched it in the fireplace. With a groan, he rose and leaned against the mantel. "That we did. Stripped him naked as his mother bore him, but couldn't find the gem. Of course, this whole time he's claiming he's been framed, that he only ran away because he was frightened when he bumped into the glass case and broke it. He says he knows no one will believe a man with a criminal record, but swears he's as innocent as a lamb and we're the ones leading him to slaughter."

"He swallowed the Queen's Tear," I said, wondering why it was left to me to point out the obvious. "It is the only possible solution."

"We thought of that," Lestrade said, favoring me with a look of reproach. "Our police surgeon gave him a draught that . . . well, let us just say it produced results in a very short amount of time. Unpleasant for everyone, but no Tear was shed, you might say. Plus, the stone was securely attached to a thin gold chain, and there's been no sign of it either."

Holmes leaned his head back in the chair and put his fingers together. "Tell me about the household, and the lady who was assaulted."

Lestrade fished a notebook from his jacket. "The house belongs to Mrs. Abigail Ames, the relic of Winston Ames, a curator at the British Museum. She's elderly, blind, and a bit daft, and was sound asleep upstairs when the whole thing happened. There's a housekeeper named Agnes who was at the market. The lady who was attacked is Miss Celeste Templeton, a paid companion to the widow. It's a female household – not a butler or footman in sight – and the widow's only son is currently living in America."

"What can you tell me about Miss Templeton?"

Lestrade scowled. "Holmes, surely you're not suggesting that a lady who was nearly ravished by a villain is in league with him? I saw the girl's wounds, they're quite real, and her dress was nearly torn from her body!"

"Still, I would like to know more details."

Lestrade rolled his eyes. "Oh, very well, if you insist – Miss Templeton has been with Mrs. Ames for a little under a month. She is a former governess, thirty years of age. Quite a good-looking lady, but nothing exceptional or suspicious in her background. The housekeeper, however, is a frightful looking woman, arms like a bear, in her fifties if I had to guess. She's silent, shifty-eyed, and not at all happy to have policemen in the place. If you insist on an accomplice, take her."

"I assume you have inspected the premises thoroughly? And not allowed false modesty to deter you?"

Lestrade's face reddened again. "Certainly not! I'll admit, I'm not fond of plundering through a lady's linen, but I did it. Even the older lady's corsets got shaken out. I promise you, Holmes, the Queen's Tear is not sewn up in a pair of bloomers."

My friend seemed to struggle against a smile.

"What about Mrs. Ames's jewels?" I asked. "Wouldn't it be simple to hide one gem among others?"

"Of course it would – and we do have some wits about us," Lestrade muttered. "We turned out every jewelry box in the house and swept through all the lady's trinkets. The stone is not there."

I glanced down at the notes I had taken. "What about the old soldier who was supposed to guard the stone? Or the owner of the museum and store? Could this be a fraud?"

Lestrade shook his head. "Gregson has been working that end, and he tells me there's nothing afoot in that direction. Impeccable credentials and genuine dismay on both their parts, and a thorough search of the premises has turned up nothing."

"Has a reward been offered?" Holmes asked.

"Not yet. The Comte is travelling in the East at the moment, and hasn't heard of the theft. Monsieur Lellouche would like nothing more than this business to be settled before word of it reaches his relative."

"So what would you like me to do?" Holmes asked. "If all of Scotland Yard's best scent hounds have failed, how could I possibly be of assistance?"

"Work your magic!" Lestrade snapped. "Time is of the essence. I believe Barney planted that stone somewhere in the house, but I won't be able to hold him much longer without evidence. And if one of the ladies is an accomplice – not that I believe it for a moment! – I can't confine them much longer either. So far, I've kept a constable at the door around the clock and none of the ladies have exited the house, but Mrs. Ames says they all have tickets to sail for America next week to visit her son in New York. The lady's almost a hundred years old, and if I hold her back and she dies, I don't want to think of the scandal." He slapped his hat on his head and made for the door. "You'll come then, within an hour? I'll be there, to make sure they can receive you."

A short time later, we were ensconced in a hansom cab, making the trip to Mrs. Ames's residence. Holmes tapped his cane against my knee.

"It is helpful, in a situation like this, to put oneself in the position of the villain. It is a useful mental exercise, to engage the imagination and, for a brief time, take the place of the criminal. You have no objections to playing the role of the sinister Barney?"

"None at all," I chuckled.

"Very well – you are now a man of low character, with a taste for acquiring shiny things. You wander into the Museum of Mineralogy and spy the Queen's Tear lying inside a glass case. Your instinct might be to smash the case and seize the diamond, but having spent time in prison, you know it is better not to be too hasty. So what do you do?"

"I begin to 'case the joint', if that is the proper slang. I watch the museum to find out when it is busy, and when the guard is either absent or might be overpowered."

"A sensible precaution. Do you seek confederates in your enterprise?"

I gave the question some thought. "If I have in the past, I might, but if all my crimes have been committed solo, then I am unlikely to change my normal course of action. The more people who know of my intention, the more chances there are for me to be betrayed."

"Excellent, Watson! You may yet acquire membership in London's criminal fraternity. Now, let us imagine that the optimal moment has come. You are suddenly alone in the museum, the guard has gone away, and the owner is distracted in the adjoining room. You smash the case, seize the stone, and do what?"

"Run for my life!"

"Of course! But a whistle blows and you glance behind to find a constable bearing down on you like a steaming locomotive! What do you do now?"

"I run faster!"

"Watson."

I could see from the sudden twist to his lips that perhaps my answer lacked merit, even if it possessed humor. "Very well, I see I cannot escape him. I will get rid of the jewel."

"A difficult task with a prime specimen of the blue-bottle type at your heels."

"So I look for any place for safety. I cross a street and see an open doorway with a lady standing at the threshold. I flee there, thinking I can get the door between myself and the officer. Then I hide inside the house or, more likely, escape through the back yard.

"You would make a very efficient criminal indeed," Holmes said, with a show of muted applause. "But permit one more question – what would you do with the lady?"

"I suppose I would push her down, or thrust her in a closet if one was handy."

"You mean you would not stop to ravish her?"

In that instant, I understood the point of our mischievous exercise. "Of course not. I would be so desperate to escape the forces of the law that I would never think to have my way with her, even if she were the most beautiful of ladies and I the grossest beast of a man. One crime at a time, I would think!"

Holmes threw back his head and indulged in a rare moment of unrestrained laughter. "One crime at a time! Watson, I believe we should adopt that as the new motto of this agency. But along with having coined a slogan, you have hit upon the central problem with Lestrade's little melodrama. A man carrying fifty-thousand pounds worth of diamond in his pocket has no time for sating his lust, no matter how helpless the maiden. It makes no sense that he would pause, even for the few moments that it took the hardy constable to summon help and break down the door."

"So the lady is an accomplice?"

"It seems likely that she is a confederate. Let us, for the moment, work on that hypothesis. If she is an accomplice, then this is not a bit of random larceny, but has been carefully planned and timed for a moment when the museum is generally free of crowds and lax in its security. The lady's place of residence is also no accident, as it is within a quick gallop from the store. The attack is an extra bit of staging to divert attention to Barney and away from his partner in crime. It is quite clever, in its daring – all Barney had to do was reach his associate, pass the gem to her, and be willing to endure the indignities that searching for the lost stone would entail. When the diamond was not found, Barney would either be released or given some minor sentence for breaking the glass and resisting arrest. He could then reclaim his prize."

"But all the residents of the dwelling have tickets for America."

"Barney may as well." Holmes buried a chuckle. "Or he may not. Perhaps the criminal is being conned. His lady-friend would have no trouble disposing of such a bauble in the American underworld, and then escaping her unsavory associate forever."

I shook my head. "You have a low opinion of women, Holmes."

"On the contrary, my dear Watson, I have a high opinion of them – they possess brains built for scheming, and nature and society has required them to become manipulators of the first order. I would not be shocked if our Miss Templeton, rather than the roguish Barney, is actually the mastermind of the plot."

This announcement did not sit well with me. It seemed a bit too arrogant, and too easily fell into Holmes's twisted notions about the untrustworthy nature of females. "Well," I said, "if you cannot find the Queen's Tear, then you may have to conclude that yet another woman has beaten you."

"Watson, old friend, that is exactly what I am afraid of."

The house we arrived at was a charming Georgian which, judging from the state of the paint and the rust along the bannister, had seen better days. The neighboring houses on the row seemed to be shrinking away from it, as if disgusted by its weatherworn condition. A hefty, broad-shouldered constable, who tipped his hat and introduced himself as Herring, opened the door. Lestrade stood in the hallway, sneering at old paintings on the wall. He motioned us toward the front parlor.

"Mrs. Ames," he said, far too loudly, speaking to the blind lady as if she were deaf as well as sightless. "I have brought in Mr. Sherlock Holmes and Dr. Watson. They are consultants who have been helpful to Scotland Yard in certain cases."

The lady sat on a small stool in a corner of the room. She was plump and jolly, clapping her hands together at Lestrade's introduction. She wore a black dress in a style that I recalled my mother favoring, and her thick white hair was braided and massed in a dozen coils around her head. Dark spectacles protected her eyes, but her smile was radiant. Clearly, the criminal incident inside her dwelling was not a cause of alarm, but for celebration.

"You've come to solve our mystery. Oh, it's the most exciting thing that has happened in this house since Harry – that's my boy – brought home a live tiger cub from India and it climbed the drapes and got loose on the street and attacked the milkman!"

Holmes bowed over the lady's outstretched hand, taking it and kissing it. "Madame is quite the collector, I perceive."

It was the understatement of my friend's career. The parlor was a veritable museum, crammed with all manner of artifacts, trinkets, and trophies. A stuffed grizzly bear rose on its back legs beside the door to the hallway, and a pair of open mummy cases, complete with linen-wrapped occupants, framed the other portal. The walls were covered in portraits, shadow boxes, and antique weapons. Glass curio cabinets filled with minerals, bottles, ornate shells, and scientific instruments stood everywhere. An exquisite model of the palace of Versailles rested on a large table next to the fireplace. The room was so packed with objects that the lady's stool was the only place to sit. I had to be cautious of my elbows, lest I upset a precious Chinese vase or topple a stuffed creature from its perch.

"Oh, these are not my things," Mrs. Ames said with a giggle. "They belonged to my late husband, who worked for the British Museum. Anything the museum rejected, he kept. And my son, dear Harry, he is a guide for big game hunters. The Prince of Wales is a client! You must see his room upstairs, where he keeps the lion, the water buffalo, and the anteater."

I glanced toward Lestrade, and noted that his expression had soured. If Holmes's theory was correct, the jewel could easily have been stashed inside one of the taxidermy beasts. There would be no way to retrieve it without ripping the trophies to shreds, an action that would hardly sit well with a man accustomed to sharing camp life with royalty.

"This is a most remarkable room," Holmes said, taking tight, careful steps and craning his head to view the many articles along the walls. "I see that the Inspector's men have not inflicted too much damage in their searches."

"I told them to be careful! It would break my heart to have anything destroyed. I have so few pleasures in life, but I do enjoy coming in here and touching these old things my husband left to me. I can't imagine what I would do if they were destroyed by the police."

From Lestrade's face it was clear that he expected her irate son to come storming into Scotland Yard with an elephant gun. He looked to

Holmes and gave a pointed cough. Holmes nodded his understanding of Lestrade's predicament.

"I am certain that we can avoid such an unpleasant outcome, Madame. But do tell me about this particular piece, Louis XIV's great castle. I assume it was your dollhouse in childhood?"

The lady's laugh was infectious. She rose and smoothed her crumpled skirts. It was easy to imagine what a charming girl she had been in the early years of the century.

"That is the oldest item in the collection. It was begun by my father, who was a footman at Versailles in the days before the Revolution. He fled to England during the Terror, and built this model completely from memory! My husband made some additions over time. Here, allow me to show you the most remarkable part."

She reached out and glided her fingers along the roof of the model until she found a secret latch. It opened and an entire wall swung free, revealing a gala ball inside the famed Hall of Mirrors. Almost a hundred dolls, each some ten inches in height and all of them dressed in eighteenth-century attire, danced before the central figures of the king and queen. The dolls' finery was astonishingly detailed, down to the elaborate embroidery of the coats and the golden buckles on the shoes.

"My husband thought we should make a present of it to the Queen, when the first little princess was born, but I could not bear to part with it." She plucked one beautiful doll free, caressing the folks of her gown. "I made all the dresses and coats for them. It was the last thing I completed, before I lost my sight."

Lestrade heaved a sigh that indicated his impatience. But Holmes merely studied the elder lady's upturned face, as if he read secrets within her sad smile.

"Watson," he said, "if you will be so kind, please pay a visit upstairs to Miss Templeton and make sure that she is well."

I nodded and followed Lestrade's lead, pausing only when he gestured toward other open doorways. Each room was packed to the ceiling with boxes, stuffed beasts, and glass cases. It would take a legion of trained curators a year to sort it all, and the lady was scheduled to leave for America the following week.

"Holmes has his work cut out for him," Lestrade said.

We knocked on the final door at the end of the upper hall, and a soft, wounded voice bade us enter. Miss Celeste Templeton was sitting up in bed. She was swathed in a heavy velvet wrapper, and was gingerly sipping at the tea the housekeeper had delivered. The elder servant – a fierce, harsh-looking woman in a drab grey dress – stared at us with cold, hateful eyes as Lestrade made introductions.

"With your permission, Miss, I'd like Dr. Watson to take a quick look at your injuries—just to make sure our police surgeon knows his business."

"Of course," she whispered meekly, opening the wrapper so that I could inspect the marks on her throat. She was a strikingly beautiful woman, with milky white skin and cascades of fat golden curls falling to her shoulders. Her eyes were large and blue, and no artist could have painted a more perfect Cupid's bow lip. But her loveliness was spoiled by the pair of livid bruises on her left wrist and at her throat, where the assailant had grabbed her and thrown her to the ground. Each place showed clearly the mark of his savage hand.

"You have been cruelly used," I said. The lady shuddered and pulled her gown back around her damaged neck.

"He was a monster. I thought he would kill me, the way he hurled me to the floor and pawed at me. Agnes . . . show the gentleman my dress."

With a grunt, the housekeeper lumbered over to a chair and lifted up a blue walking dress. Its bodice was torn to pieces and there was a long rip down the front of the skirt.

"Of course, that is just the start of how I have been mistreated," Miss Templeton said. As she shifted her gaze to the inspector, her eyes narrowed. "A half-dozen policemen have been through this room, turning it over, pawing through my lingerie! Tell me, Mr. Lestrade, have you brought twenty men this time to sniff through my private things? Or is it thirty?"

"I've brought only Mr. Sherlock Holmes. He's known for getting results."

"Results? For what? I have told you, sir, that when that beast ripped my blouse open I nearly fainted, but I never lost consciousness. I saw him run down the hallway and through the rear door. He could not have hidden that stone in this house, and I do wish you would stop pestering poor Mrs. Ames about it. We are the victims, not the criminals!"

As her voice rose in volume and shrillness, Lestrade was beating a slow but steady retreat toward the door.

"Are you really going to hold our passports and keep us from going to America? Mrs. Ames's son is expecting us."

Fortunately for Lestrade, at just that moment Mrs. Ames appeared in the doorway. Her cheeks were rosy and her step light.

"Mr. Holmes says we must all come down, right away! He has solved the mystery!"

Miss Templeton wilted back on her pillow. "I cannot. I am simply too unnerved by all of this."

"You can hear Mr. Holmes's report downstairs or at the station," Lestrade snapped, clearly grateful to have the upper hand once more. "I'm sure it doesn't matter to Mr. Holmes."

"Very well, but give me a moment to collect myself. Agnes, go on with them, if you will."

The housekeeper thudded down the stairs behind us. As we entered the parlor, we found that Holmes had managed to clear some space for our impromptu meeting.

"This will take some managing – Watson, here by me, and you over there, Lestrade, and – Agnes, is it? – I think you can just go to the doorway. Mrs. Ames, here is your stool, and now we only need . . . ah, Miss Templeton, thank you for your company. Lestrade, just behind that stuffed heron, there is a little chair. Lift it over. Wonderful."

Miss Templeton had swept her hair up and put a man's smoking jacket over her gown. The low folds of the jacket made her wound even more obvious. Holmes made comforting sounds and rattled off half-a-dozen platitudes on the evil of men as he saw her to her seat.

"Now I will make everything right again," Holmes said. "I am certain that these good ladies would prefer Scotland Yard's finest back on the beat instead of being a burdensome presence in their lives. And since their ship departs in a week, there is no doubt a good bit of packing to do. So, I will make this brief. Inspector Lestrade is an idiot."

"What!"

Holmes regarded the sputtering detective with an air of haughty contempt. "Surely you realize that Barney would not risk being caught with such a valuable gem upon his person. Such a crime would draw a hefty sentence, especially considering his criminal past. Once he saw Constable Herring in pursuit, he had no choice. He rid himself of the stone."

"But where?"

Holmes rolled his eyes like an exasperated schoolmaster. "How many rubbish containers are there along the sidewalk between this dwelling and the Lellouche Museum of Mineralogy?"

Lestrade's jaw dropped. His face turned white. "Four . . . five?"

"Fifteen. I counted. It would have been simplicity itself for Barney to fling the gem into any one of them along the route."

"But Herring had him in his sights at all times."

"Except, perhaps, in that moment when the nurse with the perambulator intervened. And even if he does not recall it, instinct would have caused the officer to look to both sides of the street before crossing. In that instant, the gem was disposed of."

"But why did he come here and attack me?" Miss Templeton asked.

"The door was open and suggested safety. But once inside . . . ." Holmes considered the lady at some length, which caused her to blush. "Forgive me for saying it, Miss Templeton, but you are a strikingly handsome woman and he is a beastly man. It was the inevitable result of –"

"Wait!" Lestrade wailed, "Are you telling me that the Queen's Tear has been lost?"

"If the rubbish has been taken up, I fear that it has."

Lestrade blistered the air with oaths not fit for ladies' ears, then turned and bolted for the door, ordering Herring to follow him. Miss Templeton breathed a deep sigh of relief.

"So our ordeal is over?"

"It is, and we can only wish the Inspector good luck in digging through the city's trash. You ladies are now free to embark for New York."

"How wonderful!" Mrs. Ames exclaimed. "What does Scotland Yard pay you, Mr. Holmes, when you work miracles for them?"

"My work is its own reward," Holmes said.

"But that is unfair. If the police will not reward you, I certain will. Please, Mr. Holmes, won't you accept a small token of my gratitude?"

She continued to babble as Holmes gently attempted to demure. Miss Templeton rose from her chair.

"I, too, am grateful, Mr. Holmes, but if you have no more need of me, I shall return to my room to rest."

"Celeste, one moment!" Mrs. Ames said. "Mr. Holmes, you must choose a souvenir to remember me by. There are so many strange and wonderful things here and – let us be frank – I will probably never return from America to enjoy them. What will you have?"

"Madame is too kind. I could not break up such a fine collection."

"I will not hear you refuse again, sir. Didn't you tell me that your niece's birthday was coming up? What was her name?"

"Dear little Martha. Yes, in fact, I must find something for her by tomorrow or she will never speak to me again. Mycroft is planning quite the party."

I reminded myself that I must not react to this revelation. Mycroft now had a wife and a daughter? Clearly, Holmes was keeping secrets from me.

"Then I know just the thing." Mrs. Ames pattered over to the Versailles dollhouse. I glanced toward the doorway, only to note that Miss Templeton had gone rigid. The hand that clutched the dressing gown together was knotted tightly, and her upper teeth were pressed against her bottom lip. Mrs. Ames opened the dollhouse to the scene of the ball, plucking a figure from its midst. "What little girl could resist such a doll? Queen Marie Antoinette, in all her finery!"

"And with her head still on her shoulders," Holmes chuckled. "Still able to wear the most beautiful jewelry imaginable."

"Mrs. Ames," Miss Templeton said, "please do not do this. Think how sad it would make your son to know that you were breaking up the exhibit. It should pass to your grandchildren."

The older lady paused for an instant, but gave a firm shake of her head. "Harry has only little boys, who could care less about dolls. Mr. Holmes's niece would be a much more appropriate recipient."

"Then choose another doll," Miss Templeton urged. "One of the other ladies. They are all so beautiful and . . . well . . . I had hoped you might give the Queen to me, as a token of gratitude for my service."

Mrs. Ames frowned. "This is not like you, Celeste. You've never said anything about the dolls, other than to complain when I asked you to help Agnes dust them!"

"Perhaps it is not the doll that Miss Templeton desires," Holmes said, "but the gem that the tiny queen now sports around her throat."

Everything happened so suddenly, so unexpectedly, that I was taken flat-footed. Miss Templeton lunged forward with the speed and skill of a viper, snatching the doll from Holmes's hand and knocking the old lady to the floor with a violent shove. Mrs. Ames fell into an open-faced cabinet, which dumped its contents over her shoulders. I leapt to her aid, only to find that Holmes and I were at the business end of a snub-nosed pistol, which Miss Templeton had pulled from the deep pockets of her robe.

"He said you might come," she hissed. Her hair had tumbled from it pins, obscuring part of her face. "Bernard warned me they might bring you in. I promised him, if you found the stone, I'd kill you."

I clutched the old lady, who gaped at her companion. Holmes was a perfect target, standing only a few feet from the murderous woman. Still, he refused to raise his hands or make any gesture of defense.

"You might wish to look out," he said softly.

"Why do you think I would fall for such an obvious ruse? Don't you think I can kill you where you stand?"

"I doubt you will have time," Holmes said, and in that instant the grizzly bear came toppling forward on its stand. Miss Templeton instinctively spun at the sound, only to be locked into the stuffed bear's embrace as it fell atop her. There was more destruction – shattered glass, broken plates, splintered wood – but the end result was our rescue. Miss Templeton was pinned down and knocked unconscious by the great bear. The gun skittered free of her grasp.

Agnes stepped forward, brushing her hands free of shed fur. "I never liked that tart," she muttered.

"Holmes, shouldn't we go in search of Lestrade?" I asked as we settled into a carriage just outside of Scotland Yard. It was evening, for it had taken us some time to settle all of the tasks in concluding the case. I had checked Mrs. Ames for wounds, and was relieved to find that she had not been harmed. We then delivered Miss Templeton to the Yard, bound with medieval chains that had been part of her employer's collection of antiquities. The purloined diamond was also in the hands of the authorities, who had summoned the museum owner to identify his stolen property. Monsieur Lellouche would have planted a hundred thankful kisses on my friend's cheeks, but fortunately Holmes was familiar enough with the Yard to make an escape thorough a back door. "If we don't find Lestrade," I argued, "he may go through every rubbish heap in London."

Holmes offered a wry smile. "Do not fret about our friend. While we were within, I slipped Inspector Gregson a note, telling him to bring Lestrade home. Of course, Gregson seemed rather out of sorts with his colleague for inviting me into the fray, so we will see how far their mutual pettiness extends."

"That was cruel of you," I scolded. "To send him on such a wild goose chase."

"It was calculation, not cruelty," Holmes said. "I felt the chances of forcing Miss Templeton's hand and tricking her into revealing her complicity were far better with Lestrade and his constable out of the house. I wished Miss Templeton to maintain the illusion that she was in charge of the situation."

"Did you think she would be armed?" I asked, a bit concerned that Holmes was willing to send Lestrade from the scene, but had no compunction about risking my life, and that of Mrs. Ames and her housekeeper.

"I assure you, Watson, that was the one contingency for which I did not plan. Women are becoming Amazons these days. I blame the suffrage movement. Once they acquire the vote, they will become desperadoes of the first order."

I shook my head at his incurable misogyny. "How did you find the gem so quickly?"

"The moment we entered the dwelling and I saw what a labyrinth it was, I had a dark moment of doubt. But when Mrs. Ames opened the palace doors, my spirit soared."

"You looked there immediately."

"As I said on the first leg of our journey, the imagination is perhaps the detective's greatest tool. I imagined myself in the role of Miss Templeton, rising from my well-staged attack as the constables ran into the garden. I would have only seconds to hide the stone, and I might not have the luxury of being left alone again for some time. Inevitably, big, loutish men in blue uniforms would come tearing through the house, upending everything. Where could I conceal the diamond?

"Then it struck me, as it surely struck her when she planned this deed – she must put the diamond in plain sight, yet in the one place a man would never think to look."

I cast my mind back to the scene within the miniature palace. "All the dolls were wearing gems."

"Precisely. There were so many artificial stones – rubies, emeralds, garnets, diamonds, all made of paste – that even if a policeman paid attention to the gala gathering of little people, he could hardly sort them out. Imagine how foolish the average policeman would feel, picking up and examining each of the figures, maybe even undressing them. It was bad enough to have to pilfer through the underthings of three ladies, much less play with their toys!"

"And Miss Templeton chose the Marie Antoinette doll because of the connection to the real queen?"

Holmes shrugged. "I doubt our thief is that romantic. More likely, it was because she could easily identify the queen, should the dolls be shuffled by careless hands. As the doll possessed a strikingly long neck, it was simplicity itself to wind the chain around the doll's throat and lay the gem on its bosom. The gem was now effectively invisible inside the tableaux. Had Lestrade not called in my services, the doll would have eventually left the premises as a 'gift' or 'token', and the curse of the Queen's Tear, if there is one, would have passed to another continent."

"Still . . . if you identified the diamond while we were upstairs, wouldn't it have been much easier to simply let Lestrade put Miss Templeton in handcuffs and be done with the thing?"

"It would have been easier, but it would also have given Miss Templeton the opportunity to cast suspicion on Mrs. Ames or the unattractive but heroic Agnes. By forcing Miss Templeton to acknowledge her perfidy and try to escape, we have tied the case up in a neat bow. Mrs. Ames and her trusty Agnes may depart in peace. And besides – once I informed Mrs. Ames of what I had found, she was eager to assist in my little charade. She found it quite an adventure, and I am gratified that she escaped unharmed but with an exciting story to tell her son."

"And you have another souvenir of a case."

Holmes pulled the Marie Antoinette doll from his pocket. Unfortunately, in the scuffle, the queen's head had come free of her neck. Holmes's lips twitched.

"Thank you for not giving the game away when I invented a phantom niece. And please do not tell my brother Mycroft that I have provided him with a wife and child . . . or the lady here might not be the only one without a head!"

It was only a few days later that I drew Holmes's attention to an article in *The Times* which credited the "intrepid and brilliant Inspector Lestrade" with solving the case, thanks to "timely assistance from Mr. Sherlock Holmes." The article concluded with a note that the Comte du Castlenau had just negotiated the sale of the Queen's Tear to the Tsar Nicholas II, who intended it as a gift for his wife, the Tsarina Alexandra.

"Let us hope it gives her no reason for grief," Holmes said, and turned to his violin, picking out a haunting Russian air.

The Adventure of Vittoria, the Circus Belle

"It is disaster, Mr. Holmes! Catastrophe! You must come to my aid or all is lost – and not just for myself, but for more than a hundred poor souls who depend on me for their livelihoods. Name your price, sir, but drop whatever business you have and come with me to Oxford. There is not a moment to lose. When I think of what, even now, might be happening to my poor dear girl, it is more than my heart can bear!"

The speaker of these impassioned words, which had come between great sobs and hard gasps for breath, was a short and stout gentleman of some sixty years. He had burst into our rooms just as we settled at the breakfast table, a perfect cyclone of garish clothing and long, grizzled hair, reeking of gin, and none too steady on his feet. I had been on the verge of heaving him bodily through the doorway when Holmes halted me, intrigued by this ungodly apparition's mention of a single name: *Vittoria.*

"So the famous circus belle has gone missing," Holmes said, making an aimless ramble around the room as our visitor, at my friend's invitation, wolfed down the remains of our morning meal. "Surely, Watson, you have heard of the lady?"

I confessed my ignorance. Holmes waved me toward the Index. Our guest, who bore the rather unlikely moniker of Sebastian Marvela, spoke through a mouthful of half-chewed rashers.

"The finest lass who ever stood upon the sawdust! She is star of our show, the most talented thespian of our age! A wonder of the universe! She has performed before more crowned heads than the Swedish Nightingale! Given dozens of benefit concerts for orphans and their schools! And at least five gentlemen of noble rank and immense wealth have bid for her hand in marriage, yet she has turned them all down, for she belongs, body and soul, to our little family – *Marvela's Marvelous Menagerie and Circus.*"

While the gentleman waxed eloquent, I quickly located the entry for Vittoria. It was at the bottom of a page, and revealed that she was a noted sideshow performer, famous for singing, dancing, playing the flute, and reciting Shakespearean sonnets.

"You have found her?" Holmes asked.

"I have. If you will forgive me for saying so, it seems she has a most unusual résumé for a circus performer. Surely a lady this gifted should be in the legitimate theater."

Marvela's face went crimson. Clearly, I had insulted his trade. Holmes, however, held out a placating hand to him, forestalling an outburst.

"If you will be so kind as to turn the page, Watson, I believe you will find her *carte de viste* pasted on the other side."

I did as Holmes instructed. A gasp of horror escaped my lips, and I nearly dropped the book on my toes.

"Good heavens! She . . . she is . . . ."

"The Circus Belle!" Marvela thundered, pounding a fist on the table. He winced. Clearly, his outrage had made him forget his obvious overindulgence of the night before, but the violent action had recalled it to him. "You must not judge her by her appearance," he whimpered. "A nobler soul has never lived."

Holmes strolled to my side. "Her condition is called *hypertrichosis*, I believe. It is fortunate that she lives in such an advanced age. Surely employment as a circus exhibit is better than execution as a werewolf."

I could not repress a shudder. The woman in the photograph was identifiable as a human female only by the shape of her evening dress. Her head and face were covered in long, tangled locks of hair, and wild brows sprouted out above her dark eyes. No lips were visible, yet I could easily imagine that if she were to smile, savage fangs would be revealed. Her gown was low, and her shoulders, bosom, and upper arms were all covered by shaggy fur. One foot protruded beneath the folds of the skirt. It too was hairy, with indecently long, canine-like nails that seemed to scratch the floor. I shut the book in a rush, but the image lingered. I feared that the beast-woman would follow me, howling for blood, into my nightmares.

"You say Miss Vittoria has disappeared?" Holmes said.

"No – she has been kidnapped! Abducted! Perhaps even ravished and murdered!"

Holmes crossed the room and poured more coffee. "Calm yourself, Mr. Marvela. We can make no progress until you gather your wits and tell us your story, from the beginning."

He groaned but nodded and, after downing another cup, began to speak with greater clarity and dignity.

"Vittoria is like a child to me, Mr. Holmes. I am, as you may have guessed – "

"Originally from America, but of Irish lineage, a former blacksmith, and a veteran of Union Army who spent much time in the southern states." Holmes made a quick motion to brush aside the man's astonishment. "It is as clear as your vowels, your thumbs, and the tarnished buttons on your coat. These things are as obvious to me as your stage name is ludicrous to your patrons. Continue."

Marvela swallowed. "Yes . . . and it was in Georgia that I found her, on a farm near the town of Valdosta. She was the youngest daughter of a family of what we called 'trash' people – poor, dirty, uneducated – who kept her locked away in a barn. I rescued her from that terrible situation." Marvela offered a sickly smile. "I paid almost a thousand dollars for her to . . . ahem . . . for her to become my ward."

The man disgusted me. "And she has been your prisoner ever since?" I snapped. "I thought the Americans had abolished slavery of all varieties."

Marvela waved a limp hand. "Of course she is not my prisoner. She has been free from the day she came of age – but I educated her, provided for her, brought her to Europe, and made her famous. She is a good girl, and would never willingly leave me."

Holmes had turned to a newspaper, flipping through it as if the gentleman's distress was invisible to him. "Yet now you have lost her. Please be precise as to the details."

"It was yesterday morning that she was abducted. We had made camp the night before in a field just outside of Oxford. Everything was normal, ordinary. We put up the tents and arranged our little caravan of wagons, fed the animals, and enjoyed our evening. Vittoria sang for us, some of those old and sad songs she learned from the Negroes in the South. But the next morning, she did not appear for breakfast. I thought nothing of it – she has the soul of an artiste, you see, and sometimes stays in her van until just before she comes on stage – and we had already experienced quite a shock that morning, for our oldest, dearly beloved lion, Leo, had died in the night. But, as we say, the show must go on! At one, we opened up our sideshows for the youth of Oxford, and we had quite a crowd of boys, all of them very excited to behold Vittoria. But when the curtain parted, she was not there!"

"You found signs of violence?" Holmes prodded, as our guest had once more lapsed into a fit of dramatic weeping.

"Yes. Her van is her private world, and someone had defiled it! The pillows on her bed were torn, the velvet curtains shredded, her lovely frocks ripped to shreds. Mr. Holmes, you must come back with me. You must find her! If you do not, the money we will lose . . . ."

"Calm yourself, sir. I need only a few more bits of data. Did none of your other performers or roustabouts witness this abduction?"

Marvela wiped his brow with a checkered handkerchief. "A few of them claimed to have seen dark figures lurking around that morning and to have heard a cry of murder. But they took these things in stride for, you see, we were adding a new scene to our performance." He fumbled in his pocket, pulling out a crumpled handbill. "A Wild West act! Half the cast is dressed as red Indians, the other as cavalrymen. There is a stagecoach, a robbery, and – "

"A rather noisy rehearsal," Holmes interrupted. "I take it the official forces have been consulted?"

"They have, but they were rude and dismissive, and said there was no real evidence the lady had not simply run away. As if she could, in her condition!"

"And what is happening at your circus today?"

"Nothing. I have given everyone the day off – though it will eat into my profits – but we must open tomorrow. After all, the show – "

"Very well, Mr. Marvela," my friend said, cutting off another flourish from his client. "My colleague and I will arrive on tomorrow's earliest morning train. Now, excuse me, but I fear I have another pressing engagement."

I knew Holmes had no plans for that day, but I played my part in the charade and, with some relief, saw the odious man through the door. When I returned, Holmes was studying the photograph of Vittoria.

"You must admit, this case will be unique," my friend said. I answered with a loud snort.

"Grotesque, you mean!"

"Not at all." Holmes held out the book with her picture. "She repels you?"

"Yes – though it is hardly her fault that she has such an unfortunate condition. However . . . ."

Holmes considered my silence. "You would prefer that she be hidden away in some institution? That she be forced to keep her talents, as well as her hirsute face, concealed behind closed doors?"

"You make me sound like a monster!" I objected. "I pity the girl."

"One wonders if we should," Holmes mused. His tone drew a sharp look from me. "But it is a capital error to theorize without data. Some research beyond the Index would be helpful. No, don't trouble yourself, Watson – this is a day for old books and yellowed newsprint. I shall be back before dinner."

Holmes clearly found information that was more interesting than food, for he did not return for dinner, much to Mrs. Hudson's irritation. I had retired and been asleep for more than an hour when the sound of footsteps in the suite alerted me to his return. Befuddled as I was, I decided to wait until the morning's train ride to Oxford to question him, but Holmes dismissed my inquiry with a grunt, pulled his cap over his eyes, and dozed throughout the entire ride to the station.

We disembarked at the celebrated university town and were quickly directed to a field on its outskirts. Marvela's circus was larger than I had imagined. A bright red-and-blue tent capable of housing several hundred people was it its centerpiece, and a series of smaller tents, each fronted by bright boards advertising some unique specimen of humanity, formed a pathway to the entrance. Despite the early hour, the air was already ripe with the smell of roasting peanuts. Stalls offering food and drink were being opened, and performers in all varieties of strange costumes were milling around. Substantial cages held sleeping tigers and a hefty bear, and I caught a glimpse of two elephants being fed their morning hay. However, the wild beasts were vastly outnumbered by ordinary horses. Nearly two-dozen were confined in a makeshift corral.

"Marvela's was originally an equestrian circus," Holmes said, breaking into my unspoken question. "He has attempted to conform his performances to the new mode, which emphasizes exotic animals and their trainers. However, a tragedy last year may have postponed this transition."

"An accident?"

"Yes. A trainer was crushed to death by an elephant."

I shuddered. "Are they certain it was an accident?"

Holmes turned his head. "What a suspicious mind you are developing, Watson! I fear I may have rubbed off on you, and not for the better. Indeed, there was some questioning of the event, as the trainer was involved in a romantic intrigue with a beautiful tightrope walker, much to the distress of her rather jealous clown husband. The performer spouses disappeared shortly after the trainer's death. But that is not our concern today."

I hesitated, watching as the denizens of the circus, the roustabouts, cooks, and performers went about their morning chores with no acknowledgement of the strangers in their midst. It seemed such an innocent place, a magic circle of childhood fantasies, especially as a calliope began pumping a merry tune. But what evil of the human heart might be hid behind such a bright façade, what hideous face lurked beneath this cheerful mask?

"Ah, I see our client has somewhat recovered himself."

Mr. Marvela was rushing toward us. He was now clad as a ringmaster, in a high hat and a bright red coat, with his yellow and blue striped breeches tucked into shiny boots. The costume made him only slightly less ridiculous than he had appeared the day before, but at least some of the puffiness had left his nose and he no longer smelled of gin. However, the garish grease paint that he had already applied to his face gave him the appearance of the cheapest and ugliest doll upon a shelf.

"Mr. Holmes, Dr. Watson – Welcome! You are just in time! We were about to begin our rehearsal for our western act, but I can halt it so you may investigate."

Holmes held up his hand. "I would not think of interrupting your company's work. Perhaps we may observe your new act now and speak with some of the witnesses to Vittoria's disappearance afterward."

"Oh . . . of course." Something about his moment of hesitation made me wonder if Marvela was about to demand we purchase tickets. Instead, he led us into the tent. The smell of sawdust was nearly overwhelming, mixed strongly with the sweat of animals and men. Marvela signaled for us to be seated on one of the rows of benches that surrounded the large ring. He picked up an oversized megaphone and barked orders. The few performers who had been lingering in the ring rapidly disappeared through another exit that was covered with a shimmering curtain.

"Ahem . . . and *now*," Marvela proclaimed, his voice startlingly altered as he assumed his ringmaster persona, "I give you the *greatest*, most *spectacular* performance of the age. Straight from the *American Plains* – innocent *settlers*, pursued by fierce *redskins*, and rescued by heroic – "

A shriek cut him short. In a storm of hooves and dust, an open wagon pulled by four shaggy ponies emerged through the curtain. The wagon was driven by a man wearing denim overalls and a huge, obviously false black beard. As he whipped his steeds, his beard whirled comically around his head. In the rear of the wagon were two clowns dressed as a woman and child. They screamed for help as their chariot made its first circle of the ring. At that moment, a host of purported Indians – young men costumed in buffalo robes, feathered headdresses, and red leotards – charged onto the scene, waving tomahawks and spears. Another circuit was completed, then another, the fierce Indians whooping for all their might and the buffoonish settlers squealing as they were chased.

Yet something was wrong. Marvela was stomping and sputtering impatiently. He raised his megaphone.

"Where the devil is the cavalry?"

He had barely spoken when a new figure shot into the ring. It was a young woman, slim, graceful, and confident, riding a splendid white stallion. She was dressed in a costume of fringed beige buckskins, and her thick auburn hair bounced in a loose braid down her back. She whipped a long gun from its holster on her saddle, pretending to pick off one of the attackers. He gave a melodramatic cry and hit the dust. The wagon drew to the center of the ring while the lithe Amazon continued her pursuit of the Indians. Round and round they went, and the lady, with each turn, performed some new stunt. She dropped below her mount's neck to fire her weapon. She stood in the stirrups. She even balanced atop the steed's rump to take aim at her moving targets.

For a finale, she somersaulted over the horse to confront the last Indian brave, who seemed poised to impale her with his flaming spear. Her gun fired a great cloud of black powder and the Indian toppled from his rearing mare with a savage shout, appearing to perish on the ground at the tip of the lady's dainty boot. She raised her gun above her head while the rescued "settlers" gave a cheer.

"Stop, stop! What was *that*?" Marvela cried, not requiring his megaphone to make himself heard. The dead tribesmen quickly rose all around him. Their leader, the last to die, pulled off his war bonnet.

"This is Laura Liberty! The Sharpshooter of San Francisco!" He grimaced in embarrassment. "Don't you remember, boss? You agreed to hire her three months ago. She's just arrived."

"I – yes, but – I thought the Sharpshooter of San Francisco was a man."

The young woman said nothing, though her face indicated she had heard such an objection before and did not appreciate its implications. The chief of the tribe turned to us and shrugged.

"I thought Liberty was a man as well – all the paperwork was signed with just an *L* for the first name. You can imagine my shock when this little miss stepped off the train late last night! But boss – isn't she wonderful?"

Marvela nodded. At that moment, Holmes began to applaud. The lady smiled with firmly pressed lips.

"She is indeed wonderful," Holmes said. "I suspect your patrons will be as surprised as you were, Mr. Marvela. She certainly adds an aspect of novelty to your circus."

"Yes, though . . . I hope she doesn't expect the salary I was willing to give Mr. Liberty!"

"As well she should not, for that would be unjust," Holmes said. I saw the maiden's tight smile slip. Holmes gave a nod in her direction, though he addressed his words to Marvela. "You should double it, sir. This lady is worth twice any man's value. Just think of all the tickets you will sell, and how the people will rush to see her."

The sharpshooter placed her delicately gloved hand to her face, but her amusement at my friend's audacity clearly shone in her beautiful dark eyes. Holmes spoke over the impresario's shocked stammering.

"Now, sir, I believe you have engaged me to find Miss Vittoria. Perhaps if you will be so good as to allow me to examine the lady's former residence? You may bring the witnesses to me there. I will interview them inside after I am done inspecting the scene of the crime."

Marvela nodded vigorously and dismissed his performers. A few minutes later, we were inside the wooden van that had served as Vittoria's home for years. The vehicle was so small that both of us were forced to stoop and take care not to collide with each other.

It was the oddest lady's bower that I had ever entered. Despite her deformity, Miss Vittoria had been the most feminine of creatures, surrounding herself with bottles of perfume, elegant hairbrushes, and pictures of theatrical beauties clipped from popular magazines and pinned to the sides of her small space. A gilded vanity was set to the rear of the wagon, and her narrow bed was adorned with silken coverlets. In contrast to its delicacy, however, the room showed signs of violence. The pillows had been slashed, their feathers scattered, and the beddings were torn. The dainty metal chair at the vanity was overturned, and the room was heavy with the scent of lavender, thanks to several broken bottles of perfume. An improvised rack held five evening gowns that had also been torn, their beads and bows ripped away and scattered on the floor. Holmes, as was his custom, examined everything with great care, and wedged himself down amid the floorboards with his lens. At his command, I took a seat upon the bed, trying to apply his methods in my mind.

"Ah – yes, just as I thought!"

"What, Holmes?"

He held out something to me. In the dim light within the van, I could scarcely make it out.

"A hair?" I asked, squinting at what he had placed in my palm.

"Yes, and a very telling one. Watson, will you alert Mr. Marvela that I am ready to interview his people? This van is perhaps a bit stifling. We should go outside."

And so, in the fresh air, seated in camp chairs, Holmes questioned a selection of the Marvela Circus performers. They were an odd and fascinating collection of individuals. The most common of them were two burly roustabouts, who said they had heard a cry of "murder" just as the rehearsal was taking place two days earlier.

"You did not find that a strange cry?" Holmes asked. The fellows glanced at each other, and after a bit of stammering, the larger of the pair answered.

"No, not since the boss was having all those wild Indians in the act. We just thought it was part of the show."

Holmes dismissed the workers. Next up was a tall, gangly man that Marvela proclaimed to be "The Human Skeleton". Indeed, he resembled a collection of sticks in a suit, with a cadaverous skull mounted above the collar. He introduced himself, very softly, as Paul Brown.

"Mr. Brown, what can you tell us?"

"Not much, sir. I saw some no-good looking fellows lurking around the wagons that day. But I was late to my stage, and I didn't say anything." He hung his head. "I wish I had."

"Can you describe these men?"

Brown shrugged. "They had on dark coats and their caps pulled low. But it was their manner, sir. Like they didn't want to be seen."

Holmes considered. "You could not make a guess as to their age?"

"No sir. I really didn't see them that well."

"But they were men, not youths?"

"I think so, sir."

Holmes sent him on his way. Our final witness was Mrs. Overton, a lady of ponderous girth. She made Holmes's portly brother Mycroft seem like a waif. Her stoutness was only emphasized by the gaudy raspberry colored frock that she wore. Unable to lower herself into the chair, she stood, swishing a bustle that would have filled half an omnibus.

"I saw three men hurrying away, and one of them had a big black bag over his shoulder. I've told this to the police already! I thought they were carrying off the lion that died in its cage the night before. I had no idea that Leo had already been buried."

Something about her tone caused me to lift my head from my notes. Mrs. Overton folded her massive arms across her chest, glaring at both of us.

"You didn't like Miss Vittoria, did you?" Holmes asked, with his usual perception into the human soul.

"I didn't kill her, if that is what you mean! But I will not lie to you – I won't cry because she's gone. It was 'Vittoria this' and 'Vittoria that', and 'Oh, Vittoria, she's so talented!' A dog who can play the flute, that's all she was or will ever be! Bah! I may be considered a freak, but I have more talent in my little finger than she did in her entire hairy body. Would you like to see my ballet poses?"

Holmes waved away the offer. "I think not. But you have been most helpful, and so I thank you."

With an angry huff, Miss Overton withdrew. Holmes asked me for my notebook, scribbled something on a page, then tore it free, disregarding my concern at having my property mangled.

"It is for a good purpose, I promise. Let us return to the tent."

Inside, Marvela was directing another rehearsal of his western show, but he brought it to a halt when we appeared. The performers gathered around eagerly as Holmes announced, in ringing tones, that he had solved the case.

"Mr. Marvela, it pains me to say this, but your Circus Belle is no more. Based on the evidence of the lady's van and the statements of the witnesses, I can tell you that you will never see Miss Vittoria again."

The entire company gasped. The clown who was dressed as the settler child began to weep.

"But – what has become of her?" Marvela asked.

"I recognize the signs of the gang led by Dr. William Wayward, the evil physician of Harley Street. He has a reputation for collecting people of, shall we say, distinctive medical abnormalities for his Museum of the Morbid. I doubt that your lady is alive now, if she was alive when she was carried from the circus. I hope you will all be on your guard, lest other members of your troupe find themselves spirited away to become permanent displays in Wayward's secret hall of curiosities."

There was a shriek and a loud thump. We turned to see that Mrs. Overton, who had slipped inside and been eavesdropping behind us, had fainted. Five of the Indians hurried over to fan her. Marvela's jaw sagged.

"My . . . my poor girl."

"I will continue my investigations in London and alert you should I learn more. In the meantime, Mr. Marvela, I suggest that you allow Miss Vittoria to live on in your fond memories of her, and focus on the continued success of your circus. Good day, and – oh, one thing." Holmes stepped forward and handed the note he had composed to the leader of the Indian tribe. "A few comments on your performance, sir. A critique, if you will, from one actor to another? Now, we bid you *adieu*. Watson, I believe we have just time to catch the eleven o'clock train."

We made a hasty departure, and within half-an-hour we were back at the station. I was burning with curiosity about this Dr. Wayward, of whom I had never heard before. Indeed, I was filled with outrage that a man of my profession could stoop to such a practice. Holmes, however, sent me into the station waiting room while he purchased the tickets. A few minutes later, he returned with a tray of coffee cups and sandwiches.

"We will hardly have time for this," I objected.

"Oh, I suspect we can devour this luncheon before the two o'clock train arrives."

"But you said – " Holmes was looking at me with twinkling eyes. I knew that expression of mischief. "What have you done?"

"Extended an invitation. Go on, Watson, have some coffee. It may take our guests some time to arrive."

"Guests?"

"Yes, two of the most intriguing individuals I have yet to meet. I may have deduced their actions, but it will be very interesting to hear their life story! Ah – I see they hurried behind us and have just walked in. Sir, Madame, won't you join us?"

Much to my surprise, it was the leader of the Indians and Laura Liberty, the Sharpshooter of San Francisco, who were timidly poking their heads into the room. Holmes waved them to the long benches where we sat.

"You truly won't tell what we've done?" the man, who quickly introduced himself as John Fitzroy, asked. The young lady settled onto the seat next to him. He had managed to wipe away most of his makeup, revealing himself to be a very handsome fellow, though a few red streaks on his brow and jaw gave him a fierce appearance. The lady, however, remained heavily painted and still clad in her distinctive frontier costume.

"Your secret is safe with me and with my companion. Tell me, Miss Liberty – how does it feel to be free of the persona of Vittoria, the Circus Belle?"

"It feels wonderful," she said. Her words were oddly accented. As she spoke, I caught the flash of sharp, almost wolf-like teeth. "Do you think I am wicked?"

"I think you are magnificent," Holmes said.

I wondered if the lady blushed beneath all her makeup. "Thank you, sir. I will tell you everything. Mr. Marvela bought me from my cruel parents when I was just a child. It is true that he provided me with books and tutors, so that I was as well-educated as a girl might be. And with him I have seen much of the world, and performed for many important people. But, Mr. Holmes, it came at a terrible cost! For every person who applauded, another snickered. Once, when I tried to take a walk in a park, my veil came loose and a group of young boys stoned me nearly to death. As I grew older, I began to long for love, as any woman would – but what hope could a freak like me have of ever finding a mate?"

"Marvela claims that men have proposed," Holmes said.

"Sick men," Fitzroy growled. "Men with strange desires. Some of them even offered to buy Vittoria – I mean, Laura – for an evening. To his credit, Marvela never forced them on her, but he promoted their disgusting proposals, had articles written about them, put it all on handbills. He used her pain and embarrassment to make money."

"You do not know how many times I thought of running away," the lady said. "But always my conscience stopped me. I felt I owed Mr. Marvela my life. I know I would have died in that barn in Georgia if he hadn't found me. And the world would not accept me as I was. So what could I do? I resigned myself to always being a lonely spinster . . . until John came along."

He reached out and gripped her gloved hand. "Laura may have had the face of a monster, but she has the heart and soul of an angel. I saw that from the moment I met her!"

Holmes nodded. "In my research, I read about her many good deeds, the charities for which she has given benefits. It must have been difficult to help others when you could not help yourself."

"Oh no," the lady answered. Her wondrous eyes glowed as she spoke. "Those were the only happy times, when Mr. Marvela allowed me to give concerts and donate the proceeds. I knew the little orphans and their schools would be aided. But always, for any good thing I did, he seemed to take the credit. It was all promotion for his freak, his . . . *belle*."

She fairly spat out the last word. Holmes leaned closer, his chin on his entwined fingers.

"Allow me to see if my deductions are correct. Mr. Fitzroy, you fell in love this lady and wanted to help her to live a normal life. But she insisted that her duty was still to the circus. Therefore, together, you came up with a plan that would allow her to achieve her freedom while remaining an important and profitable performer. Knowing that Marvela was about to incorporate a western themed attraction, you convinced him to hire a new featured player."

Fitzroy nodded. "I told him that the Sharpshooter of San Francisco was a star in America. Not to be unkind, but with the way Marvela drinks these days, I knew he would never check to see if I were lying."

"Meanwhile, you practiced your new act at night."

The lady who now claimed the name of Laura Liberty smiled brightly. "I have always loved horses. I used to ride as a child."

"She is fearless," Fitzroy added, with obvious pride.

"I have no doubt," Holmes said. "Then you took the boldest step imaginable. You enlisted a cadre of confederates." He turned with a wink. "Watson, surely you were not taken in by the vagueness of their stories. They were pat and flat, and hardly the intense – if perhaps exaggerated – memories that the sudden abduction of a beloved fellow performer would generate. All except for Mrs. Overton."

Fitzroy groaned. "I knew she would give us away!"

"Do not fault the lady. If anything, she behaved courageously by making herself seem villainous, jealous, and hateful, with a motive to have the Circus Belle removed from the scene. If Inspector Lestrade had been on the case, she no doubt would have been clapped in handcuffs – providing a pair to could be found to fit her! No, Mrs. Overton is as generous and brave as she is . . . stately."

Miss Liberty giggled. "She has been like a sister to me. She allowed me to hide in her van over the past two days. I do love her and would hate to leave her."

A train whistle blew in the distance. "And so, on the appointed evening," Holmes continued, "you caused the damage to the van and altered your appearance, being extremely careful to remove all the evidence of the shaved and shorn hair. Indeed, you were so precise that only a single clipped lock was visible to my glass. Of course, such an act of grooming presented you with a problem so – the lion?"

Fitzroy nodded. "It broke my heart a bit to give Leo his fatal draught, but in fairness he was old, blind, and clearly in pain. I think he is in a better place, if animals go to one, and his hair was exactly the color of Laura's. Nobody thought twice about it, when they found him in his cage."

"I see. And what are your plans now?"

"To seek a dentist," the lady said. "I think my new wig and my heavy make-up can continue to fool Mr. Marvela during the show. But until my teeth can be fixed, I will stay in my assigned van most of the time, pretending to be homesick!"

"And as soon as possible, we shall be married," Fitzroy said, lifting his lady's gloved hand to his lips and bestowing a passionate kiss on it.

"Then we wish you both the greatest happiness," Holmes said. "Dr. Wayward is, of course, an absurd invention – worthy of Watson's purple pen, no doubt! – but should your employer make any future inquiries, I will be certain to remain in desperate pursuit of him, in order to avenge the Circus Belle's abduction and possible murder. Come, Watson, I believe we can make the eleven o'clock train after all."

I can give a brief epilogue to this affair. For a few weeks, Marvela's ticket sales were enhanced by a new *tableau* called "The Cabinet of the Curious", in which all of his *outré* specimens were asked to hold static poses, as if they were exhibits in a museum. His western act, however, soon overshadowed this rather bizarre routine. Miss Liberty, The Sharpshooter of San Francisco, was a sensation, and even performed a special engagement of her trick riding routine before our beloved Queen, who rewarded her with a specially struck medal and a beryl broach. A short time after this command performance, Marvela succumbed to cirrhosis of the liver, and the members of his circus scattered to the winds.

Holmes, of course, insisted that I could never reveal the true identity or fate of Vittoria, the Circus Belle. Therefore, I have written this account purely for our mutual amusement, and not for publication.

To it I will attach one final note: Some years after the case, I came upon Holmes adding a new photograph to his index. It showed a striking family: The man was tall, broad-shouldered and resolute, the woman was slender and elegant, and their boy was as cherubic as could be imagined, except for the wild mane of hair that gave him the appearance of a baby werewolf.

> *I leaned back and took down the great index volume to which he referred. Holmes balanced it on his knee, and his eyes moved slowly and lovingly over the record of old cases, mixed with the accumulated information of a lifetime . . . "Vittoria, the circus belle" . . . .*

"The Adventure of the Sussex Vampire"

The Adventure of the Last Laugh

Looking back over my notes of many decades, I am struck by how seldom I recorded the more comical adventures of my friend Sherlock Holmes. Often this was from discretion, to protect those involved from further ridicule or embarrassment that publicity might bring. At other times, Holmes did not feel the cases were serious enough to merit being committed to posterity. However, upon retrieving the records of our adventure at Waterlynn, which concerned the rather bizarre self-portrait of the late Eustis Lacey, I feel compelled to offer my faithful readers a glimpse into a moment in 1882 when a peculiar client and his most unprecedented problem took us into the realm of both high art and low comedy.

"I have no means of compensating you for your efforts, Mr. Holmes," my friend's newly arrived client said. "I barely have two farthings to rub together, but I promise that if you unravel this mystery, I can make you rich beyond your wildest dreams."

Holmes turned from his perusal of the sketch above our mantelpiece, lit his pipe, and considered our rather extraordinary visitor. The young man, who had introduced himself as Ambrose Burnside Bartley, was a spectacle of an aestheticism run amok. He was perhaps thirty years of age, and his long blonde curls, each carefully oiled, trailed down over a purple frock coat and a ruffled cravat that would have made a Regency dandy proud. His crane-like legs were encased in pink silk breeches, paired with checkered stockings above green patent-leather slippers. Every item of his ensemble was spotted with stains, or patched and mended with no great skill. He was fortunate, however, to have been blessed with a handsome face and, despite his odd appearance, a genuine and pleasing manner.

"Indeed, Mr. Bartley?" Holmes asked. "While my work may be its own reward, I am intrigued by your proposition. What mystery could I solve that would elevate me to the aristocracy of wealth in such a dramatic fashion?"

The young man appeared not to hear the mocking tone that I clearly discerned, and plunged forward with painful earnestness. "Why, if you could unravel the clues in Eustis's self-portrait, and direct me to the location of the combination for his safe, which contains a trio of the world's greatest masterpieces, we would both be richer than King Midas in an instant!"

Holmes waved his guest to the sofa. "I consider myself something of a connoisseur of art, though Watson claims my knowledge of the subject is flawed and my tastes border on the crude. However, this is nothing but jealousy on his part, so let us have your problem from the beginning, Mr. Bartley."

The young man eagerly launched into his tale.

"Eustis Lacey was a dear friend of mine at Oxford, where we both studied art, with an emphasis on the works of the High Renaissance. Eustis's prospects were excellent, as he was the only child of wealthy parents, connected on his mother's side to nobility and on his father's to some of the greatest entrepreneurs of our age. But Eustis was a rebel, always at odds with his class. He broke every rule, and I have no doubt that some of his more scandalous behaviors drove his godly mother to an early grave. He was sent down twice and finally expelled for activities that are best left unspoken – only to say that a goat, a pair of lady's drawers, and an intoxicated sexton were involved.

"For a time, my friend was disinherited by his father, and forced to make his own way in the world. Fortunately, Eustis had a knack for discovering lost masterpieces in out-of-the-way shops and the homes of impoverished baronets. He regularly received commissions to travel to Italy, Spain, and France to purchase pieces for wealthy patrons. But Eustis's great goal was not merely to be an expert for hire – no, he wished to be a master himself, and to be accepted by the arbiters of taste.

"And there, Mr. Holmes, was the problem – Eustis could paint with great technical precision, but he lacked originality in his work. He was rejected by every academy to which he applied – the French were particularly insulting, and the Germans replied that he would do better to take up house painting. Even the Americans – the Americans! – refused to display his works in any of their shows. I should add that he had a real skill for drawing caricatures – you should have seen the funny sketches he used to make of our deans – but he made the mistake of getting one of his little 'wistful studies', as he called them, published in *Punch*. The Home Secretary was not the least forgiving, and after that incident there was even less chance that anyone in the British Isles would do anything except denounce him as a 'talentless amateur'. I am sad to say that my own artistic success – quite modest I must add, and mainly in portraiture of spoiled brats and aging dowagers – caused a cooling in our friendship, as Eustis experienced continued disappointments in his bid for acceptance.

"And so my friend began his sad decline. He had been restored to the bosom of his family, and his father had recently died, but the fortune he inherited could not buy him the one thing he desired: A reputation as an artist. He took to drink, and when he was sober (which I fear was not often), he amused himself with his other pastime from his college days – building all sorts of strange mechanical devices that, inevitably, involved explosives. Half-a-dozen times he nearly burnt down Waterlynn, his ancestral manor, with his little toys that caught themselves on fire.

"Then, just over a year ago, I received an invitation to a dinner party at Eustis's home. I was astonished by the guest list, which was made up of a dozen or more of Eustis's greatest critics and foils, including Professor Peter Schmitt, the sneering old instructor of art history from our college, and Miss Karen Blisschild, who has made a name for herself writing criticism for artistic journals, along with a number of other self-proclaimed experts and connoisseurs. Knowing my friend's utter contempt for these individuals, and their disdain for him, I could hardly see the purpose in the assembly. I halfway expected a brawl to erupt before the coffee was poured. Conversation was strained, to say the least, but at the conclusion of the meal Eustis rose, dramatically cleared his throat, and began a speech.

"'I am dying,' he said, without any preamble. 'I have a tumor which the doctors inform me is inoperable. Therefore, I must put my affairs in order. I will have little to leave to the world, for as some of you know I have led a profligate and wasteful life, and most of the money left to me by my sainted parents has been squandered. However, this treasure remains.'"

"He went to a large easel which had been covered with a cloth. He threw back the drapery, revealing three small paintings. One was a Madonna holding an apple, the other a still life of bread and wine, and the third a head of Zeus. An electricity ran through the room, as everyone recognized, even from our places at the table, the distinctive styles of Da Vinci, Rembrandt, and Raphael. Eustis allowed us all a moment to gape.

"'You surely see what I have accomplished – I have located three lost paintings of the greatest masters the world has known, paintings that have often been described but never found. Tonight, I will lock them a safe. The combination I will secure in a hidden place. To find the combination, you must look in my self-portrait, recently completed, which will be unveiled on the occasion of my funeral. He or she who successfully opens the safe may have what is found inside, along with Waterlynn as well! But have a care, dear friends . . . have a care!'

"At this point, Eustis replaced the drape on the pictures. He then walked over to the corner of the room and removed a second covering from a green metal safe. The squat, ugly box was wrapped with metallic wires, which in turn were attached to a strange clockwork mechanism atop it. Eustis grinned at us – I'll never forget how unnerving that grin was. I still see it in my nightmares!

"'Should you try to force this safe open,' Eustis said, 'or attempt to unlock the safe with the wrong combination, an incendiary device within the safe will activate, destroying the masterpieces! Now, fellow art lovers . . . shall we retire to the drawing room for our dessert?'"

"He herded us from the chamber, and within an hour we were all unceremoniously packed into our carriages and sent away. I was astonished, of course, and intended to appeal to him, as a dear friend and fellow aesthete, to at least allow me to gaze upon those beautiful pictures and commit them to memory. But it was not to be. A week later, his housekeeper found him expired in his bed. Eustis had left an account that would fund the maintenance of the property for a year after his passing, and, following his funeral, at the reading of the will, the strange situation he had explained to us over dinner was made even clearer."

Our guest fumbled in his pockets, finally drawing out a much folded piece of foolscap. Another round of searching produced half-moon spectacles, through which he peered.

> *To all interested parties, I declare that my greatest treasures lie secured in the green safe in my library. However, one must take note that I have devised a trap for the unwary. My safe is rigged with one of my special devices, and should anyone attempt to open it without the proper combination, the artwork inside will be incinerated. To find the combination, one must look in the self-portrait above the library fireplace. He or she who finds the combination and opens the safe is the owner of the masterpieces within, along with Waterlynn.*

"What a bizarre arrangement!" I said.

"Mr. John Lindley, who was Eustis's solicitor, was further required to open the library to guests on the first Saturday of each month, from one until four in the afternoon, to study the portrait and hunt for clues. But this funding will soon run out. The final provision of Eustis's extraordinary will stated that if no solution was reached in a year's time, the contents of the house would be auctioned and the money given to the Bethlehem Royal Hospital – better known as Bedlam, the lunatic asylum!"

Holmes smiled. "Your late friend's sense of humor was rather pawky."

Mr. Bartley ignored the comment. "I suppose that once everything is put up for sale, some wealthy individual will purchase the safe and try to open it, without having the combination in hand." Our client's agitation returned as he wiped away a sudden tear. "I have seen these paintings, and I know of Eustis' remarkable ability with explosive devices. I fear these irreplaceable treasures will be destroyed in greed and haste! Please, Mr. Holmes! Tomorrow is the final day the portrait may be inspected – I must have your assistance!"

Holmes's thin lips quivered, then abruptly turned down, giving him an expression of exaggerated solemnity.

"I presume you have rivals for this challenge?"

"A year ago, almost a hundred artists and experts descended on Waterlynn, but as every clue has been followed without success, now only three of us remain: Professor Schmitt, Miss Blisschild, and myself."

"Has either of your competitors expressed an intention to purchase the safe once the year has expired?"

"Neither of them could afford it, I suppose. They are not penniless, but they are far from wealthy."

Holmes nodded thoughtfully. "If they are truly as obsessed with obtaining the artwork as you state, then they may not let such a handicap as pecuniary difficulties stop them."

"You think they would try to steal the safe?"

Holmes put his fingers together. "I think many things are possible. By any chance would you have – ah, I see you have anticipated my request. Watson, observe – Mr. Bartley is an ideal client."

The young man had removed a rolled paper from his moth-eaten carpet bag. Holmes rose and began clearing chemical apparatus from his table.

"You have my word, Mr. Bartley, that we will be at Waterlynn at one tomorrow. I do not believe your problem presents any great difficulty."

The client's jaw dropped. "You mean – you know where the combination to the safe is?"

"I do," Holmes said. He considered the picture he had unrolled across the table. It was clearly a copy of Eustis Lacey's self-portrait. "In fact, I can state with some certainty and no false modesty that I knew the location before I ever saw this facsimile. It is an exact reproduction?"

"Yes, to every line, but – you know where the combination is?"

"I do."

"Then tell me!"

Holmes shook his head. "To do so now might tempt you to folly. Have patience, Mr. Bartley. All will be clear tomorrow afternoon. A good evening to you now, and we will see you at Waterlynn." Holmes waited until the man had made a quivering exit. "Come, Watson, what do you make of this image?"

I moved to Holmes's side. My immediate response was one of bafflement. My secondary reaction was annoyance.

"He could not have been serious! It must be some type of jape!"

In the picture, the subject faced the viewer, but the subject's eyes were crossed and his teeth locked in a disturbing rictus of a grin. The scrawny, unattractive man appeared to be clad in a strange blue toga, with a laurel wreath in his long ginger hair. In his right hand sat a monkey, while his left hand grasped a golden key. Behind him was a window, and beyond was a landscape of blasted trees and cragged peaks, with lightning striking out of a sky filled with boiling black clouds. I leaned forward, attempting to make out three figures on the horizon. They appeared to be older women, cavorting around a cauldron.

"Are those witches?"

"So they appear."

"And is that . . . a bust of Shakespeare just to the side, peeking through the shadows?"

"What a keen eye you have, Watson. It is indeed the immortal bard, lurking in the darkness at Lacey's elbow."

I grimaced. "What a hideous picture. If this is a true sample of how he painted, no wonder every gallery rejected him."

"Yet it is done with a certain level of technical precision. One cannot fault his use of perspective, or his choice in colors."

"So where is the combination to the safe in all this?" I asked. Holmes merely smiled at me, then tapped his temple.

The manor of Waterlynn was but a short train journey from London. We arrived early and enjoyed a pleasant ride from the station to the manor. The massive iron gates were locked, and our client paced nervously before them.

"Mr. Holmes and Doctor . . . ."

"Watson," I said. Our names were not so clearly linked in those early days.

"I've heard a rumor, sir. It's hideous! It's – why, I can barely believe it. To gain money this way – it is shameful!"

Holmes paid our driver, then made a show of brushing the dust from his travelling cloak. "So which one has made the marriage," he casually asked, "Professor Schmitt or Miss Blisschild?"

Mr. Bartley clutched his chest. "Sir! Are you a wizard, to know such things?"

"Calm yourself," Holmes said, "it takes no great leap of logic to deduce that if both of your rivals remain obsessed with acquiring the safe, then – lacking the location of the combination from the portrait – they will attempt to obtain the funds to purchase said safe and attempt to force it open. I spent last evening looking up their credentials, and found that they were both unwed. The easiest way to acquire sudden wealth is to marry it."

"Or kill for it," I said. Holmes smirked.

"What a devious mind you have, Watson. Clearly, I must watch my step around you."

The client ignored our banter. "Professor Schmitt is married – to Edwina Lucretia Talbert. Do you know the name?"

I snapped my fingers. "The opera singer!"

"*Aspiring* opera singer," Holmes corrected. "She has given a number of London galas, funded by her family's wealth, to underwhelming reviews. She was made for roles that require a sizeable voice, which she possesses – unfortunately she does not also possess the requisite ear for tune. But here comes the happy groom now."

A miserable little trap had pulled up, discharging a thin, sallow man with a wild mane of grey hair and a face set in a perpetual scowl. His shoulders were hunched and his coat looked worn and shabby. He peered at us through tiny spectacles, then sneered and failed to offer a hand as Bartley made introductions.

"A detective, are you? There was hardly any call for that – it is an academic matter, pure and simple. Tell me, what do you do, Mr. Holmes? Track down runaway maids and pilfering butlers? Or is your specialty finding lost dogs?"

I wondered how such an unpleasant man could have snared a wife of any description, much less one who came with a substantial dowry. Holmes calmly congratulated him on his nuptials.

"Yes, yes, she's a fine woman. Former opera singer, you know. Soprano. Still in voice. Can hit notes to break glass." He barely suppressed a shudder. "I'm used to a quiet bachelor life. Still, I suppose I will adjust."

Another vehicle approached. This one carried a lady in bright blue dress, with blonde hair and icy eyes. She waited until the driver could assist her, descending from the carriage with the cool dignity of a queen. Her profile was striking, but as she drew close I could see that most of her appearance was artifice, that paint and powder were waging a mighty war against time. Her hair was shot through with gray, and there was much of the disappointed spinster in her haughty expression. She approached us with an upturned nose, as if we were a pack of dirty farmers just returned from the field.

"Hello, Karen," the professor said, showing her none of the courtesy one would expect him to adopt toward a lady. "Where's your garish trinket?" he demanded. "First time I've seen you without it."

"What I do with my jewelry is none of your business, Peter!" she snapped, even as her hand strayed to her collar and toyed nervously with a piece of floppy lace. Bartley leaned close and whispered in my ear that Miss Blisschild had previously flaunted a golden broach bearing a yellow diamond, said to have been a family heirloom.

"Sold it, have you?" the professor cawed, ignoring her distress. "How much did you get for that piece of paste?"

"I assure you, my jewel was real, and worth more than you have earned in your entire miserable, undistinguished career," Miss Blisschild hissed, turning her attention to our client. "Ambrose, I see you have brought along friends. They couldn't be Peter's friends, as we all know he has none."

"I have a wife now," Professor Schmitt muttered.

"So I have learned," Miss Blisschild said, with bite. "It was no doubt a *weighty* decision for you to make. Let us hope the furnishings of your miserable rooms can *support* her."

Fortunately, we were spared any more barbs by the arrival of a manservant, who opened the gates and bid us to follow. The grounds of Waterlynn were thick with trees and choked with overgrown grass and weeds. Through the tangled, unkempt landscape I spotted a substantial folly, the artificial ruins of an antique temple. My mind leapt back to the painting, and how the subject had been portrayed in the garb of some type of Greek or Roman god. As we came up the gravel drive, I also noted that on the lintel of the solid Georgian home was a frieze depicting three women standing around a large pot. I seized Holmes's sleeve.

"Do you – ?"

"Yes, I see."

We were admitted into a gilded foyer by Mr. Lindley, the solicitor, a small, ferret-like man who clearly wished to be done with his duty. Despite the house's outer magnificence, inside it had an air of being stale and dusty. Boards had been pulled up in the hallway, and in places there were gaping holes in the walls. Carpets and tapestries were ripped, marble-topped tables overturned, glass cabinets shattered, their contents scattered across the scraped and damaged floors. It looked as if barbarians had arrived to sack the place, but given up on their quest midway through their pillage.

"You all know the rules, of course," the solicitor said, with the air of a bored tour guide. "The portrait remains in the library. You may study it for three hours, and seek the combination anywhere you like, but you must not touch the safe without the combination in your hands."

We were escorted into the library. It was filled with hundreds of books, though many of them had been knocked to the floor and loose pages were scattered about. A pile of broken plaster marked where some unfortunate artwork had met its demise. My eyes were drawn to a funny bit of sculpture on a high shelf. It was a golden monkey, its tail held between its teeth. A large volume of Shakespeare's plays was tucked beside it.

Much to my surprise, Holmes merely settled into a chair. The three art experts began to consider the painting, and quickly seemed to forget that Holmes and I were in the room.

"It is clearly an allusion to the folly," Miss Blisschild said. "The toga and the victor's wreath tell us that."

"And how many times have we dug up that damned folly?" Professor Schmitt muttered. "It has nothing to do with the combination! The clue is in the bust of Shakespeare!"

"Which you broke, last month," Bartley said. "We sorted through all the pieces, broke them into dust, as if we were looking for a pearl. It was a dead end."

"The toga is blue," Miss Blisschild continued, her voice suddenly sharp. "The robe of the Virgin Mary is often blue. This could be an indication of a religious tie, a direction to the combination being in a place of worship. Was Eustis a Catholic?"

"The brat was a damned pagan," his former professor snapped. "And I hope he's burning in Hades now, for all the trouble that he has caused us. If I have to listen to one more aria –"

"Have you considered the monkey?" I asked, caught up in their speculation in spite of myself. "Perhaps Eustis is saying that the monkey sculpture holds the key to this conundrum."

All three of them turned and glared at me. Even the solicitor, who had been slumped in a window seat, let out an annoyed sigh.

"That was the first thing we thought of," Bartley said.

"I'll give Eustis credit, he was more subtle than I imagined," the professor grumbled. "Perhaps the clue lies in his smile, or his gaze. He seems to look both ways at once . . . as if misdirecting us." The professor thumped his cane on the floor. "He used to cross his eyes like that in class, just to make me stumble in my lecture."

The lady folded her arms. "And he was certainly no saint. I have never forgotten that time when he asked me if I would – no, I will not speak of it! But perhaps that is also a clue – he wishes to be what he is not, so the combination must be in some place where we would not expect it."

A loud yawn took us all aback. Holmes leaned forward in his chair, elbows on his knees.

"The Scottish play."

The academic pair frowned in unison. "Yes. What about it?" Professor Schmitt demanded.

"*Macbeth* is referenced three times in the painting – in the bust of Shakespeare, the three witches, and the blasted heath beyond the window. Your deceased friend was, as the lady points out, far from a saintly figure – one who was perhaps, as his image suggests, often intoxicated to the point of ludicrousness. He is also clearly 'monkeying' with the key to the safe, casting a spell of sorts to keep you from igniting the lightning within the device, just as lightning strikes within the picture. I would suggest that the combination might be found not in a private spot, but in a public place like a public house. Correct me if I err, but I believe there is an establishment in the nearby village named 'Macduff's' and – "

Professor Schmitt and Miss Blisschild both whirled at the same time, running for the door. There was an unsightly collision at the portal, with the lady demanding to go first and the professor uttering some oaths that would have gotten a lad sent down from school. Mr. Bartley started to go after them, but Holmes seized his cane and barred the young man's exit. We heard the outer door slam in the distance.

"But you said – "

"I said a great deal of nonsense, Mr. Bartley. And, unlike Professor Schmitt, I do not wish your late friend in the nether regions. Indeed, I hope he looks down from heaven and is enjoying this moment."

"What do you mean, sir?"

Holmes rose from his chair. "The correct answer is usually the simplest. Allow me to demonstrate."

Holmes pulled a large rag and a dark bottle from his coat pocket. He poured out some liquid onto the cloth and then, before any of us could raise our voice to object, he drew up a small ladder and reached above the mantel, swiping the rag across the painting. Instantly, the gaudy image of Eustis Lacey began to dissolve in a riot of blended colors. Holmes plucked the canvas down from the wall.

"Behold. When you friend told you that the clue was in his painting, that is what he meant."

Indeed, the paint had blurred and streaked, revealing a set of numbers that were carved into the canvas. Bartley began to tremble.

"My God . . . he always said . . . critics made too much of symbolism."

"Your rivals have been led astray by their own insistence that their academic expertise outweighed Eustis's very words. Will you try opening the safe now?"

"I'm too nervous. What if I make a mistake? No – you do it, Mr. Holmes!"

The solicitor cleared his throat. "By law, the contents of the safe belong to whoever opens it. You will have no claim on the paintings if Mr. Holmes does the work."

Mr. Bartley twitched so violently I feared my medical services would be necessary. Holmes shook his head.

"I hereby give all my rights to the contents to my client. Yes, I will sign a paper to that effect. Please, sir, do sit down. I would like this task completed before your erstwhile competitors return."

We watched, holding our breath, as Holmes knelt and deftly spun the dials. There was an instant of hesitation and then a sharp and clear click. Holmes turned the handle. The green monster opened its jaws.

Within, a collection of copper wires dangled.

"Why, they're not attached to anything!" Bartley cried.

"Of course not. It was all a blind."

"But . . . why?"

"A final bit of fun, perhaps? Do come here, Mr. Bartley, and claim your prize."

The man fell to his knees and fished inside the safe. He pulled out three small but magnificent paintings. One was clearly by Da Vinci, the others I could not vouch for. Bartley began to weep.

I suddenly felt sorry for my friend. He had given up a treasure, and to a man I was not sure was deserving of it. Yet a knowing smile played across Holmes's face.

"Perhaps we should retire and leave our client alone with his masterpieces. There may be some amusement in checking to see if his rivals have torn Macduff's public house apart at the seams. Do be careful, Mr. Bartley. I would not put murder beyond either of your competitors, especially as one has parted with a favored jewel and the other has said goodbye to the peace and freedom of bachelorhood."

"You will hardly succeed in your line of work if you continue along this pathway," I told Holmes, as we arrived back in Baker Street.

"Whatever do you mean, Watson?"

"I mean, you did not even present your client with a bill – and he is now perhaps one of the richest art collectors in England. Imagine what those three lost masterpieces will go for at auction! You could certainly acquire better lodgings than these had you claimed at least one of the paintings as payment for your services."

"Ah, but I like this picturesque pile," Holmes said, as he hung his travelling cloak on its peg and took up his pipe. "It has already seen the beginning of a few adventures, and I suspect many more intriguing clients will pass through its doors in the years to come. Indeed, when you write your little tales, you may one day make this address famous."

"But the money!" I protested. "The paintings, by right, belonged to you."

"Great art belongs to the world, Watson. No, no," he scolded, as I settled at my desk with my notebook. "Do not think of writing up this little adventure. It is hardly a worthy example of my skills, and, quite frankly, lends itself more to the humorous than the deadly or dangerous, or even the bizarre."

"Perhaps you do not wish the world to know that you work for free," I snorted.

His smile was enigmatic. "Perhaps."

Three months later, upon returning from some errands, I was surprised to find Mr. Ambrose Burnside Bartley once again perched upon our sofa. He was a much changed man. Gone were the oiled curls and purple frock coat and checkered hosiery. Instead, he could have been mistaken for any dour London businessman in his black suit and high collar, with a proper leather bag at his feet.

"I had to sell it, of course," he was saying to Holmes. "That wretched manor was sinking in debt. I was lucky to get out with my shirt by the time the thing was done. Oh, hello Doctor. I've come to settle my account with Mr. Holmes."

My friend waved the suggestion aside. "You owe me nothing."

"I think I owe you everything. You see, even before I came to you, I'd made up my mind that if I couldn't discover that combination on the last day, I was going to sell the one thing of value I possessed – a miniature of Charles II by Samuel Cooper – to try and outbid the others for the safe. This miniature was given to me by my mother – its sentimental value alone – well, even now, just to think about losing it, all for nothing, makes me sob!"

He demonstrated, plucking a handkerchief from his vest. Holmes shook his head.

"I take it that both of your rivals have come to regret their hasty decisions."

"Oh, sir, if you could see the old professor! He's a ghost of himself, and gone half-deaf from all the shrieking, he says. Miss Blisschild – well, I hear she's under lock and key, awaiting trial. When she learned what happened, she tried to steal back her diamond from the fellow who bought it. No, there's been nothing but misery that has come of this – misery you saved me from."

"And the paintings," I asked. "Have you had them appraised?"

The man gave me a sour look. "I did. They are worthless."

"What? How can they be worthless?"

"Because they were painted not by Da Vinci, Rembrandt, and Raphael, but by Eustis Lacey," Holmes said with a chuckle. "Recall,

Watson, what Mr. Bartley told us about his friend – Lacey was a painter of great technical ability, but no true originality. I had every reason to suspect the paintings with which he tempted his foes were forgeries, his interpretation of paintings described in books but lost to time."

"It was a grand joke," Bartley grumbled. "I suppose if there is an afterlife, as the spiritualists claim, then he is enjoying my discomfort. So be it. I've learned my lesson, given up on art and on being an esthete. I've gone into business with my uncle, learning the trade in gentleman's woolen undergarments. Perhaps I will make something of myself after all." He turned back to my friend. "If you will not accept a checque from me, sir, perhaps souvenirs of this strange adventure will suffice?" He reached into his leather bag and pull out the three small paintings. "I am sure that Eustis would want them to belong to someone who shares his sense of the absurd. I fear I have lost my taste for any type of 'wistful studies'."

"You are certain you wish me to have them?"

"Indeed, sir. You do me a favor to remove them from my sight."

The men shook hands and Mr. Bartley departed. Holmes settled into his chair, holding the false "Head of Zeus" that had been attributed to Raphael. I asked him some insignificant question and received only silence for an answer. So it was for the rest of the evening, until at ten I left Holmes bent over his table with his lenses, examining the paintings in detail. Unable to grasp his purpose, I retired.

The next morning, I found Holmes at the breakfast table, looking like the proverbial cat that had dined upon canary. He directed my attention toward the sofa and three paintings resting upon it.

"Where did these come from?" I asked. They were the same size as Lacey's work, but each depicted Biblical characters and each was done in a distinct Renaissance style.

"It is most helpful to have insight into the character of a dead man, Watson. Think how Eustis Lacey was described by his dear friend: An artist, a prankster, a man determined to have the last laugh on a society he felt had unfairly ignored his talents. And what were his talents? Beyond his ability to paint unoriginal pieces and construct ridiculous machines, he had an eye for hidden masterpieces and a knack for concealment. It occurred to me, as I examined the forgeries in great detail, that Eustis spoke of having wasted his fortune. On what, I wondered, beyond alcohol and, one presumes, the proverbial 'riotous living'? What would have prevented him from purchasing artwork for himself to enjoy, once he had the money for it?"

I blinked. "You're right. There was certainly nothing to stop him from becoming a real collector."

Holmes inclined his head toward the sofa. "And so behold, Watson, what hid beneath the paint that Lacey applied, and which I spent last evening carefully scraping away – these are small samples of the work of Masaccio, Titian, and Caravaggio. By creating false masterpieces atop real ones, Eustis Lacey played a game of wits with his colleagues. He doubtless imagined that once the safe was breached and his forgeries discovered, the disgusted winner would hurl the spoils into the fire without ever checking to see what lurked beneath the modern pigments. Just as the combination to his safe was within his portrait, his real treasure laid within his forgeries. Dear me, Watson, you look rather pale. Should you not avail yourself of your medicinal brandy? I look forward to having these paintings appraised, and then I believe that Mr. Bartley will be surprised to find that his future is not quite so bleak after all."

The Adventure of the Awakened Mummy

My friend Mr. Sherlock Holmes was often a very difficult man. For example, it was almost an impossible feat to convince him to take a holiday, to commit to a brief respite from the noise, crowds, and crime of London. He believed the evil elements within the city would run amuck if he was absent from Baker Street for more than a fortnight. However, I once persuaded him that a brief retreat to a pleasant country house in Hampshire would be good for avoiding the nervous collapse which, as both his friend and physician, I judged to be imminent. By good fortune, an old army comrade of mine, Mr. Charles Lane, a former artillery sergeant in the Berkshires, had recently inherited a small country residence, and was gracious enough to invite us both for seven days of shooting, fishing, or simply lounging about, as it struck our fancy. Once assured that it was a bachelor household, and there would be no expectations of sociability with the neighbors, my friend acquiesced.

Trouble, however, followed us to the country.

We had been in residence less than twenty-four hours. Holmes, who favored the ever-changing metropolis to pleasant scenes of nature, demurred from accompanying Lane and myself on a morning constitutional, preferring instead to lounge about my friend's library. Meanwhile, I was delighted to set out with Lane, accompanied by his faithful dog Vino, an odd-looking canine whose heritage baffled even Holmes.

"Beagle and foxhound, but with some terrier, bulldog, and perhaps schnauzer as well on his family tree," Lane said, as we slowly made our way down the road. "Ugly creature, but always on the prowl, never losing a scent. Rather like your companion, I suppose."

I gave a hearty laugh. We were just cresting a hill, and in the distance, across the fields, I could see a gray, gothic building surrounded by an imposing wall. I pointed to it, inquiring as to what it might be.

"Ah, that is the Manor School for the Reform of Wayward Youth," Lane said. "Lads who have run afoul of the law, but aren't judged to be incorrigible, are sentenced there. A few even emerge truly reborn to good morals, or so I am told by several local notables who happen to be donors." He lit a pipe, musing for a moment upon his neighbors and his good fortune to reside among them. "Lord Hewell and his Lady live just east of the institution, and Baroness Nettle is to its west. Who would have thought an old sergeant like me would have settled in such distinguished company, heh? And there's also Mr. Topher Reilly, who lives at Ra House."

"The Egyptologist?"

"You've heard of him."

I nodded. "I attended one of his lectures when I was at the university. He presented on Egyptian tomb art." I shook my head. "I'm ashamed to admit it, but I dozed off and when I woke up, the room was empty!"

"That doesn't surprise me in the least," Lane chortled. "Reilly is a pompous old windbag. But he possesses a fine home, a fat checkbook, and a lovely unmarried daughter."

I was about to make a jest about Lane's sudden interest in all things Egyptian when Vino, who had darted away from us, came running across the field with something in his jaws. Lane shook his head.

"Ah, you scoundrel, what do you have now? It had better not be one of Lady Hewell's riding gloves. I'll end up in Broadmoor if those go missing again and . . . ."

The words died on his lips. I leaned forward, my jaw dropping in astonishment. The dog looked back and forth between us, as if awaiting praise for his discovery.

Clenched in his jaw was a withered human hand.

"How good of you to return so quickly," Holmes said, as we came bounding into the foyer of the house, sweating profusely from our gallop. "I feared I would have to order the serving lad out to find you, Lane, as you have a visitor. You also have – Good Lord!"

I thrust the grisly object into his grasp. Holmes carried it to the closest window, while Lane quickly combed down his hair.

"Who is here?"

"A young lady, fair-skinned and plump, in a great state of excitement."

"Constance!" my army companion gasped. "Did she say what she wanted?"

Holmes was lost in thought, turning the relic over and over. Lane shook his head and ran for the parlor.

"Holmes," I said. "Is it murder?"

"Perhaps. This flesh is dry and desiccated, but hardly ancient enough to have come from the Nile Valley, or the tomb of a king. Where did you find it?"

I related the story of the dog. Holmes immediately asked where Vino had come from, and I could do no better than to say from the general direction of the school, as we hadn't noticed the hound until moments before he delivered his treasure to us.

"Intriguing. But let us hear what the lady has come to consult your friend about. When young girls come driving hell-for-leather in dogcarts, something is clearly amiss."

Together, we made our way to the parlor. A striking young woman of some twenty years was sitting on the sofa, with Lane beside her. She was clearly in a state of agitation, her brown hair hanging loosely from her hat, her soft face flushed, and her eyes red and swollen. She gave a gasp as we walked inside and might have bolted had Lane not quickly caught a fluttering hand.

"No, Constance, wait – This is my friend the doctor, and his friend, the detective. Do you remember me telling you that I should be hosting these gentlemen for the week? You must share with them the story you have told me. Mr. Holmes is famous for setting things right and getting to the bottom of all kinds of mischief."

I doubted Holmes appreciated his gifts described in such a delusionary fashion, but he bowed to the lady and offered his services.

"Oh, sir – Are you a priest as well as a detective? I'm not certain which I require, for a dead man is walking and has driven my father's wits from him."

I was grateful Holmes had placed the corpse's hand on a table outside the parlor. He settled in a chair across from the nervous young woman. His slow movements seemed to calm her.

"I will not claim to be a clergyman, but if your trouble has a human source – as virtually all troubles do – then I am certain I can assist. Tell us what brings you here, in such a panicked state that a lady of fashion dons mismatched boots."

She looked down at her toes. Indeed, one boot was black, the other almost red. A pretty blush stained her cheeks.

"You are correct, sir. Let me put my problem to you quickly, for the medicine the doctor gave Papa will soon wear off, and I wouldn't wish him to awaken and find me gone. I only came here because . . . I didn't know where else to turn."

She glanced to Lane, who gave her an encouraging nod.

"My father is Mr. Topher Reilly, a member of the Royal Society and a noted Egyptologist and antiquarian. For years he lectured in London, and briefly held the Pendleton Chair at Oxford. My mother died five years ago, and after she passed away, Papa felt there was little left for him in the world. We therefore came to Ra House, so he might rusticate. However, Papa is a restless man, and retirement doesn't suit him. It seems that every other week he is travelling about the country with Sabatok-Nafi, to give another speech and demonstration."

Holmes raised a hand. "And who is this gentleman? A student or a servant?"

"Neither sir. He is a dead man."

I confess this answer startled both Lane and me. Holmes merely nodded for the girl to continue.

"You see, my father is an expert on ancient Egyptian mortuary practices. He has a collection of mummies, but they are fragile items. There was once a craze for acquiring mummies and hosting parties where they would be unwrapped – As you might imagine, the damage was irreparable, once the process was complete. Therefore, Papa wanted some way to demonstrate to students how the mummies were prepared, but without ruining his own legion of the dead. He made a special application to the Royal Society and received permission to take the body of a man who had died, friendless and nameless, in a London almshouse, and prepare it in the way of the pharaohs. Father did so, two years ago. He rewraps the body before every exhibition."

I hold myself to be a man of science, but this bordered on the macabre. "Why did he not use a statue or some kind of wax figure?" I asked, and perhaps my indignation was sharper than I intended. The lady sniffled.

"I know it sounds wicked – but Papa used the process to test his theories about the nature of Egyptian embalming, and subtle differences between the Middle and New Kingdom techniques. No disrespect has ever been intended, and no morbid gawking is allowed. Papa will not allow me to assist him, even though I could. And last evening – Oh, how I wish I had been with him!"

The girl seemed about to weep, but a glance at the clock upon the mantel abruptly restrained her tears.

"Yesterday, he had an appointment at the Manor School. The warden, Mr. Maxwell – They call him the headmaster, but in truth he is the boys' jailor – had asked Papa to give a talk for the boys who had been good for a month. Baroness Nettles and Lord Hewell attended as well, as they are great patrons of the institution and always interested in the boys' instruction. There is an old surgery in the building, for it was once an insane asylum, and Papa brought Sabatok-Nafi – as he has named his otherwise anonymous gentleman – in his casket. It is a wooden sarcophagus from the time of Cleopatra, brightly painted with images of gods and monsters and the portrait of the man who had hoped to spend eternity inside, but whose mummy was lost long ago.

"Papa said that he lectured for two hours, and that while many of the lads were very interested as he removed and then rewrapped the linen bandages, others were bored, and some, very rudely, went to sleep.

Afterward, the boys were dismissed to their room, and Papa, along with the noble patrons, were invited back to Mr. Maxwell's office for a libation. They talked longer than they had intended, for Mr. Maxwell was hopeful Papa would agree to become a patron of the institution. My father said that he would consider it, but only after I married, and my inheritance was settled. Papa arrived home at almost midnight. I had already sent the servants to bed, and so it was I who helped him shift the mummy's casket from the wagon to his study."

"How could you do that?" Lane asked. "You are just a girl, and the coffin must be heavy."

Miss Reilly shook her head and managed a somewhat exasperated look at her admirer. "It isn't heavy at all, and our mummy is almost as light as a feather, because he is nothing but a dry husk of a human. However . . . the box did feel heavier last night, but I assumed it was only because I was tired. Papa was, I confess, a bit worse for having indulged in spirits, and he wobbled so badly that I insisted he put the casket down in the hall. Fortunately, Ross, our butler, is a bit accustomed to our strange ways. I cannot imagine most butlers walking down to find coffins blocking the staircases! I tried to get Papa to go to bed, but he insisted he wished to work some more on his book, and so I left him in his study. I barely remember blowing out my candle after reaching my bedroom, I was so exhausted.

"I awoke once during the night. I could have sworn I heard footsteps, and an odd, swishing sound, like someone dragging a cloth about the floor. My chamber door creaked open. I lifted on my elbows, calling to Papa. The door closed immediately, and I suspected that Papa was lost in his own house, due to his excessive intoxication. It wouldn't be the first time such a thing occurred. I shook my head, laughed, and immediately returned to sleep.

"I awoke at six, pulled on my dressing gown, and started down the stairs. I was midway down when I halted in alarm. The mummy's case was open, the lid shoved off to the side. I couldn't imagine what had possessed my father to open it, or to leave it in such a strange fashion. I descended, looked inside, and gasped. The linen bandages, which Papa so carefully rebinds with each session, were piled in a great heap inside the sarcophagus. And Sabatok-Nafi had vanished!

"'Papa!' I called. 'Papa, what has happened?'

I heard a moan coming from the study. I ran inside and found my father crumpled upon the floor, shaking like a leaf. His eyes were wide, his face was deathly white. I screamed for Ross to run for the doctor. Meanwhile, our housekeeper came to my aid. We made Papa as comfortable as we could upon a divan, and I begged him to speak to me.

All he could mutter, between chattering teeth, was '*He walks! The mummy walks!*'"

At this point the girl broke down, leaning upon Lane's shoulder. He assured her that Holmes had the situation well in hand.

"What is the physician's diagnosis?" I asked.

"He says that Papa has experienced a terrible shock and must be watched carefully. Papa's many years in Egypt, doing fieldwork, exposed him to fevers and left him with a weak heart. The doctor gave him a sedative, but . . . Oh, I must return. Please, Mr. Holmes, come to Ra House and help us make sense of what has happened!"

The lady darted from the room, with Lane in pursuit. I went to the door, watching as she whipped her pony into a brisk trot. Holmes returned from retrieving his coat, looking highly amused. He quickly buried any hint of humor when Lane rejoined us after seeing the lady on her way.

"I have called for my carriage," Lane said. "We shall be at Ra house less than ten minutes behind Constance."

Holmes smiled. "Ah – I felt you had an understanding with the lady."

"Oh. Oh, no, I merely . . . I have hoped Constance will favor me. But at my age – "

"She fled to you in her time of need. That, I think, bodes well for your wooing. But we shall not be going to Ra House immediately. We are needed at the school."

"Why?" I asked.

"That shall be obvious as soon as we ride through the gates. Ah, what a handsome bay mare you have."

Lane drove for us, dismissing the stable lad. My army friend swallowed further questions, and I knew better than to ask any. Holmes made random comments about the fine weather and the lovely countryside. We reached the gloomy, imposing structure in less than half-an-hour.

Holmes's prediction was astute – the institution was clearly in a state of turmoil. Shouts rose from open windows, and a small cadre of lads in stripped denim pants and loose tunics milled about the yard, looking confused and angry. A guard with a club stood just a few paces away, snarling and snapping at the boys to get in line. The gate was closed, and it took several minutes before Lane was able to convince another guard – an older man who Holmes quickly placed as a former naval officer – to admit us. Lane, who had visited more than once, quickly led us to the office of Maxwell, the warden.

"My God, what a disaster!" the man, a heavy-set fellow with a dark shadow of a narrow beard across his face, swore as we entered. He was clad in an ill-fitted, greasy coat, and still reeked of the previous evening's drinking party. "We are searching in every nook and cranny of this school. How in Heaven's name could he have disappeared?"

Lane introduced us. The man scowled at Holmes.

"The private detective?"

"Consulting detective," my friend answered smoothly. "Forgive me for saying so, Mr. Maxwell, but I believe you could use my assistance."

"If you can tell me where that rapscallion has gone, I shall be very grateful indeed for your assistance. I am sure that our patrons will reimburse you. But as for now . . . What shall I do?"

"You can begin," Holmes said tartly, as he took a seat before Maxwell's desk, "by supplying me with the name of the inmate who has escaped. Who is he and how did he elude your authority?"

"His name is Howard Williams," Maxwell sighed. "He is called 'Seashore' by the boys, because he was arrested at Brighton, taken in for stealing wallets and watches from the towels of the bathers. The first night he was in residence, he tried to escape and was sent to the hole for it. I thought that had cured him of disobedience."

"The hole?" I asked. Maxwell raised his head.

"A special cell. No light is permitted, except while eating. A naughty boy may be sent there for five days, or longer if he doesn't repent sufficiently."

I saw Holmes's eyes narrow, his lips compress. I knew instantly he was thinking of his Irregulars, the little street Arabs who served him so well. His tasks kept them occupied and he paid them regularly, so they didn't need to beg or steal. But there were other lads who he couldn't help, bright children who might fall afoul of constables and become jailbirds for life. I felt Holmes was imagining Wiggins caught in such a horrible place, where the punishment would far outweigh the crime.

"Describe Seashore to me," Holmes said.

"He is small, and underweight for his age, which is almost thirteen. He has dark hair, a sharp nose, and barely speaks at all."

"How did you misplace him?" Lane inquired. Maxwell glared, clearly not appreciating the tone of the question.

"There was a lecture last night, by Mr. Reilly. Seashore – I mean, Howard – was among the twenty or so boys permitted to attend in the old surgical theatre. Afterward, the boys were told to go to the dormitory room they share in the eastern tower. We don't like to keep them in cells, though when they disobey, we do not hesitate to lock them up. Last night, we dismissed them, and then my men came to my office for a moment before returning to check on the lads and lock their door."

"Is this customary after a special lesson?" Holmes asked.

"No. Usually, the two guards would follow the boys directly. But Baroness Nettles insisted the guards have a toast with us, and they were glad to oblige. They were only here for a few minutes, certainly not long enough for any of the boys to break out of the institution. They returned to the tower and looked the dormitory chamber over. All the boys were in bed."

"And nothing memorable occurred during the night?"

"No."

A burly guard, who had been standing silent in the corner, abruptly coughed. Maxwell twisted in his chair.

"You have something to add, Byron?"

"I was walking along the wall at about two in the morning, sir, and I heard a splash outside the tower. But of course, it couldn't have been the lad."

Maxwell waved a hand. "Did you not investigate?"

The guard shrugged and looked to us for understanding. "There is a stream that runs on the eastern side of the tower. Sometimes the lads throw things from the windows into it – shoes, books, plates. They are always punished severely when they do. But the windows of their chamber are all old arrow slits. Even the skinniest of the young fellows couldn't slide through. I thought the matter could wait until the morning."

Maxwell glared at the guard. "You should have told me this earlier. You are dismissed!"

The man shrugged and walked away. The warden pulled out a handkerchief and mopped his face.

"I still cannot understand how Seashore got out," Maxwell muttered. "The boys claim they know nothing, but of course they are lying. Maybe a few days on bread and water, down in the hole, will loosen their tongues."

Holmes rose. "That will not be necessary. Mr. Maxwell, I assure you that the lad shall be dealt with, but not by you. Might you have a photograph of the young offender? Ah, thank you, this will do nicely." Holmes slipped the small image into the pocket of his coat. "I suggest that you gently chastise his associates, but don't inflict any bodily harm upon them. It would hardly be the thing to have special visitors from Her Majesty's Government witness."

The man's face turned ashen. "Special visitors?" he stammered.

"Good day to you, sir."

Holmes spun and marched out with military precision. Lane and I trotted behind.

"I say, aren't you going to visit the dormitory?" Lane asked. "I've read Watson's stories. Don't you need to walk around the premises, to make deductions?"

"That would be a waste of time," Holmes said. "I already know how young Howard Williams, fondly known as 'Seashore', made his daring escape. I know who on the outside aided him, and where he most likely is hiding. The only aspect I am ignorant of is why this individual is taking such a risk, though at least three theories have suggested themselves to me."

Lane stopped in the hallway, his jaw hanging open. I had to grab his sleeve to pull him along.

"Is he always like this?" Lane asked.

"One becomes accustomed to it," I assured him.

We returned to the carriage and Lane asked whether we would now hurry to Ra House. Again, Holmes shook his head.

"Circle the wall, so I may judge the strength of the stream."

Lane nodded and cracked his whip. The school was situated amid plowed fields, but at one corner, just below the high tower, a brook made a sharp curve before shooting out across the farming country. It was wide enough that a plank bridge was necessary to cross it. Rain had fallen the two days previous, and the waters were higher and more turbulent than was normal, for the bridge was almost flooded. Holmes didn't get out of the open carriage, instead signaling that he had seen enough.

"Thank you, Lane. Now – which road will take us to Baroness Nettles's establishment?"

"Why – we must turn around. She lives almost two miles west of the school, not far from Ra House."

"Ah, a pleasant drive then. Carry on."

I shook my head at Lane, preventing more useless questions. Holmes sank down in his seat, folded his arms, and gave the impression of a man who was thoroughly enjoying himself. I looked up to the tower where the boys were nightly locked into their "dormitory". It was a high drop, perhaps as much as seventy feet, straight down into the stream and its scattered rocks.

"I doubt anyone could have survived a fall from that window, if he did squeeze through it."

"I assure you, Watson, that wasn't how it was done."

"Then why did you wish to see the water?"

"Only to ascertain the directional flow and ponder who we might hear from next."

"I don't understand."

"The village of Thornston lies downstream. By this evening, the constables of that charming little town will have a murder on their hands. If the news travels that Sherlock Holmes is in residence nearby, they will ask me to solve their grisly case."

"Really! Holmes, this is too much, even for you. Are you now claiming to possess the second sight?"

"Watson, you and I have seen and heard exactly the same things. Nothing has been withheld. At this moment, you should be able to tell me exactly what I am thinking."

I folded my arms and gave a loud snort. "Yes, I could . . . but I refuse to do so."

My friend laughed so loudly he almost spooked the horse.

I held my peace until we approached the home of Baroness Nettles. At Holmes's request, Lane offered a bit of local gossip about the lady. She had wed Baron Nettles some five years earlier, but was now a widow. The couple had no children, and the lady divided her time between London and her country estates.

"She's an attractive person," Lane informed us, as the red roof of her house came into view. "Perhaps thirty-five years of age, with a splendid figure. Her hair is as black as ink, and she is always very well dressed. Our paths haven't crossed much, but I have seen her in church, and Constance says she is generous and kind. She is also a patron of the Manor School."

"How long ago did the baron die?" I asked. Holmes smiled at me.

"The first anniversary of his passing was last month," Holmes said. "Really, Watson, I thought you followed the society news." Holmes turned back to Lane. "But how long has the lady been in residence at this property?"

"I believe she arrived here about two months ago, but you really should ask Constance these questions." He twisted in the seat, peering over his shoulder in exasperation. "Mr. Holmes, don't you think we should be going to Ra House instead of paying a social call on the baroness? What if Reilly is dead?"

"Then the best thing for us to do would be to capture his murderer. Please exercise patience, Lane. Let us hope the noble lady is willing to receive us. I wouldn't wish for this encounter to become unpleasant."

A smart young butler took our cards and, after ten minutes of cooling our heels in the foyer, we were admitted to a room that had clearly been a gentleman's study. Baron Nettles had built his career in the colonies, and maps of various Oriental regions were hung on the walls, along with taxidermized trophies and strange weapons. His lady rose from behind a massive mahogany desk to receive us.

She was indeed a spectacular woman, fair of face with luxurious black hair set in surprisingly girlish curls about her head. Her dark-gray dress was elegantly trimmed, and a delicate gold watch hung from a chain that encircled her tiny waist. She radiated both poise and kindness, and spoke in a low, soft voice.

"It is good to see you, Mr. Lane. We missed you at church last Sunday, and the vicar's message was very interesting." She turned to shake hands with my friend. "And I have heard of you, sir. In fact, you solved a problem for a friend of mine, Lady Lyle."

"A matter of an emerald bracelet," Holmes said. "A simple case, easily resolved."

"I am glad to hear it was so elementary, as you are fond of saying. Had that bracelet disappeared forever, I doubt my friend would still be married, as her husband was so furious with her for misplacing it he threatened to divorce her! But pray, sir, what can I do for you?"

Holmes had dropped into the chair that sat in front of the desk. He had, as the lady was speaking, removed the photograph of the boy and was glancing back and forth between it and his hostess.

"Madam, you can answer one question for me: *Where is your son?*"

Lane made a sound as if he'd been shot. The lady gasped, her hands flying to her mouth. Even I, who trusted Holmes's instincts and abilities beyond all others, feared for an instant that he had made a horrible and humiliating mistake.

The baroness tumbled into her chair, gripping its arms like a swimmer seizing upon a life preserver. She swayed but didn't faint. At last, just as Lane had begun to sputter out oaths and demand apologies on her behalf, she raised a hand.

"Howard is upstairs, asleep. He ate up half the kitchen before he nodded off. I thought it best to allow him to rest."

I heard a thud. It was Lane, dropping down onto a divan at the back to the room. I stepped beside Holmes's chair, watching the lady as she slowly gathered her courage and resolve.

"Are you here to take him from me?"

Much to my surprise, Holmes shook his head.

"No, Madam. Whatever offense your child committed, he has paid for it a hundred times over. My only concern is for the old gentleman at Ra House, whose fate we have yet to learn."

Baroness Nettles put a trembling hand to her forehead. "Howard told me Mr. Reilly fainted. I imagine anyone would do the same, upon viewing a mummy that had awakened and risen from its casket."

"We shall do all we can," Holmes assured her. "Clearly, it wasn't your son's intention to harm the gentleman. But to protect your child, we must know your story."

The lady sighed. "Not even my own husband knew of him, and yet here you are, a complete stranger, asking for his history. Very well, Mr. Holmes, I shall throw myself upon your mercy.

"I was a bold and foolish girl in my youth, and I made my living with my face as a model, a beauty whose image appeared on soaps and medicine bottles. It was only a matter of time before I gave myself heart and soul to a worthless cad who promised me marriage but cast me aside when I told him I was carrying his child. I knew that if the public learned of the infant, I would be an outcast, unable to make my living. Heaven, however, had sent me an answer in the form of Lizzie Williams.

"She was my dearest friend, and she longed for children but had been unable to bear them, and her husband had just died. Together, we devised a plan. We would go on a long Italian holiday. I would give birth in Rome, and she would adopt my child as her own. For eight years all was well. Howard couldn't have had a better mother. I was introduced as a favored 'Auntie' so that I could watch him grow up. I never stopped loving him – I hope you believe this, sir! – but I knew Lizzie's home was better than any I could provide.

"When Howard was six, Lizzie married a man called Tucker. Her second husband was disliked Howard, because he was a stepchild, but was never openly cruel, and I know Lizzie wouldn't have tolerated her husband hurting him. But then Lizzie died – she was run down by a cab in London – and as he settled Lizzie's affairs, Tucker somehow learned the truth about Howard." The lady paused. A single tear slipped down her cheek. "Just weeks before her death, Lizzie had been my bridesmaid when I married Baron Nettles. Our honeymoon was a protracted one, and when I returned home, I found an abusive letter from Tucker informing me that if I didn't retrieve Howard within a week, he would be cast into the streets. My poor son had been ejected from his home with nothing more than the clothes on his back, while I was on safari with my new husband.

"Mr. Holmes, I dared not tell my spouse the real reason for my distress, because he had no inkling of the past affair which had produced my child. I loved the baron, but he had a sanctimonious streak and might well have thrown me over for my 'sin'. Any chance I had of saving my son required me keeping my husband in the dark. I claimed Howard was my late friend's child, and that I wished to find him and see to his upbringing. The lie satisfied the baron, who never objected to my efforts. I spent money like water, paying dozens of detectives, but no one could find him. I see now that I was a fool not to come to you instead, to lay my entire sad history at your feet.

"My husband passed away, and four months after his funeral my son was found – Howard had been arrested in Brighton for stealing from the tourists. My late husband's title bore influence, and I was finally able to have Howard transferred to the school here, close to my estate. When he arrived, I learned that he had been sentenced to serve five years! I visited in the guise of a generous patron, hoping to arrange some type of parole for Howard, but the warden bragged to me that he didn't care if even a royal prince was incarcerated at the Manor School – no prisoner would be released before his time.

"Howard recognized me at once. His horrid stepfather had revealed his origins, but had also lied, telling Howard that I had abandoned him. It took several visits, and many tears, before my son learned to trust me again. Howard was clever enough to keep our relationship a secret, and I feared that if I told the truth, the warden might abuse my child even further, to make an example of him to the other boys. Yet Howard's health grew more fragile every day. Therefore, I began to plan how he might escape."

The lady gestured to the walls, with their maps of the East.

"My husband told me many strange tales of his time in India and of holy men who could lapse into such a deep trance that their followers might bury them for days, and then dig them up, to great acclaim. Perhaps that is what inspired me."

Holmes leaned forward. "Please, allow me to state my perception of what happened, and you may correct me if I err."

Baroness Nettles looked relieved and gave a quick nod.

"You arranged for the lecture and by some subterfuge told your son what to do on that evening. Following the lecture, you entertained Maxwell, his guards, Reilly, and your neighbor Lord Hewell with strong spirits and a discussion of Reilly's potential status as a patron. It was essential that you keep the men occupied, for your son was busy taking the mummy's place inside the casket. Of course, he had co-conspirators, for he could hardly have removed the current occupant, wrapped himself up completely in the bandages, or lowered the lid by himself. The actual mummy was stripped and transported to the dormitory, where he took his place in Howard's bed, thereby fooling the guards when they came for a final check. The lads knew they needed to dispose of the desiccated corpse afterward, so they broke him apart and slipped him through the arrow slot, dropping him into the stream below the tower. One hand was later discovered by Lane's dog, thus beginning our involvement in the affair."

Holmes looked back to Lane, who could only nod dumbly.

"While I cannot imagine that impersonating a mummy was a pleasant task, the wooden sarcophagus wasn't airtight, so there was no risk of him being smothered. Miss Reilly noticed their burden was heavier than normal but put it off to her own exhaustion. You had already made sure that her father was too intoxicated to notice the difference.

"The pair left the coffin on the floor by the stairs. Your son waited until the household was asleep, then he freed himself. He feared that his 'uniform' from the school would give him away as an escapee, should he meet anyone along the road, and so he went upstairs in search of fresh clothing. He hadn't completely unwound the bandages, for Miss Constance heard a swishing sound, like cloth being dragged on the floor. She awakened and called out to her father just as Howard – unfamiliar with the house – opened her door. The lad very sensibly backed away and travelled down the stairs, abandoning his quest for new attire. But just as he reached the threshold, the door of Reilly's study opened and the old man, still somewhat in his cups, beheld him. Reilly collapsed and your son fled. Where is he now, Baroness?"

"I am here, sir," a small voice said. From the hallway, an emaciated child entered the room, came forward, and threw his arms around the lady. They had the same hair, skin, and striking profile. "I am so sorry for scaring Mr. Reilly. I didn't mean to do it. He gave us a very interesting talk last night, all about how mummies are made. I promise, I listened closely and didn't go to sleep, like Jacky did."

Holmes rose from his chair with an indulgent smile. "Let us see if we can make everything right. Baroness, I would suggest you that you take your son to a trusted friend in London and reclaim him when the furor of this escapade has somewhat calmed."

The lady gasped. "You will not turn him in to the authorities?"

"I think it is safe to say that Howard has learned his lesson about stealing from tourists," Holmes answered, with a wink to the lad. "He will be an upright and law-abiding citizen for the remainder of his days. I have friends in Her Majesty's government. A strongly worded letter and a visit from certain officials will prevent any repercussions upon the lads who assisted him. In fact, I predict the school will soon be under different management. Perhaps as a patron, you may even be asked to be involved in the selection of a new headmaster or mistress. As for Mr. Reilly, we should visit him now and see how he is faring."

We left the lady with her son, hurriedly preparing for a trip to London. When we arrived at Ra House, Miss Reilly raced down the steps and carelessly threw her arms around Lane.

"Papa is saved! He woke an hour ago, with a terrible headache, but able to speak. He said he understands now that it was all a dreadful nightmare and has promised to take the pledge and never touch spirits again."

"A happy ending all around," Holmes said, preventing me from descending the carriage. "Lane, it would be better to leave Mr. Reilly to his recovery," he warned, clearly not wishing us to become caught up in the household drama. "And besides, we seem to have forgotten our luncheon. You promised your cook is exceptionally talented."

Lane gave Holmes a look that indicated my friend clearly didn't understand how he was interrupting a splendid opportunity for courtship. Still, Lane bid his lady to send a note if he was needed, then climbed back into the driver's seat. The girl rushed forward before Lane could take up the reins.

"But what of our mummy? Even if Papa only had a bad dream, what happened to Sabatok-Nafi?"

Holmes leaned forward and patted her hand. "The mummy was the victim of prank committed by naughty boys at the Manor School. You wouldn't wish them to be in further difficulties, would you?"

"Oh, no! The poor little lads . . . I feel so sorry for them."

"I sensed you have a kind heart,' Holmes said. "Therefore, allow the esteemed late gentleman named Sabatok-Nafi pass from your memory into eternal rest and encourage your father to acquire a wax figure to replace him."

Miss Riley nodded and waved farewell. Lane looked back over his shoulder, once we were away from the house.

"I say, Watson, following this nosey chap around, getting into all manner of trouble, and never being allowed a moment alone with a pretty lady . . . How did you ever manage to acquire a wife?"

"Such selfish behavior is best avoided," Holmes quipped, before I could speak. We all enjoyed a laugh, and Lane whipped up the horse so that we were soon approaching his home. Just as we made the turn into his drive, Holmes commanded him to halt.

"What is it?" Lane asked.

"That is an official looking vehicle," Holmes noted, motioning toward a conveyance parked at Lane's door. "It smacks of the police."

"I've seen it in Thornston village," Lane noted. "And I recognize the man on the box. He drives for the local inspector and the constables."

"They have found the other pieces of the mummy," I said. "And now they think there has been a murder. Holmes, it seems your prophecy has come true."

"If so, they are persons best avoided," Holmes said, opening our door and leaping out, then tipping his cloth cap to my army friend. "Mr. Lane, it has been a pleasure, and I thank you for a most entertaining diversion.

The train station is just a mile in the southern direction, is it not? Watson and I shall take a brisk stroll through the woods and arrive in time to catch the five-fifteen to London. Will you be so kind as to forward our luggage? The address is 221b Baker Street!"

About The Author

A Sherlockian from age eleven, Tracy J. Revels is the Laura and Winston Hoy Professor of Humanities at Wofford College in Spartanburg, South Carolina. She is a member of *The Survivors of the Gloria Scott*, *The Adventuresses of Sherlock Holmes*, and in 2021 she was invested in *The Baker Street Irregulars* as "A Black Sequin-Covered Dinner-Dress". Along with her classic pastiche stories, she is the author of a trilogy of supernatural Sherlockian novels: *Shadowfall*, *Shadowblood*, and *Shadowwraith*. A historian of Florida, she has also published works on the state during the Civil War and the development of its tourism industry.

MX Publishing

MX Publishing is the world's largest specialist Sherlock Holmes publisher, with over five-hundred titles and over two-hundred authors creating the latest in Sherlock Holmes fiction and non-fiction

The catalogue includes several award winning books, and over two-hundred-and-fifty have been converted into audio.

MX Publishing also has one of the largest communities of Holmes fans on Facebook, with regular contributions from dozens of authors.

www.mxpublishing.com

@mxpublishing on Facebook, Twitter, and Instagram

Also from Tracy Revels – The Shadow series – Shadowfall, Shadowblood and Shadowwraith. If you like your Sherlock Holmes dark, with a fantasy twist, this series is for you. Here is an extract from the fist book – Shadowfall, which the Sherlock Holmes Society of London described:

"Dr Revels has researched deeply into English legend and Shadowfall has a delerious, almost surrealist quality, like an enjoyable nightmare"

The story I am about to tell must never be told.

If you are reading these words in some time and place far from my own, years and miles removed from the quiet domesticity of an English home in the late nineteenth century, then you will no doubt consider me a madman. You will reflect, you unknown reader who considers these scrawled line not by gaslight or electricity, but by some illumination as yet unknown to science, that Dr. John H. Watson was either a harmless eccentric or a dangerous lunatic. You will think yourself fortunate to have never known him or been forced to listen to his insane prattling. You will mock him, and perhaps invite others to laugh at his poor addled brain, which somehow conjured these disturbing images.

But I tell you they are true.
And yet they must never be known.

For many years I was the boon companion to the wisest man the world had ever seen, a man renowned for his skills in detection and famed for bringing the foulest villains to justice, even at great peril to his own life. He was a man who battled the demons of the criminal underworld, who conquered societal corruption and moral decay. He was hailed and honoured by crowned heads of Europe; indeed, he was on terms of some intimacy with the Queen herself. Everyone knew his name, his residence, his likeness.

And no one knew him at all.

This is the story that must never be told. I confess that I often, without any awareness of the truth, hinted at it in my writings, through a word I placed in the mouths of those who were amazed by his seemingly inhuman powers. But it was the truest word I ever wrote about him, the one that defined him best and the one that he embodied when he saved not only my life, but my very soul.

You may not believe this story, but I must write it down before my memories fade. My confession concerns the true nature of Sherlock Holmes.

Chapter One

It was an April morning in a year late in the century. London was finally rousing itself from a long winter's sleep, and the air was soft, filled with the fragrance of flowers bursting from window boxes. I had some errands to do, and as the weather was unusually balmy I told Holmes---who had barely roused himself to come to the breakfast table and glare at the kippers---that I would not return until the late afternoon. But in truth, it was more than business and the urge for a constitutional around the metropolis that drove me from our rooms at 221 B Baker Street.

Holmes had been in something of a fugue state for several days, answering my inquiries in grunts and snorts, lying around on the sofa and lighting a new cigarette with the remains of the last, until the atmosphere in our rooms was poisonous and intolerable. It was a familiar reaction to me. I was well acquainted with the ennui Holmes fell into when no case of merit presented itself to him, and his brain, like a finely-tuned machine, began grinding gears. At such times, I feared he would return to the cocaine bottle. I had weaned him of that vile habit some years before, but it remained a spectre in our companionship, a fiend lurking in the shadows, ready to spring. If embracing the demons of his addiction was his intention today, I did not wish to witness it. So perhaps it was as much cowardice as impatience driving me from our residence that morning.

I took luncheon in the Strand, spent some time ambling through the shops on Oxford Street, and considered dropping by my club, only to realize that I had insufficient funds should one of the lads challenge me to a game of billiards. Finding myself only a short walk from home, I decided to return and fetch the purse that I kept for just such diversions. Perhaps this would give my friend a chance to test his powers, should he attempt to deduce why I had returned so unexpectedly. My good spirits, buoyed by the beauty of the day, were such that I mentally wagered him a shilling that he could not divine my purpose. It was not, after all, my usual days for billiards.

Thus it was that I flung open the door to our sitting room without preamble or announcement, and found, to my great astonishment, that a naked woman with gossamer wings was sitting on our sofa.

There is a moment between dreaming and waking in which reality seems a thread that can be stretched, twirled and twisted into a thousand different shapes. In this instant, even the most fantastic illusion can be accepted as fact. It was in this netherworld that I seemed suspended, especially as the woman turned and acknowledged my presence with a coquettish laugh.

"So this is the famous Dr. Watson!"

"Famous for his inability to knock, I should think," Holmes answered from where he stood beside the fireplace. His voice was thick with annoyance and his eyes had never been colder. I felt myself gasping for air. I stumbled backward, grabbing at the door handle, missing it repeatedly.

"Yes, well....ah...do forgive me. I...I shall...retire."

"Watson, front and centre, man," Holmes barked, with all the authority of a general in the Afghan campaign. "There's no going back now." He extended a hand, gesturing toward the unclad woman. "I present to you Titania, Queen of the Fairies."

My wooden, nerveless legs somehow propelled me forward. The woman seemed not to sit so much as to float above the furnishing, her silky wings keeping her aloft with tiny, trembling flutters. She was as naked as Eve, her body slim and yet beautifully proportioned, her skin warm and rosy. Her long lavender hair waved around her head as if suspended underwater. Her eyes were narrow and sharply angled, directing the viewer's gaze to the razor-points of her ears. Her mouth was sensual, her lips full and flush, but when she spoke I saw that her teeth were filed like some African pygmy's. Each tooth formed a little dagger within her mouth.

I found I could not speak. How does one greet such a sensual illusion?

Sensing my discomfort, she smirked at me and extended a hand. Blindly, I bent and kissed it.

"We are gratified to see that our Sherlock has such a noble and stout-hearted companion," she said, in a voice of tinkling bells. As she spoke, she flicked her tongue, like a lizard considering a tasty morsel. "And you are a rather handsome man as well."

I felt my face grow hot. I stammered my reply. "I....thank you, Madame."

Her smile tightened. "I am addressed as Majesty."

"Oh, I...do forgive me your—"

"It does not matter how she is addressed," Holmes snapped. He grabbed my arm and tugged me away from the woman, dragging me to the fireside. With those few steps I felt like some great elastic band had been released from my chest and I could once more breathe. "The Most High Queen of the Fairies has concluded her business with me," Holmes stated, "and she is now leaving."

Titania arched a thin brow. "Is this your final word? You reject my humble plea so curtly?"

Holmes folded his arms. "It is not my intention to be churlish, dear lady. But you know how I stand on these matters. I am no longer a servant to your world. I have no intention on crossing into the Shadows again."

The woman smiled wickedly. "To refuse me is to court danger."

Holmes's thin lips twitched. "I am comfortable with danger. It is an old and familiar companion in my work."

"For you, perhaps." Titania's head turned. Her amber gaze fell on me. "But for others?"

Holmes moved between us, giving an imperious wave of his hand. "Titania, I order you away."

She laughed like a child mocking its nurse. "Really, do you think your mere words have bindings? That you, a son of our house, could force me to leave before I am willing to depart? But I will go, because I know you, have known you since the cradle. Such a puzzle will tempt you back across the Shadows." She put tiny fingers to her lips and blew him a kiss. "And there you will find me waiting."

Her wings crashed together around her. In that instant, she was gone in a vapour that smelled of forests and moss and the first unfurled leaves.

"Holmes," I said some minutes later, when I finally located my voice, "have you been conducting chemical experiments? Something that would affect the brain? Please tell me that you have been burning that dreaded devil's foot again!"

He walked to the mantle, removing his clay pipe and a plug of tobacco. "You are not under the influence of any vile chemical, Watson."

"Then what, in the name of all that is Holy, was that? Who was she?"

"Exactly who she claimed to be---Titania, the immortal Queen of the Fairies. Do sit down, Watson, you are looking rather pale."

I collapsed into the basket chair. "Holmes, this is madness. Fairies do not exist."

"How do you know?" he asked, with a short puff.

"What?" I demanded. He shrugged as he spoke.

"You say they do not exist, because you have never seen one before. But is that, in and of itself, proof that they do not exist? Mankind had never seen germs until the invention of the microscope. People believed that the hand of God caused diseases. If I were to tell you that tiny, nearly invisible creatures inside your body produced your ailments, and you were not already a man of science, would you believe me?"

My head was spinning. I kept glancing at the sofa, expecting Titania to reappear. To regain my composure, I forced myself to grab the sides of the chair until its rough texture bit into my palms.

"No, of course not, but...fairies are nonsense, stories for children and foolish people. As bad as tales of banshees and ghosts and—"

"Spectral dogs?" Holmes asked.

I lifted my head, stared at him sternly. "The hound of the Baskervilles was real. A concoction of phosphorus to the jaws gave him the appearance of the supernatural but he was merely a weapon in the hands of a greedy man, and very real."

"True," Holmes conceded, with the first hint of a smile. "But until you had him at your feet, riddled with bullets, you entertained the possibility that he might be something else. A creature of another world. A being of the Shadows."

"Holmes---please make sense," I pleaded. "Are you implying that there is some other reality, some sphere of existence beyond our own?"

The hint of amusement was abruptly banished from his face. "I am indeed, Watson. There is another world, one called the Shadows."

"Impossible."

"Not impossible. It is world filled with darkness, this space between the spaces of our own, sun-governed reality. Monsters of all forms reside there. You say that this place and these things cannot exist, because you are a rational man who sees nothing. But Watson, you use only a bare fraction of your senses. In truth, you see, but you do not observe."

I shook my head roughly. I felt suddenly enervated, exhausted. The room seemed to spin around me.

"Madness, Holmes," I whispered, rising to my feet. I grabbed the mantel for support. "You are speaking in riddles and lunacies."

"Am I?" he asked, in that old sardonic way of his. "You look rather tired, Watson. Perhaps a siesta of sorts would do you good."

My eyelids were heavy. I could barely focus to walk toward the door to my bedchamber. "Indeed, I....I will take you advice."

"Excellent. Thompson would have beaten you at billiards anyway, given your condition."

I had just enough sense to pause at the door to my room and wonder how he had known my intention to go to my club. Then darkness closed around me, shadows swallowed me, and I was grateful.

Chapter Two

I woke and was startled to find dawn rather than twilight illuminating the street outside my window. My jacket and shoes had been removed and my collar was undone, but I had no memory of attending to these details. My head pounded as if Vulcan were within, beating on his anvil. I sat up gingerly, fighting down nausea. For an instant, a ghost of a very strange dream teased my memory, despite the incessant hammering in my head. But it flitted away before I could seize it and make sense of it.

I moved slowly, and after a torturous progress I stood at last before my mirror. The sight that greeted me looked like an illustration from a 'shilling shocker,' a garish tale of horror written to amuse schoolboys. My hair stood on end and my face was a strange shade of greenish-gray. Bluish bruises ringed my eyes and my lips were crusty. Just to touch my skin caused stabbing pains. I considered tumbling back into the bed, yet I knew that I would not be able to fall asleep, lest I take a starring role in my own nightmares.

After a rather painful washing up, during which my hand trembled so violently I could barely hold my shaving razor, I timidly entered our sitting room. Holmes caught sight of my reflection in the coffeepot and turned with a mocking smile.

"Good morning, Watson." He surveyed me up and down, his expression growing ever more amused. "It looks as if Morpheus dropped you on your head, rather than carrying you in his arms throughout the evening."

Mrs. Hudson, who had been setting the table, turned and gave me an appraisal. "Good heavens, Doctor Watson, you are a fright! Are you ill?" she demanded.

"I feel dreadful," I confessed, as I settled in. "But I do not think I am contagious."

"Here, eat something," Mrs. Hudson ordered. "Food will make you better! You need nourishment."

She lifted the silver lid of the serving dish, revealing a hearty course of bangers and mash. My stomach flipped over, and it took all my self-control not to violently expel its contents across the tablecloth.

"No, please---replace the cover," I begged.

Mrs. Hudson banged the lid down, an action that seemed to open a great chasm in my head. She departed with a righteous huff, deeply offended by my rejection of her offering. I begged for coffee. Holmes was kind enough to pour and I sipped my cup delicately, drinking like an ancient invalid. I could feel Holmes' gaze piercing through me.

"Are you certain you are not sick, Old Chap?" Holmes asked, opening his newspaper.

"I think so," I muttered. Holmes rattled a page of the paper, an action that made a battery of guns explode in my head. "But I still feel terrible."

"Is there a logical explanation for this incapacitation?" my companion inquired, in the most baiting of tones. I easily grasped his meaning.

"Holmes, I know what you are hinting at and, no, I did not go out roistering last night."

"Indeed?" He waved a hand, pointing to me blindly from behind the newsprint. "The evidence before me is most suggestive: the bloodshot eyes, the facial pallor, the unsteady hands. What else would a reasonable man conclude?"

For a long moment, I entertained the idea that Holmes was correct. Perhaps I had encountered some of my old army chums and spent the evening reminiscing over my days in Afghanistan with the Fifth Northumberland Fusiliers. But there was no smell of whiskey on my breath and not even the flicker of a memory of a reunion with old comrades. Surely I would recall a few details of such an unexpected and highly pleasurable event.

"I remember nothing."

"A common side effect of overindulgence in spirits," Holmes remarked, with all the sanctimony of a Salvation Army sergeant. "Or so I have been told."

The temptation to reach across the table and punch the man was nearly irresistible. "Holmes," I defended, "I may be intemperate at times, but I have never lost my memory of a celebration, not since—" I felt a blush rise to my face as I recalled a particularly embarrassing weekend from my youth. "Not since I was in medical school! But I have never, as a grown man, been so intoxicated as to lose the memory of an entire evening." I considered Holmes, as he hid behind The Times, with my right eye. It was the only one capable of opening. "This affliction is inexplicable to me."

"Hmmm," Holmes said, with another tortuous rattling of the paper, "most mysterious."

Despite my pounding headache, my fighting spirit was aroused. I refused to let Holmes mock me without demanding that he tell me what had occurred. I had begun to suspect that one of his noxious experiments had gone awry. Indeed, I had never forgotten the words of young Stamford, the army dresser who introduced me to Holmes, that this man was capable of administering the latest poison to a colleague, just to scientifically observe its effects.

"Holmes," I said sternly, gritting my teeth against the pain of speaking aloud at a volume above a whisper, "something happened to me last night, and it has no connection to the fruit of the vine. Or to a lady's charms," I quickly added, now seeing the amusement onto his face as he folded the newspaper. "So kindly, if you value my friendship, explain to me why I have woken up feeling like a sailor just returned from shore leave."

He lit a cigarette and blew smoke at the ceiling. "I have not a clue."

"Holmes, that is beneath you, not to mention cruel. I deduce that this is somehow your fault!"

"My fault?" he asked, with an exaggerated gasp.

"Yes. You and your blasted chemicals, your noxious pipe tobacco, your music that would drive even the sanest man to Bedlam—"

"Watson!" He cut me off, giving me an offended scowl. "Why do you think I was here? I do not spend every evening in these lodgings. Perhaps I was out, tending to an investigation, and therefore did not witness your descent into drunken debauchery."

"You have no case at the moment," I protested. At least my mind was clear enough to remember that fact.

"Are you certain that I tell you everything I do?" he countered. Those words were like a sharp spear, thrust deep into my brain. For just an instant, I seemed to remember things. But they were only tissues, shadows, nothing of substance that I could grab hold of. I closed my eyes and breathed deeply.

"Of course not," I whispered. "You are a very secretive person. I still do not know how many abodes you have in London or how many aliases you live under."

Holmes' little flicker of a smile told me that he took my admission as an apology. He pulled a card from the pocket of his dressing gown.

"As it so happens, I do have a case, newly arrived upon our doorstep as you were dragging yourself back into the land of the living." He tossed the card upon the table, just beside my coffee cup. "Honest work is the best cure for your disease, Watson. Can you be ready in ten minutes?"

I lifted the card, blinking until I could read the words scrawled upon it.

Dreadful outrage at Highgate Cemetery. Please, I beg you, be discreet and come at once.

"It's unsigned."

"An astute observation, Watson," Holmes said, favouring me with a smirk. "But I know the handwriting, and a communication from Highgate can mean only one thing. It is from Charon and no other. Come now, into your armour, the battle draws nigh."

Perhaps it was his choice of words that abruptly brought my nocturnal fantasy back into sharp relief. I dropped my cup on the table, spilling coffee across the card that requested Holmes' presence at that great gathering place of the dead.

"Holmes---was there a naked woman here, yesterday?"

"My blushes, Watson."

"I am quite serious!" I countered. "Was there an unclothed, winged woman in this room, seated upon the sofa?"

He considered me with those great grey eyes. For just a moment, I sensed some debate behind them, some uncertainty. And then he gave his head a shake, snubbing out his cigarette as he spoke.

"You have it on my honour, Watson; there was no woman in these rooms yesterday---beyond Mrs. Hudson, of course, if the evidence of unsightly tidiness is to be believed. And it seems most probable to me that she would have been fully clothed while performing her duties."

"But I have the strongest recollection! Holmes, I am certain that I saw a naked woman---a fairy woman---in this very room."

Holmes rose from the table. The look of disgust on his face made it clear that the subject was closed. "Any memory that you have of a nude woman in this chamber was either a wishful dream or a wistful fantasy. I am interested in neither. Now, are you coming with me or not?"

I could do no more than accept his words. I nodded slightly, returned to my room and reminded myself of my own boast, that I was an old campaigner. To prove it I put on my coat and hat and slipped my army revolver into my pocket. Minutes later, as we rode away in a cab, I pondered my own foolish action. Who did I expect to fire upon in Highgate? Anyone there was already beyond the reach of my bullets.

Milton Keynes UK
Ingram Content Group UK Ltd.
UKHW021944151124
451255UK00009B/165